TUESDAY MOONEY WORE BLACK

Kate Racculia is the author of *This Must Be the Place* and *Bellweather Rhapsody,* winner of the American Library Association's Alex Award. She works for the Bethlehem Area Public Library in Pennsylvania, USA.

You can find her at www.kateracculia.com
or on Twitter @kateracculia

TUESDAY MOONEY WORE BLACK

KATE RACCULIA

HarperCollins*Publishers*

HarperCollins*Publishers*
1 London Bridge Street
London SE1 9GF

www.harpercollins.co.uk

First published by HarperCollins*Publishers* 2019
This edition published 2020
1

A catalogue record for this book
is available from the British Library

ISBN: 978-0-00-832695-1
ANZ TPB: 978-0-00-836661-2

Typeset in Chronicle Text by Palimpsest Book Production Ltd, Falkirk, Stirlingshire

Printed and bound in Great Britain by CPI Group (UK) Ltd, Croydon CR0 4YY

MIX
Paper from
responsible sources
FSC™ C007454

This book is produced from independently certified FSC™ paper
to ensure responsible forest management.

For more information visit: www.harpercollins.co.uk/green

For all the people I've found
(and who have found me)

CONTENTS

How rich we are in knowledge,
and in all that lies around us yet to learn.
Billionaires, all of us.

—URSULA K. LE GUIN

Brookline

2006

THE OPENED TOMB

The Tillerman house was dead. Over a century old, massive and stone, it lay slumped on its corner lot, exposed by the naked December trees and shrubs growing wildly over its corpse. It was ugly, neglected, and, despite its size, withered; a black hole of a house. If the real estate agent were the kind of person who ascribed personalities to properties – he was not – he would have said it was the loneliest house he had ever sold.

His instincts told him this would be a strange, quick sale, with a giant commission. When he'd told the owner that, out of the blue, they had a *buyer* for the Tillerman house, some guy named "R. Usher," the owner said, after a long pause, "Don't sell it for a penny less than listed." But the agent was anxious to get this over with. He had been inside the Tillerman house once before, and he hadn't forgotten how it felt.

A figure appeared on the sidewalk, rounding the corner up the street. The agent shielded his eyes against the white winter sun to get a better look. A man. Wearing a long black coat and a giant black hat, broad and furry, something a Cossack might wear against the Siberian winter. The real estate agent smiled to himself. Yes. This was exactly the buyer you wanted when you were trying to sell a haunted house.

"Hello, young man!" said the figure, waving, ten feet away

now. "I assume you're the young man I'm supposed to meet. You are standing, after all, in front of the house I'd like to purchase." A bright red-and-purple-plaid scarf was looped around his neck, covering the lower half of his face. He pulled the scarf down with a red mitten to reveal a ridiculous curling white mustache. "Young man," said the buyer, "allow me to introduce myself. Roderick Usher." And he held out his hand.

The agent, while technically younger than the buyer, resented its being pointed out to him. He was years out of school, up and coming in Boston real estate, and, yes, selling this property for the listed price of $4.3 million would be a coup, but he wasn't a young man. He was a man. He shook Mr. Usher's hand and gestured to the property. "Shall we go inside?" he said, and pressed the quaver out of his voice.

Dead leaves crackled beneath their shoes as they walked under the portico and up the front steps. The lock to the Tillerman house was newly installed, but the key never wanted to work. The agent turned it to the left gently, then the right, then the left again. "What a beauty she is," said Mr. Usher, his hands clasped behind his back, head tipped up to take in the carvings around the door, flowers reduced to geometric lines and patterns, a strange mishmash of Arts and Crafts, Nouveau and Deco, that didn't jibe with what the agent knew about when it was built. It was almost as if the house had continued to build itself long after it was abandoned. "If she's this lovely on the outside," said Mr. Usher, "I can't imagine what—"

The lock turned at last, and the agent pushed the door open.

The first thing that struck him was the smell. Of rot and garbage, of meat gone rancid, of animals that had been dying in the walls for decades. He pressed the back of his suit sleeve to his nose without thinking, then lowered it, eyes watering. The house had no electricity – when it was first built it did, but the wiring hadn't been up to code since Woodrow Wilson was president – but it did have enormous ground-floor windows on one side of the great hall, which cast light throughout the first floor and down into the vestibule. It was enough to see by. It had been enough, on the agent's previous showing with a buyer, for the buyer to take one look around and say, "Let's get out of here now."

Let's get out of here now, said the agent's brain.

"What a glorious – oh – oh my!" said Mr. Usher, and swept past him into the house. He took off his giant furry hat, clutched it in both hands at his chest, and spun back to the agent. Grinning. His front teeth were large and crooked. "My *goodness*, do you know what you have here? Can you feel it?"

He didn't wait for the agent to answer, and charged up the steps, through the archway, and into the great hall.

The agent followed, slowly. His feet did not want to move. It was exactly what had happened to him the last time he entered the Tillerman house: his body did not want to *be* here. An uncontrollable part of his brain – his otherwise rational, adult brain – reacted to this place as though he were six years old. Six years old, and pissing himself on Halloween because his big brother, in a scuffed and stage-blood-spattered hockey mask, leapt out at him from the dark.

He cleared his throat. Took the steps one at a time. Until he was standing in the half-dusk of the great hall. Mr. Usher, who'd been dashing around the room, turned back to him.

"She *died* here," he said. "Can you feel her?"

The agent managed something like a smile.

"Long, long ago, you came to Matilda Tillerman's," Mr. Usher continued, "she, the last surviving heir of all that Tillerman wealth – you came to her house to drink and to dance, to laugh and to talk, to be alive, together, in this glorious house. They *all* came here, were well met here, from every corner of this city, every nook and cranny. But something happened, nobody can say for sure what, and Matilda shut her doors. Shut out the entire world and made of her house a tomb." He sighed and laid a hand gently on one of the columns supporting the upper gallery. "And a beautiful tomb it is." Plaster flaked beneath his fingertips.

He tipped his head to the side. "Young man," he said, "I'm going to buy this house. I won't keep you in suspense any longer, so you can stop looking so frightened. But I would ask a favor. I make it a point of putting a serious question to a man whenever I meet him. Would you permit me?"

The agent, relieved to the point of tears that this showing was nearly over, would have permitted the buyer anything. "Yes," he said. "Of course."

"Marvelous." Mr. Usher dropped his furry hat to the floor. It sent up a puff of ancient dust. "I have lived for a good long while. Enough to have borne the world," he said. "And sometimes, the world is far too much for me. Too great. Too painful. Too lonely. I expect, if Ms. Tillerman will allow me to interpret her past actions, she may have felt the same. Is it selfish then, or self-preserving, to shut oneself away? At what point does one give up, so to speak, the ghost?"

The agent swallowed. He didn't know what to say. No one had ever asked him a question like that before. It made him almost as uncomfortable as the house. It was too personal. It was too—

He had, once or twice, imagined it. How it would feel to say, to his bank account and his car and his condo and his girlfriend and his job, *Go away. Leave me alone.* So he could rest, and listen, and think, and maybe have a chance, one last chance, to remember what he'd been meaning to do before all this life he was living got started.

"I'm not sure," he told Mr. Usher, "what to say."

"An honest response," Mr. Usher replied. "I appreciate that. I—"

A gust of frigid wind howled through the still-open door and lifted clouds of dust and spider webs from the walls and the floor. Delicate debris filled the air. The buyer coughed. Then the breeze caught the door and slammed it home with a crash.

The agent felt his entire body electrify. Mr. Usher jumped, and laughed.

Then: a second crash.

Smaller, closer, nearby in the house, off to the right. The agent's body twitched violently and he doubled over, hands on kneecaps. He couldn't stay here. This house was too much for him. He heard Mr. Usher walk across the great hall and pick something up off the floor and mutter to himself. *Oh, you clever house*, the agent thought he heard. *What else are you hiding?*

"Come on, dear boy," said Mr. Usher, suddenly at his side, helping him upright and clapping him gently on the back. "It's enough to frighten anyone, opening a tomb." He smiled, the curls of his mustache lifting almost to his eyes. "Makes one feel a bit like Lord Carnarvon."

The agent didn't know who that was.

"Best hope there's not a curse," said Mr. Usher, walking back down the steps toward the door and the light, "for disturbing her."

Boston

===

2012

1

THE DEAD MAN'S SCREAM

The woman in black was alone.

It was five thirty-five on a warm Tuesday evening in October. She shuffled through the revolving door of the Four Seasons Hotel, her eyes sliding around the room, unable to stick to anything but cool marble, everything tasteful and gleaming under the recessed lighting. She caught the rich murmur of voices from mouths in other rooms. The hotel staff didn't make eye contact. They knew she wasn't checking in.

The event registration table was set up, as usual, on the far left of the lobby facing the elevator bank. It was already drawing men in suits like ants to a ham sandwich. WELCOME, proclaimed a foamcore poster on a small easel, TO THE 2012 BOSTON GENERAL HOSPITAL AUCTION FOR HOPE.

"Welcome to the Auction for Hope!" echoed a tiny blonde girl, wearing more makeup than the woman in black wore in a year, gesturing her closer. Her name was Britney. She was an administrative assistant in Boston General's fundraising office and never remembered that the woman in black was her coworker. "You can check in here, and head up the stairs to your right for the hors d'oeuvres!" she chirped. "The program starts at seven in the ballroom."

"Britney, hi," said the woman, tapping her fingers against

her chest. "Tuesday Mooney," she said. "I work at BGH too. I'm volunteering tonight. I'm late."

"Oh! Of course, I'm so sorry." She waved Tuesday on, flapping her hands as though trying to clear the air of smoke. "The other volunteers got here a while ago. I didn't realize anyone was – missing." Britney's teeth were very white. She still didn't recognize Tuesday, and was, Tuesday could sense, vaguely concerned she was a random crazy off the street. Tuesday was five to ten years older than most of the other volunteers, who were generally single, young girls at their first or second jobs out of college, with energy and free time to burn. Tuesday was single but not as young. She was tall and broad, pale and dark-haired, and, yes, dressed all in black. Britney looked at her, not unkindly, as though she were something of a curiosity.

Tuesday couldn't blame her. She was, to the office, an oddity. She didn't leave her cube often, communicated almost entirely through email, didn't socialize or mix with her coworkers. Or with anyone, really. Being alone made her better at her job. It's easier to notice what's important when you're outside looking in.

She wasn't upset that the other volunteers left without her either. She'd been distracted when they'd gone, talking with Mo – Maureen Coke, her boss, the only colleague with whom she nominally socialized. Mo was also a loner, bespectacled and quiet, unassuming in the deadliest of ways. People often forgot that Mo was in the room when they opened their mouths, which is how she came to know absolutely everything about everyone.

It was a silent skill Tuesday respected.

"Starting today, your mission as a prospect researcher," Mo told Tuesday on her first day in the development office, three years ago, "is to pay attention to the details. To notice and gather facts. To interpret those facts so that you can make logical leaps. A prospect researcher is one part private detective, one part property assessor, one part gossip columnist, and one part witch." Tuesday lifted her brows and Mo continued, "To the casual observer, what we do looks like magic."

What Tuesday did was find things. Information. Connections. She researched and profiled people. Specifically rich people, grateful rich people, people whose lives had been saved or extended or peacefully concluded at the hospital (in that case, she researched their surviving relatives). The information she collected and analyzed helped the fundraisers in the office ask those rich, grateful people to donate tens and hundreds of thousands and millions of dollars; she told them which buttons to push to make that ask compelling.

Whenever the events team threw charity galas or auctions, they asked for volunteers to help with registration, crowd control, VIP escorts, and the myriad other moving bits and pieces that went into making an event run smoothly. Tuesday always raised her hand. She spent forty hours a week digging through donors' lives, trying to understand why and where and how they might be persuaded to give away their money. Thanks to the hospital's databases and subscriptions, and all that gorgeous public information lying around on the internet, she knew where they lived, the addresses of their summer houses on the Cape, the theoretical value of their stocks, the other organizations their foundations supported, the names of their children, pets, yachts, doctors, and whether or not their doctor liked their jokes. But she had never met them. She knew them as well as anyone can be known from their digital fingerprints, but volunteering at events was her only opportunity to interact with them in person. To weigh her quantitative assessment of their facts and figures against a first impression in the flesh. Without that, she knew, it was too easy to jump to conclusions.

Plus, the food was usually pretty good.

Her stomach grumbled. Tuesday's lateness meant she'd missed her comped volunteer meal, and the Four Seasons always had *great* volunteer meals. She'd worked at events where dinner was a handful of gummy bears and a snack-size pack of Goldfish crackers, but at the Seasons she'd missed gourmet cheesy pasta and bread and salad and tiny ice cream sandwiches, the kids' table version of the spread hotel catering would put out later for the real guests.

"I guess you know the drill?" Britney gestured down the length of the registration table, at their mutual coworkers, who probably didn't recognize her either. It was a good feeling, anonymity. "Just ask for their names and check them in on an iPad – there's an extra one on the end, I think. Guests can write their own nametags."

Tuesday took a seat behind registration at the farthest end, in front of the last abandoned iPad, and set her bag on the floor. Her feet pulsed with relief. She'd left her commuter shoes under her desk, and even walking the short distance from the cab to the hotel in heels – over Boston's brick sidewalks – was a rookie mistake. She wasn't even close to being a rookie, though. She was thirty-three, and she'd never been able to walk well in heels.

Her phone buzzed twice, then twice again. Then again. She felt a small bump of anxiety.

It would be Dex. Dex Howard, her coworker from another life – who could, incidentally, run in heels – and the only person who texted her.

Hey am I on the guest list?

I mean I should be on the list

Constantly.

I really really hope I'm on the list

Because I'm about to get dumped

◆

Across town, at a dark, stupid bar he hated, Dex Howard waited to be proposed to.

Or dumped.

Dumped, definitely.

He sucked a huge gulp of whiskey and propped both elbows on the bar. He knew he shouldn't be thinking like that: all or nothing, proposed to or dumped. He knew it was ridiculous and self-defeating. He wasn't about to *be* anything, other than be *met* by his kind and affectionate boyfriend of four months – the longest he'd dated anyone consecutively, ever – who'd asked to meet him here right after work. Dex had no delusions. He only had coping mechanisms, and right now his coping mechanism wanted him to believe Patrick could potentially be proposing to him, when in his heart and his guts Dex knew – *knew* – he was getting dumped.

He checked his phone. No response from Tuesday (big surprise). No other texts. No emails. No calls (who called anyone anymore, but still). The bar was called The Bank, and it was in the heart of the financial district, which meant it was full of douchebags and assholes. Dex could, when the mood struck, be either or both. It was a land of finance bros: white guys with MBAs and short hair and, now that they were in their thirties, wedding rings and bellies that pulled their button-downs tight with a little pooch of fat over their waistbands. In the corner by the window there was a cluster of young ones, fresh out of school, still studying for their CPA exams, still able to drink like this every night and come in to work the next day, half alive. The boys were prettier than the girls. They were downing pints of something golden, maybe the first keg of Octoberfest.

His phone chimed. Tuesday.

I don't see you on the list

He texted back, WHAT

Also you didn't deny my previous text

which means on some level you must ALSO believe I am about to get dumped

She didn't respond.

He'd known Tuesday for years. They'd met at work. She might be a do-gooder nonprofit stalker now, but Tuesday Mooney had started out, like him, as a temp in the marketing department at Cabot Assets, the oldest, most robust asset manager in Boston. At least that's how it was described in the marketing materials, which Dex, like the innocent twenty-something he'd once been, took on faith for the first year of his employment. After one year – during which he became a full-time employee, with benefits, praise Jesus – he would have described it as the sloppiest, most disturbingly slapdash and hungover asset manager in Boston, though he had zero basis for comparison. He only knew that every Thursday night his coworkers went out to bars, and every Friday morning most of them came in late, looking like they wanted to die and occasionally wearing each other's clothing.

But never Tuesday. She was the same on Friday morning as she was every other morning: acerbic and goth, never wearing anyone's clothing but her own.

Like the last Cheerios in a bowl of milk, he would have naturally gravitated toward her, but the universe shoved them together. In an endless sea of tall cubes they were seated across from one another, at a dead end.

"Morning, Tuesday," Dex would say, slinging his elbows over their partition. "Are we feeling robust today?"

"I'm really feeling the depth and breadth of this portfolio management team," she'd deadpan, gesturing toward her computer monitor with her palms up. "The robustness is reflected in the ROI."

"Oh, the ROI? I thought that was the EBITDA. Or was it the PYT?"

"Perhaps the PYT." She'd squint. "Or the IOU, the NYC, the ABC BBD" – which Dex took as a cue to break into "Motownphilly."

They'd both taken the job because they needed one, desperately, through a temp agency. Tuesday had something like a history BA, maybe an English minor. Dex had a degree in musical theater. He'd openly defied his parents to acquire it. In hindsight, it might have been his subconscious means of coming out to them without actually having to come out to them. His father flat-out laughed when Dex told him he'd be pursuing a theater degree. He'd thought it was a joke. His father was incapable of imagining any extension of his self – as a son surely was – spending time and money to be taught how to *pretend*, as though that would lead to any kind of career, which was surely the whole point of going to college. Dex, flush with his own inability to imagine a future for himself that didn't include a literal spotlight, told him it was his life, his dream, his decision to make – not his father's. To which his father said, "Fine. Go ahead and waste your own money," and spat accusingly at Dex's mother, *I told you not to encourage him*.

So Dex took himself to school, and took out his own loans, and studied and partied and graduated and promptly freaked the fuck out. He did not comprehend the weight of debt until it was pressing down on him. His theater school friends were either getting support from their parents or working weird jobs at all hours. Dex tried for a year to believe all you needed to be successful was fanatical self-belief, and failed. So he retreated to the safety of his minor in accounting. He had always liked numbers; music, after all, was math.

The job at Cabot was entry level and he figured it out; he was smart and worked hard and it was pretty shocking, to Dex, that that wasn't the case for quite a few of the people he worked with. The whole place felt like high school all over again, and he was still the odd arty kid no one knew what to do with, only this time he was getting paid, which helped for a while.

And he had Tuesday. Who was just as out of place as he was.

So when Tuesday couldn't stand it anymore, and jumped ship for a nonprofit, Dex jumped too. To Richmont, a smaller firm, a hedge fund with more assets under management than God, more go-getters, and better alcohol at parties. Dex hated his job at Cabot, sure, hated how buttoned down and conservative it was, how it smushed him into a cube with a computer and a tape dispenser he never used, how it had absolutely nothing to do with anything that he had once imagined for his future, or valued about himself. In finance, there was no professional advantage, for instance, to being an expressive belter. There were no head-pats for one's encyclopedic knowledge of popular song lyrics, no kudos for one's flawless application of stage makeup.

And Richmont likely wouldn't be that different. But he was terrified of giving up the safety of his salary, which was now, he suspected, easily more than twice Tuesday's. Because he had known her for so long, and in such a limited capacity – they were Drinks Friends, Karaoke Friends, Trivia Friends; he had never even seen the inside of her apartment – it wasn't weird. But it could have been. Dex didn't forget that.

He texted, see you can't say it

you can't even say 'you won't get dumped' bc you know I'm going to get dumped and it will just be this horrible vortex of pain

Dex calm down, Tuesday replied.

Your level of concern is insufficient, he texted.

"Hello hello hello!" And Patrick was there, swinging the strap of his satchel over his head and taking his jacket off in the same fluid movement. Patrick did everything fluidly, gracefully, as though he never had to think about where and when and how to move his body; his feet were so firmly on the floor they may as well have been glued. He'd been trained as a dancer. Now he was a manager at a Starbucks. That was how they met, at the Starbucks in the lobby of the office building Dex sometimes cut through on his walk to work.

Patrick moved to peck him on the ridge of his cheekbone. "Wait, I forget," he said. "Can we do this here? Oh fuck it," and kissed him, because of course he was always going to. Patrick was younger than Dex, less fearful and careful of himself in the open. Dex was only slightly older, but they had grown up in different worlds.

"Hey you," said Dex, pulling the chair beside him out from under the bar. "Welcome. Have a seat. How was work?"

Patrick rolled his neck on his shoulders. Dex watched. He had never seen such perfectly circular neck rolls. "Fine. You know, same old same old. Ground some beans, pulled some espresso, steamed some milk, almost fired Gary."

"*No.*" Dex twisted in his seat, pushed his elbow on the bar, and propped his head on his hand. "Spill."

Patrick ordered a whiskey and tonic from the bartender. He sat and shook out his shoulders like he was trying to rid himself of something unclean. Patrick had told Dex about

Gary. Gary was older, in his mid-forties. Gary had lost his job a few years ago, not long after the crash – he'd done something in finance, which made the decision to work at a financial district Starbucks particularly masochistic – and was taking classes, trying to switch careers (thank God his wife still had her job, thank God the kids were years from college). Patrick liked Gary. He showed up on time and worked steadily and well, even if he wasn't quite as fast as the twenty-year-olds who could squat sixteen times an hour to grab a gallon of milk from the low fridge.

"He stole," said Patrick. His drink arrived and he downed it in a single gulp. "I caught him pocketing twenty dollars from the till today. I saw him. He looked around first, to make sure no one was watching, and he just didn't see me. He popped open the till and took out a twenty, looked around again, slipped it into the front of his apron, and closed the register. I could not believe it. You know, when you see something happening in real life that you've only seen in movies? You think, for one second: Where am I? Is this real? Is this my real life?"

He motioned to the bartender for another drink.

"You didn't fire him?" asked Dex.

"How could I?" said Patrick. "He's stealing because he needs money. I confronted him, told him I saw what he did. He got all flushed and couldn't look me in the eye and I honestly thought he was going to throw up all over the register, me, everything. I told him if he ever stole again, I would fire him. Today, *this*, was a mistake." He pulled off his glasses and rubbed his eyes with the heel of his hand. "Mistakes have consequences, but they don't have to break us. The next time it happens, I told him, I wouldn't consider it a mistake."

Dex thought, *I would have fired that guy on the spot*.

And then, *I do not deserve the love of this entirely decent, generous grown-up*.

Patrick slipped his glasses back on and leaned to the side, his arm over the back of the chair.

"You would've fired him on the spot," he said, and grinned.

"What can I say," said Dex. "I'm a mercenary."

"You're not a mercenary. I'm too soft." Patrick tugged his ear. "I'm a sweet fluffy bunny in a land of wolves. I need to get meaner if I want to get anywhere."

"Don't ever," Dex said. "It would break my heart if you got meaner."

"Isn't that what growing up is? Shedding the fat and the fluff until you're this sleek, perfect beast, entirely the you you were meant to be?" Patrick was gesturing up and down in the space between them, and Dex realized, with a little jolt, that his boyfriend meant *him*. Patrick thought he, Poindexter Howard – who had dreamed, once, of painting his face, wearing someone else's clothes, and belting show tunes on Broadway but instead became something called an Investment Marketing Manager, impeccably groomed in cool Gatsby shirts and Rolexes and shiny Gucci shoes, who belted nothing but his pants – *was* a sleek, perfect beast, entirely the him he was meant to be. Patrick actually thought Dex was himself. He was so young and so charming and so very wrong that Dex finally realized why he'd been so nervous when he first sat down.

"Patrick," he said, "this isn't working."

◆

Tuesday flicked her fingertip up and down, up and down, over the iPad, scrolling through the guest list. Which didn't include Dex. Richmont, his firm, had bought six tickets for their employees, but he wasn't one of them. Her stomach rumbled again. She was starving. They were allowed to grab hors d'oeuvres and drinks after the program ended, but that wouldn't be for hours. At least she was sitting. At least she didn't have to staff the cocktail party upstairs, wandering among the guests, answering questions, directing them to the VIP rooms or the bathrooms. All she had to do at registration was be pleasant to white guys in suits. It was a talent she'd honed daily all the years she worked in finance.

Dex once asked if her general standoffishness, her "aversion to team sports," as he called it, came from having grown up in Salem, stewing in the cultural detritus of mass hysteria and (literal) witch-hunting. Salem's natural vibe was part of it. What happened with Abby Hobbes was part of it too, though Dex didn't know Abby Hobbes existed. Technically it was possible Dex knew the name Abigail Hobbes. He would have been a teenager in western Massachusetts when the coverage of Abby's disappearance was at its height, bleeding beyond Salem, though her story never spread as far as it might have – if they'd found her body, if the missing girl had been upgraded to a dead girl. But Dex wouldn't have had any reason to connect Abigail Hobbes directly to Tuesday. For Dex to know, at the time of her disappearance, that Abby had been her best friend, Tuesday would have had to tell him herself.

"You don't trust people in groups," Dex had said to her once, while they were out at McFly's, one of his regular haunts for karaoke. Well, Dex was there for karaoke. Tuesday was there to drink, and pointedly not to participate. "Or people, really," he continued. "But especially in groups."

Tuesday had never thought of it in those terms, but yes, she didn't trust people. People, in groups, alone – people disappointed you. That was what they did. They abandoned you. They didn't believe you. They looked through you like you were made of smoke. You had your family, your work colleagues; you needed other humans around so you didn't go completely feral, but the only person you could trust completely with yourself *was* yourself. That was, like . . . Basic Humanity 101.

"I mean . . . do you?" she said. "Does anyone? I thought that was the first rule: trust no one."

"Should you be taking life advice from a poster in the base-ment of the FBI? On a television show?" Dex asked.

"That poster said *I want to believe.*"

Dex rolled his eyes. "I trust people more than you. But only a little."

Tuesday hadn't expected to stay in touch with Dex once they both quit Cabot. But Dex wouldn't go away. He invited her to lunch. He invited her to the movies. They went to karaoke, even though Tuesday had a strict no-singing policy. They wiped the floor at pub trivia, the only two-person team that regularly took first place. She liked him; she had always appreciated his sense of humor and his intelligence. But he was needy. God, he could be outrageously needy. He texted. He chatted to her at work. In person, he required her approval of mundane choices he might have to make, her assurance that she had heard and understood him. Even the constant invitations, she suspected, had less to do with him wanting her company than not wanting to go into the world alone. Sometimes it felt like it didn't matter who she was, so long *as* she was, an audience – *any* audience – granting him her atten-tion.

She felt her phone buzzing in her bag, vibrating against her leg. Again. And again.

I did it, he texted.

IT'S DONE

WHAT IS WRONG WITH ME he was so nice and sweet and young and flexible

She paused, her thumb over the screen. She'd liked Patrick. But this had been coming for a while. Tuesday could tell, from stories Dex told her, from watching the two of them together, that they had fundamentally different versions of reality, and fundamentally different ideas of each other. They were both playing parts.

He was too young, she texted back.

Pls don't remind me, Dex texted, that I'm a decaying hag

You're not a decaying hag, she replied.

Tuesday hated texting. Hated it, for its lack of nuance and tone. She always felt she was saying the wrong thing, or saying it the wrong way. But Dex was a natural, loquacious texter, and even by his standards, he'd been texting like mad lately. It meant he was anxious. And lonely. And now that he and Patrick were no longer together . . .

She felt a cold little stab, the looming threat of being needed.

Hey, he texted. Has anyone from Richmont not showed

She dutifully examined the list. Three of Richmont's six tickets hadn't been checked in.

Anders, Grouse, and Bannerman aren't here yet, she texted.

UGH Grouse, said Dex.

I hate that guy

Why did GROUSE get an invite

He's never going to show

I'm taking his place

Won't your coworkers know you're not him? said Tuesday.

He texted back, I'll wear a clever disguise

Then: wait my whole life is a clever disguise

A flock of new suits appeared, swerved, headed toward the table. She tossed her phone back into her bag for good.

She'd worked event registrations often enough to intuit the kind of interaction she would have with an attendee the moment she made eye contact. Most people were nice. They smiled when you smiled, offered their names when asked. They were polite and looking forward to free Chardonnay and shrimp cocktail, comfortable with the implicit agreement one makes by RSVPing to a fundraiser: that at some point during the evening, you will be asked for money, and you will say yes.

Then there were people like this one. He came alone. He waited calmly, patiently, at the end of the line forming in front of the girl next to Tuesday, adjusting the cuffs on his suit, smoothing a dark tie between two fingers. The girl next to her was a Kelly – Kelly W.; there were at least three Kellys in the office. She was shy and not, like the other Kellys, blonde; her hair was dull brown, her nose small, her eyes large. Tuesday liked her. When she spoke, it was usually to make a joke so dry it made you cough. But she looked like a mouse, and Tuesday suspected that was why this particular guest was waiting in her line.

Tuesday had spotted him as soon as he crossed the lobby, moving with the confidence of someone who owns every cell of his body, every atom of the air around it, and every right in the world to be exactly who and where he is.

He was the kind of person who expects to be recognized, and likes to make a big deal when he isn't.

Tuesday was in the middle of checking in a gaggle of attorneys when he reached the table in front of Kelly W.

"Welcome to the auction," she said. "May I have your name?"

He had a face made for striking on coins: hair brushed back, broad, dark-eyed, and long-nosed. It was familiar to Tuesday. Because she read society and business columns. Because she was fond of a high forehead. And because she'd researched him.

"Bruce Wayne," he said.

Kelly W., without missing a beat, said, "Might it be under Batman?"

He laughed. It made Tuesday like him a little, which was unexpected, given everything she already knew. His name was Nathaniel Allan Arches. He was the oldest child of Edgar Arches. *The* Edgar Arches, who had turned a lot of old Boston money into a hell of a lot of new Boston money by founding Arches Consolidated Enterprises (yes, its acronym – and general business reputation – was ACE), one of the largest private holding companies on the East Coast, if not the world. ACE had started small, with a chain of grocery stores on the Cape, then exploded in the early eighties, thanks to smart initial investments in tech companies spearheaded by MIT graduates. The company had had a hand in every major personal electronic device developed over the past thirty years, from Palm Pilots to smartphones. ACE had moved through the tech world like an amoeba, wrapping itself around industries and companies and swallowing them whole, the man at its helm a seemingly unstoppable, unbeatable force of nature.

And then Edgar Arches, the force of nature himself, went missing.

Five or six years ago, now. Tuesday had still been at Cabot when it happened. He disappeared over Labor Day weekend under odd and tragic circumstances. After a scene of public drunkenness during a charity wine tasting in Nantucket Harbor, Edgar Arches and his son retreated to the family yacht, *Constancy*. Nathaniel brought the yacht back the next morning – alone. His father and the yacht's dinghy had vanished in the night. The dinghy eventually washed up on Madaket Beach, but there was no evidence of foul play – no blood, no fingerprints. There was no hint of corporate malfeasance or a scandal that would suggest a possible suicide. The family's public statement was crafted for maximum plausible deniability: Nathaniel, the dutiful son, left his father safely sleeping it off on one of the yacht's banquettes, and went to bed in his own stateroom. When he woke up the next morning, father and dinghy were simply AWOL. Nathaniel was questioned by the police, but not, as far as Tuesday knew, ever considered a suspect, because there wasn't an obvious crime. There was no body, so there'd been no murder; Edgar Arches was a missing person. The news took that paucity of information and whipped it into a froth of supposition and gossip. What had happened on that boat, that night? What had happened to the richest of rich men, Edgar Arches – the man who had it all?

But what had he really had?

He'd had a wife, Constance, who'd assumed control of ACE in his absence, and presumably still ran it. He'd had a daughter, Emerson, made internet famous by a meme of her clotheslining Paris Hilton at a Halloween party (Paris was a devil; Emerson was a unicorn). Before his disappearance, Edgar Arches was a staple on the *Forbes* list of billionaires. Constance, as the surviving scion, currently held that honor, though there were rumors – even at the time of the disappearance – that Nathaniel was champing at the bit to manage the family fortune.

Most people with that kind of life did not have a sense of humor, and if they did, it was not about themselves.

"Look under Man," Nathaniel Arches said. His voice was slow and deep. "Man comma Bat."

"Look under Arches," Tuesday said to Kelly W., soft enough not to embarrass her, loud enough for him to hear. "First name – there. Nathaniel."

He smiled like a flashbulb.

"Would you like to make a nametag?" Kelly W. handed him a permanent marker and a HELLO MY NAME IS sticker.

"Sure," he said, uncapping the marker and inhaling. "I do love a fresh Sharpie."

Tuesday's mental file on Arches, Nathaniel fluttered in this breeze of personality. Nathaniel, since his father's disappearance and his mother's takeover of ACE, had funneled his share of the family fortune into N. A. Arches, a venture capital firm that invested in biotech, the next generation of MIT-spawned companies ACE was built on. There were rumors he had dated Gisele before Tom Brady. There were rumors he had dated Tom Brady before Gisele. In every interview Tuesday had read about him, he'd sounded like an out-of-the-box corporate venture dude, a walking jargon machine. He talked about synergy, about leveraging his assets. He made not one joke, possessed not a hint of wit or irony or self-consciousness of any kind.

He'd come to her attention last month, when one of the fundraisers she worked with – Watley, who raised money for primary care – asked for research. Nathaniel had no apparent connection to the hospital; he'd given no money, expressed no interest. He was just a name Watley discovered, probably after Googling "rich people in Boston." She tried to tell Watley that good fundraising required a slightly more strategic approach, that it wasn't worth her time to research and write up a full profile on a prospect with no Boston General connections and no history of, well, anything other than being a wealthy douche.

But Watley was new to the office and eager, Nathaniel

Arches was rich as hell and his family was bonkers, and it was the dull deep end of August when everyone was down the Cape, so Tuesday dove into the cool information-soaked sea of the internet. His Facebook account was locked down, but he tweeted pictures of sunsets, the beers he was drinking, and the kind of vague motivational quotes that were usually accompanied by photographs of soaring eagles and windsurfers (REACH! IT'S CLOSER THAN YOU THINK). He *did* have a record in the patient database, but he had seen specialists (plastic surgeons, years ago), and technically that wasn't public information; it was a violation of the hospital's privacy policies to use that information to initiate contact.

So she focused on everything else. Nathaniel had been profiled on Boston.com and the *Improper Bostonian*. He barely opened his eyes in photographs. He was listed as a director of a private family foundation that gave, relative to its potential, offensively nominal donations to every nonprofit organization in Boston – the equivalent of giving a kid a nickel and telling her not to spend it all in one place. He owned no property under his own name, though he lived in the family's luxury condo at the top of the Mandarin Hotel – when he wasn't at the family compound on Nantucket – and he'd shown up on five separate lists of Boston's sexiest: Sexiest Thirtysomethings, Sexiest Residents of the Back Bay, Sexiest Scenesters, Sexiest New Capitalists (he was number one with a bullet), and just plain Sexiest.

Tuesday had compiled all the hard and soft data she could find on Nathaniel Arches, and found his self-satisfied, mega-monied, essentially ungenerous, ladykiller affect the exact opposite of sexy.

In person, though, was a totally different story.

This was why she volunteered for events.

He peeled the paper from the back of his nametag and

slapped it gently on his chest. "How's that?" he asked. "Is it on straight?"

Under HELLO MY NAME IS, he'd written ARCHIE.

"One edge is a little – higher—" Kelly W. pointed.

Tuesday stood and leaned over the registration table. "I can fix it," she said.

Archie leaned toward her without hesitation. They were close to the same height, and he turned his head slightly to the side. "I've always wondered if two heads colliding really make that coconut sound," he said, "but I don't need to find out tonight."

Tuesday gave him a long smile. "The night is young," she said, and slowly pulled his nametag from his suit. Holding the sticky corners level, she repositioned it, pressed, smoothed it flat with her fingertips.

He stepped back and held out his hand.

"Archie."

"Tuesday." She squeezed his hand.

He gave a little finger-gun wave and glided away.

Tuesday plunked back in her chair.

"Holy crap," said Kelly W. "What just happened?"

"Research," said Tuesday. "In the field."

◆

At the Four Seasons Hotel, in a ballroom full of smiling men in suits, Dex Howard waited to be hit on.

That was it, right there: that was why he'd decided to come. As pathetic as it might be, he wanted a pity pickup. A distraction from having broken up with Patrick, even though everyone – seriously, everyone, including his own subconscious – had seen it coming. They had chemistry, they had fun, but they didn't have much else. Patrick was a wet-behind-the-ears erstwhile ballet dancer turned barista. Dex was a Vice President. Richmont, which had no more than fifty employees, had fifteen

Vice Presidents. All employees who had, at other firms, started as Coordinators, transformed into Analysts, then Senior Analysts, and then, having no further room in the chrysalis, burst into fully mature Vice Presidents. He was a Vice President who Managed Marketing, whatever the hell that meant, and his hairline was receding at the same rate as his childhood dreams.

He hated to think it – it was mean, it was shallow – but Dex was pretty sure Patrick had seen him as a meal ticket, a sugar daddy, a sponsor. Dex bought dinner. Dex bought tickets. Dex bought gifts. Patrick gave: support, compliments, sex. (Not for money, Dex told himself; not like that.) He liked buying things for Patrick, and Patrick liked receiving them. That Patrick liked his money didn't mean he didn't *also* like Dex as a person. Dex took a slug of open-bar whiskey – God, he hated this thing that his brain did, the way it looked at a man who professed to want him and asked, *But why?* Then answered, without waiting for a response, *Because I can buy you things.*

At least in a crowd of *senior* vice presidents and higher, Dex's ability to buy things was relative, and puny. Though it wasn't all that different from the crowd in The Bank. It had a higher tax bracket, was older and less visibly douchey, but there was still that slightly desperate undertow of desire threading through like a hot wire. Desire to make some sort of impression, to outperform, to draw attention, or at least to numb yourself to the day you'd just had with free booze – not to mention the next day, and the next.

Tuesday, as was her wont, was suddenly, silently there.

"Are you going to spend the night drinking morosely in the corner?" she asked.

Dex tried to hide the start she'd given him.

"But I excel," he said, "at morose corner drinking."

"I'm sorry," she said. "About Patrick."

Dex shrugged.

"You should try the shrimp," Tuesday said. "Did you see them? They're grotesque. They're the biggest shrimp I've ever seen."

"That's an oxymoron." Dex drained his glass.

"Though I overheard people complaining that they didn't have much flavor." Tuesday walked with him out of the ballroom and back toward the bar and the food. "They're too big."

"Metaphor alert." Dex nabbed a small plate from the end of the buffet. "Those *are* the biggest shrimps I've ever seen. They're obscene."

"The chicken satay thingies are always good," she said. "And the dessert course here is usually phenomenal. Save room for the cake pops."

"Cake Pops and Bourbon."

"Title of your autobiography?"

"My darkly confessional, poorly received sophomore album."

That got a twitch of a grin. Dex loved it. He knew that people looked at Tuesday and saw, in order, her height, her shoulders, her pale darkness. They heard her clumping around corners, occasionally tripping over her own feet; they saw her all-black wardrobe, her shelf of bangs, and her un-made-up face, and in their heads they thought, *Grown-ass Wednesday Addams, one day of the week earlier*. Dex actually *knew* this; their former coworkers, before Dex fully defected to Team Tuesday, once asked him what the *deal* was with that bizarro know-it-all tall girl. The guys thought she was hiding a great body – I mean, no wonder she was so clumsy; she was topheavy – under black sackcloth. The girls thought her face only needed a little, like, lipstick, or eyeliner, or something. If they even bothered, they imagined that she spent all her free time watching horror movies (true), listening to The Cure (occasionally true), and writing goth fan fiction (not true, but not outside the realm of possibility).

The truth was this: Dex genuinely believed Tuesday didn't give a shit what people thought when they looked at her. But the truth was also: he spent a fair amount of his free time with her – when he wasn't with a future ex-boyfriend – and he didn't really know what the deal was with her either. He knew *how* she was. He knew she cared about him, though he also knew he cared more about her. She kept him outside. After all these years, after all this time, he knew her without really knowing her at all.

He didn't know, for example, where she came from other than geographically. He had never met her parents, or learned anything about them other than factual details: they owned a souvenir shop in Salem. She had a brother, he thought. He knew what she loved, aesthetically – the weird and macabre – but he didn't know what she feared. Or wanted. Or worried about. He didn't know where she was most tender, or why, and anytime he poked in the general direction of where her under-belly might be, she solidified, invulnerable as granite. There was something Tennessee Williams tragic about her intimacy issues that, if he was being honest with his most melodramatic self, increased her appeal. Since she wouldn't take him into her confidence, he could only romanticize her. He could only imagine how she'd managed to get her great heart squashed.

Not that anyone would ever be able to tell. A squashed heart still beat, and Tuesday categorically Had Her Shit Together. She was quick. She was bright. But Dex knew a thing or two about armor – this suit and tie he was wearing right now was a shell over his own tenderest parts – and he knew every suit of armor has a weak spot that can only be found by systematic poking. Every time Dex succeeded in making Tuesday smile, it was like seeing a rainbow over a haunted house.

He took his heaped plate of satay and shrimp back into the ballroom, and only then noticed Tuesday was plateless. He nodded toward the food. She picked up a skewer. Then another skewer. She had nothing if not an appetite. They chewed, Tuesday surreptitiously, and loitered by the rear wall. Tuesday's next responsibility was helping with the auction as a runner. If anyone sitting in her quadrant of the room won an item, she had to dash out and collect their pertinents: name, address, credit card number. The auction itself, she explained, would be pretty exciting – the auctioneer was a professional, brought in for the night; the cause was good; the crowd was well heeled, well sponsored, and well lubricated.

"We have VIP meet-and-greet tickets for the New Kids on the Block reunion concert," she said. "My money's on that for bidding war of the night."

"Really?" said Dex. He took in the room, ivory-draped tables and rows of maroon seats filling. "Big NKOTB fans here in the land of ancient corporate white dudes?"

"You'd be surprised. Hometown pride. Plus, there are a lot of parents bidding for their kids." She pulled the last bite of satay off her skewer with her teeth. "You should take a seat. I have to grab my clipboard."

"Want me to drive up the bid on the New Kids?"

"You can bid on anything you want." She raised her brows. "So long as you pay for it."

After Tuesday was gone, Dex, alone again, and embracing the reality that no one was going to hit on him tonight – this crowd was too old, too straight, too married, too professional – scanned for someone fun to sit beside, someone who might feel as out of place as he did.

"Is this seat taken?" he asked, placing one hand lightly on the back of a chair at the front of the room.

The woman sitting beside it looked up and smiled. No one else was sitting at the table but her. Dex would have guessed she was in her late thirties or early forties. Her skin was dark, her black hair fringed and pulled back; she was gloriously round, and rocking the holy hell out of a one-sleeved teal dress. On her ring finger was a yellow diamond big enough to put out a man's eye.

"Not at all," she said. "Have a seat! My husband bought this table as a sponsorship, but then we didn't invite anyone, so it's sort of a table for lost souls."

"Absolutely perfect," Dex said, and sat down. "Dex Howard." He offered his hand. "Professional lost soul."

"Lila Korrapati Pryce," she said, shaking it. "English teacher – former English teacher. Professional wife."

"You looked very lonely over here," Dex said. "A lonely little island."

"Crap," she said. "Lonely? Really? I was aiming for glamorously aloof, keeping my distance from the hoi polloi. International star, maybe. Bollywood queen."

"Ambassador's wife."

"Ambassador," she said.

"Heir to a diamond mine." He pointed at her ring. "Owner of a cursed jewel."

Lila laughed. She had a magnificent laugh. It was warm and hearty, like a drunk but high-functioning sailor's. "Professional mysterious woman," she said, "and the only brown person in this corner of the ballroom."

"Well, I did notice that," said Dex. "Kind of hard not to."

"You'd be surprised what people don't notice," said Lila. "I don't mind, honestly. I mean, I mind it in the larger socio-economic sense, but in the personal sense, I like being a little on the outside. Keeps me sharp." She cracked her neck. "You have to laugh."

"Or drink," said Dex. "You could drink."

"Oh, I do that too," said Lila. "And I forget that I'm not supposed to talk about uncomfortable things, especially with strangers. You'd think I hadn't lived in Cambridge my whole life."

"I am *very* glad to be sitting next to you," said Dex. "What are you drinking?"

"Vince – that's my husband, you'll meet him in just a moment – went to get—" She looked up and back and laughed again. "You'll meet him right now!"

A much older man approached the table, a glass in each hand – one with brown liquid and rocks, the other clear and sparkling with a bright wedge of lime – and Dex nearly choked. He was wearing a cape. A goddamned *cape*. A black cape like the kind British guys wore to the opera in old movies: secured, somehow, around his high tuxedo-collared neck, popped like a polo collar, fluttering halfway down his back. His skin was chalky and spotted, his hair was pure silver, his ears stuck out like wings, and under a nose you could only refer to as a schnoz was a peppery push broom of a mustache. His eyes were steady and warm. He looked like the kind of man who tied damsels to train tracks but only because that was his role in the melodrama, and he would never get away with it; he was there to give someone else a chance to be a hero.

"I leave for one second," he said, setting the sparkling drink before his wife, "and look who shows up. *Suitors*. Are we going to have to duel?" he asked Dex.

Dex stuck out his hand and introduced himself again. "Hello," he said. "And I hope you don't think it's inexcusably rude of me to ask if your name is really Vincent Price."

"Oh, it's hardly rude, certainly not inexcusable," he replied with half a smile. "And also true. Yes, my name is Vincent Pryce. Pryce with a Y, so you see, it's completely different. I was named years before the other Vincent Price became a celebrity. Though my people weren't moviegoing people, so they had no appreciation for the gift they'd given me." He sat and jauntily brushed his cape back from one shoulder. "And it is a gift. I've always loved his movies. *House of Wax. The Fly. The Tingler*! The sound of his voice, that rumbly, educated purr. And his characters: men of science, men of wealth, men of passion – undone! By ambition, by madness! Who went headlong, laughing, to their dooms."

"And rapped for Michael Jackson," said Dex.

"Plus, he introduced me to E. A. Poe," said Vince with reverence. "And for that, truly, truly I am grateful."

"Vince has one of the world's largest amateur Edgar Allan Poe collections," Lila said, as Pryce rolled his eyes at the word "amateur." "First editions, letters, ephemera, assorted memorabilia. Movie stuff, posters, film prints of the Poe movies the other Vincent Price made with Hammer—"

"Corman, my dear." Pryce placed a hand, surprisingly large and steady, over his heart. "He made *House of Usher* in 'sixty, *The Pit and the Pendulum* in 'sixty-one, *The Raven* in 'sixty-three, *The Masque of the Red Death* in 'sixty-four" – Lila shot Dex a beautifully arched brow – "and all the others with Roger *Corman*, my dear. *King* of American *independent* cinema." After he had composed himself, Pryce winked at Dex. "Master of cheap thrills."

"You should meet my friend Tuesday," Dex said. "She lives for creepy stuff. And she's right—" Dex waved across the ballroom. Tuesday, auction clipboard in hand, might have nodded in response. "She's right there. If you bid and win, she'll come over."

"I intend to," said Vince. "What's the point of bidding if you don't intend to win?" He took a drink. "Dex. Dex Howard. I make it a point of putting a serious question to a man whenever I meet him. Would you permit me?"

Dex, leaning forward with his elbows on the table, started. "Oh, me? You mean – of course." He laughed. "Fire at will."

Vince cleared his throat.

"Do you believe, Dex Howard," Vince asked, "that you are real?"

A beat of silence fell between them.

Dex looked at Lila. Her expression was flat, with no hint as to how seriously he was supposed to take her husband.

"Uh . . . yes?" Dex said.

"Your hesitation speaks volumes." Vince leaned into him. "*How* do you know you are real?"

Dex cleared his throat. Swallowed. Decided on:

"Because—?"

He didn't get a chance to say more before Vince charged ahead.

"Precisely. *Because*. Simply because," Vince said. "Because you have accepted the central, implicit thesis of existence – you exist as real because you know, as of yet, no other way of being. But that's the rub, aye. There are so many ways of being, of being real, of living, right now. And the true prize, the jewel at the end of the journey, is the discovery of the self. The selves, whether they be wrought or revealed, recognized at long last." Vince's voice quieted. "Tell me, Dex Howard. Who are you? How were you made, and how much of your making was by your own hand?"

Dex grinned at him. He could not help it. "I am a human," Dex said. "I was made by Harry and Phyllis Howard in western Mass. in 1978, probably during a snowstorm. I made myself—" Dex swallowed. "Do you want a real answer?"

Vince and Lila both nodded.

Dex considered. There were many answers. All of them were more or less real. Had his making and unmaking taken place on his high school's stage, when he was in the habit, yearly, of becoming fictional people? Or had his making been one great decisive action, when his father told him he could waste his own money on school and he agreed? Or—

He remembered his armor.

"On the day I went for an interview at a temp agency, I wore a suit, because a suit fit the part I was auditioning for," he said. "And they looked at me like I had three well-groomed heads and immediately sent me to temp in finance. So I guess that's when I made me, when I made this me that you see here before you."

"A fine distinction, *this* you." Vince nodded gravely. "We are many. All of us."

"Yes," said Lila under her breath. "I am aware I married a fortune cookie."

"In a *cape*," said Dex. "Well done."

◆

No one in Tuesday's section of the ballroom was bidding. She'd expected as much – she was staked out way in the back, surrounded by corporate-sponsored tables filled with midlevel executives who had already made their own, more modest contributions to the night's total. She pressed her clipboard to her stomach. She was still hungry. The illicit satay she'd snuck from Dex had only made her hungrier. She wasn't allowed to hit the buffet until after the auction, technically, but if she didn't get more to eat soon, she was at risk of passing out. Tuesday was a fainter. "Your blood has a long way to go," her doctor had said after Tuesday passed out in tenth-grade band and hit her head on the xylophone, "to get from your heart all the way down to your feet and back up to that big brain of yours. Your blood cells have to be marathoners. Marathoners have to take care of themselves."

"So you're saying I'm a giant with a big head."

"You know you're a giant with a big head," said her doctor. "Eat more salt."

The cream and gilt walls of the ballroom were broken up by enormous gold-draped windows. Tuesday nestled herself against one of the drapes, slipped out of her shoes, and closed her eyes. She always saw more with her eyes closed. Like the suit sitting at the table four feet to her right; he was angry about something. She could hear the fabric of his suit jacket sliding, pulling as he hunched his arms. He set his glass down hard. His voice – he was talking about nothing, really; work stuff – Dopplered in and out, which meant he was moving his head as he spoke, side to side, trying to catch an ear. He couldn't sit still. The other people at the table weren't listening to him. He was angry because to them, he was invisible. *I see you*, thought Tuesday, and opened her eyes.

Nathaniel Arches was standing in front of her.

He looked down at her bare feet, gripping the crimson carpet.

"That the secret to surviving this thing?" he asked. "Making fists with your toes?"

"Better than a shower and a hot cup of coffee," she replied, and balled up her feet.

A wave of noise crashed from the other side of the ballroom. Two bidders were going head-to-head for the New Kids tickets. The auctioneer pattered, *Do I hear seventy-five hundred, seventy-five hundred – do I hear EIGHT, eight thousand, eight thousand for the meet-and-greet of a lifetime, the New Kids in their home city, in the great city of Boston – do I hear – I hear EIGHT—*

"You should try it," she said.

"Take off my shoes? But then I won't be able to make a quick getaway."

"You're telling me the Batmobile doesn't have an extra pair of shoes in the trunk?"

"It doesn't have a trunk," he said. "Or cup holders." He looked down at the tumbler in his hand, half full, brown and neat. "I've been meaning to do something about the cup holder situation."

"But not the trunk."

"It's not like I take it to Costco."

Tuesday laughed. She'd been trying not to, and it came out like a snort.

—do I hear eighty-five – EIGHTY-FIVE, do I hear nine? Nine thousand? To hang tough with the Kids?—

"You're fun," he said.

"And you're very pretty," she said back, and that made him laugh.

"Fun and a fundraiser." He leaned against the wall beside her. "How's that working out for you?"

"I'm not a fundraiser," she said. "I'm a researcher."

"What do you research?"

"Prospects. I'm a prospect researcher."

"Ah, so you research people like me." He tapped his HELLO MY NAME IS sticker.

"I've researched *you*," she said. "Actually, you."

He brightened. "And what can you tell me?" he said. "About myself, I mean."

—TEN! I have ten from this gentleman here in the red tie. Yes – oh I can tell, I can tell you're a fan! But I have to ask, it's my job: do I hear ten thousand five hundred?—

"That you don't already know?" Tuesday said.

"Impress me."

She opened her mental file on Nathaniel Arches. Looked over his tweets. His investments. His vague pronouncements. The rumors. This was her favorite part of the job, a holdover from being the kid whose hand always shot up first with the answer. She loved to prove how much she knew.

She was about to say *You don't know you're rich* – because he clearly didn't; if her research had a common theme, it was incurious hunger, a dumb desire for more, as though he had no idea he'd already been born with more than most humans will see in six lifetimes—

But Nathaniel Arches turned and opened his eyes at her, wide. She had never seen his eyes before. In all those press photos, his eyes were slitted, protected, too cool. Now they were open, dark, steady. He was looking at her like he was capable of curiosity. Like he was searching for something.

Or someone.

She slid this information, full value yet to be determined, up her sleeve like an ace.

"You don't know you're rich," she said.

"You think I'm rich?"

"You're a few notches above rich," she said, turning to stare straight ahead.

"What's a higher notch than rich?"

"Stupid rich," she said. "Then filthy rich. It gets fuzzy once you're over a billion."

—do I hear eleven! ELEVEN! – Hey – hey, man, you've got some competition for biggest New Kid fan over here. You've got some competition!—

"What does a billion even mean?" Nathaniel said.

He grinned at her with all his teeth and raised his hand high.

"Fifty thousand!" he shouted.

Every face swung around and pushed them against the wall.

The auctioneer was a cheerfully sweaty guy named Tim. He had gray hair and a red nose and Tuesday had seen him call auctions before, but she had never seen him look like he did now: surprised.

The room held its breath.

"Well!" Tim shouted into his microphone, and the room let go – it exhaled, it hooted, it whistled and shouted. "Sir! Sir! Out of the back corner and into our hearts! You don't mess around! Do I hear fifty thousand five hundred?" Tim laughed. He turned back to the first competing bidders. "Guys? What do you think?"

Tuesday smiled – cheerfully, professionally – at the room. She saw Dex up front, kneeling on his chair and cackling, open-mouthed.

"You're nuts," she said to Nathaniel around her teeth.

"Takes one to know." Nathaniel smiled back.

"Fifty thousand going once!" said Tim.

"Do you even like the New Kids?" she asked.

"Not really. Do you?"

"Fifty thousand going twice!"

"Not – particularly—"

It happened then: the beginning of everything that would come after.

A dark figure on the edge of Tuesday's vision stood up at the front of the room not far from where Dex was sitting – in fact, exactly where Dex was sitting, at Dex's table.

"Sir!" Tim the auctioneer cried. He turned away from Archie and flung his arm toward the figure like he was hurling a Frisbee. The room roared. *"I hear fifty thousand five hundred!"*

The figure was a tall man with silver hair, wearing a cape – *a cape?* – a cape! Tuesday peered across the ballroom. The man turned.

"Do I hear fifty-one thousand?"

The man wobbled.

Crowds feel things before they know things. This crowd of investors and developers and venture capitalists, of vice presidents and senior vice presidents, of fundraisers and gift processors and admins and researchers, mostly white, mostly men, mostly straight, rich and not rich and not much in between, but humans, all of them humans, felt it. Felt *something*. It stilled on nothing more than premonition. It waited for the man in the cape to turn around and face it. It held its tongue.

The man in the cape wobbled again. He blinked. He didn't act as though he knew where he was. His arms were raised, tense and defensive. A woman in a striking teal gown began to rise beside him, to pull him back to her, to help him. But it was too late.

He screamed. He threw his head back like hell was raining down from the ceiling and covered his head with his arms and screamed and screamed in the otherwise silent ballroom of the Four Seasons Hotel.

His final scream died in an echo. The old man in the cape straightened. He held his hands out, fingers splayed like a magician.

"Gotcha," he said.

Still nobody moved. Nobody knew what was happening.

The old man's eyes opened as large as his lids would allow and glittered in shock, as if he'd recognized a friend long lost across the chasm of time.

Then he took two steps and fell down dead.

2

THE OBITUARY

Two days later, Tuesday's desk phone rang.

The only reason anyone called instead of emailing was because they wanted something they knew they had no business asking for.

She looked at the gray caller-ID square. KURTZ, TRICIA blinked back at her in blocky blue digit-letters. Trish worked on the events team. If Tuesday was remembering correctly, the Auction for Hope – or the Auction to Abandon All Hope, as Dex was calling it – was her baby. She was the organizer, the decider. She was the person who'd had to explain to June, head VP of the development office, that yes, a donor to the hospital, a billionaire and all-around beloved kooky Bostonian, had died, gone tits-up smack in the middle of a BGH fundraising event. And no, there was nothing anyone could have done.

People tried. Dex had tried, and was genuinely upset about the whole thing, which is why Tuesday let him get away with making morbid jokes at the event's expense. Pryce's wife – the woman in teal – had tried. They both whaled on his chest. She puffed air into his lungs. Nothing worked. Vincent A. Pryce was toast, and the next morning the *Herald* upheld its long tradition as the city's classiest rag with the headline PRYCE BIDS FAREWELL.

Tuesday picked up the phone.

"Hey Trish," she said. "Are you drunk-dialing me at two in the afternoon? Because I wouldn't blame you if you were."

"Ha ha ha," said Trish. Tuesday hadn't worked with her often, but enough to know Trish was sarcastic as hell. Everyone on the events team was. It seemed a necessary disposition for a job that was five percent emailing, five percent decision-making, ten percent constant overtime, and eighty percent shitstorm crisis management. Tuesday had nothing but respect for the events team. "I wish I were. You have no idea how badly I wish I were," said Trish.

"What's up?" Tuesday spun her chair away from her computer and propped her bare feet on a pile of binders.

"Okay, so. This morning we finally processed the auction bids, at least on the items we were able to get to before, you know." She laughed. "I still can't believe it. I mean, a dude fucking died. He *died*."

"Worst. Event. Ever," Tuesday said.

"I can hear my performance review now: 'So Trish, you've had a great year, except for how you ran literally the worst event in development history.'"

"You're looking at this wrong," Tuesday said. "What if the dead guy left us money in his will?"

"You're terrible," Trish said. "Anyway, so – you were standing next to that guy when he threw fifty K on the New Kids?"

"Yeah," she said. "It was Nathaniel Arches. I think I filled out the paperwork right. It was crazy right after, because he bid and then the guy – died – but I asked him. I remember, Archie—"

"Nickname basis already?"

"We had a moment. Or two or three." Tuesday picked at her fingernail. "I asked him if he meant it, did he honestly want to bid fifty thousand dollars for the chance to chest-bump Donnie Wahlberg, and he said yes." He'd actually said – absently, stunned as everyone else in the room – *Sure, who wouldn't*. "I told him we'd bill him."

"That's interesting. Because we just called his office, and they wouldn't pay."

Tuesday stilled. "What?" she said.

"I spoke to his secretary and she said he wasn't even *there*. At the event, I mean. I got the feeling he was there in the office and just didn't want to talk to me."

Tuesday leaned forward, squaring her feet on the carpet.

"You there?" asked Trish.

"Yeah, I'm here. What – what a flake." Tuesday turned back toward her desk, lined with her carefully indexed and color-coded binders: new prospects, old prospects, research and database policies and procedures. Information – data, *facts* – you could trust. Once you found it, it stayed put. It didn't charm you or mislead you or make you laugh despite yourself. She knew better than to trust people. She rubbed out the *not what I expected* note she'd written in her mental file on Arches, Nathaniel – good thing she'd used a mental pencil – and replaced it with *basically exactly what I expected*.

"What a dick," Tuesday said.

"That's what I was afraid of." She heard a whoosh of air that could only be Trish sighing heavily. "Do you remember who the other bidders were? The two fighting over it?"

"Sorry. I was too far away to see."

"Screw it. I'm going to take the tickets for myself. You want to come?" Trish laughed. "You know, I'm like the only woman my age who wasn't a New Kids fan. The irony, right?"

"I wasn't either," said Tuesday. "They were too—"

"Adorable," Trish said. "God, they were so cute I could puke. I skipped right past cute and went straight to Johnny Depp, do not pass Go. And the Diet Coke guy, that commercial where he takes off his shirt?"

"I'm learning a lot about you right now, Trish," said Tuesday. "I think you mean Lucky Vanous."

"You are a human Google. I love it." Trish cleared her throat.

"Thanks for nothing. I'll keep you posted if I hear anything more from our rich dick. Unless . . ."

"Unless what?" Here it came. The no-business-asking-for ask.

"If you had a moment or two or three with him, do you think you'd get any further on the phone?"

"Trish. No."

"Can't hurt to ask!" said Trish. "Thought you might not mind a reason to reach out and touch him."

"You're better than that, Trish. Or at least you're capable of making better jokes."

"C'mon, it's for a good cause." She laughed. "I'm just kidding."

"No, you're not."

"You're right, I'm not. K, gotta go, let me know if you change your mi—" And she hung up midword, presumably because another crisis was cresting in her inbox like a horrible wave.

Tuesday set her phone back in its cradle.

She hated that she felt bruised, but she did. Bruised by a grotesquely wealthy stranger who owed her nothing, and to whom she owed even less. She'd just – recognized him. No, that wasn't quite it. Yes, she'd recognized the rich man she'd researched, but there was something about him that her research hadn't seen but her gut had.

There was more dirt to dig up.

She stood and stretched. It was the low part of the afternoon, post lunch, with nothing to look forward to but the end of the day. Her fellow researchers were either away from their cubes at meetings or buckled down with their headphones on. She flexed her feet. She could get away with not wearing shoes because the prospect research department was tucked back in a weird little makeshift office, all by itself, adjacent to the first-floor lobby of a corporate office building. The main development office was up on eight. Research had been up on eight too, once upon a time, but the office kept growing – it was still growing, though at a much slower pace since the market seized in oh-seven – and Mo, looking out for her team of professional introverts, practically sprained her shoulder raising her hand when operations asked which team would be willing to move to the first floor.

It felt more like a clubhouse than an office, surrounded on two sides with huge tinted windows looking out on the little park in front, the Verizon building next door, the entrance to the Bowdoin T station, and the parade of tourists and students and homeless and smokers and the occasional period-costumed Betsy Ross or Ben Franklin on their way to nearby Faneuil Hall. The office had a propensity to flood in the winter when the pipes froze. It definitely hadn't been designed for its current purpose, but it was snug and functional enough, and best of all, nobody came to visit. Ever.

She kicked her slippers free from the jumble of shoes under her desk and stepped into them. They were plush, fuzzy, and leopard-print, her spoils from last year's research team Yankee swap; wearing them felt like nestling her feet inside stuffed animals. She shuffled over to the kitchenette and filled the electric kettle.

She dumped a packet of cocoa mix in a paper cup.

It took only two minutes for the kettle to boil.

But by the time she padded back to her desk, she had five new Outlook emails, three more in her Gmail inbox, and her Facebook wall appeared to be one post, the same, shared about ten times. Her bag was buzzing like a pissed-off bee, her phone one long, continuous thrum.

Dex was calling, wanting her attention in the middle of the day.

A cool thump filled her throat where her pulse usually sat.

"Dex!" she said, her voice a cough. "What's wrong? Why are you calling me?"

"*Read your email,*" he said. There was a long pause. "I was planning to say that and hang up," he said.

"But you didn't."

"I couldn't. Even for the sake of drama. Because did you see it? *Did you see it yet*? Like, how can it be real? Is it really a real thing? Do you think? It's wild. It's *wild*. It's some Indiana Jones bullshit and I LOVE IT."

"I have – no idea what you're talking about."

"Oh my God, READ YOUR EMAIL."

She sat down and clicked open Dex's contribution to her personal inbox.

"You're still there, aren't you," she murmured.

"Read faster," he said. Then he dropped his voice. "This call is coming from inside the internet," he growled.

"Stop distracting me." Dex's email – subject line: WHAT THE FUCKING FUCK – consisted of about fifty exclamation points and a link to an article from the *Boston Globe*. Tuesday clicked.

"Oh – it's his obituary. Pryce's obituary."

"READ. IT." Dex coughed again. "You're not reading fast en—"

Tuesday hung up on him.

She loved obituaries. Even before she'd taken a professional interest – she consulted obituaries for research all the time – she had loved them. They reminded her of Abby Hobbes. The two of them used to read the obits every weekend, until their fingers were black with newspaper ink. It was Abby's habit originally, and she'd shared it with Tuesday as easily as passing her the Sunday comics. "New ghosts this week," she'd say. They'd each pick a favorite, someone they'd try, later with Abby's Ouija board, to contact. Tuesday made her selections based on the kindred-tingle she'd get reading some small detail – how much they loved the movies, a strange hobby they had, a meandering career path – that triggered a realization of regret: she'd just missed her chance to know them. And she had; no matter how many new ghosts she and Abby tried to talk to, none of them ever talked back.

Abby never got her own obituary. Plenty of other articles in the paper, but no obit.

Vincent Pryce's was in a class all by itself.

It was preceded by a headline – VINCENT A. PRYCE, BILLIONAIRE ECCENTRIC, PENS OWN OBITUARY – and a brief explanatory lede:

Larger-than-life Bostonian Vincent A. Pryce died on Tuesday night at the Four Seasons Hotel, during a fundraising event for Boston General Hospital. His death is not being treated as suspicious. On Wednesday, the Boston Globe received a request to print the following death notice. Pryce was a frequent contributor to the Globe's public opinion pages, always by mail and always manually typed. Around the Globe, he was known for his passion for the arts, his wild fancies, and his fastidious attention to AP Style.

Given the unprecedented nature of his death and the spirit of his life, the editorial board has decided to honor Mr. Pryce's final request.

And honor Pryce's executors, Tuesday thought, and the possibility that Pryce left the paper a little something in his estate. She knew Pryce had a history of underwriting Boston institutions with financial woes, and the *Globe* had been teetering for years. She scrolled down past a photo of Pryce. He was wearing a respectable black suit and tie, but something about the way he held his shoulders, the gleam in his eye, the cackle that was surely at the back of his throat, made Tuesday think he was always wearing an opera cape, even when he wasn't.

It seemed an exhausting way to perform one's life.

The obit was a scanned image of two typewritten columns.

I AM DEAD.

You may think me mad to say such a thing. And you are most likely right, or at least not intractably wrong. I was mad when I was alive, so why should I expect death to grant me sanity?

My name was Vincent A. Pryce. I was born. I lived. I traveled the world, seeking and collecting rare and fantastic objects, strange treasures with powers I daren't describe for fear of being thought even madder. Now I have arrived at death's doormat with a full heart and full pockets. I regret the latter. Work remains to be done. Death prevents me from doing it myself.

And so I turn to you.

Yes, you: you human, reading this obituary. You are cordially invited to attend my funeral masque, to be held on Boston Common at six o'clock in the evening on the third Friday of October. Costumes are required. Save the date; formal invitation to follow.

You are also cordially invited to play a game. I have devised a quest. An adventure of intellect, intuition and imagination that begins now and will culminate on the night of my funeral. You and everyone you know are invited to play.

Is it mad to bestow my legacy on a stranger? On someone I have never met, in this life or presumably the next — though having not yet gone to that other life, at the time of this writing, I cannot say for sure whether my heirs will possess the ability to travel betwixt both. If it be madness, then indeed I am mad, for to the worthy players who dare and who dream, I shall share a portion of my great fortune.

For my fortune is great. No one person can possibly possess it all, and to the degree that I have attempted to do so over my finite years, I regret the time wasted. Of this game there will be no prize won if many do not succeed.

I have already told you where to begin. Listen for the beating of the city's hideous heart.

I am survived by dearest Lila and by all of you. Live as well and as long as you can.

In lieu of flowers, donations may be made to the Massachusetts Society for the Prevention of Cruelty to Animals.

She called Dex.

"This is amazing," she said.

"I can't believe you hung up on me."

"This is *amazing*."

"I *know*," said Dex. "It's blowing my mind. It's blowing the mind of everyone in my office. Of everyone in Boston. It's blowing the whole freaking *internet's* mind. It's—"

"Did he say anything to you that night? Anything that might – make this make sense?"

"Yes." Dex's voice was short. "He said X marks the spot."

"What about his wife?"

"I don't know, Tuesday," he squeaked. "She was maybe a little too upset watching her husband die to, like, tell me Marion Ravenwood has the headpiece to the staff of Ra or whatever."

That brought a moment of silence.

"Sorry to drag down the mood," Dex said.

"No, you're right." She took a sip of too-hot cocoa and scalded the tip of her tongue. "You're right. This is serious. Sad. I wonder if he was sick. Physically ill, but he had time to creatively settle his affairs."

"You're the one with the access to medical records, hospital girl."

"It's so . . . Spielbergian. He died and left some kind of treasure hunt. I know he's wealthy, but is he – *this* wealthy? What kind of fortune is he talking—" She tucked the phone between her ear and her shoulder and began to Google furiously: *Vincent Pryce treasure. Pryce treasure hunt. Pryce Boston.* "Holy crap. He owns the Castellated Abbey. Of course he does."

"What's the – cast – what now?"

"It's the most expensive house on Nantucket. It's a freaking castle." Her brain leaped: *I bet he knows the family Arches*. She typed "Pryce Nantucket Arches" and was rewarded with an entire page of cached articles from the *Nantucket News*.

They were – had been – next-door neighbors. Or as next-door as possible when you both own serious beachfront acreage, and as neighborly as possible when you hate each other. "Arches Files Injunction Against Neighbor's Castle, Citing 'Turret Height' Code Violation." "Pryce Submits Zoning Request for Cannon; Neighborhood Tensions Escalate."

She could have clapped. This was the kind of dug-up research diamond that made turning all that earth worth it.

"I've gotta go research this guy and figure out if he's for real. If this hunt is for – real."

"Attagirl!" said Dex. "Like tossing a whole bucket of chum in the water."

"Are you calling me a shark?"

"I'm calling you Jaws. Text me when you solve it."

There was no response.

"Tues," Dex said, "I can hear your heavy breathing. I'm going to hang up now. Happy hunting."

There was still no response. Her brain was already five clicks deep into Wikipedia.

◆

Tuesday had always been spooky. Even before Abby Hobbes moved next door when they were both twelve and Tuesday's horror movie literacy shot through the roof, the youngest Mooney had a reputation. While her older brother, Oliver, did everything in his power to distance himself from their townie-weirdo parents – wearing a tie for fun, printing out business cards on their ink-jet that read OLIVER P. MOONEY, STUDENT, YOUNG ADULT – Tuesday wore fake plastic fangs to school every day. She loved to play witch: flying around the play-ground on an imaginary broom, casting spells on unsuspecting teachers, and keeping track of the names of dozens of black cat familiars. Some kids were into it, though she usually lost them at the burning-at-the-stake-while-hurling-defiant-invectives-at-your-accusers stage of the game. When she was in fourth grade, her teacher warned her parents that their daughter was dangerously morbid.

"They think you're unhealthily fixated on death," her father told her later. Her mother had made a beeline for the box of wine in the fridge. "I told them *America* is unhealthily fixated on death *in absentia*. *America* pretends we're all gonna live forever. That everything is a sunny Coke commercial, that this grandiose experiment of a nation isn't built on blood and bones and broken bodies. Moonie, you look the dark in the face and still you dance. *You* are *healthily* fixated on death."

It was the most grown-up compliment her father had ever paid her.

She didn't have friends, really. Before Abby, other kids hadn't seemed worth the effort. She had her dog, a mutt named Giles Corey, who was too dumb to be a familiar but super-cute. She had her parents, and her parents had the shop – Mooney's Miscellany, which sold games and souvenirs on Essex Street, snug in Salem's touristy heart. She had her brother, who was wicked uptight but would at least play Monopoly with her. Most of all, she had books: she had *Bunnicula* and Bruce Coville and Susan Cooper and John Bellairs and William Sleator and Joan Aiken; later, she had all Stephen King, all the time. She had bedraggled collections of ghost stories she took out of the library again and again, and, yes, one collection of stories by Edgar Allan Poe. "The Cask of Amontillado" gave her a nightmare. She could think of no death more horrifying, more mortifying, degrading, or dreadful, than to be bricked up alive in a cellar while wearing a clown suit.

Tuesday hated – hated – clowns.

But she had always loved a sick thrill. Any thrill, really, but the sick ones – the ones that gave her vertigo, that raised her pulse and her gorge, that made her realize there was an awful lot of darkness beyond her own flickering flame – made her feel the most alive. It was why she found horror movies so comforting. Her adult life had turned out to be a series of patterns and routines. She knew what to expect of a given day, but that didn't always mean life was particularly interesting, or that she was particularly fulfilled, or that she knew what the point was, other than moving from one space to the next. At least when a guy with a butcher knife is after you, when a werewolf is loose or a poltergeist is messing with your furniture and your head, you know what you're fighting for.

So she got it. She got why this guy – this Vincent Pryce with a Y – would go nuts over occult junk. Over Poe. Would spend his life and his money collecting manuscripts and letters, rare bits and bobs from the author's own sad, melodramatic, and substance-addled life, and a whole castle's worth of funky crypto-junk. His "collection of haunted matter" was replete with mermaid remains, yeti print casts, spell books and charms, and, he claimed, "more than ten thousand haunted artifacts – objects housing the spirits of the departed," including paintings, photographs, jewelry, pipes, slippers, watches, aviator goggles, typewriters, paperweights, one toaster, and a pince-nez that once belonged to Lizzie Borden, and presumably contained her forty-whacked stepmother and/or her forty-one-whacked father.

She clicked from article to article on the web. He'd been profiled in *Town & Country*, *Mental Floss*, *Architectural Digest*. He'd made his billions as the founder and sole owner of the Vincent Mint, which sold commemorative collectible coins and plates, movie reproductions, games, and other tchotchkes by direct mail: Neil Armstrong on a spoon. Lady Liberty struck in high relief on a solid-gold medallion. A Monopoly set with mother-of-pearl inlays on the board and fourteen-karat-gold pieces. If she'd been researching him for the hospital, she would have based her assessment of his net worth on real estate (the Castellated Abbey on Nantucket was worth thirty million alone) and his history of philanthropy; he had a personal foundation that distributed millions annually to performing and visual art and literature programs at public schools across the country.

But since she was researching him for *herself*, she focused on the haunted collection. That was what made him tick, and she was sure that's what would be at the heart of this quest, and its prize. He certainly had the wealth and the inclination to give away a monetary prize, which could be even greater than his known assets would suggest – he vocally and vociferously distrusted banks and the stock market ("thieves and swindlers, all!"), so his cash was probably all in gold. Probably bricked up in a basement vault next to the amontillado. But still, that wasn't what he valued.

Money alone – that wouldn't be the prize. That wasn't what his legacy would be.

"This isn't that crazy," she murmured to her computer. A lawyer could probably treat this – scavenger hunt? game? – as a contingent bequest of a portion of the larger estate. Pryce was leaving assets, defined however loosely, to someone, but specifying that someone by conditional deed and not by name. A lawyer could help him set everything up legally, and practically, too; if there were physical clues hidden around the city, she doubted Pryce had planted them all. She checked the open record they had for him in the development database, made by another researcher long before her time. No lawyer was listed under his contacts, just his wife.

Tuesday tapped the end of her pen against her teeth.

This could be real. It was bonkers, sure, but that didn't mean it wasn't also legally plausible.

She minimized the database window and Pryce reappeared before her on the open web tab, smiling out of the photo that accompanied his *Mental Floss* profile. He was wearing a bowler and peering through Lizzie Borden's pince-nez at the photographer with a terrific grin. *I would have liked you,* she thought. *I would have liked you a lot, and I only just missed you.*

Pryce had been spooky, too. He had been plumbing the world for madness, perversity, and sensation. But also: possibility, strangeness. In searching the darkness, he was chasing the mysteries of life. Now he was passing the search along, handing it off like a baton.

She envied him a little. She'd chased plenty of things in her life – grades, her own phone line, diplomas, sex, the city, jobs, apartments, new jobs, better jobs, better sex, alcohol, different jobs, different apartments – but somewhere around thirty, she had looked around and realized she'd caught the one thing, all her life, she'd been searching for the hardest: a life on her own terms. For the past three years, she hadn't moved. She was paying her rent and her bills, chipping away at her student loans. She hung out with Dex sometimes, she tutored her neighbor Dorry, she saw her parents and her brother and sister-in-law and her niece every few weeks for dinner. It wasn't a *bad* life, not in the least. Tuesday was keenly aware that she had much to be objectively grateful for, and she was. But it was a life without mystery. It was a life without an organizing hunger, and it was slightly surprising – though maybe it shouldn't have been – that the reward for achieving one's goals wasn't total satisfaction. It was a new, vague itch. For something else, something unknown and as yet unnamable.

Tuesday was bored.

And now she—

She wanted to raise her hand.

She wanted that baton.

3

THE WOMAN IN BLACK

For Dorry Bones, Thursday nights were Tuesday nights.

Tuesday was her neighbor. Tuesday was the coolest f—ing person Dorry had ever met.

Two years ago, after Dorry's mother died and her father had to sell the house and they moved into the apartment, Dorry had started seeing a tall, pale woman who wore only black. Black T-shirts. Black sweaters. Black pants and sneakers and jeans that were technically blue but so dark they looked black. Her hair was the color of black coffee. She appeared and disappeared and reappeared again: Turning her key in a mailbox. Holding the front door. Leaving the laundry room. Once, in her pajamas – also black, dotted with tiny skulls – on the front lawn after the building's smoke alarm went off at two in the morning. The woman in black came and went and smiled a small smile at Dorry but never spoke.

Their apartment building was the kind of place that would be incomplete without a ghost or two. It was old and brick, four floors high, and wrapped like a horseshoe around a small green courtyard with pink and purple impatiens and a black lamppost in the center like in *The Lion, the Witch and the Wardrobe*. Some nights Dorry would lie awake thinking about all the other people eating and talking and having sex right next to her, right below her, right beside her and above her, right *now*, and all the other people who *had* eaten and talked and had sex in this one giant building for decades. It gave her the same fluttery feeling she got when she stood on the edge of the ocean, like that time (the last time) Mom took her to the wharf in Salem: like she was the tiniest part of something vast and old, something that had been around a long time before her and would keep rolling in and out long after she was gone. It made Dorry feel, for a second, like she was okay, and that the things in her life she couldn't control – which was basically all of it – weren't her fault. Because no one ever could control the sea.

They were supposed to have a city apartment for only a little while, to have what Dad called "options" and "flexibility." That's why he rented in Somerville instead of someplace out on the commuter rail; he could justify the expense if it was only temporary. Her dad worked in a lab at MIT, and it was super-easy for him to take the bus to work, which Dorry suspected was the real reason they rented in the city – he had never learned to drive, and never would, now, because of the accident. But she'd heard him say on the phone to Gram that it wasn't any cheaper than the house, thanks to the Gentrifying Hipsters. Her dad had a problem with the Gentrifying Hipsters. They brought a "plague of cocktail and artisanal-olive bars," restaurants with mac and cheese made from cheeses that sounded like characters from *The Hunger Games*, stores that sold actual records, and lots of friendly people with small dogs and fun hair. Dorry could see her dad's point – artisanal donuts were kind of pushing it – but she still liked it. And she especially liked the city's buses and trains and the subway, because she didn't want to learn to drive either, or move again, ever.

She wanted to stick around and haunt this place like the woman in black.

She knew the woman wasn't really a ghost. Ghosts, real ghosts, were a different thing. Dorry was old enough to know she wasn't supposed to believe in ghosts – and she didn't believe in them *that* way, in white sheets and clanking chains, like a kid. Dorry wasn't a kid. She was in ninth grade. She'd turned fourteen in August. She'd gotten her period a year and a half ago, she'd kissed someone (Wade Spiegel, who maybe would be her boyfriend if he hadn't moved to Ohio), she'd been wearing a bra since she was eleven, and for God's sake, the quickest route out of childhood was a dead parent, and she had that locked down. Now she believed in ghosts like a grown-up. Like a scientist. She believed in cold spots and strange lights and electromagnetic anomalies that defied explanation. She couldn't help it. Ever since the accident, it was the only way to believe she might see her mom again. Without, like, dying herself.

She officially met Tuesday on a lame gray Thursday during her first Somerville March. School had been whatever. She didn't hate it, but she didn't love it either. Leaving her old school felt like escaping. Ever since it had happened, they'd all been watching her, like she was a pathetic puppy, maybe with one eye and a limp. It was a relief to be the new kid, the half-Asian girl (her mom was Chinese; her dad was Jewish) who kept to herself and wasn't even on Facebook. By spring, her new-kid cool had faded to general disinterest. And the disinterest was totally mutual. She'd rather hunt around for every last bite of information she could find about ghosts. Sightings. Famous hauntings. Modern methods of detection. Contact.

But that Thursday she'd been looking forward to delivery from Café Kiraz (they actually delivered frozen yogurt; reason number eight thousand why living in the city was better than stupid old Haverhill) with Dad, and watching his *Seinfeld* DVDs. If they were watching something, then they didn't have to talk. About anything, but especially the accident and Mom and the fact that her dad was spending more and more time not at home. At least watching *Seinfeld* was a way for them to still be together, in the same room, without her father constantly clearing his throat like he was about to announce something. Sometimes Dorry worried that *she* was the reason her father was staying long hours at work, not that he'd lost track of time or whatever he was working on was so important, his usual excuses. Dorry was always in the apartment when she wasn't at school; his office at work was the only place her father could be alone. And he wanted to be alone. And the fact that Dorry *didn't* want to be alone apparently wasn't that important to him.

That Thursday, he called from the lab and said he'd be late. Really late.

"There's a pot pie and some Amy's enchiladas in the freezer. And maybe a pizza?" He sounded exhausted. She wondered if he'd eaten lunch. He was probably going to drink a lot of coffee and call it dinner. "Does that sound okay, Dor?"

Not really. But all she could say was, "Yeah, no problem. Go make science. And don't stay out too late." As soon as they ended the call, she pulled up the number for Kiraz. She'd had her dad's credit card memorized for months.

As she waited for her sandwich (turkey with green apples), her cup of minestrone, and her vanilla frozen yogurt with double Heath bar mix-ins, she began to sink. Sinking had become something of a problem lately. That was the only way to describe the feeling: one minute she'd be sitting on the couch or her bed, rereading her mother's old *Sandman* comics or highlighting entire paragraphs in her American history textbook because it all seemed important, and the next she would feel heavy, like she was made of stone. Solid and cold and dense, so dense she couldn't move her legs or lift her arms or even look up.

She started sinking after Mom died, a few days after the funeral. Everyone had gone home. Life was supposed to be normal, or whatever kind of normal was possible now. Dad was at the grocery store, and Dorry, alone, sat on the couch and felt herself pressing into the cushions. It was like gravity had tripled. She sat there sinking until her dad came home and asked for help unloading the groceries. And the weight lifted. Just like that. She thought she'd dreamed it at first.

But it came back. It usually happened when she was alone, but not always. Even if she was surrounded by people, the weight made her too flat, too slow, to tell anyone about it. So she didn't. The weight made her too heavy to care. It happened in fifth-period English. It happened while she was waiting to cross the street, at the dinner table, and that day, that Thursday when she met Tuesday, it happened while she was sitting in the recliner, waiting for the delivery guy. She felt cold and hard and heavy, and she sank without a sound.

Sound. She heard a sound. Someone was thumping down the hallway toward the apartment. *Food*, she thought, and the sink let go a little, enough for her to get out of the recliner and walk across the living room, enough for her to open the door.

It was the woman in black.

"Oh hi!" said Dorry. She was a little too excited, but it was hard *not* to be whenever the sink let you go. And it had; it was gone. The woman had vanquished it.

"Hi there," the woman said, and if Dorry had freaked her out, she was totally cool about it. She pushed her sunglasses up in her hair. She was holding keys, and Dorry realized – right then, for the first time – that the woman in black didn't just live in her building. The woman in black was her next-door neighbor. There were two apartments at the end of Dorry's hallway, their front doors adjacent to each other. She had heard muffled music through the wall they shared, had heard the door open and close, but had never met her neighbor until now.

"Are you okay?" asked the woman. "Do you want a tissue?"

Dorry's hand jumped to her cheek. Her fingers came back smudgy, damp with mascara. She'd waited until she was thirteen to start wearing makeup (Mom's rule, even if she hadn't been around to enforce it), and she still forgot when it was on her face. She'd been crying. Sometimes that happened when she was sinking.

"Oh—" she said. "Um. Yes. Thank you."

The woman dug into her bag for a plastic packet of tissues. "I'm Tuesday," she said. "Nice to meet you."

"Dorry," said Dorry, and wiped at her eyes. Her cheeks felt very hot. She didn't know why she was mortified, but she was. "I'm waiting for delivery. I thought that's who you were."

"Ah, I see," said Tuesday. "I get pretty sad waiting for delivery too."

What Dorry did next happened because she'd been sinking, and because she wasn't sinking anymore. And because this *whole time* the ghost had been living right next door.

She threw herself at the woman in black. She wrapped her skinny arms all the way around her and hugged like she hadn't hugged anyone in months, which she hadn't.

And the woman in black – Tuesday – hugged her back.

That was the beginning. By now, Tuesday Thursdays had settled into a simple pattern: They ordered Indian. They talked about Dorry's classes and homework, per her dad's wishes. She wasn't flunking or anything, but Dorry knew she could be doing better. She'd always been a straight-A to A-plus kind of kid until the accident, which had sort of redefined what did and did not feel important. Homework was definitely the latter. And she *had* been doing better in school since Tuesday Thursdays started.

But it wasn't because Tuesday was knowledgeable about the War of 1812 or vectors or *Animal Farm* or quadratic equations (though she was); it was because Tuesday was her friend. And a grown-up, but the sort of grown-up who made growing up look pretty great. Tuesday came and went when she pleased. Tuesday bought her own groceries and washed her own dishes. She took care of herself. She had a job in the city at the big hospital, and from what Dorry understood, she was great at it – and she cared about Dorry. Having someone care about you makes you want to give a shit, especially if you're having trouble caring about yourself.

And she had great taste in music and movies and TV. That was the *real* tutoring Tuesday did: every Thursday, Dorry got a new lesson in the culture she'd missed out on because she hadn't been born yet. Tuesday had introduced her to every season of *Buffy the Vampire Slayer*, even the bad ones. To *Twin Peaks*, which Dorry didn't really understand, though that seemed like the point. They started *The X-Files* over the summer. Dorry loved it so much she dreamed about it. It made Dorry want to grow up, because the world was big and strange and exciting, and as long as you had your true partner – and you loved each other so much you couldn't even, like, *discuss* it – you would live to fight another monster. You might meet a miracle.

But tonight the pattern was off.

Dorry pressed her hand to Tuesday's door. It vibrated. Usually when her neighbor was playing music this loud, Dorry knew better than to knock. It meant Tuesday was working. It meant Tuesday was working so hard she wouldn't notice if a bomb went off.

But it was *Thursday*.

She knocked three times. Nothing. She held her ear to the door and heard half a lyric – *luctantly crouched at the starting line* – that sounded like . . . Cake? Was that the name of the band? Dorry was a little obsessed with the nineties. Tuesday had been treating her to what she called the BMG Music Service experience, which, so far, included a lot of Cranberries, Tori Amos, and Cake. Dorry knew that Tuesday played Cake when she really wanted to concentrate, when she needed the rest of the world to fade away.

She felt a little hurt. But then curiosity swallowed her hurt and she balled up her fist and pounded on the door until it rattled, until the Cake – *HE's going the dist* – cut out. She heard foot thumps and then the three friendly clacks of Tuesday throwing her door's bolts and chains back.

"Hey," Tuesday said. "Sorry, I got distracted with this crazy – did you see this thing?" She stepped aside for Dorry to enter. "This obituary treasure hunt thing?"

Dorry dropped her purple bag on the floor next to Tuesday's pile of shoes. The buttons on the straps clattered and clinked. "Nope," she said. "You forget I don't have any friends. Or any Facebook friends." She could make a joke about it because she *did* have a friend – Tuesday – even if she didn't have any friends at school. But she really didn't have Facebook, or Twitter, or anything. Dorry had a phone "for emergencies," from her grandmother. But she'd never signed up for Facebook because her mother was still out there, smiling like nothing ever happened. Once she'd asked her friend Mish from her old school, who did have an account, to show her her mother's page. It was still up months after the funeral, and full of comments like RIP, thinking of you all, what a beautiful person, gone too soon, from people Dorry had never heard of. It was weird. She didn't know how to feel about it. And she didn't know what was worse: that pictures of her mom, pictures of *her* and her mom, were haunting the internet forever for anyone to click and comment on, or that one day her father could check a box and make it all go away.

"I forget," said Tuesday, "you're the last Luddite teen in America."

"It does not make me a Luddite," Dorry said, "to not want to give it up to Mark Zuckerberg."

"Dear Dorothea." Tuesday put a warm hand on her shoulder.

"The first time you share your private information with an internet monolith is a very special, magical—"

"I'm saving myself for Tumblr," Dorry said.

Tuesday closed her door and pulled her phone out of her back pocket. "Usual?" she asked, and Dorry nodded, though nothing about this Tuesday Thursday felt usual. There were short stacks of paper all over the living room floor, lined up across the coffee table and the couch cushions.

"What's the big deal?" Dorry asked.

"A very rich man died," Tuesday said. She put her hands on her hips and faced the neat piles she'd made. "In his obituary – he wrote it himself – he promised to leave part of his estate to whoever follows his clues. It's like a treasure hunt."

"Can he do that?"

"He did it," said Tuesday. She squatted down and narrowed her eyes. "His obit says to 'listen for the beating of the city's hideous heart,' which is a reference to Poe's 'Tell-Tale Heart.' You know that story?"

Dorry nodded. She'd just read it in English. It was basically a New England English class requirement, to read Poe in October. "Guy goes crazy because the old man he's taking care of has a big creepy eye," she said. "So crazy guy kills the old man and hides the body under the floorboards. But then he confesses like as soon as the police even *breathe* on him, because he thinks he can hear the old man's dead heart still beating under the floor."

"Poe's narrators are always drama queens. 'I admit the deed!'" Tuesday muttered. "'Tear up the planks! here, here! – It is the beating of his hideous heart.'"

A black and white blur galloped out of the bedroom and straight through the papers.

Tuesday gently smacked her own forehead. "I am a terrible cat mom. I haven't fed him yet."

"On it," said Dorry. The tuxedo blur – Gunnar – was

sprawled on his back on the kitchen linoleum, looking very weak and hungry, or as weak and hungry as a slightly overweight cat can look. "Talk about drama queens," Dorry said, and rubbed the thick white fur of his belly. His eyes slid closed.

"So anyway," said Tuesday, her voice echoing toward the kitchen, "I thought 'The Tell-Tale Heart' might be the decoder ring, the key to deciphering – whatever the clue is. If it were a straightforward substitution cipher, you know, a jumble of seemingly meaningless letters that he gave us and said here, crack the code, someone would have cracked it in five minutes. But the clue *itself* is hidden. Under the floor. Like the old man. All we can hear is the beating of its hideous heart."

"Which is only in our minds," called Dorry over the plinking of cat kibble into Gunnar's dish.

"He said he already told us where to begin, so I printed off every letter to the editor he ever wrote, of which there are many. I've spread them out by month and year." She looked up. "How do you feel about reading a bajillion letters tonight?"

Dorry walked back to the living room. "What am I looking for?" she asked.

Anything. Anything that didn't seem quite right, that called attention to itself. Or, as Tuesday said with a shrug, any jumble of seemingly meaningless letters. Dorry threw her legs over the arm of the couch and Tuesday took her cat-scratched leather chair, and for the next thirty minutes, they read.

Dorry was surprised that it sort of bummed her out. This guy – Vincent Pryce – seemed pretty cool. He made a lot of dumb jokes, but he also really, really cared about things. He cared about teaching theater and music in elementary schools. He cared about scholarships for kids to attend summer programs and prep schools and colleges. When a handful of parents tried to get *The Diary of Anne Frank* taken off their kids' summer reading lists, he went ballistic.

Pryce also had strong opinions about, of all things,

Valentine's Day. On February 13, 2006, he wrote, "Please – this holiday makes a mockery of one of our greatest capacities as humans, perhaps THE greatest function of the heart: to love and to be loved." On February 10, 2007: "Ask yourself: why do many of us feel compelled to spend this day proving we love each other, something we could be doing any other day of the year without the absurd theater of chocolate roses or edible underwear?" February 14, 2008: "Roman godlings, bare-bottomed. Flowers that smell of sugar and rot. Hearts. Candy hearts. Chocolate hearts. Stuffed hearts with cheap lace edging. Hideous hearts, all."

Hideous hearts.

Dorry grabbed a pen and began to circle.

Tuesday's buzzer rang.

"Thank the Maker," Tuesday said, and pressed the button under her intercom to let the delivery guy up. She was in the kitchen, clanking silverware against plates, when Raj – their normal Palace of India Thursday-night delivery guy – knocked on the door. Dorry, distracted, opened it.

It was not Raj.

It was a white guy. Tall. Lanky. Dark hair that was somehow annoying – kind of fake-looking and wrong, like a wavy helmet of snapped-on Lego hair. His whole face was long, prickly with five-o'clock shadow, except for his smile, which was soft and wide. He was wearing jeans and sneakers that looked like the kind the rich kids at her old school collected – because that was a Thing, collecting sneakers – and a bright white T-shirt, bright blue V-neck beneath a beat black motorcycle jacket with a rip in the sleeve. He smiled at her, then thought better of it.

"You're not Raj," she said.

"No, but he said to say hi. And to give you this." He had a rumbly voice. He handed her the usual brown paper bag of food, order slip and receipt stapled to the folded flap.

"Tuesday," Dorry called. "Could you—"

She could feel Tuesday standing behind her.

"You're not Raj," said Tuesday, and then, sharp, "Did you pay for our food?"

The man nodded.

"So you could pay for our food but you couldn't pay your auction bid?" She paused. "Actually, that isn't much of an argument."

"No, it isn't," said the stranger. "It is far, far easier for me to pay thirty bucks plus tip for Indian than fifty thou for New Kids tickets."

"Do you know this guy?" asked Dorry. "Or should I call nine-one-one?"

"I haven't decided yet," said Tuesday.

"Well. You should decide," said Dorry. "Because the food is getting cold and I'm hungry."

"This will only be a second," Tuesday said. "Take the food." She looked at the stranger. "You," she said, "aren't coming in. But I want to talk to you."

Dorry cradled the food bag and walked in her sock feet to the kitchen, listening the whole way.

"How did you find out where I live?" Tuesday's voice was quiet but firm.

"You of all people should know how easy it is to find someone's address," he answered.

"Okay, let me rephrase: where the hell do you get off coming to my apartment?"

Dorry set the bag on the counter. Gunnar, having followed her into the kitchen, gazed up at her expectantly. Dorry lifted him into her arms, which wasn't at all what he'd been hoping for.

"—apologize."

"Bullshit."

"I knew you'd say that," he said. "Which is why I brought this—"

Dorry didn't need to hear more.

She bolted into the living room, Gunnar bouncing in her arms. "Don't you TOUCH her," she shouted, "or I will throw this cat at you."

The stranger was holding a piece of paper between his first two fingers. Tuesday was reaching for it.

Gunnar sort of sighed.

"He has claws," Dorry said. "And he knows how to use them."

"It's okay," Tuesday said. "This is a classic example of money having its own rules."

Dorry shifted Gunnar's weight. It was like holding two bags of warm flour wrapped in a sweater.

"Money has its own sense of what is and is not appropriate human behavior," said Tuesday. "For example, money" – she indicated not-Raj, who gave a stupid little wave – "thinks it's okay to show up at a stranger's apartment so long as he's hand-delivering a check for fifty thousand dollars."

"Does that mean I can come in?" he asked.

"No," said Tuesday.

"I meant to pay. I swear. My secretary gets requests for money all the time, so she turns them down out of hand. I forgot to tell her this one was legitimate." He shrugged. "It was a crazy night. And I am truly sorry for the trouble I've caused." He looked down at the floor. "Still making fists with your toes, I see."

"Stop staring at my feet," said Tuesday.

The stranger flushed. It made Tuesday smile one of her small smiles, the kind that meant she was playing around. That was enough for Dorry to relax a little. She set Gunnar down on the sofa, next to Pryce's letters about Valentine's Day.

"To be honest—" said the stranger.

"Please do," said Tuesday.

"I have a proposal for you. I assume by now you've heard about Pryce's quest."

Tuesday nodded.

"I know a lot about him. He's – he *was*, I guess – a family . . . acquaintance. I've seen his collection. And, assuming some 'portion of his great fortune' includes the collection, I can personally vouch that it's worth whatever we can do to make it ours."

"Pretty liberal use of the plural possessive there, Arch," said Tuesday. She crossed her arms and propped herself against the doorframe.

"I know things," he said. "You know things, and what you don't know I bet you know how to find. The check I just gave you – I can write another one, just as big, if you agree to help me with Pryce's game."

"No," said Tuesday.

He opened his mouth in a perfect O. Dorry leaned into the silence growing between them. Because she knew Tuesday, she knew it was a deep-thinking silence. But the stranger – Arch or whatever – didn't know that. He panicked.

"I'll double it," he said. "One hundred thousand for your help."

"I'm charmed that you take my silence for hardball," said Tuesday. "Trust me, you'll know when I'm playing hardball, and that wasn't it." She stared at him. "Why me?"

"Because you're smart," he said.

"Unlike," said Tuesday, "the horde of lawyers, accountants, private investigators, and public relations handlers your family has on retainer."

"They're smart but you're smarter."

"I doubt that." Tuesday narrowed her eyes.

The guy frowned. Then he muttered, "I met you, I liked you, I feel bad that I flaked on the fifty thousand. And, well: nobody in my . . . *complex* family knows who you are, which means you can operate with a degree of anonymity."

"Fine, that's why me. Why you? What does the collection

have that you can't get somewhere else? You're almost passing for aspirational middle class in this J. Crew catalog drag right now—"

"*Hey*," the guy said, and smoothed his blue sweater over his stomach. "This is not J. Crew."

"—but I bet you've got four figures in loose change in your pockets. From a financial standpoint, to you, Pryce's 'great fortune' has negligible value. Forgive me for questioning your motives, but contracting me for this is like – if I were to contract Dorry here to help me hunt down a pack of gum."

"I would do that," said Dorry.

"I know you would, kid," said Tuesday. "No, not even a pack of gum. It would be like me hiring a PI to find a *wad* of gum under a desk. So why do you, dirty, filthy, stinking-rich Nathaniel Allan Arches" – with every adjective Tuesday lobbed at him, he nodded – "want a wad of used chewing gum?"

He tugged on his right earlobe, and Dorry blinked. A tell. He had a tell. The next thing out of his mouth would be a lie, or, if not a direct lie, something that wasn't entirely the truth. Her mother had had a tell: whenever she was about to drop a Wild Draw Four on Dorry in Uno, she tapped her fingers on the cards.

He inhaled. His chest rose. *So many tells*, thought Dorry, and looked at Tuesday, who had no tells, or at least none that Dorry had ever noticed.

"Why does everything have to be about money?" he said. "Honestly, and I would expect someone who roots around in the digital drawers of rich people for a living to know this already, if you have enough money, it stops meaning anything. You can't touch it or taste it or feel it. Then the things that matter become what you *can* touch, or taste, or – feel."

"Objects, you mean. Something *in* Pryce's collection," Tuesday said.

"Let's just say" – his already deep voice lowered, which

made the bottoms of Dorry's feet tingle – "that the value is sentimental."

Tuesday didn't respond.

"One hundred fifty thousand," he said. "Final offer."

"One hundred fifty is my retainer, plus expenses," said Tuesday. "I want a working partnership. We split the detecting, the legwork, fifty-fifty. If we win, we split the reward fifty-fifty. I'll take half, you take half. Or you can buy me out, for however much Pryce's estate is currently valuing whatever the prize turns out to be." She smiled. "But for no less than five million."

Dorry's throat dried up. She made a little coughing sound halfway between a gasp and a laugh.

"Oh, *now* you're playing hardball," said Archie.

"Still not," said Tuesday, grinning. "But closer." She stuck out her hand.

Archie paused.

"Why does everything have to be about money?" Tuesday said. "C'mon, I know you're good for it. I've done the research."

He slid his hand into hers.

"We start tonight," said Tuesday. "Because you know anyone else who's serious has already started too."

◆

So Archie came in. He introduced himself to Dorry with a handshake, and Dorry felt herself start to giggle, because seriously, a handshake? Then her hand went sort of rigid in his warm grip, and after he let go, her first thought was *I did that wrong*. Or did she? How was she supposed to shake a guy's hand, a guy who wasn't her dad's coworker, wasn't her mom's old college friend, wasn't saying, while they held her cold hand, *I'm so sorry for your loss*?

They all sat at Tuesday's rickety Ikea table and ate and strategized.

"Tell me about Pryce," said Tuesday.

"He was a weirdo. A true-blue, first-class, dyed-in-the-wool weirdo." Archie dipped a piece of naan into the malai kofta sauce. "New money, vulgar money. Barely tolerated. And I really don't think he gave a fuck. Oh—" His eyes darted to Dorry.

Dorry snorted. "Dude," she said, "you kiss your mutha with that fucken thing?"

"This is your influence?" he said to Tuesday. "Look what you're doing to the youth."

"I believe the children are our future," said Tuesday.

Dorry cleared her throat.

"Oh *children*," said Tuesday, "do you have something to say?"

Dorry felt herself blush. She did. She had a lot to say. She coughed. "Um, I think I might – know where to start looking."

Tuesday's head jerked like a bird's. "Wha— that's *great*. Where?"

Dorry looked at Archie, blushed again, and looked back at Tuesday. "Do you really trust this guy?" she asked. She didn't, but she trusted Tuesday completely.

"I trust his money," said Tuesday.

"I want a cut," Dorry said.

Tuesday cackled. "And that," she said to Archie, "is hardball. You got it, kid. I can't spend five million all by myself."

"Actually, you can," said Archie.

"Well, I have no plans to go to college again. Dorry needs it more than I do."

Dorry knew she was still blushing – she could feel her face almost pulsing, and a cool tight spot in the middle of her forehead – and when she stood up, she shook a little. Even if Tuesday only shared *one* million dollars, it meant Dad could afford the apartment for as long as they wanted. It meant they would never have to move back to the suburbs, or buy a car or have to drive one. And if neither she nor her father ever learned to drive, they could never hit a patch of black ice and smash through the guardrail of a bridge and sail into the river below. They could never be missing for two days in a blizzard, sealed under ice and snow.

They could never drown in freezing water with their seatbelt still on.

She grabbed the letters she'd been reading before Archie knocked on the door. Gunnar was sleeping on them (of course), and was less than pleased to be displaced. "Pryce had a real problem with Valentine's Day," she said, handing the printouts to Tuesday. "Every year, he wrote about what a sham it is. He calls candy hearts hideous hearts."

She heard Tuesday suck in a breath.

"I started circling the first words, then the first letters, of each Valentine's clipping. In order. So far I have P A R. It could be spelling a word, right? And didn't the obit say something about hearing the city's hideous heart?" She was talking too fast. "We'd have to find them all to be sure, but I bet – I bet the first letter of every Valentine's letter spells Park. As in Park Street."

"Park Street station. The oldest subway in America. Of course," said Tuesday. "Where else but under the ground would the old city's heart be beating?"

"Where else?" said Dorry. Her own heart was leaping like it would never stop.

4

THE CITY'S HIDEOUS HEART

Tuesday, on the sidewalk outside her apartment, snapped her bike helmet's chin buckle.

She couldn't believe she was doing this.

But *of course* she was doing this. It was the most fun she'd had in an age.

"Archie," she said.

Nathaniel Arches turned around. "What?"

"I never told you my last name," said Tuesday.

"I never told you mine either."

Fair point.

"Are you so surprised by my resourcefulness?" he asked.

"Your resourcefulness," she said, "is borderline creepy."

"Isn't your whole job borderline creepy?"

"I don't cross the border. I have a code of ethics. I don't, for example, show up at the apartment of someone I have researched."

"You just write up dossiers about us that we don't even know exist."

"Dossiers that help the people I work with strategically persuade you to become just slightly less rich, so the hospital can build a nice new oncology suite. Besides," she said, "you knew. You *know*. You gave those interviews." He pulled his own helmet over his head as she continued. "You tweeted those memes. You put an idea of yourself out there for me, for anyone, to find."

"Did you ever consider," he said, "that I was using my resourcefulness to impress you?" His voice was muffled by the helmet, but his eyes were visible, the same eyes she'd recognized in the ballroom of the Four Seasons. "And that with our powers combined—"

He threw his leg over the motorcycle, parked illegally in front of her building's driveway. Tuesday didn't know much about bikes, but she knew his was a Ducati, and that it was very cool.

"Your game needs work," she said.

The first glow of sunset was disappearing over the top of her apartment building when she climbed on the bike and locked her arms around him.

"Seems like it's working okay," he muttered, and ripped the bike to life. She was charmed, begrudgingly; it was the cheater's way of getting the last word.

They rode through the blue night air, up and over the Somerville streets, on the crumbling elevated highway, past the Museum of Science, crossing the Charles River into the white lights of the city. They swung low through the winding snake of Storrow Drive, pulled off at Beacon, looped around the Public Garden, and slalomed down into the parking garage beneath Boston Common. There was so much beneath the ground in Boston: cars and tunnels and tracks and subway trains. Literal garbage, under the Back Bay – an entire neighborhood built on landfill. No wonder Pryce started his hunt here, at the center of the city, on the corner of the Common, in one of the oldest subway stations on earth. Everything began beneath the ground.

Archie cut the engine. "That tickles," he said, and Tuesday realized her phone, tucked in her inside jacket pocket, was vibrating. Dorry, probably. She'd been pissed to be left behind, but she'd backed off once Tuesday pointed out that (a) her father would have a fit if he found out his daughter's tutor had taken her on a wild treasure hunt, (b) they needed someone at mission control, someone who could call the police if they stopped making contact, and (c) only two people would fit on the bike. "I'll give you the first two," Dorry'd said. "But the third reason is crap. It's a T station. I don't need to ride with you guys to get there."

But it wasn't Dorry. It was Dex.

Did you solve it yet you're killing me

She felt a little guilty. For forgetting about him. And for not, with a fleeting adolescent protectiveness, wanting to share.

Yes! Park Street. Heading there rn, stay tuned

It was officially blue-dark in the Common when they came up out of the garage, only a little past seven, though, so the paved paths were still full of people. The closer they got to the station itself, the brighter and noisier it was. Under a street-lamp, two guys in bandanas banged syncopated beats on upturned plastic tubs while a third did the worm on the side-walk, the last of the day's buskers, playing, now, for the locals. Drumming in the city made her walk differently. It loosened her hips. Brought her back into her body, ready to bend and to move.

Her phone buzzed again.

WHAT you mental minx

I knew you'd figure it out

She texted back, Next Dorry did, not me, and felt a pop of pride for her neighbor. Dorry was a good kid. The best kid she knew. The kind of kid who made having kids seem particularly great, if you wanted to have kids, which Tuesday didn't.

"So what are we looking for?" asked Archie.

"I have no idea."

"Then let's go see what we can find," he said. "Maybe it'll scream at us."

Park Street had two entrances, gray iron-and-stone structures like twin mausoleums dropped at the edge of the Common, heralded by the symbol of the Massachusetts Bay Transportation Authority: a capital T in a black circle, branded on white like the M on an M&M. Tuesday and Archie took the right entrance, flowing with the human tide down yellowedged steps to the first of two levels of trains. The upper Green Line platform held the remnants of rush hour, exhaustedlooking commuters, eyes glazed, ears sprouting white buds and wires, lazily poking at their phones or burying their noses in books. A girl with pink and purple hair – Berklee student, for sure – was slow-jamming the theme from *The Simpsons* on tenor saxophone, smooth and sweet, and a youngish man with dark hair silvering at his temples smiled at her. He dropped a crisp bill into the instrument case open for change at her feet. It floated down like a leaf.

Tuesday stalked along the right side of the platform, dodging T riders, following the yellow rubber edge all the way to the end. Nothing. "I don't know what I expected," she muttered. "Kilroy saying 'Vincent was here'? 'Follow to clue'?"

"Um," said Archie, pointing over her shoulder. "That seems pretty close."

On the other side of the tracks, spray-painted and dripping on the dirty white and gray plaster of the wall, was a black bird. Head up and stiff. Wings folded back. The very silhouette of a raven, if it were sitting, say, on a bust of Pallas above one's chamber door. A shaky scrawl in white chalk floated above the raven's head. She had to step closer to read it: *The prince of darkness is a gentleman!*

"I mean," said Tuesday. Her pulse picked up speed. She imagined the platonic ideal of a lawyer, three-piece suit, leather attaché, leaping over the tracks with a stick of chalk and a raven stencil, shaking a can of spray paint like a maraca: Pryce's helper. Leaving clues around the city. "We shouldn't be worried that it seems too easy, right? Pryce wants us to follow him. He wants people to solve it. He's not trying to hide."

The painted raven's beak and one spindly foot, raised, were pointing toward the dark of the tunnel, beyond the platform, where the tracks disappeared on their way to Tremont Street station.

She took a picture on her phone and sent it to Dorry.

Dorry responded in four separate texts:

O

M

F

G

"I have no idea," said Archie, drawing Tuesday by the elbow to conspire, "what sort of security cameras are set up here, but I'm willing to make a run for it down the tracks to see what we can find."

"I'm less worried about security cameras than I am about – well." Tuesday rolled her head to indicate the other people milling on the platform. "We're about to become the definition of see-something-say-something."

"They're not going to see or say anything," said Archie. "Look at them. They're zombified. We wait until another train pulls into the station and they'll all turn to look at it like—" He whipped his head to the side. "*Squirrel.*"

She swallowed. She felt a little dizzy. A little too warm. A little shaky.

On the internet, when she was researching, she was fearless. She would chase the tiniest clue down any number of research rabbit holes. This was just a forty-foot walk down a dark tunnel. Where she wasn't supposed to go, technically – but, unlike the internet, once she was gone, there would never be any trace of her. No IP data, no browser history, no nothing. Online, she left tracks. Only in the world could she actually be invisible.

This was real, and her body was reacting accordingly.

She cleared her throat. "We have options," she said. "We should discuss them. One: we wait for a break between train cars, and we sneak down the side of the tracks. Two: one of us sneaks, and one of us distracts. And I suppose there's a third option, where we locate the station manager and tell him what we've found and wait for the police to come and supervise the whole thing."

Archie's lips slid slowly into a grin. "I don't want to do that," he said.

"You are bad news," said Tuesday. "But I don't want to do that either." Her heart bumped. There was a whole world underground, of access doors and unused passages, old stations and tunnels. How deep was Pryce going to ask them to go?

Five million dollars could bail her out of jail more than a few times.

She looked across the tracks at the DANGER DO NOT CROSS signs posted every ten feet. She looked at Archie. He was rocking back and forth on his limited-edition Pradas, tenting his fingers like Mr. Burns, looking more mad scientist than sexiest new capitalist. It made him hotter. Stupid hot. One step removed from filthy hot. Tuesday's taste had always run to the Doc Browns of the world, the wild-eyed renegades and rule breakers. But Emmett Brown broke rules because he wanted to find new roads. Archie broke rules because he thought, as did so many born under a dollar sign, that the rules applied to other people. This was less attractive, philosophically.

But it wasn't *un*attractive.

The metal-on-metal shriek of a train approaching on the opposite track made her decision for her.

She grabbed Archie's hand and ran into the dark beyond the platform.

Her feet kicked up stones. She crossed over a tie with each stride. She didn't stop until they were well inside the tunnel, far enough not to be seen from the station but not so far that the station's ambient light couldn't reach them. Tuesday instinctively hopped over the rail and threw herself flat against the wall, and then realized the wall must be disgusting – all the walls were black with grime, the whole place had needed a power wash for half a century – and flinched forward, her foot connecting with an empty plastic cup. It bounced up and over the rails, clear dome winking in the low light, and rolled to a rest against some kind of train machinery. A signal box, maybe, or a breaker, levers sticking up out of the ground.

She looked behind her. No klaxons. No shouting. No reflector-stripe-uniformed T personnel blinding her with a flashlight.

She let go of the air in her lungs.

"Told you," said Archie. This time, he took her hand. "Come on," he said. "Watch your – watch your feet. You don't want to step on a rat."

"New York has rats," Tuesday said. "We have cute little mice."

"I doubt you'd want to step on one of them either."

She heard shuffling and then there was light, tiny but piercing, from Archie's iPhone. She pulled her phone out of her pocket and fired up her own app.

"So we're here," she said. "Huh."

"Not as magical as you'd hoped?"

Yes and no. They were a few yards away from the junction that brought the station's twin tracks together, en route to

Tremont, and the parallel rails coursed through the darkness, crossing, shining, melting together, iron arteries flowing from a metal heart. It was also full of garbage. Dunkin' Donuts cups and Coke bottles and wrappers and plastic bags and assorted other, unnamable detritus. She felt it before she knew it was happening – a shift beneath her feet, like an earthquake's ghost – and the train that had been pulling into the station when they made a run for it coasted down the opposite track, through the junction to points beyond, clacking through the darkness like a great green mechanical caterpillar.

She threw her phone's light up on the wall. Dirt. More dirt. Here, a door, with an MBTA PERSONNEL ONLY sign, half open – a storage closet. Inside, buckets and tools and wires and plastic yellow CAUTION/CUIDADO signboards with graphics of flailing stick figures. Next to the door, more dirt and graffiti, all in caps: YANKEES SUCK.

"Hey!" Archie's voice carried from ahead. "I found – I don't know. Over here."

Tuesday followed his voice around a corner into an alcove, clear from the path of the train, partially made of brick. Bright, clean brick. So clean it couldn't possibly have been down in the tunnel for very long. And over the brick, someone had spray-painted more graffiti, though the sentiment was some-what more refined than YANKEES SUCK:

IN PACE REQUIESCAT

"Rest in peace," said Archie.

Tuesday put her hand on the bricks. The mortar felt loose, powdery.

Shit.

"This is it. This is what we're supposed to find. There's – I hope to God there's only a clue bricked up inside and not some poor schmuck. Buried alive." Her stomach was doing something she wasn't sure it had ever done before. It felt very dense, like it had its own specific gravity, distinct from the rest of her body. "In a jester's costume," she croaked.

"Ah," said Archie. "The cask of amontillado marks the spot." He nudged her with his elbow. She tried to nudge back.

But she felt sick and weak, and all she could think of was the last time she read "The Cask of Amontillado." In high school, under duress in English Ten. Ms. Heck's class.

With Abby Hobbes.

Abby used to sit at the desk behind her. Abby kept up a running commentary throughout class, even though they both loved it, and loved Ms. Heck. Not being able to shut up was how you knew Abby Hobbes loved something. And Abby *loved* that "The Cask of Amontillado," with its pathetic, drunk clown buried alive, was Tuesday's Achilles' heel. *Are you seriously freaked by this? This is so tame. This is lame. It's masonry. It's a drunk asshole and a psycho and unnecessary home improvement. "For the love of God, Montresor!"*

Tuesday could still hear her cackle. Focus on the task, she told herself. Focus. There's nothing here that can actually hurt you. It's theater. It's a game. It's one hundred fifty thousand dollars plus expenses in your pocket. It's the possibility of five million more.

"We need a tool, a hammer or something."

"How about an elbow?" said Archie. "Or a shoulder?" And he threw himself sideways at the wall.

It did not work.

Tuesday laughed a weak laugh and felt, for the moment, better. When she realized Archie was smiling at her, and that he hadn't really expected to break through, she thought seriously about pushing him up against it and sticking her tongue down his throat.

Focus, she told herself.

They found a hammer and a rubber mallet in the supply

closet. Tuesday took a picture of the graffiti, one without and one with Archie ("Should I make finger guns?"), and sent them to Dorry, who responded immediately: !!!!!!!!!!!!!!!!! Then they stood in front of the bricked-up wall, weapons raised like bats. Tuesday paused.

"This is not how I expected my night to turn out," she said.

"Me neither," said Archie.

They swung.

Tuesday had never tried to break down a wall before, but she could tell right away this wall had been built to fall. Whatever the mortar was, it was still soft; the bricks started to give on the second swing. By the fifth swing, they'd knocked whole chunks clear. They pulled the wall down with their hands, brick by brick.

Her feet felt the earthquake-ghost again, stronger this time, closer – vibrating down their track, not the opposite one. "Careful," she told Archie. "I think a train is com—"

Archie chose that exact moment to shine his phone on the black hole they'd been making.

And on the corpse of Abby Hobbes hanging inside.

Strung up by her wrists. A multicolored ruff around her neck. Her face a bloated gray moon. Lips black. Soft rotten holes instead of eyes. Found. After all these years vanished, found. Found dead and bricked up in a tunnel underground.

Tuesday didn't scream. Later, she would be proud of herself for at least that.

What she did was turn and bolt out of the alcove like an electrified rabbit, toward the oncoming path of a Green Line car that would have splattered her across the tracks if Archie hadn't lunged after her, flung his arm around her waist, and yanked her back from the edge and into the pile of dust and bricks.

The train *ding-ding*ed.

"We've been made," Archie gasped.

The train car's brakes squealed, then shrieked.

Tuesday couldn't move. She couldn't breathe. She couldn't close her eyes. She couldn't—

It couldn't be.

It could not be Abby.

"Are you okay?" Archie asked.

She scrambled off him and onto her knees, wrapped her fingers over the edge of the broken brick wall, and peered inside.

A red emergency light flashed.

And no, of course.

Of course it wasn't Abby. Abby wasn't here. Abby wasn't anywhere.

This was a dummy. A blank mannequin, obvious now in the low red glow, hanging by its handless wrists from some kind of metal frame. It was dressed in full motley, garish red and purple and green and yellow harlequin, with a twisted jester's cap, bells on every twist. Hanging around the dummy's neck, alligator-clipped from each side like a dental patient's bib, was a furl of parchment.

Archie leaned above her, into the hole, and retrieved it.

Tuesday heard shouting down the tunnel. Far but drawing closer.

"They're coming," she said. Her voice was too loud. She pressed her lips together.

"Take this." Archie shoved the parchment into Tuesday's hands. "For, uh, various reasons – I've got to go. I hate to, but I do."

"What are," said Tuesday. "What are you talking—"

She looked beyond the alcove. The train that had almost punched her card was stopped fifty feet up the tracks, purring mechanically in a pool of red and white light. In the other direction, she saw three uniformed T personnel booking it through the station, almost to the tunnel's entrance.

Her body took over. It pushed her to her feet, it pumped her legs. She ran. She was aware of her fingers curling around the parchment. Of the sound of Archie's feet crunching through gravel, of the whirring beast of the train car on her right as she passed beside it.

She was not, however, aware of the crosstie until it caught the tip of her sneaker.

Tuesday felt the world shift. She thrust out her arms, but it was too late. She whipped straight down on her face.

Archie's footsteps at least had the decency to stop.

"Are you okay?" he hissed.

"I'm not dead," she said. The palm of her right hand and both forearms were studded with bright points of pain, rocks and gravel and please dear God (*Montresor*) nothing worse. Her ankle hurt. She'd wrenched it. She pressed herself up on her elbows.

"They can't know—" Archie's voice rose. "Not yet."

"What—" Tuesday frowned. Of course. Of fucking course. "You have *got* to be kidding me," she growled.

"Tomorrow," he said. "I'll find you." And then she heard his footsteps again, faster, farther, until Archie had melted into the black.

She lay on her back. She unrolled the now-bedraggled parchment and had time, just, before the cops were upon her, to snap a picture of it, a series of obscure symbols written in neat black pen:

"A freaking secret code," Tuesday murmured.

Aww, said Abby Hobbes, sharp, in Tuesday's rattled head. **You got a love note from the Zodiac.**

◆

The first thing Tuesday did – after the police handcuffed her and led her up the stairs, out of the station, and into the back seat of a cop car; after she successfully convinced them she was *not* a terrorist, that her goal in the tunnel was treasure hunting, and that the parchment they'd taken as evidence was in fact the first clue in that rich dead guy's game; after they decided not to charge her, because she was white and well spoken and a woman and obviously no threat to anyone; after she realized the only person – the *only* person – she could call to pick her up without either jeopardizing her employment or terrorizing her parents was Dex, and Dex said, gleefully, "I always knew one day you'd call me from jail"; after Dex came for her, around eleven, wearing his white *Miami Vice* jacket and Ray-Bans, his costume screaming *I am living for this ridiculousness,* a message that filled her with both gratitude and shame, that she'd been so worried that this slightly over-bearing but essentially decent human would need *her*; after Dex escorted her out of the precinct and through a small but aggressive throng of news media who'd gotten wind of her, because intrepid Bostonians had tweeted pictures of the scene, of Tuesday in handcuffs, even of the parchment, meaning the whole freaking internet knew what Tuesday had risked her stupid neck to find; after Dex, loving every goddamn second of this, told them his client had no comment and hustled her into the cab he'd paid to wait; after they were finally alone, and Dex said, "Jesus God, girl, what. The fuck. This town loses its shit over a couple of Lite-Brites under bridges and you decide to tear down the T?" and all Tuesday could do was shrug and shake her head because she was so exhausted she felt like vomiting, and she didn't know so many unbelievable things could happen in the same night – the clue and its solution, a brush with death, and that jackass abandoning her – not to mention the thing that was the least believable of all, seeing Abby Hobbes, *hearing* her, Abby's voice so *clear* in Tuesday's head, a place it hadn't been for more than fifteen years; after Dex walked her up to her apartment and got her a glass of water before leaving (but not before examining every room, nodding, saying, "This is exactly like I imagined, exactly") and Tuesday finally saw Dorry's texts – you are so badass, went to bed (big chem test tomorrow), DYING TO HEAR WHAT HAPPENED!!!!!!! – and realized, with a twinge, that she was perhaps the worst role model in the world – after all of that, the first thing Tuesday did was get out her Ouija board.

Technically, it was Abby's Ouija board.

Tuesday had stolen it from Abby's room during the wake. No. It wasn't a wake. What do you call it when everyone goes back to a house after a funeral to eat cold cuts and prepared salads and make strained conversation? A memorial? But could it even be a real memorial if there hadn't been a real funeral?

It wasn't a real funeral. There had been no official death. There was no obituary. There was no body. Abby was still considered a missing person. Even so, one morning they'd lowered an empty casket into the ground – empty except for a pair of purple Doc Martens, a few photographs, and the High Priestess card from Abby's Rider-Waite deck, which Tuesday had slipped in when Abby's dad, Fred, wasn't looking. (She couldn't bury the whole deck; dropping the whole deck in would have meant that she'd given up hope, and she hadn't, not then.) By noon, Tuesday was at her presumed-dead best friend's house, dragging a chip through French onion dip. Tuesday was sixteen. Abby was sixteen too. She would have turned seventeen in November if she hadn't disappeared in July.

Tuesday's parents and her big brother Ollie were eating chips too, and Ms. Heck, their English teacher, and a bunch of people from school and the neighborhood and of course Fred, who was vibrating with grief. Tuesday could almost still feel the pain of watching Fred hovering, fluttering, asking if he could get people anything to drink, trying to take care of everyone else so he wouldn't have to stop, not even for a second.

All funerals are for the living, but this funeral, this premature burial, was explicitly for Fred. He was already a widower. Tuesday didn't know if there was a word for the surviving parent of a (presumed) dead child, but now he was that too. He had tried to hope for the rest of July and most of August, and that was enough; he couldn't live with the uncertainty. She'd heard her parents talking about it, late, on the back porch, a little drunk. "He said he'd rather proceed as though she were dead than live with false hope," her dad squeaked. "Can you – can you imagine? Is that pessimism? Is that – what *is* that?" And her mother said, "It's a ritual. A rite. A motion to go through simply to move."

Tuesday, at the memorial, fled to Abby's room, which looked exactly the same as it had every day of Abby's life, or at least all the days of her life during which she and Tuesday had been friends. Matted purple shag carpet, a black bedspread with purple pillows. Taped to her sloped ceiling, a blue and black and white movie poster: a woman, buried to her waist in the ground, trying to pull herself free but held down by a disembodied arm, a rotting hand wrapped around her throat. *I'm going to be one of the evil dead, Tues. None of this nice dead business for me.* Sneaks and platform clogs lined up at the end of the bed. A pile of clean socks and T-shirts stacked on her dresser.

You would never guess that two months ago she had vanished off the face of the earth.

Or off the edge of Derby Wharf at least. Into the water, probably – into the cold Atlantic, all while Tuesday was fast asleep in her bed. Tuesday was supposed to be staying over at Abby's, but they'd had a fight. Sort of. It was a dumb fight. Abby had wanted to go out to the light station at the end of Derby Wharf that night, and Tuesday didn't. For years, they'd walked out during the day – it was their usual meander around town, down by the old counting house and out the long concrete stretch of the wharf to the tiny white light-house at the end. They'd lean against the light station and scuff their feet over the crumbling stone and most of the time they talked, but sometimes all they did was sit and watch the sea and the sky. Tuesday would only be able to articulate later – years later, with the language of time and adulthood – that that was the first time she understood it was possible to be with another person and not feel at all alone.

That June, right after school ended, they started going out to the light station in the middle of the night. It had been Abby's idea – of course – but Tuesday needed little convincing to get on board. They each filled their backpacks. Abby with candles and matches and a spell book she'd found and, naturally, the Ouija board. Tuesday with sweet and salty snacks, Oreos and chips and two bottles of chilled Sprite and, once, two teeny bottles of cherry-flavored vodka she'd found at the back of her parents' liquor cabinet. They snuck out of their houses, two girls in the dark world, packing spells and candles.

She knew her parents would have freaked out, but she didn't care. They weren't trespassing – the wharf was a national historic site, and it was open twenty-four hours; she'd checked at the visitor center. And they weren't actually summoning, like, demons. They were trying to talk to people who had died – recently, in town, or historically, at sea, always with limited success (*This Ouija is broken*, said Abby, *we need a better board*) – yes, but mostly they were talking to each other. Making each other laugh. It was a ritual, all right: they were tasting their own freedom. And they were getting away with it.

The reason Tuesday hadn't wanted to go *that* night was because it was raining. And because, earlier that day, Abby had asked Tuesday what she thought about trying to contact the ghost of Abby's dead mother. Tuesday had said sure, but her gut went tight and cold and dug in its heels. She didn't want to have to tell Abby the truth: that she didn't really *believe* believe in this stuff. And that she felt a strange breed of shame – shame for the plain dumb luck that her mother was still alive when Abby's wasn't.

"Wimp," said Abby. "It's just rain."

"Rain is cold," said Tuesday. "And it's not supposed to rain tomorrow."

It seemed like an airtight argument.

"Well then, I guess I'll see you tomorrow," Abby said. They were in the Hobbeses' downstairs den, watching *The Evil Dead* on video for the zillionth time, and though Tuesday wasn't done with her bowl of vanilla ice cream and jimmies and radio-active-red maraschino cherries, she knew Abby had told her to leave. So she left. Hours later, tucked warm into her bed and tired of fretting, she figured, when she saw Abby tomorrow, that they'd do what they always did: pick up where they left off.

But the next day all the Salem police found was Abby's backpack, heavy with the previous night's rain, leaning against the white concrete of the light station. And Abby's fringed scarf – Tuesday could still picture her haggling with a cart seller on Essex Street – caught around the station's high metal railing, a black banner flying twenty feet in the air.

If Tuesday hadn't left Abby's house – if Tuesday had gone to the wharf, or even just asked what was so special about *that* night, and why Abby wanted to go – she would have seen. She would have known what had happened to her best friend.

She might have stopped it from happening.

But she didn't.

Seven-odd weeks later, she finally did something. The day of the memorial, in Abby's closet, on the tall shelf next to her sweaters, was a short stack of board games, shelved in order of how often they were played: Life, Clue, and on top, Ouija.

It was the same Ouija box that Tuesday, wrists and pride still smarting from the police's handcuffs, balanced on her lap a lifetime later. The box was old, foxed and squashed, dark blue with a lighter blue sketch of a hooded figure, one hand raised. Good old William Fuld's mysterious oracle, a quality product made by Parker Brothers, right at home in Salem, Mass. She hadn't taken the board out in years, hadn't wanted the reminder (as though she needed a reminder), but maybe she should have. It was like seeing an old friend. Abby had personalized the edges of the board with pictures cut from magazines, a *Sgt. Pepper* collection of heads and shoulders: Lydia Deetz. A winged Claire Danes. Three different Keanus, a John Lennon, a Morrissey, an Edward Scissorhands, a Wednesday Addams. Anjelica Huston as the Grand High Witch. The 27 Club: Hendrix, Cass, Joplin, Cobain. Mulder was glued upside down, next to the sun in the upper left corner, a word-bubble connecting his mouth with the word YES; Scully was opposite, glued beside the moon, saying NO. Abby had sealed everything flat and smooth with a coating of clear nail polish. It still smelled, chemical and teenage.

She rubbed her eyes. God, she was tired. And confused.

She set the Ouija board on her knees and placed the plastic planchette, yellowed with age, a short nail spiked through the clear viewing hole, on the board. Gunnar, purring like a fiend, rubbed up against her leg.

She coughed.

"Abby," she said, and she was worn so thin that just saying Abby's name out loud made her throat tighten and her eyes sting and she cried a little. She coughed again. "Abigail Hobbes. Calling Abby. Abby Cadaver. It's me. It's Tuesday Mooney." She twitched her lips. "Your living best friend."

Gunnar bonked his forehead into her shin.

She rested the tips of her index fingers on the planchette and closed her eyes.

"Abby," she said, "I thought I saw you."

She breathed in and out.

"And then I – heard you."

She lifted one lid to peek. Nothing. Gunnar was lying on his back now, furry limbs splayed like a little murder victim. He blinked at her.

"Abby, are you there?" she asked.

Silence.

"That's settled, then," said Tuesday. She laughed, but it wasn't from amusement. She was relieved. And disappointed. And worried. She had no idea if she was losing her mind.

Again.

5

BLOODY MARYS

Friday.

Tuesday's alarm went off at the usual time. Her arm shot out from a mound of duvet and smacked Snooze with a great deal of violence.

Before any discernible time had passed, it went off again.

And this time she remembered the night before.

Her brain sprang to life, dinging like a pinball machine. She had chased Pryce's clue into the bowels of Park Street – *ding!* – and found a secret code – *ding!* – with a wealthy, obscenely attractive stranger – *ding-ding!* – who also – ran away and left her to the cops?

Had that really – had that—

She pulled her duvet up and over her face. Her lips cracked into a demented grin. Tuesday, alone in her apartment, cocooned in her bed, began to laugh. It came out first like a strangled hiss, air pushing between her clenched teeth, but the more she thought about it, the more absurd – she was exhausted, but it was – she was – her head was full of helium. The laugh pushed itself up and out into a full-throated cackle.

Tuesday Mooney was awake.

And now that she was awake, she had some decisions to make. Like: Should she call in sick? Or was calling in sick delaying the unavoidable; was it better to suck it up and get the worst of the "yes, that was me you saw on the internet in handcuffs" conversations out of the way before next week?

She stopped laughing and sat up straight.

Her parents.

It was too early to call her parents. Any call from her before eight a.m. would scare the daylights out of them, but she should probably try to talk to them before they saw it somewhere. Complicating matters was the fact that her parents had recently discovered Facebook. At her brother's insistence, they'd created a page for Mooney's Miscellany, which was really a way for Ollie to post pictures of the rare action figures he traded and sold out of the store on weekends. Her father thought Facebook was hilarious – "Six people liked what I had for breakfast. What a world!" – and her mother mostly used it to take personality quizzes. "Guess what?" she'd say, as though passing along hot intel. "If I were a Muppet, I'd be Gonzo."

Did they look at Facebook at home before opening the store at ten? She didn't know. She turned off her alarm and glared at her phone. She could check her own Facebook app and see how bad it was. She loved the internet, but she loathed feeling so fucking available. So exposed. And so goddamn distracted.

Gunnar howled from the kitchen.

She didn't want to call them.

She didn't want to have to explain any of this. She already knew what they'd think, even if they didn't say it. Especially if they didn't say it. It would ooze into all the cracks and crevices between their words.

And they would be right, this time, to be worried.

Her phone rang. The screen filled with a picture of her parents' dog, Giles Corey III, pressed to sleep under a mound of couch cushions.

She slid her fingertip across the phone.

"Is this my daughter the terrorist?" her mother said. Sally

Mooney had a voice like dark maple syrup, sweet and deep. And she *was* Gonzo; she invented strange, mostly useless things (an automated toast butterer, a case for golf pencils) and held firm beliefs about the healing powers of various Stevie Nicks songs. Tuesday didn't need an online quiz to tell her that her mother was a weirdo.

"I was really hoping I could break it to you guys," she said.

"There's this thing, dear terrorist daughter, called the internet. It's faster than the speed of a daughter's admission of guilt."

Tuesday tucked herself farther under the covers. "I don't feel that guilty. Lucky, yes. And ashamed, maybe? That I got caught."

"It's true, we raised you to be slipperier than that. Are you okay? Ted – Ted, pick up the phone. It's your daughter the terrorist."

The line crackled and her father's higher voice – nerdier, brighter, the voice of an overly enthusiastic cartoon squirrel – broke in. "You say terrorist, I say anarchist. Moonie! What the hell happened?"

"I—" And here it was: the wall. When asked for an explanation, Tuesday found herself unable to provide the truth, whole and unvarnished.

For a variety of reasons. Despite being on social media, they weren't tech savvy; they wouldn't know how to tweet Archie's involvement to the world (not that she felt any great desire to protect him at this point). But every time she so much as glancingly mentioned a man, in *any* context – Pete, her mail carrier; Alvin, her bus driver; Fancy Hobbit, the short, curly-haired, bowtie-wearing stranger she saw most days on her commute – both of her parents turned into giggly preteens. For as resolutely nontraditional as they both claimed to be, for all the talk of dream-divining and heart-following, and the gently radical dogma that had permeated her childhood (the fourth little pig lived off the grid, which is why the wolf never bothered him in the first place), when it came to the question of relationships, a conservative streak ran deep. They only wanted her to "fall in love," to "be happy" – as if the only way she could possibly be happy was by securing an explicitly sexual romantic partnership – but she wasn't looking for excuses to get their hopes up, particularly when their hopes were theirs and not her own. So she said:

"Dorry and I figured out the clue. How could I not go for it?"

Elision was the best kind of lying. You didn't even have to lie, just selectively tell. She selectively told them about the editorials, the hideous hearts, the raven in Park Street. She told them about the clown mannequin.

She did not tell them that it had, for a moment, worn the decaying face of Abby Hobbes.

"Oh Moonie," said her dad, who had never forgiven himself for hiring a clown for her third birthday. "I am so sorry."

Her phone buzzed against her ear.

It was Dex: guess who's on the front page of the metro.

She felt her entire body try to sink into her mattress, desperate to become one with her bed.

Gunnar galloped the length of the apartment and sprang onto her feet. Then he sat, deliberately thumping his tail, flattening the duvet, and stared at her.

"The world is telling me I have to get up and get this over with," she said. "I promise not to make too much more trouble."

"Don't make promises you can't keep," said her mother. "But be careful. You know you're our favorite daughter."

"I'm your only daughter," she said. They'd been reciting the same joke, like a benediction, ever since Tuesday was old enough to understand why it was supposed to be funny.

"Moonie," said her father, the brightness of his voice

dimming. Tuesday pulled the duvet back over her head. There was never any question of telling them that she'd seen and heard Abby – never, ever would she do that – but she didn't have to. Abby was always just below the surface.

"Be careful," he said, "only daughter."

◆

An hour and change later, though only nominally more awake, Tuesday swung into her cubicle. She set the first of what would necessarily be many, many cups of coffee on her desk, and noticed someone had taped the front page of that morning's *Metro* to her computer monitor. Under the headline TREASURE HUNTER IN THE HUB was a full-color photo of *her* – holy shit, she really was in the *Metro* – being escorted out of Park Street station by two of Boston PD's finest. She looked . . . good. The night was mostly a blur; it wouldn't have been surprising to see herself with a slack jaw, a gaping mouth, a Quasimodo hunch. But she was straight and tall – her head back, her hair blowing around her face like a lion's mane. She was taller than both officers, dwarfing the policeman on the right by about half a foot.

And she was smiling, like she had a terrific secret, which, as far as she knew, she still did. Twitter was cluttered with pictures of the raven and the prince of darkness graffiti that led down the tunnel, but no phone in the universe other than hers had a picture of Pryce's secret code.

The same someone who had taped it up had written RESEARCHERS – THEY'RE JUST LIKE US! in black Sharpie over the headline. *They get so wrapped up finding stuff that the cops have to haul them away!*

Tuesday meandered over to Mo's open office door.

"You know I recognize your handwriting," she said.

Mo adjusted her glasses. "A life of crime agrees with you," she said, and grinned.

The rest of the day was a variation on that theme. Ollie, who wrote the Mooney sibling book on rule-following, emailed to ask (only half ironically) why she'd brought shame to the family, and whether she was still coming for Olive's fifth birthday party in three weeks, and if so, could she bring her refrigerator pickles, by Olive's special request? Facebook's little red notifications climbed from ten to twenty, then to fifty, as she was tagged and messaged and liked and commented on. She signed out.

At one o'clock, after the office had ostensibly moved on, she'd been able to accomplish the bare minimum of work, and she realized, a little late, that she was starving for lunch. Her desk phone rang. It was an outside line.

She picked up the receiver.

"Hello." It was a woman with a Boston accent thick as fudge. "Is this Tuesday Mooney?"

"Who is this?" asked Tuesday.

"Brianna McGuff, *Boston Globe*. I wanted to ask you a few questions about the—"

"No comment," said Tuesday, and hung up.

She stared at the phone. They'd found her. Of course they'd found her. The *Metro* had printed her name; she wasn't hiding. And she, of all people, knew how very easy it was to find someone. She suddenly had the sensation of standing on the edge of a tall building in a strong breeze, in a great voluminous dress that flapped and ballooned and threatened to launch her over the ledge, a lone woman on the wind.

Only she wasn't alone. She only looked, to the world, like she was alone.

She opened Nathaniel Allan Arches's record in the development database – and remembered (crap) that she still had his check for fifty thousand dollars. She'd take it over to Trish later. There, populated in all the usual demographic fields, was his address at the Mandarin Hotel, his address on Nantucket;

there was his age (thirty-nine) and his birth date (November 3 – his fortieth was approaching). There were her own research notes, all about him – his career with N. A. Arches, all the interviews and gossip and blind items and Boston's sexiests. Researching a prospect always made her feel that she was getting to know them. She'd gleaned a sense of what he was like, what might make him tick – and it didn't jibe with anything she'd learned from spending time with him in person. Well, except for his tendency to flake like a complete dick. That seemed about right.

Her gut pinged. The barrage of information he spread across the internet was a smokescreen. Camouflage. A careful construction of a self, probably more truth than fiction but an incomplete picture, PR designed to distract from the salient facts she already knew. First, Vincent Pryce and the Arches family had an ongoing feud. When asked what was so compelling about Pryce's game, why Archie wanted to win it so badly – when asked *about* Pryce, point-blank – what had he selectively told her? The prize held great sentimental value. Pryce was a wacko.

Elision, as she knew, was the best kind of lying.

The second fact was just as undeniable, but it snuck up on her. It was hiding in plain sight. It was what she had recognized that night at the Four Seasons, and then again outside her apartment.

Archie's father had disappeared.

Archie knew how it felt for someone in his life to up and vanish.

It didn't make her trust him any more, but it explained what she saw in him.

◆

Dex smoothed Tuesday's *Metro* front page over his desk blotter. He thought, *I know her,* and not for the first time that morning, danced a little in his seat. He knew someone famous. Or infamous, at least, for the fifteen seconds every commuter spends scanning the picture above the *Metro*'s fold.

Dex had never been on the front page of anything.

He stopped dancing.

Dex had a meeting he didn't want to go to and a pair of Jimmy Choos and a bottle of whiskey in his bottom drawer. He'd been trying very hard not to get drunk or cross-dress at work (as much), but this week had been difficult. First, he watched a guy die. No, first, he broke up with Patrick. His sweet, flexible ballerina, who, although visibly upset by the request, had taken Dex at his word and didn't contact him thereafter. Dex liked breaks to be clean. Dex didn't like complications. Dex would have absolutely continued to have all kinds of sex with Patrick after they broke up – and, given the events of the past few days, it would have been great, inspired-by-proximity-to-death sex. He didn't want to *do* that anymore, the same way he didn't want to open Grindr and feel, with every swipe, exponentially disposable, duplicable, and depressed. But he would have, if Patrick had made it easy by making the first move. Because Dex, God forbid, could not make anything easy for himself.

So he missed his boyfriend, though he knew he didn't really want him (other than Like That). And then Vincent Pryce died. The man with the cape and his fantastic wife, Lila, who had become extra-fantastic in her shock and her grief. As soon as her husband went down, after five seconds of stunned silence, she'd shouted, "Is there a doctor here? Anywhere?" She wasn't crying. Dex didn't see her shed one tear. "Oh, come ON," she said. "You cannot tell me there is not ONE doctor in the house. I don't care what kind of doctor you are, you all took the freaking oath." And she dropped to her knees on the carpet, flopped like she was wearing gym togs instead of a one-sleeved gown, flipped her husband over, made a tight ball with her hands, and pounded his chest like she was driving a fence post into the ground.

Dex remembered everything about those minutes with precise, pinching clarity. Kneeling across the body from Lila, telling her he wasn't a doctor but he wanted to help, taking turns thumping Pryce's chest. The mentholated old-man smell rising off the body. Lila muttering, *Come on come on come on you old idiot come on don't do this don't DO this*. The doctors came forward – it was a hospital fundraiser after all – but the EMTs whisked him off, as if it weren't too late, not yet, though of course it was. One of the EMTs was desperately cute, had a dimple that winked even when he looked dour, and they put the body on a stretcher and wheeled it away, Lila trailing behind.

Dex sighed. He folded the *Metro* so he couldn't see Tuesday, then unfolded it, then folded it again. If he was being perfectly honest, he was more than a little jealous she had gone adventuring with someone else. He was frustrated and sour that he hadn't been next to her in the *Metro*, in full color above the fold. Sure, he was *thrilled* that she'd called him from jail, and that, at long last, he had stepped inside her apartment. But. Tuesday told him about Rich Boy last night – about the pact they'd made, the five million dollars or at least the potential promise thereof – and it was all he could do to stop himself from saying, *Was I not the person who told you about this treasure hunt in the first place?!* Which was ridiculous; even if Dex hadn't told her, Tuesday would have found out; just because he told her about it didn't mean he had exclusive rights to what she *did* with that information; and it was actually pretty exciting to be close to that kind of wealth, to have a leg up on the competition an Arches could surely provide. Jealousy was a too-sensitive teenager's reaction. If it had been any other week, it would have passed through him like a cool breeze. Instead, it was lodged in his chest like a little chip of ice.

He just – wanted to play. Dex, all his life, had wanted to feel that he was part of a team, a member of the cast – an integral member of an ensemble that appreciated his comedic timing, his showboating, his *talents*, before they withered to dust. Though he supposed the vast majority of humans felt like unpaid extras. Milling about, uselessly waiting to be discovered, recognized for their innate yet invisible value, but doomed never to be anything but human scenery. Maybe *that* was his team, and he was already on it. Had been on it, in fact, forever.

He looked at his watch. It was ten o'clock. The meeting, scheduled for ten, would actually start in fifteen minutes.

Dex turned toward his computer and checked his email. At the top of his inbox was a message from Lila Pryce.

To: p.howard3@richmontinvestments.com
From: lilakorrapatipryce@gmail.com
Subject: Brunch?

Hi Dex,

I've started this email several times. Every time it gets weirder. At first it was like, "Dear Sir, I would like to cordially invite you to my home in Beacon Hill for brunch." Then it turned into "Dear Person I Barely Know, You tried to resuscitate my husband, and even though that didn't work out, I'd still like to get you drunk by eleven a.m."

I am having trouble calibrating my gallows humor.

So here is my final attempt:

Do you like brunch?

I hope you're not doing anything tomorrow (Saturday) and can join me for brunch. As a thank-you, because I saw how hard you tried to save Vince, but also because, in another timeline, a timeline where the most exciting thing that happened that night was a chance meeting of lost souls, I'd still be inviting you over for brunch. Though in that other timeline, we would have exchanged cards at the end of the night. I wouldn't have had to Google-Fu your email address from the Richmont website.

(By the way, if this is not the Poindexter Howard whom I met at the Four Seasons on Tuesday night, my apologies.)

I can't guarantee I won't be a disgusting mess, but I promise carbohydrates and the finest bloody mary bar you've ever seen as an offset. Brunch is at 10:30. My address is 13½ Louisburg Square.

And you can bring your friend Tuesday, who found the first clue. I would have loved to meet her at the fundraiser, but since we live in this timeline I would love to meet her at brunch.

Lyle KP

Dex accepted the invitation immediately.

To: lilakorrapatipryce@gmail.com
From: p.howard3@richmontinvestments.com
Subject: Re: Brunch?

Is "do you like brunch" code for "are you gay"? Because yes. But really, what sane human, gay, straight, or otherwise, does not like brunch? Whoever they may be, I do not wish to know or associate with them.

But I would be honored to associate with you.

I will be so bold as to accept the invitation on both my own and Tuesday's behalf, with assurances that she would love the chance to know you better as well. No matter the timeline.

Dex

◆

"I forget what we decided," said Tuesday. "Are we pretending this brunch is or isn't part of Vincent Pryce's game?"

Dex stepped over a hole in the brick sidewalk that looked thirsty for his ankle. They had just turned off Beacon and were ascending Walnut, heading straight up into the heart of Beacon Hill. "God, this neighborhood is one giant booby trap."

It was Saturday morning. They were both hung over, which was unusual. In fact, if Dex was calculating correctly, the night before had been the first time he had ever met Tuesday Mooney for drinks and she'd become visibly intoxicated. Even when they were self-medicating finance newbs, Tuesday had never given the impression of being remotely overserved. It had seemed like a superpower.

But she was very obviously, now, a human.

The day before, she'd texted *him*. He came back from his boring meeting and was bursting to text her about Lila's brunch invitation, but lo and behold, Tuesday had beaten him to the punch. Dex just about tipped out of his ergonomic Staples chair in shock. She never texted first.

Hey Dex. I owe you drinks, multiple. McFly's?

McFly's was a beater of a bar dangling off the ass end of Charles Street, an equidistant cab ride from their respective apartments in Somerville and the South End. It was dark and sticky and the stools wobbled and it served undergraduates from Suffolk and Emerson – there were always several faces in the crowd that could've been peeled off a bottle of children's sunscreen: glowing, innocent, slightly dazed – but critically, for Dex's purposes, it was the last Friday-night karaoke venue in greater Boston that had not blacklisted him. He had a tendency not only to hog the mic, but to hog the mic by playing karaoke roulette. It was a game of his own invention: he sang songs of his choice in the style of an artist chosen by the whims of the Shuffle feature on his iPhone. That was the whole game, and that was how he came to know the genius of, say, belting Rage Against the Machine's "Killing in the Name Of" in the style of Barbra Streisand. It was a very dumb and very entertaining game that Dex could play all by himself but chose not to. It was objectively obnoxious.

Not, Dex thought, unlike himself, which was why karaoke roulette was so essential. Singing like a giant, showboating, asshole chameleon – an undeniably talented one, but still – was one of the only ways he could remind himself of, well, who he was, and what he loved. He sang like an attention-seeking missile and remembered everything that weeks and months and years of pretending to care about money and how to sell it to other people had conspired to make him forget. Whenever he wrapped his fingers around the mic and opened his mouth, he, Poindexter Howard, was *back*.

Tuesday Mooney, however, when he sat down across from her that night at McFly's, was . . . different.

She buzzed, and not because she'd already started drinking. She flickered, almost, like her attention couldn't settle. And she blushed – her face went full tomato when she thanked him, again, for coming to fetch her from the police.

"Of course," Dex said.

She cleared her throat.

"I guess I'm not used to—" She shrugged. "I mean, I could've called my own cab, but I – anyway. I appreciate it."

Dex poked her in the arm.

"Don't get mushy on me, girl."

They ordered another round. After a thorough debrief of everything that had happened that week – the end of Patrick, the Auction to Abandon All Hope, and Tuesday's night with Rich Boy/Poe Boy (a pun Dex made without even trying, and about which they giggled for a solid sixty seconds) – Dex felt a little better. Jealousy was like indigestion: it cleared with crackers and conversation. The invite from Lila helped. He had a card to play now too. And he wasn't such a monster that he could begrudge Tuesday a thrilling Thursday with a slab of man meat who truly was, in the common tongue, Hot as Hell. She'd shown him the pictures on her phone to prove it.

That girl needed to get laid yesterday.

"He said he'd 'find me' today," Tuesday said, slurping up the last of her third G&T.

"How romantic," said Dex.

"He didn't." Her words were clipped and quiet. She looked down at her glass. Dex paused, waiting for more. But Tuesday pressed her lips together.

"What a dick," he said casually. She exhaled, clearly relieved that he wasn't going to press for details. At least not those details. Instead, he flicked to the next picture on her phone. "So this is the secret code," he said.

"Sure is," said Tuesday.

"Fat little ankh, funky arrow, coffin, eyeball, butthole. Maybe you chant this stuff naked around a bonfire on the solstice." He snickered. "Sixty-nine, dudes."

"That's not the number sixty-nine. That's the astrological symbol for Cancer."

"Sure it is," he said. "Filthy little crustaceans."

"I spent most of the afternoon trying to crack it." Tuesday rubbed her whole face with both hands, pulling her cheeks down like something Edvard Munch would paint. "And it doesn't make much sense. The ankh is an ankh – life. The coffin seems like it's just a coffin. You've got the astrological symbol for Jupiter in there, infinity, a heart, a cartoon cat, a dollar sign – there's no consistency. It's a bunch of random symbols. It's wingdings."

"Have you tried reading them like they're emojis?" Dex hunched over the glow of her phone. "Life arrow coffin. That has a certain trajectory." He took a sip of his own gin and tonic. "What does Cookie Monster's eyeball stand for, really?"

"Gold," said Tuesday. "It's the alchemical symbol for gold. Hey." She hunched lower beside him. "You're not wrong about that trajectory – life to coffin. Birth to death. Unless we find, like, a decoder ring somewhere, this might be our best—" She jerk-bobbed upright on her stool and wove closer to him. "Poindexter Howard," she said, drilling her eyes into his, "we need a plan."

"A plan?"

"We shouldn't go to brunch tomorrow without a plan."

Dex swung his giant forehead around and pointed it at hers. "Why is that?" he asked.

"Because." She was a little slurry now. "We're going into the dead man's den. There may be clues."

Dex frowned. "I'm pretty sure," he said, "the living widow invited us because she's, like, sad. And wants company."

"But we should have a plan anyway. In case she's sad *and* there are clues." Tuesday sucked down the dregs of her drink. "What song did you choose?" It was nine-thirty. McFly's had filled. The karaoke DJ was setting up.

Dex hadn't. He'd been too focused on this slightly different iteration of Tuesday – fuzzier around the edges, sloshing out of her typical container – to think of a request.

"How about I choose for you," Tuesday murmured, and it was Dex's turn to blush. She'd been in the audience for karaoke roulette before, sure, but she had never given any indication that she wanted to play along. He was stunned. And thrilled.

Tuesday pulled her phone out of her bag. Her face, reflecting the light of the screen, glowed in McFly's grubby darkness. Then she laughed. She turned the screen around for Dex to see.

His rendition of "I Don't Know How to Love Him" in the style of John Denver and the Muppets was both one of his crowning karaoke roulette achievements and one of his last clear memories of the evening. They drank more gin and more tonic. They listened to a lot of ear-bleedingly awful karaoke. When Dex finally slithered into his bed, around two-thirty in the morning, he was grinning and spinning.

But then Saturday dawned far too early and far, *far* too bright, and these stupid brick and cobblestone streets were – Jesus, who thought these were quaint? People who had People to carry them around in litters?

"This brunch," he said over his shoulder to Tuesday, "is a social call. We're not assuming anything, but we're also not assuming nothing either."

"You are so hung over right now," said Tuesday.

"Takes one to know one," said Dex.

◆

Louisburg Square was a block of adorable warm brownstones, some undulating with turrets, all with charming wrought-iron fences and grillwork, huddled around a long green park. Number 13½ had an intercom in place of a doorbell, and Dex, after ringing, hadn't even announced their presence before the door buzzed open. They stepped into a dark, shining space.

The floor was black marble buffed to a high gloss, and the walls, above a mahogany chair rail, were papered with purple-black and navy blue damask. A weak chandelier hung too high above them to do any good. Tuesday's head was still tender from gin and lack of sleep.

Looking at the white bear-mop of a dog sitting in the middle of so much darkness was like looking straight at the sun.

"Where are its eyes?" whispered Dex.

"I don't know." She'd pushed her sunglasses into her hair on the stoop, but slid them back down. "But I don't think you should be trying to make eye contact."

The beast greeted them with unusual stoicism for a dog: it raised its snout and snorted, once, in their direction.

"Hello?" Lila Korrapati Pryce's voice emerged, before she did, from what could have been a shadow but was more likely a dark-papered hallway. She was wearing a shocking-pink T-shirt, sweat-pants, and no shoes. Her toes were shiny cherries. Tuesday pushed her sunglasses up into her hair again. She opened her mental file on Pryce, Lila Korrapati and scribbled: *freshly pedicured*. Lila looked tired but eager, like she was expecting a cluster of old friends from college rather than one person she barely knew, and another she'd never met. But her eyes were bright and she smiled, and Tuesday believed it. She was happy to see them. It was real.

While researching her late husband, Tuesday had given Lila a brief pass, so she had the basics – fortyish; born in Cambridge; went to Harvard and had been, prior to marrying Vincent Pryce, a high school English teacher. Tuesday, independently of Dex, had made a firm decision about her plan for this brunch: it was an unmissable opportunity for field research. *Grieving*, she wrote in her mental file. *Obviously. But also glowing*.

"This is Roddy," Lila said, setting her hand on the dog's head. It disappeared into his hair.

"This is Tuesday," Dex said, putting his arm around Tuesday's shoulder and squaring her in Lila's direction. Tuesday shook Lila's hand. *Confident grip. Warm. Eye contact. Wry twist of her mouth, as if to say: I know you are not Dex's Roddy.*

But Lila actually said, "I'm glad it was you."

"Me?" said Tuesday.

"I'm glad it was you," Lila repeated, "who found the first clue."

Tuesday stretched her lips into a smile and nodded, hoping her silence would do exactly what it did.

"Something about you," said Lila, "reminds me of Vince." She propped her hands on her hips. "Shall we brunch?" she said, turning back toward the shadow hallway. "I have a brunch room. A whole room for brunch. Sometimes, when I am totally out of fucks to give." She tilted her head, and for a moment Tuesday wondered if she'd completed her thought without vocalizing it. But then she continued, "I eat dinner in there."

Dex grabbed Tuesday as they followed their host down the dark hall.

"I'm sorry," he whispered. "I didn't mean to create a parallel between you and the dog."

"Well, you did," said Tuesday.

The hallway opened into a small room, not quite as dim as the foyer – the ceiling was high, and tall windows overlooked a spiny black wrought-iron fence and the square beyond – but still wearing that dark damask. The various accoutrements of brunch were laid on a sideboard: a linen-lined basket of assorted bagels and a row of white ramekins gleaming with purple, pink, and orange jams and jellies; a platter of fruit and sugar-dusted pastries; a bloody mary bar, with hot sauce, Worcestershire, olives and horseradish, pickles gored with tiny plastic swords, a shining silver ice bucket. There was a platter heaped with French toast, a platter heaped with sausage patties, and a platter heaped with scrambled eggs. It was enough food for the three people who entered the room and the one person who was already in it to subsist on for several days.

The man already in the room – Tuesday pulled out a fresh mental file – was sitting at a beautiful old wooden table (easily, Tuesday assessed, an antique; likely worth several hundred thousand). He looked to be in his early to mid-thirties, trim, ruddy, dark-eyed, and intensely adorable in a human teddy bear sort of way. His hair was short and still mostly dark but beginning to lighten. He looked huggable.

And familiar.

He pushed back from the table.

He hadn't yet straightened before low bells rang from the foyer.

Lila wobbled a little. "Huh," she said. "I wonder who that is." She looked at the man, who still hadn't stood, let alone introduced himself. He frowned at her, shook his head the tiniest bit: *Why are you looking at me?*

"Grab a mary," Lila said. "Roddy and I will be right back."

Dex shrugged at Tuesday and addressed himself to the brunch bar.

"What a spread," he said. He looked back over his shoulder at the stranger, who finally rose all the way up. *Deliberate*, Tuesday wrote in his file. *A careful man.* She doubted he was Lila's sibling – at least not biologically; he was white – but they were clearly comfortable with one another. They could speak without words.

Ex? she scribbled. *Love unrequited?*

"How do you know Lila?" Tuesday asked.

The man smiled. "We met at work," he said.

"Aww," said Dex, flicking his head toward Tuesday. "So did we."

"I'm Tuesday," said Tuesday, and this time the stranger held out his hand and she shook it. He had warm hands. A little sweaty.

"Bert," he said. "We taught together, Lyle and I. She taught eleventh-grade English, I still teach music. I conduct the orchestra."

"How long have you been friends?" Tuesday asked.

"Six years," he said. "No – seven. We met through work, and then we were roommates for a few years. Until she met Vince."

"And how long were they together?" Tuesday asked.

Bert hesitated. Not, Tuesday suspected, because he didn't know the answer, but because he was sensitive too, maybe more sensitive than she herself was, and he recognized a researcher when he saw one.

"Sorry," Tuesday said, though she wasn't.

"Tuesday can be an intense conversationalist," Dex interrupted, handing her a very large bloody mary with a bendy straw and a giant pickle-olive-pickle-olive shish kebab balanced across the rim. "But I can vouch for her good intentions."

"*I'm* sorry," said Bert. "Small talk isn't my favorite, even under the best of circumstances. And these circumstances are—" He waved his hand. Conducting, maybe. Trying to pull an answer, like a refrain, out of the air.

"Strange," said Tuesday. Bert nodded and laughed a little.

He shoved his sleeves up, crossed his arms, cupped his elbows in his hands. He had nice arms and hands, no matter how sweaty, and a tattoo on the inside of his right forearm. Tuesday couldn't tell quite what it was. He squeezed himself. He was nervous. She would have put good money on nervousness being one of his natural states.

Dex handed him an unasked-for bloody mary, and Bert beamed.

Bert was Dex-nip. Tuesday knew Dex couldn't help himself when the boys were cute, couldn't shake his *Tiger Beat* aesthetic ("Too much Marty McFly, too young," he'd once explained), but maybe Bert couldn't help himself either. Not with a boy like Dex, silver-tongued and charming, who made you drinks you didn't have to ask for.

She licked the tip of her mental pencil and summarized: *work spouse, roommate, friend, Dex-nip.*

He was so familiar, and she didn't know why.

"Have we ever met be—" was all she got out before Lila's voice returned to the room, also in the middle of a sentence: "—do join us, we have so much food. Right through here."

Two familiar-looking women followed in Lila's wake whom Tuesday *did* know, though she'd never met them.

Her mental pencil, stunned, hovered in midair. Her senses crackled, then tuned themselves up to eleven.

The first, the younger, didn't give Lila a chance to speak for her. She advanced into the room and slid a disturbingly porcelain hand into Tuesday's.

"Emerson Arches," she said.

Everything about her was disturbing and cool. She didn't blink. She was thin and composed, wearing a rose tunic under an oversized, oatmeal-colored cardigan and what would have been tackyass jeggings on a BU student yet were perfectly chic skinny jeans on her. She was blonde, but not originally. Her dye job was impeccable, her hair immaculately treated and moisturized, but it looked wrong against her dark eyes, the slap of freckles on her nose, and the boozy blush of her cheeks. Her brows were two dark bolts. Her teeth were a little sharp. She was uncanny.

Kind of like her brother.

"Lyle was telling us all about you," she said, and Tuesday wondered, as she always did when someone used that particular phrase, what she was supposed to say in response. Thank you? That's nice? Emerson's voice was low, slow; her accent didn't have enough affect to be affected. "And your recent notoriety. It's nice to meet a fellow meme."

Tuesday made a note. Sister, like brother, had more of a sense of humor than she would have expected.

"Nice to meet you too," Tuesday said. Dex shot in front of her and pumped Emerson's hand hello.

"Dex Howard," he said. "Financier."

"And this," said Lila from behind, her voice a little thick, "is Constance Arches."

Emerson stepped aside to reveal the only woman who could possibly have given birth to her. She possessed the same contained fierceness, a tigress in a shell of cashmere and six figures' worth of tasteful jewelry. Tuesday's mental file cabinet slid open. So this was Constance Arches. Chief executive, in her husband's continued absence, of Arches Consolidated. *Forbes*-anointed billionaire head-of-family. Not legally a widow (yet) – but did she, as the surviving Arches, carry forth the feud against Vincent Pryce? Was she here to call Lila out? She had a sharp white bob, no bangs. Her eyebrows were light but penciled. Her facade was vaguely Anna Wintour, dipped in liquid nitrogen. Constance caught Tuesday's eye and held it. And held it.

"Hello," said Tuesday. She was full of a sudden and tremendous desire to break everything.

"We brought muffins," said Constance.

Tuesday's eyes fell to the pink box this woman was cradling, tenderly, as if it were a sleeping child, in her arms.

"Vincent loved muffins," Constance continued. She looked down, and Tuesday felt palpable relief. Constance Arches was carrying an extraordinary amount of pain. That layer of ice was a necessary containment; if her insides got out, she would immolate.

"He loved brunch," Lila said gently.

"Minimum effort," said Constance.

"Maximum enjoyment," finished Lila.

A heavy silence settled over the room, thick as dust. Quiet

enough to hear Dex's straw reach the bottom of his first bloody mary.

"Who wants another?" he asked.

◆

Dex preferred to be useful. His definition of usefulness was more elastic, more encompassing, perhaps, than the average American's, but there was no time that required the deployment of an elastic definition of usefulness quite like the aftermath of a death. It was useful for Dex to make a second round of strong bloody marys, and it was useful for him to serve both Lila Pryce and Constance Arches a plate of food at their respective seats. It was useful for him to keep making eyes at that adorable Bert, to quicken the blood, his own and someone else's. It would be useful, also, to keep Tuesday in check, to remind her that she was not Miss Marple, that this was an informal brunch and not an interrogation. His brain was getting progressively more bloody maryed, and so was Tuesday's. He suspected it was making them both become more themselves.

Therein lay the danger.

"Please, everyone, have a seat," said Lila. "Wherever you like – only – Dex. Over here. Next to me."

Interesting: next to Lila, but *between* Lila and Bert. Dex set the last of this round of bloodies in front of Lila and took his assigned seat. "Poindexter," he said, finally introducing himself formally, officially, usefully to Bert. Dex was a romantic cynic, not a cynical romantic; he didn't *actually* believe in love at first contact, but Bert shook his hand, said "Hi," and looked him in the eye – and Dex could see that he was half embarrassed about Lila's ham-fisted seating-nudge, but, beneath that, he possessed a steady kind of honesty, a gentleness, a desire, always, to believe in good. And Dex thought, *It's you.*

At last.

And there was no worry or rush or panic or any of the things he usually felt when he met someone he was going to fall in love with. Only a warm opening in his chest that could have been happiness.

"Hey," Dex said.

Or maybe it was the bloody mary.

"I'm dying," said Emerson. Across the table, or in another galaxy, Dex didn't know anymore. "To hear more about this game." Dex looked up. Tuesday was sitting across from him, between Lila and Emerson. "First. How did you crack the first clue? How did you know to go to the T station?"

"There was a hidden message," Tuesday told her, "in Pryce's letters to the editor of the *Globe*. And then there was – a – sign, a symbol to follow, in the station itself."

"Did you take pictures? You must have." Emerson took a refined but serious gulp of bloody mary. "Can I see?"

Tuesday hesitated. Weighing, Dex knew, the pros and cons of sharing this information. God, she was always herself; she couldn't not be if she tried. Finally she pulled her phone out of her bag.

"Have you seen that anywhere else around town?" Tuesday asked.

"What is – is that a raven?" Emerson leaned forward. "What is it pointing at?" She pointed her own finger.

"Down the tunnel, the tracks toward Boylston. A section of wall had recently been fake-bricked up."

Emerson started to chuckle. Then she swallowed it, as though she were acting out of turn. Dex had recognized her immediately, before she'd introduced herself. He didn't know as much about richies as Tuesday did, but he *did* work in finance. He wanted to bask in her presence – she was tailor-made for his tastes: an impeccable, sophisticated, and slightly ridiculous creation of a self – but it was almost as if she wouldn't let him. Or anyone, really. There was a dead seriousness about her person that Dex suspected she could put on and take off like a piece of haute couture, and, at the moment, it was bolted to her body. She was coiled, a cobra in Tory Burch flats, capable of striking to kill.

Emerson's finger moved over the screen and flicked to the next picture.

Tuesday started and pulled the phone away.

Dex thought, *Dick pics*, and snorted. Tuesday was the only person he knew with figurative, not literal, dick pics on her phone: of Archie the dick, pics she felt compelled to hide from his sister.

It was time for him to intervene.

"Constance – may I call you Constance?" She was sitting at the far end of the table, across from Lila. She nodded. "How did you know the deceased?"

Everyone at the table stiffened. Dex felt his spine straighten in sympathy.

Bert coughed into his fist.

"We were neighbors," Constance said. "On the island."

Tuesday gave Dex the sliest of side-eyes. *There's so much more to it*, the look said. *I'll tell you later*.

"He built the Castellated Abbey in, what – the mid-aughts?" Tuesday asked. "Was that when you first met?"

Constance turned her head slowly. Dex could practically hear the clockwork whirring in her neck.

"Yes," she said.

Emerson took another elegant slurp of bloody mary.

"Have you figured out the next step yet?" Emerson asked Tuesday quietly, as if there were enough people around the table for them to have a casual side conversation.

"No," he heard Tuesday say to Emerson. "Not yet at least."

"The prince of darkness," quoted Lila, smiling dreamily, "is a gentleman." She hadn't touched her bloody mary or her plate of food.

"Do you know what that means?" Tuesday asked her. Far too aggressively for the occasion, Dex thought critically, and kicked his leg in her direction beneath the table. He didn't connect with anything but air.

Lila didn't seem to mind. Or if she did, she hid it. She shook her head and propped her elbows on the table, on either side of her still-full plate.

"Nope," she said. "I don't have a clue."

"Are you lying?" Tuesday pushed.

"Tuesday," Dex warned, but Tuesday didn't look at him, and Lila laughed. It sounded genuine enough, but still. What use was asking a widow, to her face, if she was lying? First of all, it was rude. Second of all, of course she was lying – not as Tuesday thought, but to herself – faking it until she made it, telling herself she was okay, that she preferred the company of strangers and neighbors to curling into a fetal position on the floor and crying herself unconscious.

But then. Lila didn't look like she was faking anything. She looked kind of – how to describe it—

Luminous.

"I'm not lying," Lila said. "Vince was an exceptional secret keeper." And she looked at Constance – Dex caught it, and it caromed like a rubber ball around his buzzing brain – and Constance looked back. A powerful intelligence passed between them. It wasn't combative. It was a kind of vow, warm and solid. It had weight and mass; Dex practically felt it push against his sternum.

Constance placed her napkin beside her half-eaten plate.

"Emerson," she said, "we've paid our respects. We ought to leave Mrs. Pryce to her guests now."

The standard departing pleasantries were exchanged. Thank you for stopping by. Of course you didn't intrude, do come back. Anytime. Dex stayed in the brunch room. His vantage at the table allowed him an unobstructed view of Lila leading Emerson and Constance back toward the foyer. It happened so quickly, Dex could have – if he hadn't been in a state of drunken high alert, tender to the world, to Bert beside him, to Tuesday's socially suicidal tendencies; if it hadn't been for his bloody maryed brain – he might have convinced himself it didn't happen. That he hadn't seen it. But he had.

Constance Arches's bony fingers threaded through Lila's and squeezed, hard.

And then let go.

6

HUNCH DRUNK

Tuesday and Dex sat on a bench in the Common, drinking coffee out of borrowed travel tumblers, squinting into the brilliant fall sky, listening to the leaves and watching the people, wondering whether anything that had just happened would make more sense with sobriety.

Tuesday doubted it.

Lila didn't come back from leading Emerson and her mother away. They all heard the door shut, and then, in the silence that followed, a muffled little sob.

Bert cleared his throat. He asked Tuesday and Dex if they wanted some coffee. "Lyle," he called gently to the foyer, "we'll be in the kitchen. Come in whenever you're ready."

She croaked an okay.

The kitchen was unlike any room they'd yet seen in the townhouse. It was full of light. Real, live light. "It burns," said Dex, shielding his eyes from the glass back wall, panes gleaming with late-morning sun, overlooking a small backyard patio and garden. It wasn't gothic and gloomy, but it wasn't Nancy Meyers kitchen porn either. Empty tomato juice bottles clustered on the island, cool granite dotted with red, like a vegetable splatter movie. It looked like the kitchen of someone messily eating her feelings: the countertop held a rogue's gallery of salty snacks – Pirate's Booty, pretzels, pita chips, white cheddar Cheez-Its – at least four packages of Trader Joe's Joe-Joe cookies stacked like books, and an empty pint of Ben and Jerry's so clean it was probably licked.

"Regular, I assume?" Bert pointed at the coffeemaker.

"Yes, God," said Dex. "Double regular, extra regular, intravenously, yesterday."

"I'll see what I can do." Bert was absolutely low-key flirting, and Tuesday patted herself on the mental back. He was self-possessed, anxiety aside, and kind, and, if the salt running through his hair wasn't premature, age appropriate. But she wasn't quite prepared, if Dex asked (which he undoubtedly would), to make a recommendation. Bert was hiding something. She knew it.

She recognized it plain on his face.

"So." Tuesday cleared her throat, wrapped her hands around the cool stone edges of the island, and leaned forward. "What was that all about?"

Bert didn't turn around, but his shoulders rose slightly, like he'd been jolted with a tiny current. He poured water from the carafe into the top of the coffeemaker.

"Arches," he said. "That was all about Arches."

"I know about the feud," Tuesday murmured.

Bert did turn around then, and raised an eyebrow. She chose to interpret it as a sign that he was impressed.

"Frankly," she continued, "I wouldn't eat those muffins."

Dex, leaning beside Bert against the counter, cranked his head in her direction. "Tuesday," he said.

"I think the muffins are probably fine," Bert said.

"Forget about the muffins," said Tuesday. She apologized again, and said, "I get awkward when I meet new people. Who know famous people," which was technically true. "How long did you say Lila was with Vince?"

"About four years." Bert was easier now, talking about his friend. Telling her story. He hugged himself again. "Three years married this month. They just had their anniversary." He shrugged without letting go of his own arms. "She has a tendency to overthink things, and she was just getting used to it."

"Overthinking?" asked Dex. "Marriage?"

"Money," said Tuesday.

Bert smiled at her. "Two points for Tuesday." The coffee-maker gurgled. "Vince owned eight houses. The cheapest one – he's got another apartment on Beacon Hill, over on Pinckney – is worth over two mil. She went from our little piece of triple-decker heaven in Somerville to a castle. From working like a dog for peanuts to not working at all, and having anything she wanted. It was unreal. And honestly, it's not like she's even used to it – she was just kind of figuring out how to be okay with it. How to get the hang of being wealthy without it making her crazy or an asshole or a crazy asshole." The corner of his mouth lifted in a grin that immediately drooped. "Then *this*."

"What?" asked Tuesday. "What's *this*?"

He shrugged his shoulders higher and held out both arms, palms up, in the universal gesture of *the hell do I know?* "All this? Vince dying? And leaving behind this – game?"

"Nice tattoo," said Dex. Bert blushed and crossed his arms again, covering the tattoo, but not before Tuesday finally saw it close-up: one of John Tenniel's famous illustrations from *Alice's Adventures in Wonderland,* the White Rabbit, standing on its hind paws, wearing a checked coat and looking at a pocket watch.

She reopened her mental file on him. "Bert," she said. "What's your last name?"

"Hatmaker," he said.

Dex hooted. "*That's* a name. Bert Hatmaker. I didn't know real people had names like that."

"Isn't your name Poindexter?" Bert deadpanned.

Sly and dry. Good but nervous. Knows more than he's telling. Tuesday paused, mental pencil over mental paper.

"Dex becomes me," Dex said.

Bert smiled at him. Dex smiled back. *Put Dex on the case,* Tuesday scribbled in her file. *Not that he isn't already.*

"What we're dealing with here – from what you're saying," Tuesday said, "is some very complicated grief. While she was adjusting and overthinking, was she ever a crazy asshole to you?"

"Huh?" Bert twitched. "No, she—" He shot up straight. "Lyle!" he said. "Coffee's on."

Lila stood behind them in the kitchen doorway, one hand on the wall. She spoke to Bert as if he were the only person in the room.

"How much did you tell them?" she asked.

◆

Dex frowned at his travel tumbler, then smiled at it, because it belonged to Lila or Bert, and returning it was a reason to see either or both of them again. Soon.

"See, we didn't need a plan," said Dex, stretching his back against the bench. "It was a social call. And they sang like social canaries."

"Just because you didn't have a plan," said Tuesday, "doesn't mean *I* didn't."

Dex peered at her sideways. She was worrying her thumbnail between her teeth.

"What are you thinking?" he asked. "Or overthinking."

"Whether those canaries sang us the truth."

He saw no reason to doubt either of them, but then, Dex never did. Trusting no one was Tuesday's job.

And Lila had put on a trustworthy performance. She was an actor – Dex knew one when he saw one – but just because it was a performance didn't mean it wasn't true. Still sniffling from whatever had passed between her and Constance Arches in the hallway, Lila entered the kitchen from stage left. Her bare feet slapped on the tile floor. She repeated her question to Bert.

"How much did you tell them?"

"Not much," Bert said. "I was waiting for you."

"We should tell them," she said.

"Well, we kind of have to now," Bert said.

Lila sighed. "Booty me," she said, and Bert tossed her the bag of Pirate's Booty. She caught it and yanked it open in the same graceful movement.

"The morning after Vince died," Lila said, scooping a handful of Booty into her mouth and talking around it, "a man dressed as Edgar Allan Poe came to my door. Pale as hell, half-drunk pouchy eyes, Victorian suit, stuffed bird sewn to his damn shoulder. Told me he had a message from the beyond." She swallowed. "It was maybe seven-thirty. I'm wearing – I think I'm wearing these exact sweatpants. My life feels like an impossible surreal nightmare, and this fucker rings my bell before eight a.m., and for a hot second I think I'm going to gouge his eyes out with my thumbs."

She paused. The bag of Booty crinkled as she lowered it to her side.

"Then he starts—" Her chin trembled. "Wait," she said. "That's not where the story starts. I need to back up." She inhaled slowly with her eyes closed. "I met Vince at karaoke," she said, and Dex couldn't stop his own intake of breath. A romance after his own stupid heart. "I was out with a friend—" She nodded at Bert, and Bert pressed his fingertip to his chest and mouthed, *She means me.* "After a peculiar night. A peculiar, shattering, liberating night." Lila paused again. She composed herself once more and stood, firm, ready to launch her monologue to the back of the house.

"A new teacher on staff, Heather," she said, "asked if I wanted to go with her to the Museum of Fine Arts for their evening cocktail hour – a famous hunting ground for older, wealthy men looking to bag young nubile things. I like art, I wasn't currently bagged, and Heather was new and looking to make a friend. So I went with her. It became very clear, very quickly, that she didn't want to make *a* friend, let alone *me* as a friend. She wanted to get bagged, and didn't want to look so desperate to be there alone. It was a strange evening, fairly inane; I talked to a lot of old white men who thought my eyes were here." She moved her hand in a circle over her chest. "Heather wasn't getting bagged. When I suggested we bag the *mixer* and hit the falafel joint around the corner so the night wasn't a total waste, Heather got – riled. She said to me, 'You would rather eat falafel than get married.'"

Dex snorted. He covered it up, not sure if he was being rude.

"No, it's hilarious," said Lila. She chewed a few more bites of Booty. "It was the worst insult Heather could imagine. When she said it, her face went still as an assassin's. She shot to kill. And we hardly knew each other! But I heard those words, and I knew they were the truth, and they set me free.

"'Yes,' I told Heather. *Yes*, I would rather eat delicious falafel at the joint around the corner than flatter my way to an intimacy with someone for whom marriage is a financial transaction, young flesh for old, security for heirs. *Yes*, I would rather enjoy creamy tahini, a soft pita, those perfectly fried little balls, than torture myself about what was or was not happening in my life when my life was good. *Yes*, I rejected marriage – as an abstract, arbitrary signifier, as a legal and social status that determined my value, as a bullshitty benchmark I'd blown past years ago anyway. *Yes!*" She raised a fist in the air. "I wanted pleasure. *Yes*, I wanted companionship. *Yes*, I wanted a life of meaning. Yes, *this* was thirty-six, goddammit, tonight I wanted falafel and tonight it would be mine. I *would* rather eat falafel than get married."

Dex said, "I want to clap. Can I clap?"

Lila continued. "It wasn't Heather's fault – she didn't know my life. I didn't know hers. And whatever natural anxiety she had about coupling could've only been made worse by the garbage we've all been eating all our lives, every piece of fairy-tale cake we've choked down that rewards a girl – for her kindness, her wit, her courage – with a wedding. As though a wedding is a marriage, as though marriage is itself a trophy." She shook her hair back over her shoulders. "So I left, grabbed my goddamn falafel at the joint around the corner and called my friend and asked what he was up to."

"I was dating a guy at the time," said Bert, and Dex noted, as he was surely meant to, all the information contained therein. *I date men. I was dating someone at that time whom I am dating no longer.* "Who hosted karaoke at a bar in Brookline."

"So I walk into this karaoke bar, still eating my falafel," Lila said. "It was so good, salty and rich, crispy and soft, like deep-fried freedom and truth and acceptance. It tasted like the known, owned self. It tasted like fuck you, patriarchy. And halfway through savoring this falafel, I heard him. Vince had—"

All this performance was bravado. All of this drama was camouflage.

"—a perfect tenor. Perfect pitch." She looked down. "He sounded like Paul McCartney. This fantastic old man with silver hair, wearing a frigging cape, got up and sang 'No More Lonely Nights.' And he made the whole room turn toward him, all our hearts on a string."

Tuesday sat back on her stool and crossed her arms.

"I complimented his cape," Lila said. "Later, when he was offstage, I said, 'You don't see many capes in the world today. They're difficult to pull off.' His speaking voice was lower than his singing – I liked his big ears and his big nose, a little Cary Grant, a little busted Harrison Ford; his eyes were intelligent but kind, with a glint – and he said, 'Am I? Pulling it off?'"

She sagged a little.

"I know how it looks," she said. "Young woman – well, not as young as some – marries much, much older wealthy man. Trophy wife. But it wasn't like that. I didn't want to get married. I wanted, more than anything in the world, love." Her throat caught. "The kind that lasts longer than life. So, the morning after the auction. A man dressed as Edgar Allan Poe wakes me up and he – he's a Singing Poe-a-gram. He sings the first song I ever heard Vince sing, and it's the first time I notice the refrain. *I won't go away,*" she said, her tiny voice thickening with uncried tears, "*until you tell me so. No, I'll never go away.*"

Her voice cracked.

"You get the point," she said. She splayed her fingers and mimed a waterfall from her face. "Weeping. Because Vince was still here. *Is* still here. He's dead but he won't go away. Like this – today. He's been sending me food every day. Pizza and takeout and catered brunch just shows up at the door. He's feeding me. I mean, that's partly why I invited you." She shrugged at Dex. "I need help eating all this stuff.

"Anyway, the poor singer looked terrified that I was snotting all over him, but he was sweet, gave me a tissue. Then he told me he'd already been tipped and asked if I needed a hug. A hug. From a faux Poe." Her voice clotted again. "That was Vince." Lila pushed the tears out of her eyes with her thumbs.

She blinked. "Shit. Shit – ouch. I got – I got Booty in my – *shit.*"

Bert turned on the faucet. Lila crossed to the sink and dunked her face under the tap to flush her eye.

"That's quite a story," said Tuesday.

"I know." Lila's voice echoed out of the stainless steel basin.

"Vince was theatrical," said Bert.

Lila righted herself, blinking, water streaming down her face and matting one side of her hair. "Vince was a lunatic in all the best ways. He's not done with life, despite being dead. He's not done with me, or you or you, or anyone who takes him seriously enough to play this game."

Dex's fingers tingled. "Are you saying we're in danger?"

"God no!" Lila said. "I'm just saying if you want to win, even if you just want to play, think like a lunatic. A theatrical lunatic."

"With a romantic streak," said Tuesday.

"Shouldn't be difficult," Dex said. Out of the side of his eye he caught Bert, tucking his chin to his chest and blushing again.

Dex could see that Tuesday's assessment of Vince as a romantic – which, of *course*; no one sends a soft-rock Poe-a-gram from beyond the grave unless they believe not even death can conquer love – impressed Lila. Over her shoulder to Bert, she said, "I knew these were the horses to back."

"What about the Arches family?" Tuesday asked.

Lila's face went still. "What about them?" she said.

Tuesday shrugged. "You tell me."

Lila thought for a moment. A bead of water from her wet hair slid down the side of her face, and when she spoke, it didn't sound a bit scripted.

"Stay far away," she said, "from Nathaniel."

◆

"Is this how a pawn feels?" Dex asked. *Probably*, thought Tuesday. A pawn. Or a rook. Were rooks the same as ravens? She didn't know how to play chess. A ratty city squirrel raced out from beneath their bench and bounded anemically over the Common's leaf-strewn grass. "Are we being used?"

"At the very least we're getting sucked into some bizarro family drama." Tuesday tapped her fingers on her tumbler. "Disappearances, deaths. Long-standing grudges, rivalries beyond our control."

"The Arches and the Pryces aren't exactly the Hatfields and the McCoys."

"That's exactly who they are," said Tuesday. "In a higher tax bracket." She jiggled her leg. "And not to be a pedant, but the plural of Arches is Archeses. Feels weird, doesn't it?"

"Yeah," said Dex drily. "The plural form of their last name is what feels weird about them."

Lila – or Lyle ("we're in nickname territory once you've seen me in sweats") – had sketched the details of Vince's relationship with the Archeses, or at least what she'd been around to witness. They were neighbors on Nantucket. She had only ever heard stories of Edgar Arches; he'd disappeared before she met Vince, but she knew him as "a craven bastard" who had fought tooth and nail to restrict the construction of the Castellated Abbey. The Arches family, when Vince moved to the neighborhood, thought Vince was vulgar, tacky, a blight; Vince thought that reaction suggested the Archeses were "morally bankrupt snobs of the highest order." Dex said that made them sound kind of fun, which made Bert laugh, which made Lyle and Tuesday exchange a glance.

Lyle, personally, had had the most social contact with Constance and Emerson. They crossed paths at charity events, at galas, at auctions, on sidewalks in the posher neighborhoods. "We're from completely different worlds," Lyle said. "Different universes. I think visiting my bereaved ass was the very last thing Constance Arches wanted to do this morning, and yet it was the Thing To Do, so she did it. But they don't scare me." She inhaled. "Nathaniel, though – I've met him a few times. I always come away with the impression that he doesn't understand I exist. I mean, I *don't*, functionally, exist for him. He doesn't have to deal with anyone who looks like me or thinks like me or lives like me – I guess *lived* like me – and what he doesn't already know, he can't imagine, so I might as well be – nothing." She tapped the side of her head with her fingertip. "He's hollow," she said. "And he's always . . ."

"A dick?" said Dex.

Lyle smiled. "Well, yes," she said. "But I was going to say he's always hungry."

All things considered, all bloody marys consumed, it had been, for Tuesday, a successful research brunch. Her mental file on Archie was getting fatter (and odder) by the minute. Plus, she had fresh details on Emerson – witty – and Constance – taking Pryce's death harder than one would expect. And, sure, she'd accidentally shown Emerson a picture of her dumb brother making finger guns in the bowels of Park Street, despite having promised Archie she'd keep him a secret. But she *also* had two shiny new mental files. One on Lyle Korrapati Pryce, and one on Bert Hatmaker.

"So, Bert," Tuesday said.

"What about Bert?" Dex asked.

"I've seen him before. I know him from – something." She sighed.

"From my vision board, probably," Dex said. "I projected that Secret, and boy howdy."

"I don't trust him," said Tuesday.

"Oh, good," said Dex. "That must mean he's a human being." He paused. "What was that line of Shakespeare chalked over the raven again, that Lyle said? 'The prince of darkness is a gentleman'?" He pulled his phone out of his pocket and tapped at it with his thumbs.

Tuesday nodded. "*King Lear*," she said.

"Act three," said Dex, "scene four. Edgar's 'Poor Tom' monologue."

"Drama nerd," said Tuesday.

"Huh," said Dex. "Says here that Poe's parents, both actors, met in a production of *Lear*."

Tuesday slurped her coffee. "The internet takes all the effort out of detecting, doesn't it?"

"His mom was great. Legitimately talented. His dad was . . . less great. Total piece of work. Chucked being a lawyer for the stage, then got routed by the critics . . . huh! He was born here! Poe was born in Boston. I did not know that."

"I knew that."

Think like a romantic, theatrical lunatic.

"You know, the theater district is like . . . right on the other side of the Common," Tuesday said. She pointed. "Right over there. Boylston and back." She had officially reached the sleepy stage of drunkenness. Day drinking, while more practical once one reached a certain age, did have the unfortunate side effect of knocking her out cold by two p.m. Her muzzy half-awake brain, however, was often capable of some of her best thinking. Which reminded her.

"Lyle's pregnant."

Dex did the next best thing to a spit take, blasting air into the lid of the tumbler. "How can you – did she pee on a stick when I wasn't looking?"

"For a fully stocked grief kitchen, something was conspicuously absent."

"What the *hell*. Do you ever turn off?"

"Wine," said Tuesday. "Booze. Empties. And for a bereft widow, she's oddly luminescent."

"But, like, bloody marys. We were drunk," Dex said. "There was definitely alcohol flowing in that house."

"Oh, *we* were. Drunk. But was she?" asked Tuesday. "Did you see her drink anything?"

Dex paused.

"Just a hunch," said Tuesday.

"The plot thickens."

"The plot's the thing in which we'll catch the king."

"Wrong play," said Dex. "And butchered quote. Come on, let's walk. I have a hunch too."

◆

Dex had hunches all the time. He didn't tell anyone about them or test them to see if they were correct, so they were probably less hunches and more oversensitive delusions, but they *felt* true. Tuesday's hunches, her leapfrogging trivia brain and lady detective intuitions, were in a class by themselves (though Lyle's being pregnant seemed – actually – it didn't seem at all impossible), which might explain why he didn't bother sharing any of his, under normal circumstances.

But this circumstance was abnormal. This circumstance was Dex joining the Team, because Tuesday was a pathological loner, and though she was slightly looser and chummier than usual, she was never going to invite him. This was Dex, coming off a booze buzz, courting a coffee buzz, made whirrier by a simultaneous Bert Hatmaker buzz, the swirling, possibility-twirling, heart-hammering potential of a crush. Had Patrick ever made him feel this light, even in the beginning?

It was thinking about Patrick that made Dex's hunch bite. He stood up.

"Where are we going?" Tuesday sniffed as he pulled her to her feet. "What is your hunch?"

"Wikipedia says Poe was born somewhere on Boylston Street."

"Do you believe everything Wikipedia tells you?" she asked.

"No, but my hunch does." He drew her closer, walked a little faster. "The second clue is a line from *Lear*, the play Poe's parents might've been in when they met. It's a line of dialogue spoken by a character named Edgar, I mean – think like a theatrical lunatic."

"Pryce wants us to go to the theater. *A* theater. But which? There are . . . a lot."

"There are only two theaters on Boylston Street." He paused for dramatic effect. "And only one underground."

Patrick had told him about it. Patrick knew a flock of musical theater kids from Emerson College. Emerson's main campus had been expanding down Boylston for years, engulfing the Colonial Theatre, transforming empty commercial spaces into residence halls and classrooms. And at the end of the block, casting an urban legend over the student body, was the M. Steinert & Sons building: a stone-and-brick edifice with a six-foot metal G-clef sign, a piano showroom on the first floor—

"And an old, old theater in the basement," Dex said. "Like, fifty feet below street level."

"You're making that up," said Tuesday.

It was possible, but not probable, that Patrick had been making it up. He'd mentioned it early in the game, when they were still trying to impress each other with everything they knew, everything they thought was important or interesting or worth sharing with each other. But Patrick, sweet, credulous Patrick, was a wretched liar. Unlike Dex, who'd sold more than a few lies in his time, like that he'd been to the Castro ("Of course I have! What kind of traveling homosexual do you take me for?"), that he'd seen *Grey Gardens* (he had *now*), or that he had *never*, ever, so much as slightly nudged another car in a parking lot and driven away without leaving a note. They had been harmless lies. Flirtations, almost. And Patrick's wide-eyed gullibility made him especially fun to string along.

"Patrick said he knew a kid who knew a bunch of people—"

"Naturally."

"—who snuck into the theater to get high."

"Naturally," she repeated. "Emerson kids."

Dex, at the corner of the Common, looked across Boylston to the building on the other side of the street, with its grand recessed entrance, gray cement columns, and the shining street-level windows of a music store showroom. He could just make out the raised edge of a grand piano. Above the first floor, around the side and front, the columns supported carved stone arches.

"Arches," said Tuesday.

"Don't you mean archeses?" said Dex.

"No." Tuesday squeezed his arm. A little bell chimed inside Dex because Tuesday Mooney – Tuesday Mooney – was not only voluntarily touching him, she was *latching*. She pointed at the building, at the front door, which was closing behind someone. "Nathaniel Arches just went inside."

"You are making that up," said Dex.

Tuesday squeezed his arm again, harder, half glanced at the pedestrian WALK sign – Dex assumed out of habit more than any conscientious desire to follow traffic ordinance, because it said DO NOT WALK and the next thing Tuesday did was walk anyway, dragging him to the island in the middle of the intersection of Boylston and Charles. "Nice hustle," said Dex, "for a death wish!" and Tuesday said, "Go. Go go go go go" – and they ran across Boylston to the other side of the street.

Dex was gobsmacked. In all the hours they'd spent sitting across from each other's cubes, all the after-work drinks, the movies, the trivia, he had never seen her act this way. He had never seen her this – *emotional*. About anything (or any*one*). She had enthusiasms, yes; there were things she loved (scary movies, solitude, solving shit), but this was more than enthusiasm. This was electrified. Tuesday Mooney was scurrying – scurrying after a *man* – and ten haulassed steps up the sidewalk, Dex yanked his arm free and called her on it.

"I am not," she said.

"You are *too*," he said, laughing. "This is *textbook* scurrying. I can hear rapid-fire xylophones." Dex grinned at her with every tooth in his head. "He must be really cute."

"He's a hell of a lot less cute when he's going rogue," she said.

"For God's sake, you don't even know that was him."

It was him.

Dex knew it was him the second he reappeared, sauntering down the concrete steps of the building in question, arms and shoulders and hands all casual, tucked into the pockets of his motorcycle jacket. He was tallish. Thinnish. Darkish. Broadish in the shoulders, with a long nose and the kind of forehead Dex remembered was Tuesday's kryptonite ("*Working Girl* Harrison Ford," she'd explained once, which required no further explanation). Privilege rolled off him in waves. He was walking straight ahead, and for a second Dex thought he was going to cross Boylston in the middle of the street, trusting the traffic to swerve.

"Archie!" yelled Tuesday.

He froze. When he turned, for a second, he didn't look a thing like Nathaniel Arches, Prominent Bostonian. He looked younger, his face a cold-water smash of excitement and terror, but by the time Tuesday and Dex – who was now one hundred percent on the scurrying bandwagon – caught up to him, that face was gone. He just looked like a rich white douche. An unconventionally handsome rich white douche, but a rich white douche nonetheless. He removed his hands from his pockets. They fluttered, nervous, then settled into the shape of twin finger guns.

Douche or not, he was even more perfectly ridiculous than Tuesday had described.

"I was going to call you," Nathaniel Arches said.

"Poindexter Howard," Dex said, grabbing one finger gun by the barrel and shaking. "Friend to the friendless."

"No, you weren't," Tuesday said, ignoring Dex. "What are you doing here?"

Archie gnawed on his lip. "Waiting?" he said. "For . . . you?" Then he frowned. "Were you going to call *me*?"

"I might have," Tuesday said, "if you hadn't run away before we exchanged numbers last time."

"Oh, come on, you can find my number. You don't need me to give it to you. I thought we were partners." Archie jerked his chin at Dex. "But it looks like you've found another."

Tuesday opened her mouth, stunned.

Dex bloomed. "Sir," he said, pressing his hand to his heart. "Oh, sir. You flatter me. And to think that *I* was feeling jealous about the two of *you*."

Tuesday turned, her fingertips on his arm. "You were?"

"A smidge," Dex said.

"Wait, *who* are you?" asked Archie.

"Dex," said Dex.

"We just met your sister," said Tuesday. "And your mother."

There – it was back, for only a second, the other face that Archie had, the one that popped up like a coked-out gopher whenever he was truly taken aback – but Dex didn't have time to observe it before the doors behind them, the doors they had come to enter, swung open. A man in a jacket with a security guard patch on the arm walked out. Adjusting his Sox cap against the sun, he turned and headed up Boylston toward Tremont.

Archie checked his watch. "Dunks run," he said. "Right on schedule." Then, off Tuesday and Dex's silence, "I told you I was waiting."

He took the steps two at a time and caught the door before it closed.

"Come on," he said.

"Come on," said Dex to Tuesday, who was squeezing his arm again.

They walked into the lobby – a room that had no business calling itself a lobby. It was a cramped, dark little hall, with windows overlooking the piano showroom on the right and an empty chair – those butt dents belonged to the Dunks-jonesing guard, no doubt – facing an elevator at the far end. On the left was a staircase, marked off with a velvet cordon, that went up into the light of day and down into darkness. Someone nearby was tripping chromatically across a piano's keys.

"That's perfect," whispered Dex. "That's the perfect music for descending creepy steps. Let's go."

Archie swung one long leg, then the other, over the cordon.

"How did you figure this out?" Tuesday asked him.

"I didn't know that I did," he said, and offered his hand. Tuesday glared at it and swung her own long legs over the rope without assistance, but Dex took it. "And they say chivalry is dead," he said, giving Archie's long, cool fingers a squeeze.

The steps led to a landing, turned, led to another landing, and turned again, the piano growing fainter as the light disappeared. Tuesday pulled her phone out of her pocket and opened a flashlight app.

"Chivalry may be alive, but romance is rotting," Dex hissed. "Can we not find a femur to wrap in rags for a torch?"

"*Who* are you, again?" asked Archie.

"Poindexter Howard," said Dex, "inveterate adventurer."

"We're out of earshot even if the guard comes back," said Tuesday. "So talk. What are you looking for?"

"You mean, out of life?" Archie's low voice wrapped around them in the darkness. "In a job? In a partner?"

"You know what I mean."

"I don't know."

"Does that answer apply universally?" asked Dex. He hopped, tripping over what he didn't know. They'd spiraled down a few more flights and now had reached a passage lined on either side with what looked, in the light of Tuesday's phone, like a burial ground for Bankers Boxes. Everything was wet, musty, funky. "Smells like shin guards down here."

"Dex," said Tuesday, "this was your plan. Take it away."

Patrick had never told him how his friends had broken in, only that they had, the implication being that it couldn't be so difficult if it was within the grasp of a pack of stoned under-graduates. Dex turned on his own flashlight app and threw light up and over the walls. The floor was carpeted but not plush; the walls were chipped plaster, weeping water. "This can't be the main entrance, can it?" Dex said. "It was suppos-edly a real theater, a music hall open to the public, but this is – claustro. This must be for hands, employees, the talent. So we're not looking for anything grand."

"We're looking for a back door," said Archie.

Dex bit down hard on his tongue.

"You have no idea the amount of self-control he's exercising right now," Tuesday said to Archie, "to not make a filthy joke."

"It would be too easy," said Dex. "Beneath me. Low-hanging fruit."

"Well, now everything sounds filthy," Archie drawled.

"Jesus, he is charming," Dex said to Tuesday. "Charming like a psychopath. Are we sure he's not going to murder us down here?" He paused. "That's a legitimately horrifying thought. Please don't do that to us, Mr. Arches. I haven't drunk half of what I intend to before I die."

"What's that?" Archie pointed at a break in the wall of boxes, a gap darker than the cardboard-colored shadows on either side. Dex turned his flashlight. In the wall was a door. A crappy old plywood door with a crinkled paper sign with NO ENTRANCE written in shaky capitals, begging for a Sartre joke Dex suddenly hadn't the heart to make. This was happening. No amount of nervous quipping was going to still the tremor in his hand as he reached for the knob. No amount of patter could distract from the fact that he was opening a door he had no business opening.

He exhaled, wrapped his fingers around the knob, and turned.

It did not move.

"Shit," he said. "It's locked."

He felt a hand on his arm in the darkness, nudging him aside. "Back a little," Archie said, before pumping one of his long legs into the air and kicking the door open before either Dex or Tuesday could think, let alone shout, What the *hell*—

The door bounced off something on the other side and swung back into the frame. The knob had broken through the plywood; it was recessed, smushed in like a thumbprint cookie.

"Or we could have used that," Tuesday said, shining her light on an eyehook screwed into the doorframe, and the key dangling from it.

"Where's the romance in that?" Archie pushed the door open again with one arm. "Adventurers first," he said, and Dex took another breath and stepped through.

They were no longer in a hallway but a storage room, maybe, an antechamber on the outskirts of a much larger space. A balcony. A balcony, with several tiers like cake layers, for now-absent seats. Dex stepped down one, then another. There were columns and a curling metal railing in front of him, and more cardboard boxes, though not stacked so high as in the hallway. Tuesday called out that she'd found stairs, and Dex and Archie followed her down the curving darkness.

"Oh Dex," said Tuesday. "Look."

Her phone flashlight was puny, but it was enough. There was a mural on the back wall of the theater: an audience of figures in Grecian robes listening to a standing figure on the shores of a lake that was still bright blue after all this time. Dex's dusty heart stirred, caught in his chest. His eyes prickled. What a terrible thing to bury such beauty alive. The rest of the paint was chipped and dulled by water and time, but the mural was spectacular, ageless and so big Dex had to back up to take it all in, which he did without realizing he was backing up to the lip of another short flight of stairs, flanked by more columns – Tuesday caught him just in time, or else he would have tipped ass over heels, down the stairs into the mass of filing cabinets and chairs and piano benches and music stands and dead pianos, rotted skeletons of keys and wires, and – oh God, was that a toilet? Dex wiped his brow with the back of his hand and looked out into the auditorium, which was small and oval. The air was cool, but the walls seemed to glow orange, and he felt safe and close, as though he were a yolk floating in an egg.

"The acoustics in here must be insane," said Tuesday. She walked down the last steps to join Dex on the auditorium floor, shining her light on the junk all around her, the railings, the walls. Archie followed. Once she was standing in the center of the floor – seatless as the balcony, who knew when the seats had been removed – she lit the walls in a slow circle. Massive columns, deep niches. Walls feathery with flaking paint. Each niche was marked with the name of a composer in delicate letters, surrounded by decorative hand-painted borders: BACH. MOZART. BEETHOVEN.

This was a recital hall. For music, not for theater. Dex didn't see a stage, just a flat floor with space at the front for a piano, a quartet, a soloist, and though a stage could have existed and been removed at the same time as the missing seats, dramatic productions were not what this space was built for. It was underground, sure, and Pryce (and Poe) had a fondness for the subterranean, but the clue was a snippet of Shakespeare. *Lear*. Dex pondered. This didn't seem quite right.

Maybe his hunch had been drunk.

Dex turned back to see Tuesday flash her phone's light straight into Archie's eyes. "We need to talk," she said.

Archie raised a bent arm, shielding his face like a capeless vampire. "Ouch, jeez," he said. "You don't have to torture me."

"*Were* you going to call me?" Tuesday asked Archie, gesturing to the garbage heaped around them. "You've obviously known about this theater for at least a day. Long enough to know when the guard makes his daily coffee run."

"All I did" – Archie backed up into a filing cabinet – "was figure out that Poe's parents met doing *Lear*, and that Poe was born here."

"And that brought you *here*, specifically?" Tuesday said, lowering her light.

"Yes. When I say Poe was born here, I mean right here. That alley next door? It's called Carver Street. Edgar Allan Poe was born on Carver Street."

"How do you—"

"I'm *resourceful*," he said. "Remember?" He pushed a hand through his hair and stopped halfway, grabbed it, gave it a tug. It stood. It was practically a mane. "And yes, I put that together and didn't tell you about it, but it's not like I wasn't *going* to." He swallowed. "I Googled the addresses adjacent to Carver Street, and all this stuff about the underground theater comes up, which seemed like the kind of thing Pryce would've loved. But it was all – supposition. So I came on a recon mission."

"I like supposition. I'm *great* with supposition." Tuesday set her phone on a chair, light shining up, and crossed her arms. "You said you'd find me yesterday. I did not hide. Yet somehow you did not find me."

Archie made a deep noise midway between a grumble and a growl.

Dex took a slow, centering breath. He mulled. Carver Street. What a fantastic name for a street. What a perfect place for Edgar Allan Poe to be born. What a hopeful sign that his hunch hadn't been so drunk after all. He pressed down hard on a piano bench and, satisfied with its sturdiness, sat. He crossed his legs. Rubbed the first knuckle of his right hand with his right thumb. From where he was sitting, he had a full view of the giant mural, of the figures standing by the water.

Or were they on a heath?

Tuesday's voice cut into his thoughts: "—thought we were partners, and the terms of partnership were—"

Archie: "—don't remember signing anything—"

Dex tuned them out. Not all the way out, because they were amusing, and Archie's voice was a gorgeously soothing bass. Tuesday went for the destabilizing non sequitur – *What's wrong with your ear?* (what indeed?) – and Archie, after a beat, responded with a classic – *What's wrong with your ear?* Tuesday shot – *It's a reasonable expectation of a partner to NOT abandon me to the freaking Boston PD* – and Archie shot back: *I didn't abandon you, I was trying to* protect *you—*

Dex perked. *Oh you sweet, stupid man,* he thought. He had broken not one but two of the Tuesday commandments: Thou shalt not gaslight. *And* thou shalt not condescend.

He looked up. Tuesday's lips were pressed flat and her eyes held something that wasn't quite murder but close – manslaughter, maybe, or negligent homicide. But she looked *amazing.* In this cold, wet piano mausoleum, she burned like a coal. And Dex, distracted by Pryce's puzzle, caught up to what had been happening right in front of him. Tuesday was *fighting.* Implacable, unflappable Tuesday – his favorite emotional iceberg was on fucking fire.

And Archie – more of his hair was standing up now, and higher too, brushing Barry Gibb-ian heights. His lips were tilted in a kind of smile, because he was the kind of man who laughed when he argued, and his shoulders were up high, around his ears, his hands out in front of him, fingers splayed so he could hold his own words and present them to her like a hot dish. It seemed that being intensely frustrated was the most fun Archie'd had in months.

They'd been arguing about something Dex had been only half paying attention to – oh, it was about trust, being on the same page, about not "unnecessarily going it alone," which was a hilariously ironic argument considering Tuesday had come up with it – with a fierceness and a flush that could mean just one thing: they were desperate to bone but hadn't quite admitted it to themselves yet.

Dex laughed.

They both turned to him.

"Stop overthinking it," he told them.

A bell rang in the back of his brain.

He saw it.

◆

Dex squawked.

He raised his arm and pointed at something behind and above Tuesday and Archie, and Tuesday whipped her head around to follow. All she saw was the wall. No, it wasn't just a wall. It was a niche pressed into the wall, a slightly rounded space offset by columns. She saw the name BACH lettered in what had once been white at the top of the niche, surrounded by an intricate hand-painted frame, also in dusty once-white paint, of flowers and vines and—

Tuesday's jaw dropped. It actually dropped, flopped loose with her open, astonished mouth. It didn't matter that, ten seconds ago, she'd wanted to rip Archie's head from his shoulders (or his clothes from his body; it was getting progressively more difficult to tell where one desire ended and the other began). All that mattered was that they were exactly where Vincent Pryce wanted them to be.

She turned back to Dex.

"We don't need a decoder ring," she said.

"What," said Archie. "I don't—"

Dex stood from his piano bench and walked straight back, sliding between Archie and Tuesday, sheer glee radiating off his body. He stood with his back to the niche and pointed straight up at the painted border.

"Sixty-nine, dudes," he said.

"You're going to have to explain a lot better than that," said Archie.

"Look," said Tuesday. "Look at the design, the border around Bach's name."

Archie stepped closer. Dex grinned fanatically and hopped a little, still pointing up.

"Do you know the difference between a code and a cipher?" Tuesday asked.

"Here we go!" Dex clapped.

"What people think of as codes are, most of the time, really ciphers," said Tuesday. "Ciphers replace each letter in a hidden message with a sign or a symbol. A code replaces each *word* in a message with a sign or symbol. Vincent Pryce gave us a secret code. And this, all of this—" She gestured to the air. "This concert hall is the secret code decoder room."

Dangling on the edge of the faded painted border around Bach's name, someone very recently had painted the astrological sign for Cancer in bright white paint. Beneath that, also in bright white paint, the same someone had painted the word "clock."

"The symbol for Cancer is code for the word 'clock,'" said Dex. "And we need more light."

They hunted. Archie traced a string of yellow-caged work lights back to a small generator and flicked the switch. Tuesday warned him they might be sitting in a pool of seeping groundwater. "Don't electrocute yourself," she hissed, and he smug-smiled at her like he'd caught her accidentally caring about his safety and wasn't it adorable, and she rolled her eyes and immediately, in the new low light, saw another symbol: the ankh. Painted on the side of a rusting green filing cabinet listing in the corner of the room. She circled the cabinet. There was a symbol on each flat side – the ankh, the bent arrow, the coffin – and beneath each symbol, a freshly painted word.

"The ankh . . . means *life*. The arrow is *after*. The coffin is *death*," she said to herself, and then, louder, to Dex and Archie and the whole haunted room, "Life after death."

Dex found, to his eternal delight, the asterisk ("butthole!") in the border painted around Mozart – *game*. Archie found both half-moons, facing left and right – *before, the*. And scattered throughout the mural like hidden pictures, they found infinity (*well*), the cat (*alone*), the tombstone (*ages*), the circle (*seek*), the star (*play*). Tuesday tapped each of their discoveries into her phone notes, then sat quietly on the steps and began to decode. They were missing a few: the dollar sign, the equal sign, the heart. Though maybe those symbols didn't need decoding, because they meant what they meant.

She looked up and caught Dex's eye as he crossed the room, still searching. He grinned extravagantly at her, all teeth and joy, and for a split second she saw him as a child, six, seven, on Christmas morning. Or – she knew this to be a part of his personal history – watching *Newsies* for the first time. She laughed. Child Dex would have played witch with her, she realized; child Dex would have loved it.

She had missed his childhood, but she had known him, and been known *by* him, through what felt like two or three ages of her adult life. It was suddenly astonishing to her, her friendship with Dex. Outrageously lucky that she was friends, still friends, with the sole legitimately witty coworker at her first adult job, who just happened to be assigned the cube opposite hers. Without meaning to, or trying, she and Dex had been friends to varying degrees for more than—

Ten years.

Ten years, and they hadn't gotten bored of each other. Ten years, and she'd seen almost every side of Dex, every boyfriend, every gripe about his job, every voice he could borrow and bend, and there were *still* sides to him. Ten years, and she honestly couldn't think of anyone else she would rather be with here – here, in this basement theater, together. Maybe this was how adult friendships happened: by accident, embroidered over time, visible only from the height of years.

She smiled at him, bewildered and grateful.

"Tuesday," said Dex, wary, "why are you looking at me like that?"

"Because," she said, tucking what was precious safely away, "we found the theater. We cracked the code." She stood on the steps, the mural to her back. "We're missing a few symbols, but I think we can fill in what they mean based on context. The equal, for example, probably means 'equals,' the dollar sign probably means 'dollars,' and the ampersand probably means 'and.'" Archie propped one elbow on the rusty green filing cabinet and grinned at her like he was going to bust. Dex pressed his palms together and hopped up on his toes. "The cat," she continued, "means 'alone' and the starburst means 'team,' so I'm interpreting that to mean we can play by ourselves or in teams. The only one we're missing that doesn't seem completely obvious is the heart."

"Play?" asked Archie. "Play what?"

"Only you," said Dex, "would look for another explanation for what a heart means."

Tuesday grinned at him and cleared her throat. "You ready? All together now:

"Life After Death

"A Game for All Ages

"Alone or in Teams

"Objective: Seek well before the clock (equals) twelve.

"Receive thirteen thousand (dollars) and (heart)

"How to Play: Use your imagination."

Dex opened his mouth. He held out his hands, fingers flexed expectantly.

"Fantastic!" he said. "What the fuck does it mean?"

Tuesday shrugged. She felt like giggling. She was sober, or

at least the most relatively sober she'd been in hours, but even so, her head was light and loopy.

"It's a game," she said. "For all ages. We use our imaginations to play it."

"Where's the money coming from? Is someone going to give us thirteen thousand dollars?" Archie asked. "Where – how do we get it?" And then, off Tuesday's face, he said, "I'm not focused on the money, I'm focused on how the game works."

"Maybe it's here somewhere?" She gestured at the room. "We haven't looked everywhere yet. There are plenty of places to hide – I mean, look at all the boxes."

What had Dex said, right before he saw the symbol on the wall?

Stop overthinking it.

She hopped down the stairs and crossed the cluttered floor to where Archie stood, leaning against the filing cabinet with the name of the game, ankh-arrow-coffin, Life After Death, painted all around it. She pulled open the top drawer; it was empty. The middle drawer was empty too. But the bottom drawer, which she could open only so far, since it was surrounded by cardboard and old paper and assorted other garbage, was heavy with manila envelopes. Several dozen neatly filed, front to back. She pulled the first one out.

The envelope itself felt like any other manila envelope, but the flap was sealed with a glob of black wax and pressed with an elaborate symbol:

"That's him," said Archie, close over her shoulder. He was giddy almost, buzzing like a neon tube, lit by something deeper than the excitement of finding a clue. His voice rose so high, so quickly, it cracked. "That's his – see the V, the A, and the

P? That's—" He coughed into his fist. "That's Vince," he said again, his eyes bright.

Dex pulled the file from Tuesday's hand to peer at the wax seal. He wasn't paying any attention to Archie.

But Tuesday was.

Her mental file on Arches, Nathaniel floated open.

Didn't just know the dead man, she wrote.

Archie coughed again. Knuckled what might have been a tear from the corner of his eye, with a hand that had the slightest tremor.

Might have loved him.

7

DEAD PEOPLE

Dorry flicked her highlighter back and forth between her fingers until it blurred. She didn't really *get* highlighting. Everything seemed important, every tiny detail – that's why those sentences were there, to be noticed! – so she painted every sentence in smooth stripes of yellow, blue, and pink. When whole pages in her biology textbook turned fluorescent orange, she kind of wondered if she'd missed the point.

But weren't all the points the point?

She squared the report on her desk. One more read and she would take it to Tuesday. She wanted to highlight *the whole thing*, but she resisted. She'd worked on it every free second since Thursday night – when she wasn't in school (and sometimes when she was, like in study hall), or while eating or sleeping or Having That Talk with Dad (he *super* freaked about the picture of Tuesday in the *Metro*, which Dorry had to take off the fridge and stick in her desk drawer). The report was thirty pages long. It was the longest thing she'd ever written. She'd had to go to the Staples in Harvard Square to buy another printer cartridge because there were so many photos in the appendix. The title page read, in a drippy *Buffy the Vampire Slayer* font she'd found online, THE HAUNTED LIBRARY OF VINCENT PRYCE: THE COLLECTOR AND HIS COLLECTION.

Tuesday hadn't asked for it, but just because no one had assigned it didn't mean it wasn't the best work Dorry had ever done. She hadn't known she could feel this proud of something she wrote. And it wasn't just the writing that she thought was good; it was the information. Mr. Pryce's collection was *amazing*. No wonder Archie wanted it so bad. No wonder he'd said it had sentimental value. It was starting to mean the world to Dorry and she'd never seen it, hadn't even known it existed before three days ago.

Everything she'd found was online, in newspapers and online articles and on Wikipedia. Maybe she could turn this in instead of her final research project for English class. But no: she didn't want to share this information. It was sensitive. It was for Tuesday's eyes only (and Archie's, she guessed, since they were partners). And it wasn't for a grade. It was for millions of dollars.

Whenever she allowed herself to imagine she might actually *get* part of millions of dollars, her stomach did this funny hover-drop. It was so weird. What did millions of dollars even feel like? She'd tried to get her dad excited about that, to explain that that was why Tuesday had been arrested, not for doing anything (really) bad. He'd looked at her like she'd grown a unicorn horn or giant bunny ears, like he didn't quite believe or understand what he was seeing when he looked at her. He said that Tuesday was making some questionable choices and he wasn't sure how appropriate she was as a tutor. Which made Dorry so mad, her hands curled into fists.

"It's not like she's teaching me to be a terrorist," Dorry said.

"She's teaching you to get your hopes up," he said, "too high," and somehow that made Dorry even madder. How high Dorry's hopes were was on *Dorry*, not Tuesday. They were *her hopes*. So she said that just because Mom had always been the hopeful one, the one who got excited about stuff, didn't mean that no one else in their family could get their hopes up about the possibility of crazy awesome things. She was the kind of angry that made her want to be mean, so for a second it felt great. But her father's eyes skittered around like he didn't know where to look anymore, and just as quickly she felt terrible. She apologized for it later, but she and Dad were kind of avoiding each other still. Maybe because they both knew she had a good point.

It wasn't fair that Dorry couldn't get her hopes up.

Because it wasn't fair to pretend that the possibility of crazy awesome things, like the collection, didn't exist.

She flipped open the report cover. She'd started with a biography of Vincent Pryce. Just a short one, a prologue before you got to the good part, mostly taken from his bio on the *Forbes* list of billionaires. It listed his age (seventy-four), the source of his wealth (self-made, owner of the Vincent Mint), and his infamous extracurriculars; he spent his early retirement, already "wealthier than any individual human has any right to be" (his words), collecting rare and occult artifacts and books from around the globe.

She put in a little about his house on Nantucket and a picture of him, standing in front of a bookcase so full it looked like it was about to topple. He had a toothy grin and a big nose, and ears that stuck out almost as much as his hair. He looked like she'd imagined while she was reading his editorials: like a cranky crackpot who lives in a basement apartment with thirteen cats and a bunch of hamsters. The kind of guy some kids think is a child-eating troll but other kids suspect, correctly, is a secret wizard. She'd written:

Mr. Pryce's life before his retirement was pretty normal. He did not have any children and did not get married until he was very old. He made all his money as the owner of the Vincent Mint, which sold special coins and plates honoring celebrities and dead presidents through the mail.

Because of the Vincent Mint, he became a billionaire. He once said, "Money has meaning when you put it to work."

He retired when he was forty-one and started traveling the world, looking for artifacts. He became famous for his haunted collection, and many rumors about his "secret double life" were passed around. People said he was a grave robber, a thief, and "a modern pirate in the style of Captain Kidd" (www.nantucketdirt.com). One thing is clear: regardless of how he collects his objects, he has a lot of them, and they are strange.

She scribbled out "collects" and "has" and wrote "collected" and "had."

Her mom had been a collector of little things. Literally little things: miniatures. Tiny hats and shoes and clocks and books and plates and furniture, fit for a dollhouse, perfect for a mouse. A walking stick no bigger than her thumb with a duck carved on the handle. A suitcase with real leather straps, a real clasp, small clothes inside. Some her mother made herself, teensy cakes and dim sum and candy and fruits from polymer clay and nail polish. Her mother had displayed her collection in glass-fronted shadow boxes, one in every room in their house. Dad didn't unpack any of them after they moved to Somerville. The entire collection, hundreds of itty-bitty things, fit in one box, which Dorry kept taped shut, in her closet.

Mr. Pryce's collection was a lot bigger.

Mr. Pryce built his mansion on Nantucket to be large enough to hold his collection, which is "a spectacular library of curious stuff" (*Mental Floss*). It contains over twenty thousand objects, such as many rare books and letters written by Edgar Allan Poe, but also mummified mermaids, Sasquatch hair, and an unhatched sea serpent egg. Many of the objects are haunted. They provide a way of seeing or contacting or talking with ghosts, or they hold a departed spirit itself. For example, the portrait of Eugenia Meisner not only watches people as they cross a room, it speaks when they turn their backs. The Earhart goggles are aviator goggles that Amelia Earhart left behind before her final flight (from which she never returned). If you look through the goggles when a ghost is present, you will see the ghost. The Peggy Luna Shure is an old-fashioned microphone that electrocuted a singer named Peggy Luna, who was supposed to become a star. If you talk or sing into the microphone, her ghost will talk or sing back.

In this report, I have organized the objects in Mr. Pryce's library as Weird (mermaid mummy), Haunted (the portrait of Eugenia Meisner), and Tools, which are subcategorized as either Seeing (the Earhart goggles) or Interacting (the Peggy Luna Shure).

Thirty pages later, Dorry had barely *begun* to express everything important about Mr. Pryce's greatest hits in each category. And these were only the objects that were mentioned in articles: Lizzie Borden's pince-nez (seeing). A pot of blue ink that put a writer into a trance so they could talk with spirits (interacting). A glove with a finger bone sewn into the pinkie (weird). His collection even included a whole haunted house. It was somewhere in Brookline, the home of a family of real estate speculators named Tillerman. According to ghostsof-newengland.com, Matilda was the last living Tillerman, a "wealthy spinster who sealed herself up inside her mansion to die, taking the whereabouts of her vast fortune to her grave." But Mr. Pryce called her an artist. The exact quote, in an article from the Brookline Historical Society's newsletter, was "I have obtained the last masterpiece of the artist Matilda Tillerman." Which Dorry remembered because it was so sad and cool to call a haunted house a work of art.

But the Earhart goggles were her favorite. They were so *neat*-looking, shiny silver frames, lenses big and bug green. She'd feel tough wearing them, brave as an ace pilot. She doubted they had anything to do with Amelia Earhart. She wasn't a dork; she knew a bedtime story when she heard it. And she knew that, scientifically speaking, ghost-seeing goggles weren't part of the standard ghost-hunting tech; they couldn't detect electromagnetic fields or changes in temperature. But they clearly had *some* value. Mr. Pryce had paid a lot of money for them, and he featured them in his collection. What if they couldn't be explained but could be, like . . . experienced? Wasn't it good science to at least *try* them? For herself?

What if they were possible?

She flipped the report closed.

Her dad was zipping up his jacket in the living room. It was the only room that wasn't either of their bedrooms, the kitchen, or the bathroom. The smallness of her space, compared to their old house in Haverhill – which had had a den *and* a living room, plus a dining room and a basement, and an office where her mother kept all her art supplies – still surprised her sometimes. "Hey," he said, "Dor. I have to go to work for a bit." He rubbed the side of his nose with his knuckle – *his* tell. He probably didn't have any actual work to do. He just didn't want to be in the apartment with her.

"On Sunday?" she asked.

He nodded. "You know how it goes. Science cares not for weekends."

"Okay," she said, and thought, *Liar*. "Go make science."

He opened the door. Muted music, familiar, filled the air from next door. Dorry turned her ear toward it, thudding beats, a man's low voice (*—should have hidden it, shouldn't you—*). What song was that? She should know. Tuesday must have told her.

Her dad turned back.

"Dor," he said, "I don't want you to get involved. I mean it."

Her cheeks burned. She looked at the floor. Her fingers got all sweaty on the report cover again, sweaty and slippery.

"Or get your hopes up."

She bit the inside of her cheek.

"I don't want you to go over there," he said, "for any reason other than homework."

There it was. The worst, stupidest, dumbest, meanest part of their fight. Dorry looked up – still all fiery and hurt – and her dad laughed at her. A little dry laugh that wasn't happy, sure, but he *laughed*.

"And we both know you're going over there as soon as I leave," he said. "I just wanted you to know that I know."

He shut the door.

Dorry made a fist with the hand that wasn't sweating on the report. Dammit. *Dammit.* Now she felt *worse.* Of course she was planning to go over. Of course she could see Tuesday whenever she wanted to – they were neighbors – but now she felt . . . like a little kid. A little kid, *so* predictable, sneaking something she'd been forbidden, like Tuesday was a cookie. A stupid kid who thought she was pretty smart but really wasn't. And now, if she wanted to prove her dad wrong, she'd have to stay. She'd have to spite herself to spite him. When had her dad gotten so good at messing with her head?

"Terrorist," she called after him, not loud but not quiet either, hoping, kind of, that he'd heard.

◆

Tuesday heard the Boneses' door shut. Footsteps plodded down the hall. Heavy steps. That would be Dr. Bones, not Dorry. She looked over at her stereo. She was playing Depeche Mode loud enough to try any neighbor's patience, and she was already on Dr. Bones's shit list.

Not that she blamed him.

She stretched her long legs out straight across her couch. It was a love seat, really, plush but unfussy, upholstered in dark red velvet. She spread her toes. Plucked at the fabric.

Gunnar was dozing in a pool of sun on the back of the sofa, a black and white loaf of cat, his head turned toward the window's light.

His fur was warm when Tuesday rubbed it. "What the hell, Gun," she said. "What the hell was this *week*. A week ago this time, I was—" A week ago she'd spent Sunday – she didn't even remember. She did not remember what she was doing one week ago today. Laundry, probably. She might have read a book or watched television. Gunnar splayed his front knees and dropped his little furry chin flat to the sofa, moving from loaf pose to camel. A week ago she'd been bored, and now she was not.

Tuesday heard a knock on her door.

She'd been expecting it. Even so, she closed her eyes and pretended, just for a second, that she hadn't heard. Pretended that her favorite kid, her Next Dorry, wasn't about to press the point that the good Dr. Toby Bones had driven home.

He'd stopped by yesterday in the late afternoon. She'd only been back from the day's adventures for fifteen, twenty minutes. He must have been listening for the slam of her door. It was light out still. She, Dex, and Archie hadn't stayed long once they found the envelopes – about as long as it took to have a discussion about how many they could, in good conscience, take.

"The rules of the game state we can play alone or in teams," said Archie. He was kneeling in front of the filing cabinet, thumbing through the long stack. "Look, there are *tons* in here. We can take three. It's not unethical."

"Actually, it *is* unethical to take three. It's not *irrational* to take three." Tuesday snapped the wax seal off an envelope and reached inside. "You and I have an agreement; we're a team. If we took three we'd be rationally obeying the rules to the letter but not honoring the spirit of the game."

"Literally," Dex said, and high-fived her for the pun. "What would Vincent Pryce want?"

Archie sniffed. "As many players as possible," he said. "As many as—" He began counting under his breath.

"Fifty," he said. Then he looked up at the envelope in Tuesday's hands. "Fifty-one."

"Fifty-one." Her brain chewed on the number. "Fifty-one envelopes. Fifty-one teams or individual players. What does fifty-one mean?"

"Area Fifty-one," said Archie. "Secret government base."

"Seventeen times three." Dex crossed his arms. "The square root of two thousand six hundred and one. Six fewer than Heinz's varieties." He paused. "You know, I'm quite struck by how much faith Vincent Pryce had in people. Like, all these envelopes are here on the honor system." He looked at Tuesday. "He's sort of the anti-you."

"Vince," Archie started, and stopped, like he'd forgotten what he was going to say.

"We should take at least two, though," said Tuesday gingerly, because she knew Dex would be sensitive about exclusion. "So we can compare what's inside each envelope. Starting with—" She pulled out a banded stack of crisp twenty-dollar bills.

"There's your thirteen thou, Arch," she said. She dug back in, though the envelope felt empty. But it wasn't.

She held up a single playing card. A queen of diamonds.

The card didn't look tampered with. There were no obvious changes or hidden messages on either the face or the reverse. It was an ordinary, impassive, flower-gripping queen of diamonds.

"Since it's strategic for us to play on two teams," Dex said, eye-balling her knowingly, "pass me one of those." He held a hand down toward Archie.

Dex's envelope held an identical banded stack of bills. And a seven of hearts.

"Magnificent," said Dex.

They left the theater. Climbed back up to the lobby. The guard was gone again. Tuesday paid little attention to all of it. Her brain was focused on the card. On the money. On fifty-one players. What it might mean. What Pryce might be asking them to do.

She did not have a clue.

"We should have a plan. Let's divide and conquer," Dex said, once they were out on the sidewalk. "What are we looking for again?"

Tuesday looked down at her notes. "Seek well," she said, "before the clock equals twelve."

"I'll look for wells," said Dex.

Tuesday frowned at him. "I think Pryce was speaking metaphorically."

"Then I'll look for metaphorical wells," said Dex. "You look for clocks. Archie?" Archie turned toward him and raised both eyebrows. "Wells and clocks are spoken for," said Dex. "Look for something else."

"Fifty-one," said Tuesday. "What about the significance of fifty-one?"

Archie nodded. He was clearly working something out in his mind. What he was really going to look for, maybe, without telling her or Dex.

"I'll keep the money," she said, waving the envelope in front of his face, "until we figure out what to do with it."

Archie nodded again.

"And we should keep in touch," Dex said, "so no one can accuse anyone of going rogue." He pulled his phone out of his pocket and asked for Archie's number.

"What do you need my number for?" asked Archie.

"Um," said Dex, "so we can keep in touch. Paranoid much, Rich Boy?"

Archie gave Dex a number. Tuesday didn't have the contact information from Nathaniel Arches's record in the database at work memorized, but she knew exactly what she'd be cross-checking first thing Monday morning.

Dex dropped his phone back into his pocket. "Let's touch each other's bases," he said. Then he nodded crisply at them both and about-faced to walk home down Tremont.

Leaving her alone with Archie. Standing outside the Steinert building. Facing each other. For the first time since he ran away into the bowels of the MBTA.

"I'm heading to Somerville," she finally said, pointing across the Common. "Taking the Red Line from Park Street."

"I think it's best we steer clear of Park Street station," Archie said. He had a wide mouth. It took a long time to curl at the corners. "At least together."

Tuesday's bag buzzed. Archie jumped and reached for his butt. It was Dex, still walking – hell, she'd be able to see him if she turned around – texting to the group: TESTING TESTING TESTING. Then, in a separate text, just to Tuesday:

Girl you're welcome

How many times have you been out with this big bag of sex

And *I* had to get his digits for you?

Tuesday dropped her phone back in her bag, and they headed toward Park Street. They walked together, but they didn't talk. Which was odd, because even though she'd unloaded every barrel of words she had at him in the theater beneath the street, Tuesday had more to say. To ask. About Vincent Pryce. About Pryce's monogram, and what had happened to Archie's eyes, and his hands, and presumably his heart, when he saw it. Usually she didn't have a problem saying what was on her mind. But she sensed a magnetic field pushing at her from Archie, a sort of attraction-repulsion polar dead-lock. She was sure there was more he wanted to say too; he just didn't know where to start, or whether to let her go first

because he could feel *her* field. And so they made it all the way
to the T station without having said anything at all, until:

"So," said Archie. He looked at his feet. "You met my sister?
And my mother?"

Yes. God. A year ago this morning. Tuesday nodded. And
briefly explained that she and Dex had been at Lyle Pryce's
for brunch.

"You didn't tell them anything – about." He gestured –
toward her, the station entrance, all of Boston, the air. His
hands were large and his fingers long and graceful.

"Probably more than I should have, but nothing about you."
Nothing explicitly about you, at least. "There's a chance your
sister saw a picture."

"You were showing—" A line appeared between his
eyebrows. "Why do you have pictures of me?"

"Because I took them when we were down in the tunnel."
And Tuesday made finger guns and shot them at him.

"Shit," he said. He covered his mouth with his hand, tapped
his fingertips against his cheek, and didn't say anything else.

"Where are you heading?" It wasn't close to what she
wanted to ask, but it was at least a rational question.

"Home," he said. He tugged on his earlobe, nodded toward
the Park Street Church and parts beyond. "Over there," he
said. "Beacon Hill."

Tuesday's mental file riffled.

Home wasn't Beacon Hill.

She didn't call him on it. She told him to have a good rest
of his weekend, that they'd talk soon. Then she descended
underground to the Red Line train to Alewife, shot across the
Charles River, got off at Harvard Square for the longer walk
home, all the while wondering: Why would he say he lived on
the Hill when all her research indicated that he lived at the
Mandarin Hotel, in his family's condo? Was he trying to avoid
his family? Was he trying to snow her, worried that she'd blown

her own cover, wrecked her anonymity? (Not that showing up in the *Metro* hadn't done that already.) Or was he still lying – and if so, why? What was he hiding?

A bolthole?

An accomplice?

These were the things she was still stewing over late Saturday afternoon when Dr. Toby Bones knocked on her door.

Tuesday liked Dorry's dad. A lot. She wasn't sure what he did, but he did it in a lab or a biotech company near MIT. He wasn't very tall – Tuesday dwarfed him, and Dorry would be taller than him too, soon – and he was nerdy and bald, but he embraced his nature with dark-framed glasses and crisp collared shirts, pressed khakis and soft brown shoes. He had a nicely shaped head and dark eyes, and if he had a bit of a gut, he didn't carry it with shame. He talked fast. Sometimes she saw a glimpse of Dorry in him, like when he looked away when he was describing something complicated, as if he were working it out as he spoke, and to make eye contact while he did so would overload his CPU. From stories Dorry had told about him, both from before and after Dorry's mom died, Tuesday had a fuller picture of the man: He was sad. He was brilliant. Talking – especially about how he felt, but words in general – wasn't his strongest suit. But he was trying to do what he thought was right for his daughter. Even Dorry could admit that, even if they didn't have the same idea about what that meant.

As soon as Tuesday saw his face on Saturday, she realized he was trying to do what was right for everyone. She saw it in the lines by his eyes, the draw of his mouth. *Concern.* Not just for his daughter – though principally for Dorry, of course – but also for her. He sat next to her – very close, because the love seat offered no other kind of seating – and expressed genuine concern for her, for Tuesday, getting involved in what was obviously a publicity stunt, and an irresponsible, potentially dangerous one at that. And now she had a *criminal record*? (Not quite, she told him.) What about her job? What about her *future*? (Tuesday raised a brow. Toby might have a decade on her, sure, but she wasn't his kid or his sister or his girlfriend or his wife or anyone, really, who might give him the benefit of the doubt when he condescended to her.) Consider what you're doing, he said. Really think about it. Were all the risks she was taking – well, risks worth taking?

He'd told his daughter that he didn't want her involved in any way, and he didn't want Dorry to come over for any reason other than tutoring. She'll still try, he said, but please dissuade her.

"I understand," Tuesday told him, because she did. "I promise to be the grown-up."

So now, a day later, after finally opening the door to Dorry's knocking, she knew she couldn't step aside for her to enter the apartment.

"Hey Next," she said. "I talked to your dad."

Dorry made a fist. With one hand, but it might as well have been her whole body.

"Sorry," said Dorry.

"You have nothing to be sorry for," said Tuesday. "He's right."

"Maybe," said Dorry.

"What've you got there?" Tuesday asked.

Dorry hesitated. Then: "Here," she said, and whipped a plastic folder at Tuesday from behind her back. "It's incredible. The collection is *incredible*. We have to – you have to—"

Tuesday took the report. Read the cover. Flipped it open. This kid. This *kid*. "You're a girl after my own heart," she said, smiling. "Nice job, Dor. I'd say this more than qualifies you for silent partnership."

"There's, um – I mean. Yay! For partnership." Dorry hugged herself. "I mean I'm still interested in a cut, money-wise. But

there's also. There's a thing. It's on page – let me show you—"
Dorry flipped through the pages upside down. "If you guys
win, and Archie's okay with it, and you are, I'd really like – um.
This." And she pressed a fingertip to a picture of a pair of
green-lensed aviator goggles.

"Funky," said Tuesday. "What do they do?"

Dorry licked her lips.

"See ghosts," she said.

Tuesday chilled.

This kid.

Dorothea Bones, whose mother had died. Dorry didn't talk
much about her mother, but when she did, she looked dazed
and far away, overwhelmed with the sheer weight of the loss.
The absurdity of it. Dorry's brain could not compute it, would
not accept there was nothing to do with this feeling but endure
it. So she fought for answers, for certainties, however small,
that she might be able to grasp. The overwhelming grief of
missing someone without hope that they will ever return –
Tuesday knew that feeling. And she knew how much pain lay
in trying to make sense out of senselessness. In discovering,
no matter how much you've already lost, there was still more
to lose.

Dorry was so young. And so full, of hope and of need.

Her father was right.

"Dorry," Tuesday said, "you know, you can't really see—"

"Oh!" Dorry let out a raw laugh. "I *know*. I mean, I'm not
a—" She looked away from Tuesday. To the side. To the floor.

"I know," said Tuesday.

She tried not to look at Dorry's face when she closed the
door.

◆

No good ever came from ghosts. From seeing or talking to
them. Tuesday knew.

The disappearance of Abby Hobbes, the July they were both sixteen, hit her like a car or a fastball or a bullet. It yawned, opened the ground beneath her feet. The police came and talked to her, and to her parents and Ollie too. Nobody had a clue what had happened. Where she'd gone, or why, or with whom. That she'd slipped into the sea made the most sense – but where was her body? Why hadn't it washed up anywhere? Even if you drowned, you didn't disappear.

Tuesday had made it through Fred's fake funeral by stealing Abby's Ouija board. She'd made it through the following week, the week before the first day of junior year, by making color-coded binder and notebook combinations for every class in her schedule and by sleeping twelve hours a day. She'd made it through the first month of school by force of habit, goosed by the anxious energy of everyone else, the kids in her classes, her teachers, the principal, even, worrying they might have to talk to her about it, worrying that she would force the conversation by painting a pentagram in the front lobby in gasoline and setting it on fire, because didn't she and Abby do, like, spells together? What did one witch do when the other half of her coven vanished without a trace?

Tuesday didn't know what to do. At all. Every day she woke up (again), and every day she went to school (again), and every day she turned in homework (again), and every day she took notes (again), and every day she went to her locker (again), and every day Abby wasn't there (again and again and again), and it never, ever made sense. Tuesday hadn't expected to have a best friend. "Best friends" occupied the same imaginary territory as fairies or leprechauns, mythical things kids (girls especially) were told they should be looking for. She certainly didn't *need* one – between Ollie and her parents and the other honors arty kids at school (the ones who weren't freaked out by all her black clothes), she wasn't lonely, she had people to talk to, to sit with at lunch. But Abby and her dad Fred moved next door when Tuesday was twelve, and from the very beginning it was just *there*.

Attachment. Abby was the first person Tuesday met and liked right away – the day she moved in, carrying a huge stuffed black cat into the house, draped over her shoulders like a stole. "Hi!" Abby called, waving from her porch to Tuesday, sitting on her own. "This is Beelzebub. Lame excuse for a real cat, but I'm allergic. My whole face turns into a balloon. It's wicked." Abby was the first person who didn't share her DNA that Tuesday trusted. Maybe it happened because neither of them needed it, really; Abby might've been down a parent, but she was more independent than Tuesday. Or maybe it happened because neither of them was looking for it. It could have happened for no particular reason at all, other than the happy accident that two twelve-year-old neighbor girls living in Salem, Massachusetts, should be weird, should be smart, should share more than a passing interest in witches, monsters, ghosts, movies, mysteries, murder, and magic.

They'd only been best friends for four years. It was just so goddamn unfair.

And it didn't make sense. It didn't make any sense *at all*. There were Those who said Abby'd gotten mixed up with witchcraft, Satanists, cultists – it was Salem, after all – and had been human-sacrificed. There were Those who said she'd show up eventually, kids like that always did. Overwhelmingly, there were Those who said Abby killed herself. It looked like a suicide, like a goth teenager flinging herself into the sea, and of course it could only be what it looked like. But it wasn't, because Abby wasn't really her ripped tights and black lipstick, because ripped tights and black lipstick weren't anything but clothes and makeup. She was strange, she was macabre, she talked about being dead, being a ghost, sure, but excitedly, nerdily, the same way she talked about her witch ancestor and Sam Raimi. Even when she talked about her dead mom, and wanting to call her on the Ouija board, it wasn't like—

Just because you wanted to talk to dead people didn't mean you wanted to be dead yourself.

They'd watched a video in health class, and Abby didn't do any of the things the suicidal kid did. She didn't cancel plans. She didn't fade. She didn't give away her things. She shook Tuesday down to get her things *back* – a pair of purple Doc Martens with glitter soles, her copy of *Something Under the Bed Is Drooling*. Abby'd already bought all the fabric for her Halloween costume that year, yards of black and purple satin. She was going as the Grand High Witch from *The Witches*, had shown Tuesday her sketches: a cape with a high neck, elbow-length gloves, and a black cocktail dress she would never sew.

All September, Tuesday sleepwalked through her days, itching to crawl into bed and lose herself to unconsciousness. But then as soon as it was time to sleep, she couldn't. Her brain turned. Over and over and over, it turned on what had become the central mystery of her sixteen years: What had *happened* at the light station? And where was Abby now?

It wasn't until October that Tuesday thought about Abby's Ouija board again. She'd taken it after the memorial out of nerves and instinct, out of a desire to keep some part of Abby safe, or at least to herself. But now the whole experience – the police, the funeral, the memorial – was wrapped up in a black cloud, thick and still, that only the occasional detail pierced: an unfinished bowl of ice cream. *I guess I'll see you tomorrow*. A board game, stolen.

Only it was more than a board game. It was a telephone for talking to dead people.

Tuesday hadn't believed in it like that, as a literal link to the other side. Ouija boards were like Tarot cards: they didn't tell you anything your subconscious didn't already know. But the night she thought of it – it was well past midnight, she had a history quiz the next day, and the more she insisted to herself to go to sleep go to sleep go to sleep, the more awake she stayed, until the thought slipped in like a dead leaf beneath a door (*Ouija board, use it, use it*), and she was suddenly, completely, perfectly awake. That night, the night she remembered she had the board, she was suffering from such a ferocious desire to believe it may as well have been true belief itself.

She dunked her head over the side of her bed. The Ouija board was underneath. This whole time she'd been sleeping on it. She crossed her legs. Unfolded the board over her knees. All those paper faces that Abby cut out – Mulder and Scully and Keanu and Winona and Wednesday – Tuesday's first thought was *If this works, you'll know. For sure. If this works, you'll know she's dead.* She swallowed. Set the planchette on the board and her fingertips on the planchette. Her hands were shaking.

She sat there quaking until after one-thirty (screw her history quiz, just screw it), but the planchette never moved. She was relieved at first, and then disappointed, because – she felt it too. She felt it as deeply, as instinctively as Fred that Abby wasn't just missing. Abby was dead. So she tried again the next night. The planchette didn't move. She tried the next, and the next, and the planchette didn't move, until the eighth night, at thirteen minutes after midnight, when it finally swooped in a figure eight, then spelled S-U-P-T-U-E-S.

Tuesday burst into tears. **'Sup, Tues.** And she could hear her, she could *hear* Abby in her head, clear over the sound of her own furious, ugly crying. It didn't make sense. It wasn't rational. But it was real. It was Abby Hobbes, saying **'Sup, Tues.**

Once the connection was made, Abby didn't shut up. Tuesday heard her even when she wasn't using the board. In math class (**thank God I'm already dead, pre-calc would have killed me**). At the video store (**I can't believe I never** made you watch *Suspiria* while I was alive). At home, over dinner (your brother is like REALLY into action figures, isn't he). And every time Tuesday tried to ask – What *happened* to you? – she clammed up. Later, she'd say. Not now.

Three weeks after she started talking to the ghost of Abby Hobbes, Tuesday took a good long look at herself in the bathroom mirror. She didn't look like a teenager having a psychotic break. She didn't look like she was delusional. She looked better than she had since July: she was pale (because she always was), but she'd lost the translucence that Ollie called her jellyfish skin. The shadows under her eyes were purple instead of black. "You're getting better," her mother said, cradling Tuesday's head in her palms, locking her eye to eye. "I think a few spins of *Bella Donna* on the old turntable and you'll be yourself again."

She let her mom put on Stevie Nicks. They danced around and it did feel good, but Sally Mooney was wrong. Tuesday would never be herself again. She could only be a new self, a new Tuesday, a Tuesday who believed in best friends but whose best friend was dead.

A Tuesday who talked to her ghost.

On a Wednesday in November, while Tuesday was waiting for Ollie to drive them both to school, kicking pyramids of built-up slush from the undercarriage of his car, Abby told her, I don't remember.

The slush plopped to the ground.

"What?" Tuesday said out loud.

I don't remember.

"You mean," started Tuesday, and Abby let it all go in a rush.

I don't remember. I don't remember anything about the night I died. I thought it would come back but it's all – blank. It's my death, my own death, but I can't remember it and I need your help. I need your help.

"Why?" Tuesday's breath was a cloud.

I need your help to find out who killed me.

That hit, too. Maybe harder than Abby's death, because she'd become so tender in the intervening months. She felt like an idiot for not seeing it sooner. She had taken everything she had seen and heard from the news, from the police, from her parents, and from everyone at school, and balled it up into a wad of meaningless noise. But there *was* an answer. *Something* had happened that night at the light station out on Derby Wharf, something that took her best friend out of the world.

And Tuesday could find out what that something was.

Or *who* that someone was.

The only time she felt like crying about it was that first day, on the ride to school with Ollie – crying, out of relief, out of grief, out of rage. If he noticed – which he probably did; he was as sensitive as she was – he didn't say anything. By the time he threw the car into Park in the student lot, Tuesday was still. She was full and clear with purpose. He was the first person she told.

"Abby was murdered," she said, "and I'm going to find out who did it."

To his credit, Ollie still didn't say anything.

Abby's ghost was zero help. She didn't remember anything, even when Tuesday pulled out her Ouija and lit all of Abby's black candles and talked to her for hours – walking her through the day she disappeared (a normal summer day until their stupid argument; they got breakfast at Red's, read the obits, Tuesday came over that night). Did she remember meeting any freaks that day? (**Define "freak,"** said Abby, and Tuesday said, "That is not helpful.") Abby couldn't say who killed her or why, but she said a whole hell of a lot else: **Is Mr. Mack ever going to retire? Ancient creeper is like ninety percent dust. Wear the floor-length skirt with the heeled lace-up boots, yeah? What sorcery is this stew – man, your dad can cook. Gus Rousseau has got to be the biggest**

**skeeze to ever slime his way around Salem. And isn't he
older than your brother, didn't he graduate? Why the
hell is he haunting his old high school?**

"You should talk," said Tuesday, and Abby said, **Har har
har. Also he is not even remotely cute.**

"Yes, he is."

No he is not. Grossville, Tuesday, grossville.

The fact that Abby couldn't provide additional information,
Tuesday had to concede, was a fairly clear sign that she wasn't
communing with the dead so much as exhibiting what a book
on abnormal psychology she found in the Salem library called
"classic signs of dissociative identity disorder." Abby, not
unlike Tarot cards, couldn't tell her anything she didn't already
know, because "Abby" wasn't anything more than a schism in
Tuesday's psyche. But she didn't want to interrogate herself
too closely. She wanted, she needed, to trust the sound of her
best friend's voice. She didn't think she could bear it if Abby
went away again. And regardless of what Tuesday needed to
believe to get through the day, that her best friend had been
murdered – that her life had been taken against her will – made
sense. A whole lot more sense than anything else.

"What should I do, Abby?" she asked the Ouija board, her
fingertips on the planchette. It had been swooping in a figure
eight, not landing on anything in particular, fluttering for the
fun of it. It was late November now, almost Thanksgiving.
Tuesday used the board every night before she went to sleep.
Abby talked to her all day long, board or no, but the movement
of the planchette was a comfort, the glide of its felt feet over
the board's papered surface familiar and soothing. "If you
don't have any suggestions about how to start finding your
killer, do you have any other advice?"

The planchette dove into another eight.

Don't you know it's dangerous to use the board alone?
said Abby.

"I don't think *Witchboard* is an accurate representation of proper Ouija usage," Tuesday said. She snickered, then felt a pang, because even though Abby was around, it wasn't the same as actually having her here. Watching awful eighties horror movies starring Tawny Kitaen with a voice inside your own head wasn't the same as watching them with your best friend – your best friend who muttered *Bitch stole my look* every time Tawny's increasingly wild mountain of red hair appeared onscreen. Abby was a flame redhead. "You know," she'd said when she still had a living body, "once upon a time this hair alone would've gotten me burned at the stake."

Tuesday addressed the board. "Are you saying you're going to possess me?" she asked.

The planchette slid up and sat over NO.

"What are you saying, then? Anything?" She paused. "What should I do, Abby?"

The planchette wove loops through the letters and spelled out F-I-N-C-H.

"Scout?" asked Tuesday. "Atticus?"

Detective, said Abby. **Detective Finch, moron.**

Tuesday hadn't known that a detective looked into Abby's disappearance. She certainly hadn't known that detective's name. She lifted her fingertips from the planchette. The hairs prickled on the backs of her hands, her wrists, then the prickle ran up her arms and across her shoulders and straight up the back of her neck. "Abby," she said. *"Holy—"* And Abby said, **Mary Mother of God.**

A week later, she was explaining to her parents it was on a tip from Abby Hobbes (no, really – *that* Abby Hobbes) that she had broken into the Salem police station – which had gone about as well as one might expect, and certainly worse than Tuesday had hoped. But that was only the beginning of the bad. The Much Worse was still to come.

All because Tuesday wanted to talk to a dead person.

And now, so did Dorry Bones.

Dorry was a girl after her own heart: a smart, strange, searching girl. If Tuesday could protect her from a Much Worse of her own, she would, even if it meant breaking the heart that they shared. A broken heart hurt like hell, but it kept beating.

A lost mind was something else entirely.

8

THIS MEANS SOMETHING

It wasn't until the following Tuesday – Tuesday the day, not Tuesday the person – that the underground theater got that much closer to being officially, publicly discovered. Tuesday the person was, that Tuesday morning, sitting in her cube at work, procrastinating. She had a queue of research requests, but none of them pressing or particularly interesting; if you've researched one midcareer lawyer in Cambridge, you've researched them all. Far more urgent was the desire to apply her imagination, as instructed, to Pryce's game. To *seek well before the clock* – turns? strikes? Was there some nuance she was missing? – *equals twelve*. She'd been trawling the internet for clocks in and around the city of Boston. Clock towers at universities. Public clocks in town squares. Expensive antique clocks up for auction at Skinner's. Historically important clocks on display at the Museum of Fine Arts. "Clock" was the only noun in the code preceded by a definite article, so, logically, Pryce had a specific clock in mind: *the* clock. So far she'd learned that Boston was full of clocks, of all sizes and functions, but none of them had any obvious link to Pryce or to Poe.

She blew a puff of air into her bangs. She thought it would be simpler to track down a clock rather than address the larger, vaguer, more all-encompassing part of the objective. What *did* it mean to "seek well"? To play the game strategically, with clarity of purpose? Or was Pryce pointing his players toward a broader understanding of what it meant to do anything well, or to *be* well, or to—

She looked over at her cooling second cup of coffee. Too early. It was too early, and she was too undercaffeinated, for philosophy.

A chat window popped up in the lower right corner of her computer screen. Someone else procrastinating at work, half a mile and fourteen floors away.

DexHoward: what does it even mean, really
"Seek well"
I think I'm coming around to your metaphorical wells

Tuesday exhaled again. Dex, ever since the decoder room, had been reading her mind. Or she'd been reading his.

Or they were both getting obsessed.

TuesdayMooney: The search for wells
Not going so well?
DexHoward: ha ha ha
TuesdayMooney: My gut really says he's using "well" as an adverb and not a noun
And it's up to us
(The players/seekers)
To figure out what it means to seek well
DexHoward: Figures
It would have been so nice if we were looking for a literal hole in the ground
But of course we're looking for "enlightenment"
And I have to work for my enlightenment
Why can't it like
Come in the mail

Tuesday sat back in her chair, tucked one foot under the opposite knee, and the warm growl of Archie's voice bubbled up from somewhere in the back of her brain. He wasn't saying anything in particular. He didn't have to. He was always there lately, like a daydream she couldn't (and didn't want to) stop having, or a riddle she couldn't (but wanted to) solve. The number he'd given Dex didn't match any of his known contacts in the fundraising database. She looked over at her cube wall. She'd pushpinned a copy of Pryce's obituary into the fabric, between an old Christmas photo of Ollie, her sister-in-law Vivian, and little Olive, and a single-serve pouch of Spam that had magically appeared in her desk drawer one day, because Mo was both a great manager and an obscure prankster.

Her desk phone rang.

She looked at the display: an outside line. She'd been screening her calls, at work and on her cell – the only people who called her now, it seemed, were her parents and reporters who'd managed to track down her number. She hadn't given any interviews, hadn't made any statements. There was nothing to say. The game was news, not her. And even then it wasn't really *news* news. It wasn't Afghanistan or the Arab Spring or Occupy Wall Street. Ms. Heck, her tenth-grade English and journalism teacher, would have called it meat for the monkeys, a gawker piece. The interesting but inessential human interest story of how one rich lunatic lived, died, and spent his money.

She'd been avoiding Facebook too. She'd received dozens of new friend (ha) requests and unsolicited messages, many of them genuinely bizarre, some of them threatening. She'd deleted her Twitter account, which had gotten terrifying, terrifyingly fast. It was liberating, frankly, to disappear from social media so deliberately. She had no interest in fanning flames or being famous, at least not for this. She just wanted to figure it out.

And, sure, get bought out by Archie. Five million dollars wasn't nothing. Five million dollars meant – it meant she could change her life, if she wanted. And Dorry could change hers. It meant she wouldn't have to be or do anything she didn't want. It meant she could wipe out her student debt, for starters. Beyond that, it meant – she didn't even know yet. It meant she would have time to figure out what she'd like to do for the rest of her life. Or for the next few years, at least, before she got bored again. And she would never have to swing into her cube, or log on to her computer, or open her email, or research another midcareer lawyer in Cambridge ever again.

God, it was an appealing thought.

Her phone kept ringing.

"You going to answer that?" Her cube neighbor's voice floated across the aisle.

"My fan club is kind of annoying," Tuesday said, and her coworker chuckled, and Tuesday decided what the hell and picked up the handset.

Before she could say anything, a terse woman's voice took control. "Hello," the voice said. "I'm calling for Tuesday Mooney. Is this Miss Mooney?"

"It is," Tuesday said, though "Miss" always made her itch.

"Nathaniel Arches would like to meet you for lunch. He's free at twelve noon. Are you available?"

"Uh." Tuesday's brain blipped. "Yes?"

Why hadn't he texted?

"Excellent. We'll have the car to your location by eleven forty-five. That's One Bowdoin Square, correct?"

"Yes?" she said again.

"Do you have any food allergies?"

Tuesday's mouth opened but the words weren't there. She looked at the photo of her brother and Viv and Olive, at the obituary, at the Spam.

"No?" she finally said.

"Excellent," the woman repeated. "Have a pleasant day."
And she hung up.

Tuesday lowered the handset. Pressed it against her
shoulder. *What.*

The chat window at the bottom of her monitor flashed.

DexHoward: WHOA
WHOA WHOA WHOA
Someone else found a raven
WE'RE NOT ALONE
I REPEAT
WE
ARE
NOT
ALONE

Tuesday felt a whoosh of dizziness as she clicked on the link
Dex sent next, which meant she was close to passing out. It
also meant she was a lot more personally invested in this
competition than she had previously admitted to herself.
Dammit, she wanted this. She wanted this for herself, and
she wanted it *with* Dex and Dorry and Archie. And nothing
made her want a thing more than the threat of it being taken
away.

It was a public Facebook group page. Under a photograph
of a hissing black cat was a header in capitals: WE R THE
BLACK CATS. *We're playing Vincent Pryce's game*, the group's
description read, *and you should too. IF YOU SEE
SOMETHING, POST SOMETHING.*

The group had sixty-six members. They all considered
themselves Black Cats, but within that there were subgroups,
clusters of treasure-hunting gangs like pub trivia teams, repre-
senting their corners of greater Boston. The Smoots had MIT;
the Gay Mafia covered Eastie; the Highlanders, Somerville;

the Green Monsters and Challahback Girls, Fenway and Brookline. Adama Is a Cylon – the name of a trivia team she and Dex had gone up against more than once, which couldn't be a coincidence – had parts of Cambridge. The more she dug, the more motivating and heartening they seemed, the gangs of Boston, all working together. She could hear Dex: *See, Tuesday? Not all humans in groups are a bad thing.*

She supposed groups of collaborative nerds were an exception.

The earliest posts (the group hadn't even existed a week) were of—

Tuesday.

Pictures of her, and of the raven and the quote from *Lear*, snapped and circulated from Twitter. Her, coming out of Park Street station with a cop on each side. Her first instinct was not to read the comments – the first rule of retaining whatever faith you had left in humanity was *Never, ever read the comments* – but she couldn't help it.

She read the comments.

Tim Burton's Lady Indiana Jones and the T Station of Doom #hero #fuckshitup

Who is this woman???

And then – these were her people, all right: resourceful, internet-literate geeks – a link to her professional profile on LinkedIn. She inhaled. And, not for the first time, was intensely grateful no one who didn't already work for the hospital knew the location of her little satellite office.

Subsequent posts included links to articles about Pryce, some conspiracy boondoggles and a few smartass memes, and then, after a few days, someone posting as Lisa Pinto said: HEY GUYS what about the Shakespeare? Like that has to be part of the solution right? And then the most recent post, the one Dex had sent her.

It came from a Highlander named Ned Kennedy, who had

ventured beyond his home turf of Somerville into downtown Boston. It was a picture of a brick wall with another spray-painted raven, tilted so that its beak and leg pointed down at the ground, as if it were saying *Peck here*. Above it, instead of a line from *Lear* in chalk—

"The code," Tuesday breathed.

The symbols that had been on the scroll, the instructions to Life After Death that had given her her head start, were sketched in white chalk, one symbol per brick. And shared on Facebook for all the Black Cats and their friends to see. The photo was captioned:

Heeeeey look what I found. GUESS WHERE I AM!!!!! Ok ok I'll tell you: alley off Boylston, between burrito place and piano store. Poe born here. I have no idea what the hell any of this means but it seems important. K now Imma get a burrito.

Dex chatted her again.

DexHoward: Whelp
There goes our lead
Also how did we not see those??

Tuesday sat forward in her chair.

TuesdayMooney: It rained
DexHoward: what does that have to do with anything
TuesdayMooney: It rained on Sunday
And on Friday too
Meaning it keeps washing away the code
Meaning it comes and goes
Until someone living re-chalks it
DexHoward: well
. . . hell
TuesdayMooney: but now that it's on the internet it's not going anywhere

She chewed her thumbnail.

> **TuesdayMooney:** Archie just had his assistant make a lunch date with me
> **DexHoward:** His assistant?
> **TuesdayMooney:** He is important, Dex
> **DexHoward:** Tell me something I DON'T know

Tuesday tried to smile. It helped ease the uncertainty rippling through her stomach.

> **TuesdayMooney:** I just wanted someone to know
> It feels . . . off
> **DexHoward:** Mooney-sense tingling?
> I'll release the hounds if I don't hear from you
> **TuesdayMooney:** Thanks Dex
> And yes, I'm tingling like crazy
> . . . not like that
> **DexHoward:** Sure
> Right
> Uh huh

◆

The sky was perfect October blue when she left the office, but Tuesday didn't look up. She looked down at her phone instead, at the text she'd tapped to Archie but hadn't sent.

> Um you had your ASSISTANT call me?

It seemed stupid to text him when she was going to see him any minute.

And yet.

She put her phone away in her bag, message unsent.

She didn't understand him or what he was doing, but she

wanted to. She wanted to fit all his pieces together, mesh the data she'd found online with the information she'd collected in person. She was maddeningly close to creating a complete picture of a person, on the brink of understanding who the hell Nathaniel Allan Arches really was. And once she knew who the hell Nathaniel Allan Arches was, she suspected she'd be that much closer to knowing who the hell Vincent Pryce was – and knowing Pryce, she thought, would be the key to his own game. Who Pryce was, what and whom he loved, and why he did what he did with everything he had would tell Tuesday how to win. And with the code exposed, it was only a matter of time before more players found the underground theater. And decoded the rules for Life After Death. And picked up their money and their cards. She could feel the clock, which she couldn't find anywhere, ticking faster.

Yes. She nodded to herself. That was it. That was where this jittery anticipation was coming from. She was loitering outside her office building, swinging her bag nervously at her side, teetering on the edge of discovery. While the whole city breathed down her neck.

A town car floated up to the curb like a gleaming black cloud. She didn't move toward it.

The driver's door opened and a trim man in a white shirt and thin black tie climbed out. He opened the rear door and gestured for her to approach.

Oh, so *this* is how you die, said Abby Hobbes.

Tuesday flashed cold.

Abby.

Back in her head for the second time in less than a week.

This is not how I die, she thought back at her. *This is how I live*.

Abby didn't respond. Tuesday walked toward the car, slid inside, and sat down, and when she looked up, Archie was watching her from the other end of the seat.

He was wearing a dark, chalk-stripe suit, a white shirt so crisp it seemed capable of slicing his neck, and no tie. The suit likely cost more than a year of her take-home pay. His hair had been slicked back with fistfuls of product. It made his face longer, sharper, his eyes smaller. He was drenched in a cologne that made her eyes water. So this was what he looked like, and smelled like, when he was himself.

"You're not what I expected," he said.

The car pulled into traffic. Tuesday's body rocked back against the seat.

She didn't know what to say to that.

Archie looked at her like he had never seen her before, and wasn't quite sure how to process her as a piece of visual information, how to connect her head and face and neck and chest and trunk and lap and legs and toes. When he looked into her eyes, he did something unfamiliar: he clenched his jaw. Two dimples appeared on either side of his face. How had she not noticed those before? Then he brushed a hand through the side of his hair. It wasn't slicked back, it was short; it was shorter than it was supposed to be because—

"Holy shit," said Tuesday. "You're not Archie."

He laughed an irritated sort of laugh and looked away from her, out the window at the passing city. His voice was deep but colorless. "That's what he's calling himself?"

"I don't – know—" Tuesday's mental files were frozen. They didn't riffle. They didn't flutter. This information was beyond them. "If you're not Nathaniel Arches, then who are you?"

"I *am* Nathaniel Arches," said the man sitting beside her. "That asshole is my little brother."

Tuesday sat.

And stared.

He patted her knee. "Don't worry," he said. "I'm still taking you to lunch."

◆

Afternoon hours in the office were, for Tuesday, the most challenging. Lunch made her full and sleepy. Lunch sucked away her motivation. After lunch, without even lunch to look forward to, the afternoon was long and dull and Tuesday's brain was at its natural snoozy nadir.

That day, after that lunch, Tuesday returned to the office something close to high.

Or drunk, maybe. It was a little hard to walk. It was a little hard to focus, and, yes, she'd had a bourbon, neat, with the bloody steak Nathaniel Arches had ordered for her, but it wasn't the booze or the red meat. It was the new information, all the radical recalibrations she had to sort and process and confirm. It was nuts. It made sense (even though it was nuts), and her professional pride was smarting, but she couldn't – it was possible, surely, but – why hadn't—

How had she overlooked Edgar Arches *Junior*?

"How do you find what you don't even know to look for?" Nathaniel had said – not about his brother, or at least not consciously, but it had struck Tuesday as absurdly on the nose. "*You* don't. You can't, because you don't know how. But I do. That's what makes me so good at my job. That's what *elevates* N. A. Arches, that's why it stands head and shoulders above the pack. That's what makes me *better*." His own relative yet absolute awesomeness was a theme Nathaniel returned to with some frequency. "It's like a goddamn sixth sense. I can see the future in some shitty nothing company. I can see a way forward that makes a profit. It's not something you learn; you just have to know." He took a sip of bourbon. "It's something you're born with."

This Nathaniel Arches was everything Tuesday's original research indicated he would be. The blurriness that had appeared around her first impression – the fuzz of Archie – resolved, and the callow, shallow, outrageously self-involved billionaire asshole snapped into focus. He was less cartoonish, observed in the flesh. He gave off a certain magnetism, possibly the kind of charm they talked about when they talked about everyday sociopaths. His face was like a too-perfect, vaguely plastic copy of his brother's. He didn't blink much. Tuesday suspected everything Nathaniel said and did was in the service of taking exactly what Nathaniel wanted from the world while giving the world back as little as possible.

He had taken her to a steakhouse in the financial district, unmarked by any sign. It wasn't the kind of place you went to be seen; Nathaniel, Sexiest Scenester that he was, knew those places, and had, she suspected, deliberately not taken Tuesday to any of them. The dark green walls and carpet swallowed sound. What light there was shone off the polish of dark red wood. It was redolent of old white men. Tuesday could have walked there from her office in under fifteen minutes, and she guessed Nathaniel worked in the gleaming glass building that towered above it, but that, she knew, was not the point. Not the point of this lunch date, and not the point of Nathaniel Allan Arches.

He smiled at her. She did not smile back.

"It's why I should have the company," he said, still smiling, perhaps even wider, at her discomfort. "As my father intended."

"You mean you're entitled," she said, "to Arches Consolidated."

"What other company is there?"

Many others. Again: not the point of Nathaniel Arches.

"You're probably wondering why I reached out," he said.

He squared his shoulders toward her. Laid both palms flat on the shiny surface of the table and then turned them up, as if to say: See? I'm an open book. I'm opening for you right now.

What a fucking prince I am.

"My sister," he said.

Tuesday had already assumed as much, but let him continue.

"She met you at Lyle Pryce's this past weekend. She saw

some – evidence, apparently. In your possession." He cleared his throat. "Eddie is our little brother. Like most little brothers, he has always been a gigantic pain in the ass."

"What did he do?" asked Tuesday.

Nathaniel didn't answer her directly.

"Even without my sister's – intelligence. So to speak." Nathaniel pulled the sides of his mouth back in a grimace. "I knew my brother was back. He's been harassing me for years. Stupid things. Taunting – postcards."

"Postcards." Tuesday frowned. "He harasses you with . . . postcards."

"Just because it's stupid," he said, "doesn't mean it isn't harassment. Quite recently, the harassment became more intense." He locked his eyes on hers. "He's acting like a child, but that doesn't mean he's innocent. Or harmless." He swallowed. "He's never been innocent or harmless, even when he *was* a child."

It was an exceptional performance. There was just enough truth, Tuesday's gut said, to convince a less suspicious person it was wholesale fact. But it wasn't.

She just couldn't tell which parts.

"What has he done?" she repeated.

Nathaniel frowned at her. "I'd rather not get into the gory details."

"You're going to have to give me more," Tuesday said, "if you want me to help. And you do want me to help. Don't you?"

Nathaniel pulled his arms back off the table. Sat up straight. He jerked his chin in the direction of an unseen waiter who immediately made himself visible with a fresh bourbon.

Her mental pen, which had been scribbling furiously over a fresh file, paused.

"Tell me where he is," Nathaniel said, "and I will give you five hundred thousand dollars."

"I don't know where he is," she said.

"I don't believe you."

"Believe me or not," said Tuesday, "it won't change the fact that I have no information to give you."

"Seven hundred and fifty thousand dollars."

"Why do you think you can buy what doesn't exist?"

"Because everything can be bought." Nathaniel took another sip. "Everything, and everyone. Even you. I know where you work and what you do. I know you know about me. About my family. I know you know about my brother, things that I don't have access to. I want to hire you. I want to pay for your services."

"You want me to sell him out," Tuesday said.

"For a fee." Nathaniel shrugged and smiled a toothy smile. "Let's not pretend you have a moral compass. Like I said, I know what you do for a living."

Tuesday laughed. It would have been impossible to continue without the release.

"Is this really the game you want to play?" she said. "I'm a particularly adept professional Googler. And yes, I gather publicly available data about persons without their knowledge, for the sake of *charity*. What do *you* do, in the world? Without anyone's knowledge?"

Nathaniel's lids lowered to slits. He raised his glass. Took a sip.

"One million," he said. "Cash. For my brother's whereabouts."

She looked down at her steak. Pink and wet and half eaten. She didn't have the stomach for it.

She looked up at Nathaniel.

Her mind skittered back to something he'd already said.

About the company. The only company. That should be his, as his father intended.

His father, Edgar.

Senior.

Her brain leapt.

"I'll think about it," she told him.

Which was not a lie. He tossed the last of his bourbon down his throat, and she thought about it. He passed her his card, said some curt words about not thinking too hard or too long, and she nodded. They stared at each other for a long beat. Nathaniel said, "So I guess we're done here," and stood, and left her, and she thought about it. She spared a brief thought to wonder if she was dine-and-dashing, rationalized that Nathaniel likely had a tab, and then Tuesday left too, and walked back to her office, thinking about it. Thinking about the only company, to Nathaniel, that mattered. Once owned by Edgar Arches. Currently overseen by Constance. Tuesday thought about Archie. Who had led her to think he was Nathaniel. Who had charmed and manipulated her into never questioning who he said he was.

Had he ever said he was Nathaniel? Or had *she*—

She'd had Nathaniel on the brain, because she'd researched him. And she saw only what she expected to see. But then why did Archie—

What was the point of lying to her?

She didn't know whom or what to trust. And when Tuesday didn't know that, she retreated to the only thing that had never let her down.

Back in her cube, she decided to start with the ultimate authority. The internal database only she, and not, say, an Arches – whether an Archie or a Nathaniel or an Emerson – had access to. The information was not online. The information was private.

The information could not be manipulated.

She opened the hospital's records. She had access; it was part of her job to confirm whether people had been patients. To confirm their addresses and birth dates. Their identities. It wasn't an invasion of privacy but a legitimate function of her position, using their personal information to do her job, and do her job only.

Who said finding Edgar Arches Junior wasn't her job too?

It was surprising how wrong it didn't feel to fire up the patient database. It was so old it still had a Unix interface, didn't respond to the mouse but only to key commands, like the first amber-screened computers she had ever used. She typed ARCHES, EDGAR into the search field. It felt *better* than not-wrong when the database spat back two records. For two ARCHES, EDGARs. One born thirty-five years after the other.

She opened the first record. Full name ARCHES, EDGAR ALLAN JR.

Found.

Found.

ARCHES, EDGAR ALLAN JR hadn't had an appointment at the hospital in over a decade. Not since he still saw his pediatrician (Dr. Anton Phillips – still practicing, a favorite, a legend, children regularly went to him through their college years). Edgar Junior's birthday was April 11. He was going to be thirty-two next spring. Emergency contacts listed – his parents. ARCHES, CONSTANCE ALLAN (relationship MOTHER, occupation HOME). And ARCHES, EDGAR (relationship FATHER, occupation ACE).

Tuesday stared at "ACE" for a long time.

It was an acronym. An acronym for Arches Consolidated Enterprises. She knew this. She had known this the whole time.

Vincent Pryce told her to use her imagination.

Vincent Pryce gave her the queen of diamonds.

She found an ace on her own.

9

LIBRARY VOICES

Dex passed under the vaulted mosaic arches of the Boston Public Library, checked his watch for the thirtieth time, reassured himself that if it was at a library, it wasn't strictly a date – but it wasn't *not* a date either, and it was perfectly okay to have become the kind of person who met guys for dates at the library; it didn't mean he was old or a dweeb or an old dweeb.

It was six o'clock on Wednesday. Tuesday had returned from her lunch with Archie the day before in a state of cagey high alert. Dex could tell something had happened, but Tuesday wouldn't tell him anything. At least she respected him enough to admit something *had* happened. She was looking into it; she'd let him know what she knew when she knew more. And in the meantime, she'd suggested this mission: get in touch with Bert Hatmaker, return Lyle's insulated beverage tumblers, squeeze every last drop of information out of him that he could.

Why not just ask Lyle? he'd chatted. Because duh, she said, you'll have way more fun squeezing Bert.

This was true. He'd emailed Lyle to ask for Bert's contact information, to follow up on something they'd talked about over the weekend. Simple interpersonal skullduggery, the kind he excelled at, and she'd responded within an hour. He then wrote his opening salvo to Bert (rabbithat80@gmail, how adorable) without breaking a sweat. But as soon as he sent it, his pulse accelerated by a good ten beats per minute. Every minute, every *second* he spent waiting for Bert to respond, he felt that he was on a precipice in a wild gale – wearing a fabulous gown, vintage Valentino, midnight blue – clinging to an outcropping of shaky rock over a vast wasteland populated by the ghosts of his exes, and if he didn't manage very quickly to unlock the secrets of human flight, he was going to plummet to an intensely glamorous death. Then Bert wrote back. And Dex had to fight the urge to squeal.

This behavior was unusual and troubling.

The library was Bert's suggestion. He had an errand to run downtown after school, and they could grab a cup of coffee at the library café. *A coffee date*, Dex had thought. *How freshman year!* He had gone on his first real date his freshman year of college, in the late nineties, to the Starbucks at the student union. At four in the afternoon. He and Theo, a boy from his Introduction to Musical Theater class, had never discussed it in those terms, before or after. They had both been sort of walking toward the union after class, and talking about how they liked coffee, and Dex could tell – hoped – guessed – that Theo was also gay, and liked him like that, a hope that was confirmed by four thirty-five that same day, back in Theo's dorm room. For a date that had started out ambiguous and furtive, it had suddenly become very *un*ambiguous and terrifying, and then wonderful, but never really romantic. It was more surreal than real, but it felt really good and really gay and, three weeks free of the only small-town closet he'd ever known, Dex took every gulp of the world he could get. So was this library date, this promise of coffee in an intellectual setting – was this the universe offering him a second *real* first-date chance? Or was it just a coincidence?

Dex didn't believe in coincidences.

Wait. That wasn't true at all. Dex believed in coincidences, and fate, and signs and wonders, and the great interlocking gears of the universe telling him to do things, and though he'd gotten pretty good at ignoring what the universe was telling him to do (most recently: quit your soul-sucking job and open a karaoke bar!), it didn't mean he couldn't still hear it screaming.

He turned down the hall toward the library café and Bert Hatmaker was already there.

He was wearing neatly pressed pants, a genuinely distressed denim jacket and something collared, and blue and green and argyle beneath it. Very Cambridge prep, Dex remembered – right down to his shoes, which were the most expensive things on his body. And like that, Dex's anxiety was gone. What poured over him instead felt a bit like the calm assurance he'd first experienced in Bert's presence at brunch, and also a bit like how Dex imagined the first signs of a stroke might feel.

Bert turned and waved a little, but did not advance, which meant Dex actually had to walk toward him. Dex had to move his feet and either look away awkwardly or maintain eye contact for the length of the hallway, staring Bert down like a deranged lion eyeballing a gazelle.

Bert looked flustered. "It's closed," he said, shrugging and pointing a thumb back at the café door. "I just assumed it would be open."

"Library's not too big with the after-work crowd," said Dex, thinking of The Bank and all those golden girls and boys drowning their finance salaries in golden beer.

"I don't see why not," said Bert with a twist of a smile.

Dex tucked his hands in his pockets. Yes, Bert made him feel calmer. Made him feel like he didn't have to put on a show. Though that produced its own kind of uneasiness, because if Dex wasn't putting on a show, he wasn't quite sure who to be. "Run your errand?" he asked.

Bert nodded. "I did." He smiled. "You too?"

"Oh – right!" and Dex opened his messenger bag and brought out Lyle's travel mugs. Bert tucked them inside his own bag, and when he looked back up at Dex, he seemed a little let down, his face betraying a hope, maybe, that this meeting wasn't just another errand for either of them. Dex had never met an adult man so obviously in earnest. He wanted to make a warm nest for him, a shelter from the vulgarities of the world and all the bigger, crueler animals that would chew him up and spit him out.

"They probably wouldn't have let us take coffee into the library anyway. Want to look around?" Dex asked. Bert brightened.

Two birds with one stone, Dex thought. He could interrogate *and* flirt. This was an excellent distraction. He otherwise would have spent his Wednesday night breathing into a paper sack in frustration over everything Tuesday was withholding.

They walked outside, following the loop around the library's open courtyard. Connecting the original old library with its modern addition, the courtyard was a gorgeous square arcade with a shady sheltered walkway, tables and chairs looking out over a garden, and a fountain with a statue of a pixie, perhaps, or some other breed of mythological creature, dancing whilst taunting a baby with some grapes. The fountain was turned off, whether for the night or the season, Dex couldn't say. He didn't remember the last time he'd been here, but he remembered the feeling: of being outside and inside at the same time, the air cool and light as the stone surrounding you, the city at a distance but audible everywhere, like you were tucked deep in its stone heart.

"I should come here more often," said Bert. "It's hard when you work and live on the other side of the river. There's no real reason to come into Boston proper."

"Don't you visit Lyle?" *Thrust*, thought Dex, though everything he knew about fencing metaphors came from movies. "Or does she come to visit you?"

"We usually meet somewhere. There's a townie restaurant in Porter Square that she loves, right on Mass. Ave. The Newtowne Grille. I think she likes it because no one recognizes her, or if they do, they don't care. She's been going there for years, and they have no idea." Bert cocked his head. "I mean, they know who she is – they know she's the girl who gets a whole pitcher and a cheese pizza all to herself, who plays the same song on the jukebox every Wednesday night. But they don't know who she married." He sighed. "They might now. Her face has been in the news enough."

"What song?"

"'More Than a Feeling,'" said Bert, looking him straight in the eye when he said it.

"Well, of course," said Dex. "Boston girl."

"Indeed." Bert hunched closer to Dex's shoulder. They had reached the end of the loop and were about to reenter the old library. "She's taking Vince's death a lot better than I would if I were in her shoes. Hell, she's taking it better than I am in *my* shoes."

"I'm sorry," said Dex. "All the" – insanity? hoopla? – "the *activity* of his game makes it easy to forget it's happening because he died. Do you think that's why he did it, to keep people preoccupied in the early stages of grief?"

"Possibly," said Bert.

"I'd say something wise and comforting about death," said Dex, "if I had anything wise or comforting to say about it. Tuesday's the one—" *with the philosophical approach to morbidity,* he almost said, but stopped, because he was the interrogator, not the interrogatee, and it was almost full dark in the courtyard, and despite the fact that Bert Hatmaker was pointedly – *pointedly* – brushing against him as Dex held the door open, he was creeping himself out. He wanted to be inside. Where electricity reigned and the mosaic ceiling was tiled with writhing vines and the names of dead men

(EMERSON, ADAMS) who had nonetheless achieved a kind of immortality. He let the door slam shut behind them.

They walked up the main stairs of the building – McKim, Bert called it, like the building was an old friend (*And he says he doesn't come here often*, thought Dex, doing his best to think like Tuesday) – past the white stone lions on their plinths, the murals of dancing nymphs, ladies in togas and capes swanning about gardens and lakes, the water so blue it reminded him of the mural in the underground theater, hidden and rotting away. For a moment Dex was full of an artist's indignation, that these murals – which were great, he meant no slight – should be seen and the others should fade forever.

Maybe it was the company. Maybe it was the whole game, making him suggestible and sensitive to ridiculous notions he'd grown a hearty hide against years ago. He'd dipped a toe in the visual arts, painting, film and video, en route to his performance degree, and he'd found the fine-art nerds both delusional and charming; they legitimately believed they were creating objects meant to last. Performance, by comparison, had always felt more authentic. Performance was alive, so performance had to die. A piece or a song or a play was designed to last for only as long as it took to perform, to begin and end and echo in the mind. But he had to admit there was something noble, too, in the pursuit of permanence, and something beautiful and sad about how much art had been lost and forgotten by time.

Dex followed Bert into a gallery on the right. There were more murals, red here rather than lake blue, vaguely Arthurian. Lots of knights and ladies-in-waiting and crowns and long gowns.

Bert planted himself in the middle of the room, then about-faced toward the doorway they'd just entered. The wall above depicted a mural of three distinct scenes: the left was a king's hall of courtiers in earthy browns, and the right, bright, with touches of blue and yellow, was some sort of holy conga line. Dex could make out angels, maybe, brandishing candelabras, a spear. A figure in red held a platter with a halo above it over her head, and at the front of the line was a crowned queen brandishing something so magical its glowing rays burst from beneath the hankie covering it. In the middle, directly over the doorway, was an old man lying on a bed, wrapped in a blanket of rich black fur that would have looked magisterial on Joan Collins. To the left of the bed was a young man in a blood-red cloak with blond hair and a troubled face.

"What's this?" asked Dex. He pointed to the man in the bed, the man in the cloak, the woman with the platter. "Father, son, holy roast?"

Bert turned. "I'm going to pretend you never said that."

Dex grinned. "Pretend all you want, dear."

"That's Galahad." Bert pointed to the man in the cloak. He was speaking quietly, which had to be for show because they were the only two in the room. "Do you know his grail story?"

"If it doesn't involve Harrison Ford and Nazis," said Dex, "or a castle full of lady virgins into spanking and oral sex, then no."

Bert just looked at him.

"What?" asked Dex, though he knew perfectly well what. He could feel it in the air between them, a charge between their lips and their skin: Bert thought he was funny. He made Bert want to laugh. Everything Dex said had the improbable effect of making this man actually like him more.

"This panel—" Bert cleared his throat. "This panel is Galahad's first visit to the castle of the grail under the Fisher King. The grail is there, but no one can see it – I forget why; the king committed a great crime long ago, so they're cursed with not being alive, but not dying. Despite being pure—"

"Overrated," said Dex. "Sorry, go on."

"Galahad couldn't see the grail either. He had to figure out from these apparitions" – he pointed to the conga line – "what it all meant. But it was too soon. He was too young to solve it. He had to spend the rest of his life questing in order to understand the first, the only, the organizing mystery of his life." Bert turned to the next panel. "He figured it out eventually, and came back to the castle, freed the king. Galahad got the grail in the end."

"Those," said Dex, pointing to a panel on the other side of the room, of the man in the red cloak bowing before a crowd of queens. "Those are the randy virgins, aren't they?"

"Yes," said Bert. "But that's not the point."

"What's the point, then?" Dex looked back over his shoulder.

"We spend our whole lives becoming worthy. Of ourselves. Our mysteries, our solutions, the fruits of our quests."

Dex turned slowly to face him. His heart ached something marvelous. "What are you trying to tell me?" he said.

"Did you find it?" Bert looked like he was happy but it hurt. Like he wanted to tell Dex everything in the world but simply couldn't.

Dex blushed. "It? You mean" – he dropped his voice to a whisper – "you mean the theater? The room and the symbols and the code?"

Bert didn't respond. He inhaled and looked warmly at Dex with that beautiful face of his, and Dex realized this wasn't a real date. This was only a prelude.

Dex wanted to take this man out for real.

"Yes," he said, answering all of the questions, his own and Bert's. But there was so much more to ask. "What do you know abou—" was all Dex got out before Bert crossed the tiles between them and kissed him, softly and perfectly.

"My friends call me Rabbit," he said, and left, taking every word Dex could think to say with him.

◆

Someone screamed.

Dorry jumped from the book where she'd buried herself. She'd been down so deep – and she was in the library, where you got shushed for talking, let alone screaming – that her first thought was that she'd imagined it, heard it at the back of her head. She *was* reading about ghosts. She might have fallen asleep and not realized. She was tired enough; she hadn't slept much lately. She felt awful that Tuesday was avoiding her – something was up, and Tuesday hadn't told her a thing. The wall their apartments shared had shivered from Tuesday's music for hours the past two nights, angry, thumpy electronic beats that made her father sort of bop his head even as he asked Dorry, "You like this garbage?"

The library screamer screamed again.

It was more of a whoop that time, and a partial phrase, —*oly shi*—!, followed by the sound of footsteps thumping upstairs from the librarian's desk. Low voices met somewhere off to her left. Dorry was curled in a chair on the second floor of the Somerville Public Library – a balcony that surrounded the main floor, ringed with non-fiction stacks – with her back to one rounded window. It was that late-afternoon dip between the end of school and the time when she knew her dad would start to worry that she wasn't home. But she didn't want to go home at all. It was Thursday, and she was afraid Tuesday would be too busy or too on Dorry's dad's side or too – whatever (even though she had a paper in English and a test in math, real reasons to meet with her tutor). Part of her wanted to be a baby and pretend that if she just stayed here in the library, hidden among the art books, she wouldn't have to deal with any of it. Libraries had always made her feel like a kid, in a good way: secret and safe and taken care of, rocked to sleep in a cocoon of books.

But she was going to have to deal with *something*, apparently. She craned her neck to listen better. The screamer had been close, in the corner to her left, and whoever it was still seemed excited, even if they'd stopped screaming. Whoops threatened to bust free from the few words she caught – *sorry, understand, of course of course* – as the screamer apologized to the librarian who had rushed upstairs. Then she heard *Vincen – Pry* – And if she'd been dreamy-sleepy before, now she was awake.

She leaned so far over that the chair began to tip.

She saw the librarian first. She emerged out of the far corner, turned left, headed back down the stairs to her desk. And after the librarian came Ned Kennedy.

She knew Ned. He was in her English class, but he was at least a year older, a sophomore, probably. Dorry had tested so well when she changed schools that they'd bumped her up a year. Ned was wiry, with brown skin, black-framed glasses, and super-short hair. He didn't say much in class, but when he did, it was funny, a joke that wasn't obviously a joke, the kind that made the teacher (and Dorry, in her head) laugh. She didn't know much else about him. He played trombone, she thought. Or maybe he was in the art club. She got an arty vibe from him. He was wearing a gray hoodie, unzipped so Dorry could read QUESTION REALITY – REALITY was printed upside down – on his purple T-shirt.

He was gripping his phone in his left hand. The screen glowed between his fingers.

She got the same tingly feeling she'd had when she told Tuesday and Archie about the first clue: a premonition that this, this moment, was a beginning. If Tuesday was shutting her out, if she didn't want to play Pryce's game with Dorry anymore, Dorry would just have to play with someone else.

"Hey!" she whisper-hissed. "Ned!"

Ned's head whipped toward her, independent of his body, which took a beat to catch up.

His face was blank.

Of course: he had no idea who she was. Dorry was just the new girl who sat behind him.

She motioned for him to come closer.

He pushed his glasses up his nose with a finger.

"I'm Dorry," she said, keeping her voice as low as possible. Sound carried all over the library, over the side of the balcony, way across the stacks. "I sit behind you in English. Newish girl." She raised her hand in an instinctive, stupid wave. "Hi."

"Hello," he said. He didn't say more, but an . . . *and?* floated on the air.

If he wasn't going to come to her, she would go to him. At least he didn't back up as she approached. And though it didn't feel as true as it had a week ago, she knew – assuming Ned Kennedy had been whooping about *this* Vincent Pryce, not the other Vincent Price – exactly what to say.

"I'm a friend of Tuesday Mooney's," she said.

His face changed. It lifted, like a curtain.

"No way," he said.

Dorry nodded. "Yes way," she said.

Ned tucked his chin down and sort of laughed into his chest, like he couldn't believe he was having this conversation. Like it was some huge lucky break for him to have run into her. Someone who knew Tuesday. A girl who knew the girl who'd uncovered Pryce's first clue.

"Dorry," she said again, and stuck out her hand, because despite the fact that the most interesting thing about her was that she knew Tuesday, she had a name and she wanted Ned to know it. "Dorry Bones."

Ned slipped his hand into hers. It was warm and dry, and he said, "Ned. Ned Flores Kennedy. Of the Union Square Kennedys," like it was a joke Dorry was supposed to get. She didn't get it. But she didn't let on.

He propped the hand still holding his phone on his hip and shook his head.

"So you're really a friend of Tuesday Mooney?" he said. "I mean, I want to trust you, you've got a real—" Ned waved his free hand in the air, almost like he was trying to get a better whiff of her. "You've got a real trustworthy air."

Dorry didn't know how to respond to that. She smiled encouragingly.

"It's just that – I guess, if you're a friend of Tuesday's," Ned said, "do you know – do you know who I am? I found the secret code down the alley and posted it? I'm a Black Cat, repping the Highlanders?"

She did not. She wished she did, for how disappointed Ned looked that she didn't. He explained: The Black Cats were a collective of self-organized teams all over greater Boston, Cambridge, Somerville, Brookline, Jamaica Plain, who had agreed to share information about Pryce's game in the hope that one of their number might solve it – and, after solving it, share the wealth. They started as an open group on Facebook, but had gone private after Ned posted that picture of the code in the alley downtown – because, as one of the group's leaders put it, "we're a cooperative, not a class-action lawsuit; let's keep our individual shares healthy." His sister, Cass, was one of the leaders, and Ned's eyes got shiny when he talked about the other one, Lisa Pinto. (If Dorry had to guess, Ned had *definitely* had a crush on her at some point. Boys could be so transparent; sometimes you could see straight through them.) They'd been trying hard to recruit Tuesday, but she hadn't responded to any of their messages or requests on Facebook.

"We have room for one more," Ned said, "especially if that one is your girl Tuesday." He looked at her. "Or two more." He sort of wince-laughed, like he was embarrassed he'd left her out, had never meant to. "I bet we have room for two more."

So *this* was what Tuesday had been keeping from her: a secret code. More players, finding more clues. Her father had asked Tuesday to cut Dorry off, and boy, had she ever. And, yes, he had asked Dorry not to get involved with Tuesday.

But he hadn't actually said anything about not getting involved with someone else.

"Did you solve it yet?" she asked. Her voice rose; she couldn't help it. "Do you know what the code means?"

"You want to get a drink or a slush or something? At the LP?" Ned asked, bobbing his head in the general direction of Highland Ave. and the convenience mart down the street. "And no, I do not know what the code means yet. But I know something else," he said, and smiled so brightly, Dorry caught it like a cold. She grinned back. And nodded. They tromped downstairs to the circulation desk, where Dorry checked out her book (*Famous Ghosts and Where to Find Them: New England*), and then they left the library. Dorry noticed that Ned was leaning closer, and realized he was looking at the buttons on her bag. All bands that Tuesday had introduced her to, because everything that was cool about her she had learned from someone who was a lot cooler: The Cure, Nine Inch Nails, Cake. They stopped on the curb to let a car pull out of the parking lot, and Ned reached out and touched one of the buttons so he could read its tiny letters, which said, NUKE A GAY BABY SEAL FOR CHRIST.

He laughed. "The poor gay baby seals," he said.

"My dad loves that one," she said. "He worries that we've lost our sense of irony. Like, as a country."

"My dad would probably agree," said Ned. "But I don't know if he's worried about irony as much as he's worried about other stuff. Like coastlines. Species. He teaches biology. Right here." He hitched a shoulder at the high school they were currently walking in front of. Somerville High was a giant stone castle spreading along Highland Avenue, between the library and the city hall, across the street from the LP convenience mart. Another thing that was way, way cooler about living in the city instead of the suburbs: you got to go to high school in a building that was old enough to be haunted. "I spend most afternoons hanging out at the library, waiting for a ride home with him. I kind of hate the bus. And it's getting dark earlier every day."

It was strange that Dorry had never seen him there before. She hung out at the library all the time too, usually in art history, because the chair was big and cozy. She told him so.

"Well," said Ned, "you might not have seen me, but I've seen you. Disappearing around a corner, sort of flashing out of sight, melting into the wall, with your boots and that bag and – kind of like Kitty Pryde." Ned sniffed. "You know Kitty Pryde? From *X-Men*?" He shook his head again. "She's wicked cool."

Dorry's cheeks reddened. So he *had* known who she was when she introduced herself. She might not have been brave enough to say hello if she'd realized she wasn't a stranger to him.

The LP mart always smelled a little like her grandmother's fridge, funky from years of cutting the moldy bits off food she should have thrown out but couldn't, because part of it was still good. It was familiar and gross at the same time. She asked Ned what he wanted, and Ned blanked for a second, and then asked for a chocolate milk. When she brought two bottles of chocolate milk back up to the counter, he looked relieved, like he was worried chocolate milk had maybe been the wrong choice, the little-kid choice, but the fact that she had chosen the same meant it was the right choice after all.

They sat inside the brick bus shelter across the street and clinked their milks together.

"Do you read comics?" Ned asked. Dorry turned toward him. "If you do, you should check out Rodney's Comics, in Davis. Rodney is the best. You'd like him, I bet. He's super-smart and mysterious and – he's not a Black Cat, which is too bad because he has this way of figuring stuff out. He knows everything, *everything*, not just about comics and superheroes and movies and TV, but the world, the patterns, the rules that everything's constructed on. The invisible forces pushing and pulling and shaping what we all take for granted, or don't even see." Ned pushed his glasses up the bridge of his nose again. "Like," he said, "the first time I showed up at the comic shop with these glasses, Rodney sort of nodded at me, slow, and said, 'The thing people forget about Superman'" – Ned paused for effect – "'is that those red and blue Underoos aren't his costume. Clark Kent is.'"

Ned mimed a bomb going off in his brain, held his fist to his temple and exploded it with a soft *pshhhhhh!*

Dorry smiled. So he had a Tuesday too.

"Are you in costume right now?" she said. "Is Ned Kennedy your secret identity?"

"Is Dorry Bones *your* secret identity?" he said, and Dorry smiled into her chocolate milk. She shifted on the metal bench. She didn't know what to do next. Sitting next to Ned felt both normal and super-weird, because they didn't know each other at all and yet it felt like they did. Like maybe they were already friends. She hadn't been friends with a boy since preschool, and those friendships existed mainly in stories her mom had told her. ("Andrew was your favorite; we had to pack extra snacks because you shared so many with him.") Would it be different to be friends with a boy now? Like, could you even *be* friends with a boy without it leading to, you know, sex stuff? Especially when the boy was really cute, and it was kind of hard to talk in front of him, and when you did, your ears got hot?

"This bench is making my butt chilly," Ned said.

"I'm not on Facebook," Dorry said. And grimaced. Why had she said that? She could be so awkward it hurt.

Ned said, "You know, if you're not on Facebook, you're a ghost. Officially." He swigged his milk. "Maybe Dorry Bones is your secret identity, and Ghost Girl is who you really are."

They sat at the bus shelter and watched the light at the corner turn from red to green.

"So," Dorry said, asking herself, *What would Tuesday do?* And answering, *Tuesday would investigate.* "What do you know? How did you find the secret code? What did you figure out that *isn't* the code?"

Ned laughed. "Whoa," he said. "One question at a time."

Dorry rolled her eyes back. She was half frustrated, half excited, half nervous, half elated. She was too many halves. She was twice as much as she usually was.

"Seriously," she said. "I'm really serious." So Ned made a really serious face, pulled his mouth down in a flat line, adjusted his glasses, nodded, blinked, rubbed his chin with his fingers. "I'm *serious!*" Dorry laughed, and pulled her hand inside her sleeve and smacked him with the empty cuff.

"I know something happened," she said. "I know you figured something out in the library." She pushed her voice and her face to be firm, adult, cool, and in control – and it was so sudden and funny and *so not her* that after a beat they both exploded. And Dorry could sense Ned's joy bubbling.

"I did," he said. "It's kind of against the rules, the Black Cat rules, to show it to you. But." Ned stared at her, straight at her, without blinking, and Dorry stared back, daring herself not to look away first. "But if I keep it to myself one second longer, I'm going to—" And he made that bomb sound again, only this time he mimed his whole body blowing up.

He pulled his phone out of his pocket. "Okay, so," he said, "the code was written on the side of a building downtown that's built in the spot where Poe was born. Which I went looking for because that Shakespeare thing, the prince of darkness and whatever? Poe's parents met while they were both acting in *King Lear*. And as I'm reading up about how Poe's parents met, I find out he was born here. Right here." He pointed a finger down at the ground, thought better of it, pointed out of the bus shelter in the general direction of the city across the river. "Well, right over there. In an alley between a piano store and a burrito place.

"So I go there. And I find another painted raven and this, like, secret code written in chalk, so I know I'm on the right track. At first I thought you could, you know, crack the code by figuring out what the symbols were, but that didn't go anywhere. And I was in the library today when it occurred to me to, like, figure out what the *building* was." He tapped at his phone and passed it to her to see. Dorry chewed on her lip.

It was a gallery of pictures on a site called Flickr. She tapped the first picture to enlarge it: an old door with a piece of paper stuck to it: NO ENTRANCE. She swiped to the next picture. The photographer had gone through the door. It was hard to tell, on Ned's phone, exactly what she was seeing. A room cluttered with old-fashioned metal chairs, piled in a heap. She swiped again. Stairs, looking out toward a big dark room. She swiped again, and the room got bigger. The room got huge. It was rounded and orange-red, full of more chairs and boxes, and shadows, and high arches all around the walls.

She still didn't get it, but she couldn't stop swiping through the pictures. The room was rotting, dusty, falling apart, but every curl of paint, every tilting three-legged chair, every shadow and scuff, made Dorry's throat ache, like she was going to cry.

"That's in the basement," repeated Ned, "of the building next to where Poe was born. And the raven with the code was pointing down, like it was saying 'This way.'"

Whatever this room was, Tuesday knew about it, knew what it was. Dorry felt it in her bones. And Dorry knew it now too, knew it *separately* from Tuesday.

She wondered if Tuesday had gone down there. She wondered what she'd found.

"So." Ned tapped the screen, still in her hands. He had a

dark blot on his right index finger that might have been ink, and he was so excited, he was shaking. "Um."

Ned jiggled his leg.

"What are you doing?" he blurted. "Right now? Like, do you want to go check it out? With me?"

A spear of adrenaline pierced Dorry's heart.

"I'm." Her mouth was dry. "Supposed to go home soon."

Ned stiffened. "Oh," he said. "I mean. That makes sense. That's cool. I can go – by myself, I just thought. You know, if you weren't busy."

"Not that—" Dorry handed the phone back to Ned. So this, she thought, was probably how it felt to be asked out. She'd never been asked out in her life, and though she wasn't being asked *out* asked out, she had to assume it was a similar experience. She felt dizzy. Excited. A little suspicious. She wanted to say yes – she did, she did – and she wanted not to believe the tiny voice in her brain that said: *He'd rather ask Tuesday. Tuesday knows how to win. Tuesday has been in this strange dead room and knows what to find there. He's only asking you because you're right here, right now. Because you're the human clue that gets him closer to her.*

She was supposed to go home. It was supposed to be Tuesday Thursday. But what if today was a new day entirely, and Dorry could choose what to do with it?

"Not that I always do," she said, and grinned at him with all the boldness she could pretend to possess. "What I'm supposed to."

10

TAKEOUT AND DELIVERY

Edgar Allan Arches Junior, comfortable in the knowledge that the deliveryman wouldn't arrive for at least thirty minutes, stretched out across Vince's black velvet sectional sofa and reviewed his notes.

They were not conclusive. They were mostly lists of plans he had to perpetually cross out and rethink. He collected them in a small reporter's notebook; Archie had a deep appreciation for the act of writing something down instead of typing. A love of paper goods and pens. It was a predilection – some might call it an affectation, to which Archie would say, Have you met my family? – that he'd had since childhood. But he had fully committed to leaving only a paper trail for the past six years, years he had spent avoiding most humans, in person and online, making plans and crossing them out, pretending his life had any direction or purpose beyond *disappear completely*.

That plan had changed only recently, and it wasn't going great. He flipped back to the first page.

Talk to Vince @ 4 Seasons auction for hope

He knew about the auction. It happened every year. He knew his family, because they were always invited to these kinds of things, would be on the guest list but highly unlikely to attend. And he knew Vincent Pryce, because *he* was always invited to these kinds of things, would be on the guest list and highly *likely* to attend. Approaching Vince, after so many years gone, seemed a far less terrifying prospect than approaching his sister. Or his mother.

Or his brother.

He didn't have the heart to cross *Talk to Vince* out.

Archie couldn't afford to think about it. The guilt would suffocate him. Instead, he flipped to the next page, where he had written:

—Tall girl
—Researcher @ hospital
—Intel on Nat?

He hadn't had to write it down, because he would never forget, but his fourth bullet would have been *Nice feet*. He pictured her bare feet, long and slim, against the swirling maroon and gold carpet of the ballroom at the Four Seasons. Dark red shining toes curling into the plush pile.

Archie stared at the portrait over the gray marble fireplace, of Vince in a canary-yellow cravat and smoking jacket the color of old blood, staring vaguely into the middle distance. *I'm sorry*, he thought; *I am so, so sorry*. Then he flipped his reporter's notebook closed, laid it on his chest, and drummed his fingers on the cardboard cover. His stomach gurgled. He was hungry.

It was Friday. All week, Tuesday hadn't called. Or texted. Neither had Dex, but Tuesday's silence was louder, especially since there had been very serious developments. Someone found the code on a wall and posted it to Facebook; it went viral. Other people found the underground theater. Just yesterday, when Archie walked down Boylston Street, the Dunks-jonesing security guard and a cop had been supervising a crowd lined up to get into the Steinert building, though all the envelopes were (reportedly) gone. The *Globe* began profiling players and teams who self-identified, had even printed the decoded rules of the game. And the formal invitation Vince promised in his obituary had blanketed the city overnight, in the form of beautiful black and red broadsides, stapled and taped and glued on light poles and T tunnels and store windows:

To THE LIVING AND THE DEAD OF Boston:

You are cordially invited to attend the funeral masque of

VINCENT A. PRYCE.

The third Friday of October.
Six o'clock in the evening.
On Boston Common.
All are welcome. Costumes required.
Seekers may request an audience with the Widow at nine o'clock,
where they may yet hope to play their hands.

The funeral was exactly one week away. They had been given new, maddeningly obscure information – "play their hands" had something to do with the playing card, probably – and they had forty-nine competitors. They had yet to figure out how to play, how to seek well, where the clock was that was primed to strike, or even to decide what the fuck they were supposed to do with the thirteen thousand dollars Vince had given them – though Tuesday could very well have already spent it, could have figured it all out, for all Archie knew.

Because she was silent.

Deafeningly silent.

Maybe it was for the best. The less he saw of her, the fewer lies he had to keep track of, the less of a distraction she was. And the less danger she was in. The more time he had to contemplate . . . other things.

There was a knock on the door.

He lifted his head from the arm of the sofa, curious. Delivery guys usually called his cell from the courtyard below. And it was too fast; either House of Thai had discovered a way to bend space-time or—

Another knock, followed by a muffled voice.

"I know you're in there."

Tuesday.

Archie didn't move.

Archie didn't know how he was feeling, but he was feeling something, all right. Something warm and weird and intense. He sat up, tight.

"I can wait all night."

She didn't sound angry. Or like she'd brought anyone with her. Dex. The cops.

Emerson.

His mother.

"That's not true, actually," she continued. "I have to go home at some point to feed my cat."

He swung his legs from the black velvet cushions of the couch to the floor. His own bare feet sank into the deep pile of the rug.

"Come on. Let me in."

Then she said, "Edgar Allan Arches Junior."

He froze. Every part of Archie stopped thumping, and for a moment he was petrified, fixed, weightless and breathless. On Vincent Pryce's silly black couch in his silly Hot Topic by way of *Architectural Digest* apartment. It had been six years since anyone had called him that name.

So she knew. He didn't know how she knew, but she knew. And, sure, hearing his name always burned, but his name from her lips didn't make him angry. He didn't feel the sting of having been made, the fear of being cornered, though Tuesday's presence meant both of those things were true.

This extraordinary feeling that Archie was feeling – now that he thought about it – was relief. He didn't have to lie anymore.

Well, he didn't have to lie about *everything* anymore.

He stood. Shuffled across the carpet, through the living room into the foyer. Wrapped his hand around the doorknob. Turned his wrist. Opened the door.

Tuesday was standing in the hallway, holding a brown paper bag in her arms.

"I brought dinner," she said.

"How did you find me?" he asked.

"You of all people," she said, "should know how easy it is to look up the real estate holdings of recently deceased billionaires who buy investment properties on Beacon Hill using the limited liability corporation Roderick Usher Real Estate. May I?"

He stood aside. She walked in. His blood, just beneath his skin, felt like it was percolating. He was a little feverish. She kept her shoes on. Which was disappointing, but sensible – the rugs were all black – and Tuesday was nothing if not full of sense.

She crossed into the living room, taking in the heavy purple drapes, the portrait of Vince over the fireplace, the surrounding books and curios in glass cabinets and shelves. The skull with the arrow through its temple on the mantel. The stuffed two-headed bat under the glass dome in the center of the coffee table, flanked by old issues of *Vanity Fair* and the *Weekly World News*. Tuesday nodded, like this was what she'd expected, and turned her attention to him. Which was the moment Archie realized he was wearing the same smoking jacket from the painting – Vince's jacket, the color of old blood – over jeans and a T-shirt, because the condo was a little chilly, and—

She narrowed her eyes at him in a way that he couldn't decipher.

Then she disappeared around the bend of the dining room

into the kitchen. He heard her opening drawers, the fridge, the freezer, closing them again. She reappeared, still clutching the brown bag. She set the bag on the dining room table and rested her hand on the back of a chair.

"We should talk," she said.

He didn't move.

He didn't want to talk.

She sat down first. He took the chair opposite. Out of her messenger bag she pulled a white three-ring binder. She squared it neatly on the table in front of her, interlaced her fingers, and stared at him.

"On Tuesday," she said, "your brother took me out to lunch."

Oh fuck. Fuck fuck fuckity fuck.

"He offered me – well." She tilted her head. "First he told me you're not him. Then he offered me a million dollars if I told him where you were hiding."

Archie's hands went tacky with sweat.

"So I found you," she said. "In the patient database, first. It was a little more difficult to find you here, in the city, in this condo, though you'd already given me everything I needed. When you said you were heading home to the Hill on Saturday, and the way you reacted to Vincent Pryce's seal – I guessed that you, unlike your father, didn't exactly hate him. So it wasn't too much of a leap to think that you, intelligent and resourceful, might be lying low in one of the dead man's vacant properties." She gestured at him. "And here you are. Lying low in one of the dead man's vacant properties."

Archie swallowed. "I bet," he said, and his tongue got stuck in his dry mouth. "I bet you're pretty pleased with yourself."

"I'm terrifically pleased with myself," Tuesday said. "I solved you. And I was so pleased about solving *you*, I decided to keep going. To see what else I missed." She flattened her hands on the binder. "Here it is. Everything I could find. About Arches Consolidated, its filings and financial statements, its press. All of your houses and charitable foundations. Every jerkwad aphorism Nathaniel ever tweeted, every time Emerson showed up on *Perez Hilton* with a cocaine halo MS-Painted around her head—" She flipped to the end. "In the appendix.

"Everything I could find about you, which isn't much."

"What can I say?" His throat was papery. "I'm an offline type of guy."

"And everything I could find about your mother, and your vanished father."

Archie's heart gave a funny little contraction, like it had forgotten how to beat.

"So what did you think?" he said. "Of Nat? The real Nat."

Tuesday squinted at him again. He was getting better at reading her expressions, and this one clearly meant she was thinking something she didn't want to say out loud.

"He was exactly the man I thought he would be when I first met you, and thought you were him," she said. "Acquisitive. Spoiled. Incurious. Vain." She narrowed her eyes again. "That's why you hired me, isn't it? Because I could tell you things about your brother. Things you didn't know, recent things, because – you've been gone for, what?"

"Six years," said Archie.

Her face flushed deep with sudden satisfaction. He thought of all the things he still hadn't told her. He might tell her just so he could watch her make that face again and again.

"Six years," she repeated. "Six—" She opened the binder, licked her fingertip, and flipped through the fat stack of three-hole-punched pages.

"You've been gone since your father disappeared," she said.

He returned her steady stare.

"What else can you tell me about Nat?" he asked.

"You really don't want to talk about him, do you?"

"Nat?"

"No," said Tuesday. "Your father."

"First tell me one thing that happened to Nat in the last six years," said Archie.

"Plastic surgery," she said. "A lot."

"No!" Archie said, laughing despite the weeds of fear trailing through his bloodstream. It helped. "And he was always the pretty one."

"He's pretty something," said Tuesday. "I mean, it's good plastic surgery – you'd never know. He just looks—" She shrugged. "Younger than he should. He looks like you, I guess. Even more than you look like him."

"The Arches line is strong."

"Come closer," she said, crooking a finger. She lifted herself to kneel on her chair. She leaned toward him.

Archie did the same. He kneeled and moved forward, walking his palms across the table. When he lifted them, they left sweaty shadows.

Tuesday brushed his hair back from his forehead. Tucked it behind his ears. Pressed his ears flat to the sides of his head. It felt so good to be touched. Blood warmed his face.

"Pinned his ears," she said. She let Archie's ears spring back. Then she cupped them, one in each hand, rounding them, pulling them toward her. She ran the tip of her finger down his nose – his long, lumpy bloodhound nose, the nose that Nat broke after Archie broke his – and said, "Nose job." She frowned in concentration. "Clench your teeth?" she asked, and he clenched, and she brushed her fingertips along the lines of his jaw. "Possible fake dimples." Then she pressed the pad of her thumb against his fat bottom lip.

"He's pretty boring," she said.

Over the years, in his darkest moments – waking up still drunk, still wrapped around a girl whose name he had made a point of never knowing, or, later, after a long late shift, alone on a bus or a porch, knowing there was no one, possibly anywhere on earth, who cared if he lived through another night – Archie would be forced to admit something to himself. Just because he could, occasionally, pretend not to care, the truth never went away; the truth never stopped being true. He might have run away from the money, from the business, from his family, but he couldn't run away from his own stomach. To never be satisfied was an Arches trait at the genetic level; to want, regardless of how much he already had, was his legacy. What made Archie different was the flavor of his hunger. It was less tangible than money, more common than power. He had tried, almost all his life, to exist without it.

He didn't need other people to know him. He didn't need someone to touch him. He didn't need to be connected to anyone or to anything.

But he could no longer pretend he wasn't hungry.

Because he was starving.

"I have some questions," Tuesday said. "But first" – she nodded at the brown bag – "let's eat."

◆

While ferreting out Vincent Pryce's second Beacon Hill address on Pinckney Street (which she knew existed because of something Bert Hatmaker had mentioned at brunch) from Boston's online property records, Tuesday had decided to bring sandwiches. When Archie had come to her place unannounced, he'd been bearing food. It seemed only appropriate to return the favor.

Plus, she wanted to confront him on a full stomach. No, confront wasn't quite the word. She wanted to show him what she knew, what she'd discovered on her own, and then discover everything she didn't. She'd been close, before, to solving one Arches, but now she was close to solving *two*. It was delicious. She wanted to know more. She wanted to know everything.

And he was interesting. He was the first interesting man

she'd met in – she swallowed a bite of turkey and cheddar – in so long, she'd almost forgotten how it felt to *be* interested. She'd lived for years now, and happily, freed by the realization that she didn't need to believe the books, the television shows, the commercials that told her, if she was single, there was something wrong with her. That if she liked it, she was lying to herself. If she chose it actively and indefinitely, if she didn't think of her single life as a holding pattern, a prelude to the next (coupled) life, then she was – what even *was* she? A nun, repressed and suspect? A witch, dangerously free? A spinster with a cat, pathetic and irrelevant?

In other words, confused.

But she wasn't confused. She knew who she was, and who she was was herself. She took care of herself. She came home to herself. She was enough, herself.

So to meet a person who was truly interesting, who presented both a mystery and a challenge, whose life was extraordinary to her yet familiar – she had not seen that coming. Archie was novel. She had never known anyone quite like him, in person, at least – she'd known any number of people in his tax bracket, his level of society, from facts and strange details collected and analyzed. But she had never felt anyone like Archie look at her, and (try to) lie to her, and, with very little persuasion, reveal to her a kind of malnourished need – to not be such a goddamn stranger – he was desperate to feed. His need didn't feel overwhelming to her, though; it was far more overwhelming to him, and if he was asking anything of her at all, it was to not be overwhelmed alone. And – he was a mystery. A mystery she knew she could solve. It might not have been the healthiest attraction. She didn't care.

She didn't know what would happen. She didn't know what, precisely, she wanted from Archie. Only that she wanted more.

"It's your turn," she said.

He stared at the sandwich on the table in front of him.

"What?" she said. "Do you not like ham and Swiss and honey Dijon?"

He shook his head.

"I love it," he said.

She raised a single eyebrow. "Don't worry," she said. "I only use my powers of intuition for good."

He stared at her.

"It's your turn," she repeated.

He picked up his sandwich. Opened his mouth.

Tuesday sighed.

"You don't want to talk about your father for one of two reasons," she said. "Either because you miss him very much, or you're very glad he's probably dead."

He chewed.

"Junior," she said.

"Don't call me that."

"Junior?"

"Call me Archie," he said. "Eddie – Edgar – that was *his* name." He lowered the sandwich. "My father was not a good man. Nathaniel . . . whom you've described to a T, by the way." He looked down at the bread in his hands. "Nathaniel was always more his son."

Archie's eyes traveled to the backs of his hands. Tuesday saw a scar on his first right knuckle, a lump of tissue, a jagged white line like a check mark. He rubbed it with his thumb.

"He's been gone for six years, and I still – see him," Archie said.

Tuesday's insides jangled.

Archie's voice was very low. "Sometimes I hear him."

I know, she thought, helplessly, though Archie didn't elaborate. He didn't have to. She knew just how that felt, and it didn't feel sane.

"It's a little disturbing," Archie finally said, "to hear my – vanished asshole of a father calling me—" He dropped his voice and drained it, dried it up into a husk. "Junior," he growled. "Whenever I'm about to do something I know he would just . . . hate."

"Like what?"

"Like this," Archie said. He widened his eyes at Tuesday.

"What's this?" she asked.

"Spilling the family guts," he said, "to a money grubber."

"I told you," Tuesday said, "I'm not a fundraiser."

"You're really more of a stalker."

"I'm really more like a private eye," she said. "And I'm not here for the money."

"We have a verbal agreement that says otherwise."

"You're the money I'm here for," she said. "You're filthy rich with secrets. That's what I'm here for, now."

Tell me, she thought at him. *Trust me.*

Archie's chest rose with a long inhalation. "Six years ago, over Labor Day, my father got drunk and shoved my mother into the bar cart," he said. "This was not unusual for Labor Day. Or any weekend of the year, really. What was different about that year was the summer that came before it. That summer—"

"What?" said Tuesday. "Why did you stop?"

"You're not writing this down," he said.

"I'm not writing it down anywhere you can see," she said.

He cleared his throat and continued. "That was the first summer my father began seriously grooming Nathaniel to take his place at Arches Consolidated. Nat had been there for years, but without much power. Summer intern. Junior analyst. Cutting his teeth. That summer, Dad let Nat hold the reins. And Nat was great at it, of course. He had learned how to be an excellent asshole from the most excellent asshole in the business. He went straight to work on a company they were prepping to sell, streamlining, trimming the fat. Eliminating positions. Demoralizing people so that they worked harder and longer, even though there were fewer of them, so that the company's financials looked fantastic. But they weren't, like. Real."

"The corporate crash diet."

Archie nodded. "Nat's job performance wasn't the problem, as far as I could tell. Well. Not in the traditional sense." He took a bite of his sandwich.

"He was too good," Tuesday said. "Too powerful. Too young."

Archie nodded, still chewing.

"Your father felt threatened by his own son."

Archie swallowed. "You're a little spooky."

"It's not that difficult to put the pieces together," she said. "I'm sure your father liked to think he was unique, but he really wasn't."

"He was in an extra rage that Labor Day. Against his own decline. His death. I think he actually believed that, because of who he was and what he had, he wouldn't die. Not because he took great care of himself, because he didn't, but because he couldn't imagine being anything less or other than what he was." He rubbed the scar on his finger again. "So he shoved my mother into the bar cart, and while I was helping her up he pushed me down and I sliced myself open." He held up his finger. "Emerson stitched me up. Like she always did. Nat, I don't know – he took a swing at Nat too. He took a swing at all of us. And—"

He looked up at her. "I think you know the rest," he said.

Tuesday propped her elbows on the table. She *did* know the rest.

"That was the day," she said, "he and Nathaniel went to a private wine tasting at the Blue Whale, a restaurant by the wharf. On Nantucket. He was already drunk. He got drunker. Made a scene." Archie nodded. "Your brother – wait a minute." Tuesday flipped through her binder, to her freshly researched and recreated timeline of Edgar Arches's disappearance. "Your brother called him a 'drunk clown.'" She looked up at Archie. "I thought that was a fun detail."

Archie didn't respond.

"He went ballistic," said Tuesday. "And then Nathaniel hauled your drunk clown of a father away to the family yacht to sober up."

Archie clamped his lips together and nodded.

"There's more," she said.

"There is." Archie looked down at the table and tugged his earlobe. It was almost charming, how bad a liar he was. "Sometime during the night, my father and the dinghy both disappeared. Dinghy washed up. Father didn't. The company board granted my mother, as the CEO's next of kin, emergency powers. Control in his absence. Whenever he returned, alive or dead, the original succession plan would kick in." Archie inhaled again. He looked away. "I left. I couldn't – I didn't want to be a part of my family anymore, or get caught in the press and all that – shit. Needed a fresh start. For six years I slept in random beds and worked whatever jobs I could, in ware-houses, hotels, boats. I'm a decent short-order cook now. It wasn't easy, but it was better than being an Arches. Junior."

She thought she knew what he was going to say, but she wanted him to say it.

"So why are you back now?"

"Because in the next year my father can be declared legally dead," he said. "Which will negate the emergency powers and activate the original succession plan."

"Nat gets control."

Archie nodded.

"Of a multibillion-dollar company."

He nodded again, half closing his eyes.

"And that," said Tuesday, "really chaps your ass."

Archie flinched.

Tuesday smiled. Of course he thought he was the whitest of white knights. Of course he thought this was his destiny, his mission, the justice he alone could seek. He was a prince who'd paupered his way around and returned in secret, shut out his sister and his mother (who, everything in Tuesday's research suggested, had done a more than decent job running the company financially and ethically, and might be a terrific ally, if only he gave her the option). He flew under dramatic cover of his brother. All so he could pull off the greatest gotcha in the book: *The forgotten prodigal returns! And he's way less of an asshole than his brother!* After all, the world he'd been raised in had never disabused him of the notion that he couldn't, if the spirit moved him, be Batman.

"Um," Archie said, vaguely flustered, "I'm not sure what you—"

Tuesday went in for the kill.

"What does all of this have to do," she said, "with Vincent Pryce?"

◆

Everything.

Everything that happened that summer had everything to do with Vince.

What Archie had told Tuesday was the truth. It was true that his father was in an extra rage that Labor Day, on the heels of Nat's success, at the first hint of his own obsolescence. It was true that his father had pushed his mother into the bar cart, and it was true that Archie had almost lost a finger, and it was true that his sister, his Swiss Army knife of a sister, had literally stitched him back together. Teenage Emerson had taken a slew of survivalist courses, which turned out to be far more applicable to both their lives than Archie's piano lessons. She had sterilized the needle with their father's World War II Zippo.

It was all true. It was enough, Archie thought, for Tuesday to know.

Even though it was only part of the story.

The rest of the story was Vince.

Archie first met Vincent Pryce on a chilly morning in mid-May when Vince brought a plate of cookies to the front door of the Archeses' house on Nantucket. "Hello, neighbor," Vince said, brandishing the plate. "I'm building the castle next door."

Archie, uncharacteristically, had answered the door. He was mostly sleeping and drinking at the time, nominally keeping his mother company but more committed to wallowing in his quarter-life crisis, which was manifesting as a perpetual hangover. He knew about the gaudy pile next door. He knew it made his father insane. Which predisposed him to like this stranger a great deal. He was primed to like anything, or anyone, who might make his father angry, or at the very least make things more interesting. Life on the island, life in the house, was luxuriously dull (except when his father was home, which wasn't often). Nat was in the city, working. Emerson was out in Los Angeles for the summer, doing – something, Archie didn't know. They had a cook, Maria, and a landscaper, Georgio, and Maria's cousins Cristela and Jan cleaned the house once a week, though Archie and his mother lived in only five of the twenty-five rooms: their individual en suite bedrooms, the kitchen, the TV den, and the library, because it had the bar cart and the books, Archie's and his mother's addictions of choice.

Archie had a series of private tutors when he was a child, but most of what he learned about the world outside his family came from reading his mother's paperbacks: Stephen King and Michael Crichton and John Grisham and Danielle Steele, and for a while he had been obsessed with Mary Higgins Clark, for the suspense as much as the glimpse her books provided of the terrors of being a girl. The blind dates who murdered you with your own shoe. The women framed as unfit mothers and never allowed to shed that false accusation. The men who, once you became financially dependent on them, and once they impregnated you, turned out to be violent psychopaths. (He suspected this was uncomfortably close to his own mother's life story.) He was fascinated and horrified. They were thrillers about powerlessness, which, at the age of twelve, he understood too well, though he knew he could never get pregnant (thank God). He'd wanted to ask Emerson if she was afraid of these things too – blind dates, motherhood, having no money of her own – but *he* was afraid to ask, afraid she would tell him to mind his own beeswax. She had taken a lot of judo in addition to her survivalist training, but unlike half of the rest of their family, she'd never once hit him, and not because she wasn't capable. Besides, that was the Arches way: never to speak, in actual words, of anything more personal than how they felt about dinner. As much as Archie would have liked to know his sister better, he did not possess the words.

Now, at twenty-six, he drank gin and tonics with his mother and watched *The Price Is Right* every morning at eleven, and the days passed, and he didn't do anything with them, and part of him didn't care, and the part that *did* care, the hungry part, the starving part, existed in a suspended state of numb paralysis. This was the only life he had ever known. It was easy and predigested. He was rotting from the inside out, though he would only be able to name that sensation later.

Much later.

But it all started with that first plate of cookies Vince brought over, which were the best cookies Archie had ever eaten. They were chewy and buttery with big soft lumps of chocolate. "What are you eating?" his mother asked. "One dollar," said a contestant from Des Moines, and Archie passed his mother the plate. "Neighbor stopped by," Archie said through a full mouth. "He's weird."

"Weird how?" his mother asked.

"He was wearing a top hat," said Archie.

Vince came for lunch. His mother had extended the invitation when she returned his plate, something Archie didn't know she'd done until Vince reappeared with it at the door, heaped, again, with cookies. He was wearing a pith helmet and a Hawaiian shirt with interlocking pink flamingos on a black background, and they drank gin and tonics and ate lobster rolls on the great patio overlooking the sea.

Vince came back a week later. Vince came back three days after that. Vince kept coming back until he was coming daily. At first the intrusion was annoying. Archie resented the interruption to his self-centered wallow, begrudged feeling half awake at lunchtime, whenever Vince was in the house. Vince was strange and smart and funny; Vince was warm and nice and the opposite of his father. Vince made his mother laugh. Archie had forgotten what that sounded like, or felt like – to hear his mother laugh. Her eyes sparkled. Which was such a stupid cliché, but it was true. His mother's eyes crinkled and filled and caught the light. Every day Vince asked him what he thought about things; he actually cared about Archie's opinions. Vince prodded him, one question at a time, to imagine other lives for himself. What did he think about the law? What did he think about piloting his own hot-air balloon? What did he think about becoming a librarian?

"Archie," he said – it was Vince who had first called him Archie – "tomorrow you could be anyone. Imagine that."

It wasn't that Archie suspected his mother was having an affair with Vince, though he wouldn't have blamed her. He'd forgotten she could be this other person, this lighter person, who hummed to herself, who looked at the sky and the ocean, who noticed the world with something like hope, and he didn't care who or what was making it possible. Vince had snuck up on them both. In the span of a month, the weirdo next door had become a person who made their house feel, improbably, like a kind of home.

Archie loved that this friendship was theirs, together. It was like he had a secret other family, a family that was easy – not easy the way being an Arches already was, but easy because it was safe. Because it was made up of people who took care of one another.

Of course it couldn't last.

Of course his real family would ruin everything.

"In Pryce's collection," Archie told Tuesday, "is a copy of my father's will."

She made a face.

A skeptical face.

"You don't believe me?" he said.

"No."

"Why don't you believe me?"

"Because it doesn't make sense."

"Not everything does," he said. The lie was twisting his gut so hard he would've been embarrassed for her if she didn't notice. Why had he made the lie more complicated than the truth? Wasn't the first rule of lying to keep it simple?

"Granted," she said. "But it really doesn't make sense. That your father would give a copy of his will to a man he publicly and violently disliked. Unless Vince got a copy without your father knowing, which also – doesn't make sense. Unless—"

Archie sat completely still and watched. He was better at the second rule of lying: once you're down in the hole, stop digging.

"Unless this has something to do with your mother. Or your sister." She hooked her front teeth into her lower lip. "What does the will say?" Tuesday lurched forward, hands gripping the binder. "How do you even know he has it?"

"I saw it. Six years ago. Before I left." Tuesday looked at him. Archie looked back. He could have searched her face forever. Could have hunted the dark arches of her brows for clues, the full roll of her lips for hints. Her face didn't so much conceal the riot of the mind behind it as it did contain and frame it, like a door to a strange new universe. He hated that the only way he could talk about his life was to lie. He hated that he could lie, even to her. But Nathaniel was a fucking monster, and this was the only way he could think to throw her off the scent. "I don't know what the will says. I don't know if it reinforces or rewrites the succession plan at Arches Consolidated," he said. "But I think it's worth finding."

"That's what you want, from Pryce's collection." Tuesday didn't look away. She didn't blink. She flushed, again, with the satisfaction of knowing. Despite not knowing the half of it. "That's why you're playing this game."

"Yes," said Archie. He smiled because he couldn't help it. He was playing several games at the moment, and if he was very lucky, he might possibly win them all.

Something rattled twice.

"What's that?" asked Tuesday.

He looked away from her, over his shoulder, and the room felt cooler. His cell phone chatter-pulsed and flashed on the coffee table.

"You have a flip phone." Tuesday sat back with a smirk. "Like a drug dealer."

"Like someone who prefers to be slightly less—"

"Like a drug dealer."

"Available."

"And here—" She flipped through the white binder until she found the research she was looking for. She marked it with the tip of her finger. "*Boston* magazine says you're one of the city's five most eligible heirs."

"You're thinking of my brother." Only: *I am not my brother*, he thought. He tapped his chest with the tip of his own finger. Light, like it was funny. "I'm the spare."

"Who can tell you apart?" Tuesday said.

Archie shrugged.

Ha ha ha.

My brother and I.

The killers.

She nodded at his still-vibrating phone. "Are you going to answer that or let it go to your service?"

"I ordered delivery before I knew you were bringing takeout," he said, wondering, after all of this, how he could have any appetite at all. But he did. He could've eaten the table. He could've eaten the chairs. Just so long as it meant he could use his mouth, his lips, and his tongue for some activity other than lying. "How do you feel about Thai?"

Tuesday pushed back from the table and turned so he could see when she slid off one shoe, then the other. She dug her naked toes into the deep plush of the rug. Archie's face filled with heat.

"Still hungry," she said.

11

MUCH WORSE

On Tuesday morning, Mo popped her head over the wall of Tuesday's cube and asked her to step into her office.

There was no reason to suspect Mo's request was unusual – not considering everything else in Tuesday's life at that moment. Dorry had blown off tutoring, and when Tuesday did pass her in the vestibule that weekend, she was texting and giggling and bumping, gently, into the mailboxes. Then Dex – who'd been enthralled to learn, via text, that Archie wasn't Nathaniel but another Arches entirely (good lord, he'd texted, he's a mess, a perfect mess, how do you attract these ridiculous should-only-exist-in-Wodehouse imposter menfolk, and Tuesday had responded, he is literally the first man like this I have ever met) – had blown her off too. He had some funky irons in the fire that required his complete attention, and when she responded, ???, he'd replied, two can play the withholding game – which stung. She wasn't used to wanting Dex's attention, let alone wanting it and being rejected. It dropped her into a blue mood that only the developing Archie situation, in all its abject novelty, was capable of snapping her out of.

The Archie situation was a Situation. Archie had a *scheme*. A scheme to use Vincent Pryce's game to get back what he thought was his, or at least to make sure it didn't fall into his brother's nefarious hands – or something to that effect.

Tuesday knew he was still lying to her. But enough of the truth was out between them now that the difference was palpable. Archie was wearing his own skin. He was warmer and looser. For the first time, she knew she was playing Pryce's game *with* him, that even if there wasn't absolute honesty between them, their interests were aligned. They were ticking in rhythm, giving and taking.

"What's the point of this game?" she had asked him. "You knew him. What would Vince mean by 'seeking well'?" They'd moved on from the Thai to dessert – a pint of chocolate ice cream left in the freezer, which might well have last been eaten by Vincent Pryce himself. "What's the money for?"

"Use your imagination," said Archie.

"I know. That's what Pryce—"

"I *know*," said Archie. "I'm saying, there's no trick to it. Vince was big on imagination. On being able to step into other lives. Other futures. Other worlds. Imagining other things and people and ways of living and letting that . . . change you, I guess." He shook his head. "He was trying to get me to snap out of it."

"It?"

"My life. My life of obscene—" He scrunched up his nose. "Just – disgusting – waste. We didn't use our money to build anything, or help anyone, or make anything better. We used it to insulate ourselves, and it was suffocating. I mean – use your money however the hell you want, and if that's how you want to live, like, sure. But I didn't want to live that way. I don't."

"That's why you left."

"I have the Arches nose." He drew his finger down from his brow. "And I have the Arches hunger. But I did not want to live like an Arches. Like my brother. Or my father—"

Every time he mentioned his father, every single time, the part of Tuesday that knew how it felt to live with that kind of unfinished thought thrummed. She was dangerously close now to telling him what she hadn't told another soul – not for half her life. She almost said: That's what I recognized the first time I saw you. Not your brother but your father. Your father, and the weight of his absence. *I know.*

I know how it feels to be haunted.

But she didn't.

She left him not long after. She didn't kiss him. She wanted to, but she also wanted to prolong the inevitable, stretch that feeling between them like warm taffy, because *that* game was its own kind of satisfaction. All weekend, they texted. They sent jokes. Ridiculous ideas about how to play Pryce's game. How about a down payment on a precision driving machine? said Archie, and Tuesday replied, I'm not parking anything precision on the street in Somerville. Next she suggested they get drunk and clean out a dollar store. Archie thought that didn't entirely fit the brief. Let's spend it all on balloons, said Tuesday. Then WAIT HALT I'VE GOT IT, said Archie, followed by a picture of the green and red retro sign outside Modern Pastry.

I've always wanted to see what thirteen thousand dollars' worth of cannoli looks like, he said.

It looks like heaven, she said. Also if you're in the North End you're close to my office BRING ME PASTRY

And he *did*. That Monday, at three in the afternoon, Archie sent her a text that would have been deeply alarming in almost any other context, which was how Tuesday knew she had officially gone around the bend.

Look out your window

A small cardboard pastry box tied with blue and white string was sitting on the outside ledge of her cube's floor-to-ceiling window.

Yes, since confronting Archie on Friday night, Tuesday had become the kind of person who flirted stupidly via text. She felt a little delirious. But even in her delirium, she insisted on a plan: dinner on Tuesday night at Vince's condo. Archie would cook. They would decide what to do with the money, and what they would tell Lyle Pryce when they were granted their audience. Tuesday felt certain that, with all the energy they were bouncing off each other, she and Archie would come up with a plan that was as good as anyone's. As good or better, because Archie had known Vince, and Tuesday had met Lyle. They had an innately better hand than the forty-nine other players and teams – the *Globe* was cataloging and interviewing them daily – and they only needed to figure out how to play it well, together.

For that, they would use their imaginations.

Given all that, there was no reason for her to suspect Mo was calling her into her office on Tuesday morning for any reason other than to watch a new stupid cat video on YouTube.

Mo let Tuesday walk ahead of her and closed the door.

That was strange.

"Whoa," said Tuesday, sitting down. "What's up?"

Mo didn't say anything. She sat behind her desk, which, Tuesday noticed, was clean.

"Did you – straighten?" Tuesday rolled back in her chair – freely, unstopped by stacks of paper and old issues of *Town & Country*. "You only straighten when—" When someone important was stopping by. But why would someone important stop by for a meeting that would also include Tuesday? And Mo, sitting at her clean desk, tucking her hair behind her ear, looking—

Somber.

"Oh," said Tuesday.

"Do you get it now?" asked Mo.

"I get that it isn't good," said Tuesday.

"It's not good," said Mo.

"What—" Tuesday's mental files flipped, fluttered, shuffled like cards. All she felt was breeze. "What's going—"

Mo's door opened and three people joined them. The first, June MacRea, the big boss, the VP, head of the whole development office, took an extra chair Tuesday now noticed behind Mo. The second was a woman Tuesday didn't recognize. She was wearing a blazer over her dress and she wasn't smiling.

The third person was Nathaniel Arches.

He looked even sharper than when he'd taken her out to lunch. Glistening. Slippery, almost. Or maybe that was because, in the meantime, she'd gotten more familiar with his brother – his lumpier, softer, stranger brother. Nathaniel was an uncanny mirror now, bright and careless as a knife. He sat in the rolling chair beside Tuesday, brushing at his impeccable suit. This early in the day, he was practically dew-dropped with aftershave. He slotted his hands neatly together, finger on finger – his knuckles were raw, like he'd been working a heavy bag – straightened his shoulders, did not look at her.

Tuesday's fingertips went cold.

"We have an unfortunate situation," said June.

Tuesday had always liked June, though before this morning they'd hardly spoken a dozen words to each other. She was probably in her mid- to late sixties. She was slim, tailored, and wore a lot of tweed, and rumor had it that she purposely downplayed her skills on the golf course with male donors of a certain age – those male donors who agreed to go golfing with her in the first place. Because of this, Tuesday primarily felt frustration on her behalf. But at the moment, when it was becoming clearer and clearer that Tuesday was in some serious shit, what she felt was a gut-deep shiver of reverence.

"Tuesday," June said, and Tuesday twitched a little. "We have to let you go."

The coldness in her fingertips shot up both arms. She looked at Mo, desperate, not caring if it showed. She looked at the stranger, and thought, *HR*. She had to be from the hospital's administration. An impartial witness to make sure—

"We have evidence that you've spent a fair amount of office time and resources on a project not related to your employment here," continued June. "You violated patient privacy, accessing medical records for reasons unrelated to your job, which, as you well know, is illegal. Coupled with your recent publicity—"

"She means," said Nathaniel Arches, out of the side of his mouth, "those pinups in the *Metro*."

It was not Tuesday's imagination that both June and Mo bristled at "pinups." Which made everything clear: this firing was not their choice. Their hands were being forced. This firing was the express desire of Nathaniel Arches, because he could, because it was their job to do what the money wanted. And because Tuesday, like an idiot, had given him all the ammunition by – *holy shit*—

Mo opened one of her drawers. She pulled out the three-ring binder of research Tuesday had last seen on the dining room table of Vincent Pryce's Beacon Hill apartment.

"Do you recognize this?" Mo asked. She flipped the binder open.

"Yes," said Tuesday, though she didn't know how she still had the power of speech when all the air had been sucked out of her body.

She had left it.

Left it for Archie.

"Keep it," she'd told him. "Read it. Let me know what I missed."

"I sincerely doubt," he'd said, "that you missed much of anything."

"Except *you*," she said.

She'd trusted Archie to keep it to himself.

She had trusted him.

"You," said Nathaniel Arches, "are an odious woman."

Tuesday's hands and arms no longer felt like ice. Now they felt like rubber bands.

"I," she started, but her voice had evaporated. She tried to swallow, and when she continued it came out like a wheeze. "I am good at my job." She addressed June and Mo. "And I sincerely regret that I abused the tools of this job to perform a different task than what I was hired for. And I did." She made two fists. "I did everything you said. That was arrogant and careless, and I'm sorry. It's appropriate to fire me. It's egregious that this—"

Her pulse hammered.

"—it's egregious that this asshole gets to be here while you do it," she said, and Nathaniel laughed. "What did he do, bribe you?" She looked at June. "He brought you the binder and made you a deal, right? Fire me while he watches, and he won't sue? Maybe he'll make a gift? Six figures? Maybe more?"

Tuesday showed all her teeth to Nathaniel. "How much am I worth to you?" she hissed.

Mo's face was bright red. She looked anguished. "Tuesday," she said, "please don't make—"

"I won't," she said. "I understand why I'm being fired. I'll be fine. Six figures can do some good. I'm one person. One person, one person who is actually guilty, is an acceptable loss." She rested her fingertips on Mo's desk. "I would do the same," she said quietly.

"We have to ask you to clean out your things right now," said the stranger from HR. Her voice was surprisingly high. "Maureen will escort you out."

Tuesday nodded. She stood. Stepped over Nathaniel's outstretched legs, resisted the urge to clock him in the mouth with her elbow. The world was water. She was slow and far away. Mo brought her a cardboard box from the copy room.

One of her coworkers popped her head out of her cube. Her face asked *What's going on?* and Tuesday's face answered *Exactly what it looks like.* Into the box went her mug, her headphones. Her fuzzy leopard slippers. The Christmas photo of Ollie and Viv and Olive. The packet of Spam. The six pairs of shoes fornicating under her desk.

Pryce's obit.

She put on her scarf and her coat. She nodded at June and the woman from HR. She could see Nathaniel Arches through the glass front of Mo's office, leaning forward, elbows on knees, smiling with his eyes closed, like he was listening to a sublime piece of music.

Mo walked with her through the building's lobby. Tuesday couldn't look at her until they reached the revolving glass door. By then, Mo's eyes were wet. Whether they were tears of anger or sadness, and directed at whom, Tuesday didn't know.

"Mo," she said. "I'm so—"

Mo closed her eyes. "It was great. It was great research," she said. "I knew it was you. I could tell right away; no one else uses that many semicolons." She shook her head. "That was so dumb. So *dumb*, Tuesday. You *know* how dumb that was, don't you? For someone so fucking smart, how could you have been so *dumb*?"

"I know," said Tuesday. "I know."

"Don't do anything dumber," said Mo. "Now get out of here." She dropped her eyes to the polished marble of the lobby's floor. "Go on. Scram."

Tuesday hitched the box in her arms.

Her legs didn't feel like legs.

"How much?" she asked.

"How much what?" said Mo.

"How much did he pay," she asked, "to get me fired?"

Mo was gray, the color of heavy clouds. "You got yourself fired," she said quietly. "And he watched for free." Sudden, intense pressure rose up Tuesday's neck, flooding her face, pinching her temples. Tuesday's heart beat on either side of her throat. And Tuesday thought – how – how stupid she was to think she was worth anything at all. She pushed herself through the revolving door – with a box, so stupid, everything she did was stupid and worthless – and outside the day was crisp and sunny, the sort of perfect fall day she would usually spend taking a long walk to the North End for lunch.

Tuesday was neither ice nor fire. She was numb.

She made it as far as the little park just outside the building's entrance.

She set her box down on a bench and sat beside it.

And sat.

And breathed.

The park was empty except for the pigeons, the tough city birds – aggressive, bedraggled – that made it their home. She watched them flap around the feet of the benches, scrapping among cigarette butts for the last crumbs of the morning's muffins and donuts. Rats of the skies, Dex called them.

Oh God, her parents. Her brother. She was going to have to tell people she'd lost her job. No, not lost – it wasn't like she'd misplaced it, been let go, downsized with severance; she had behaved unethically and had thought she could get away with it. (Had she thought about it at all?) But she had been caught and fired. She deserved it. She truly did – even for her actual job, it was illegal to look at Nathaniel's medical records for any reason other than to confirm he'd been a patient. It was illegal to confirm, to write up, and to share with someone outside the hospital that he'd had extensive plastic surgery. She had violated his privacy. It didn't matter that he was an asshole. She was, in this situation, an asshole too.

The shame was sour and cold, and she was sore with it.

Could you collect unemployment if you'd been fired? She had savings, enough for a few months' expenses, but was she burned, tarred, marked now? Could Mo give her a reference? She had no master's degree, had a history BA, a minor in film studies, a ten-year meandering career writing, editing, researching, analyzing. She could get another job. Any job. She could buy her own insurance, thank you, Massachusetts. Shit. What about Christmas? Christmas was coming. Oh *shit*, what if she had to move back in with her parents – what if she had to work at the store – and she still had so many goddamn *loans—*

She put her head between her knees. She was not going to faint. No she was not.

Archie.

She sat up. Pulled her phone out of her bag and texted him. Her hands were sweaty.

Archie what the hell happened?

Are you ok?

Call me

How? How had Archie been so careless? Careless enough to give Nathaniel Arches the means, motive, and opportunity to kneecap and humiliate her, just because Nathaniel wanted to and just because Nathaniel could?

He didn't respond.

Archie, she texted again.

She had tapped, this is an emergen, when she heard a throat clearing.

She looked up. Nathaniel Arches was standing over her, red-knuckled fist to his mouth as he cleared his throat again.

Before that day, Tuesday hadn't realized there were so many distinct stages of shock. She'd felt cold fear. She'd felt loose, disconnected shame. Now she was – she didn't know what she was, only that her hands were shaking so hard she could barely hold her phone. Which was silent.

Because Archie wasn't texting her back.

"You never called," Nathaniel said.

Tuesday didn't respond.

"It's too late now," he said. "I've decided to go in a different direction."

Archie wasn't texting her back.

She glared at him. Goading was the only power she had left.

"Well." Nathaniel smiled at her. "I wish you all the best in your future endeavors." He walked toward a black town car idling at the same curb where he'd picked her up six days ago.

Six days.

She had wrecked her life in *six days*.

Told you, said Abby. **Told you this was how you died.**

Cold, thick and painful, poured across her shoulders.

This was not how she died.

No.

She didn't watch Nathaniel Arches go. She turned back to the little park instead. A ratty pigeon was sitting on the bench across from her. It cocked its head and cooed. It was a dumb bird, incapable of seeing humans as anything but droppers of food, but to be noticed at that moment, to be cooed at with what looked like tenderness, made a tiny bone inside Tuesday snap.

Her last thought, as helpless as the tears that followed, was that she wanted to talk to Dex.

◆

It was the second time in her life she'd cried in public. The first time, she'd had more than a pigeon for an audience.

She was in the final month of her sixteenth year. It was December, a week before Christmas break. The board in Mr. Mulrooney's homeroom was festooned with silver tinsel, and an antique print of Ebenezer Scrooge humbugging his way down a London street was stapled to the bulletin board above the assignment calendar. Abby Hobbes had been missing for almost six months. Tuesday had been communicating with her regularly, with and without Ouija assistance, for almost two.

It was a Wednesday. It was two weeks after Tuesday, failing to get any traction – or any response whatsoever – from the mysterious Detective Finch, had taken dramatic action. She had called the Salem PD multiple times, sent letters, identifying herself as a friend of Abigail Hobbes. She had some questions for Detective Finch. *For school,* she said, *for a project,* because she needed a reason that sounded more legitimate than *because I got a hot tip from a dead girl.* None of the messages she left with the desk sergeant and none of her letters were answered.

You know what you have to do, said Abby.

"Not exactly," Tuesday answered. "But I know what *you* would do."

The police department was a neat brick building on Margin Street, almost brand new, about a ten-minute walk from her parents' shop on Essex. It was a Saturday afternoon. She'd worked, under duress – it was supposed to be Ollie's day, but he had "something to do," which meant "a session of Magic: The Gathering at Chip's house that might yield a glimpse of Chip's hot older sister Hallie, home for semester break." As soon as Leon, the evening-shift guy, showed up, she bolted. Her entire plan was lifted from Mrs. Frankweiler's infamous mixed-up files. She would hide in the bathroom until the police station closed for the night, then sneak into the detective's office unnoticed.

She did not realize that a police station never really closes. She'd been crouching on the toilet in the public women's restroom, butt perched on the tank, one sneaker on either side of the horseshoe seat, calves cramping, for thirty minutes before she realized her mistake. She was going to have to improvise.

Tuesday left the bathroom. Loitered in the hallway. Assessed the situation. She could see the front desk and the front door. On the other side of the desk was a hallway with a sign that she couldn't quite read. The front door swung open and a disheveled-looking man, hair flying, patting down his pockets as if he'd already lost his keys, approached the front desk, muttering about goddamn parking tickets. The desk sergeant greeted him by name – "*Hey* DICK!" he said, laughing (because apparently even grown men found the word "dick" hilarious in any context) – and Tuesday moved. She slipped behind him – he was pretty tall, parking-ticket Dick – and down the hallway beyond. The sign, now that she was close, read RECORDS.

Not a bad place to start.

The door to the records office was locked. So there *were* parts of the police station that closed. She was surprisingly not nervous, even though she was definitely somewhere she shouldn't be, doing something she shouldn't be doing. She was excited. Excited almost to the point of laughing, and sort of pleasantly frustrated by the locked door. It was a challenge. It felt like a game. She wanted to win.

She swung her backpack around her shoulder to her stomach and unzipped the front pocket. Her wallet was inside. What could she sacrifice? She decided on her Blockbuster Video card; her library card was too precious. The Blockbuster card was still new and stiff, perfect for doing that credit card trick. She slid it along the frame between the door and the jamb, brought it toward the knob, and wiggled.

She could hear herself breathing.

She was breathing too loud.

Something in the latch caught, and she *did* laugh.

Holy shit, said Abby, **look what you did!**

"Hey—" said a voice behind her, quiet at first, and then, when the voice realized what it was seeing – a teenage girl breaking into the Salem PD records office with a Blockbuster Video card – it shouted "HEY!"

But Tuesday was already gone.

At that first, gentle hey, the fear and trepidation she should have been feeling all along exploded in her solar plexus. Adrenaline shrapneled through her and she *ran*. Her sneakers squeaked when she cornered into the front hall; her elbows, her knees, her heart pumped. She squeaked again by the front desk and threw the full weight of her body against the crash bar on the door, and if anyone had been on the other side, she would have pulverized them. But nothing got in her way. She escaped. She didn't turn around as she ran straight up Margin Street because she was exposed – the street was open sidewalks and strip malls. She would be easy to follow if she were being followed – was she being followed? She didn't have time to turn around and see. She ran and ran, all the way back to her parents' store, to Mooney's Miscellany, which seemed random at first, gasping for breath, holding herself upright on the postcard rack, sick, stomach-cramped, and panicked, until she realized some deep, lizard part of her brain had led her there to hide, had been too afraid to go straight home. A confrontation was already waiting. She had never gotten away at all.

She'd left the Blockbuster card in the door.

The store phone rang and Leon picked it up.

"Yup." She could barely hear him over the blood booming in her ears. "Yup. Yup." He looked at her. "Yup." Then he held out the receiver. "Yer ma," he said.

For a moment she thought she was going to throw up all over the floor of Mooney's Miscellany. Instead, she fainted. Fainted dead, and took the postcard rack down with her.

The consequences of her adventure, as her parents called it, were various and wide-reaching. She was grounded, for a start. "Immediately and without hope for parole," her father said, and her mother said, "For at least two months. We'll revisit for good behavior in February." Her parents escorted her to the police station to apologize, and to explain herself, to none other than the infamous Detective Finch. Finch had been catching up on paperwork that Saturday and, irony of ironies, *she* had been the shouter, the very person who caught Tuesday in the act, who discovered the incriminating Blockbuster card. She wasn't the cop who'd interviewed Tuesday over the summer, but she looked a little familiar – Tuesday might have seen her around Abby's house, talking to Fred, after. Mostly she looked pissed. She was short and stocky. Her cheeks had a permanent flush and some freckles, her nose was perky, her eyes very blue. She looked like an angry leprechaun. Tuesday figured she'd have to be pretty tough to be that short and that cute, not to mention that female, and still be a detective.

"Hello," she said to Tuesday. They were sitting in a room next to the chief's office. It was probably his special interview room, for when he needed to shake down people like politicians. It was way cozier than Tuesday had been expecting. The carpet was squishy and blue, the drapes were bright red and fancy, like bunting, and there were three framed seals on the wall. The middle seal was the Salem police insignia: an outline of a witch on a broom flying across a crescent moon, the founding year 1626, the words THE WITH CITY. The table was so shiny she could see herself in it.

"Hi," she said, looking at her reflection.

"Please look at me," said Detective Finch, and Tuesday looked up and murmured sorry.

"Sorry doesn't get either of us anywhere," she said. "An explanation does. What were you doing?" She didn't sound as pissed as she looked; she sounded concerned, curious, like she wanted to help. Maybe she always looked pissed no matter what she felt. Maybe her face couldn't help it.

"I was trying to – find information. A record on Abby. Abigail Hobbes." Tuesday tucked her hair behind her ears. This room made her feel like a little kid.

"Your friend. I bet it's been hard. I bet it's been very, very hard to lose a friend like that." Detective Finch sounded positively *nice*. "Has it been hard to feel okay? To feel like yourself, since?"

Tuesday nodded. She felt her mother's hand on her back.

She wasn't going to cry. She took a breath.

"Abby's dead," she said. "She was murdered."

Detective Finch was still.

Her parents went from stern and supportive to fully agitated. "What?" her mother said. "What are you talking about?"

"I don't have any proof and I don't have any suspects. But I know. I *know*," said Tuesday. She looked at Finch. "You have a theory. Don't you?"

Finch didn't flinch.

"Tuesday," said her father, hovering over her left shoulder. "That is a serious thing to say. I'm not doubting – *you*, per se, but – why? How do you know – we're all still hoping—"

"Fred isn't," said Tuesday, a little surprised by how nasty her voice sounded.

"What do you know?" asked Finch.

"Well." Tuesday swallowed. She was starting to feel more like herself, more grown up. It had something to do with the way Finch was watching her. "I know Abby wasn't suicidal. I know it could look like she was, but that's just how she dressed and what she loved. And I know she didn't do drugs and she wasn't in any kind of cult. And."

"And?" said Finch. "How do you know, about the drugs?"

How cliché does she think I was? said Abby.

"She told me," said Tuesday.

"She told you," repeated Finch. "She told you what? When? Was someone threatening her? Was she afraid? Did she have any boyfriends?" Tuesday shook her head no, no. No.

"I mean she told me – uh."

Put me in, coach! shouted Abby. **I'm ready! I can do it!**

"She told me a little before Thanksgiving."

Finch blinked.

"A little before—" Her father's voice skipped. "This. Thanksgiving?"

"She talks to me," said Tuesday. "All the time. It started – I have her Ouija board, and one day she just – said hey. And now she doesn't shut up, frankly."

Real nice, said Abby. **Like I have anything better to do than chat your ass off all day. I'm DEAD.**

No one was speaking. Finch had lost her seriousness, her intensity. She was looking at Tuesday coolly. *This* was what she looked like when she was legitimately pissed off.

"Oh Moonie," said her father. His voice was kind. Too kind. "Why didn't you tell us? We can deal with this."

Tuesday said, "I understand it sounds—"

And that was the moment Tuesday realized she'd opened the door to the Much Worse.

The Much Worse was gentle. The Much Worse was cottony and condescending. The Much Worse was *Oh honey*. It was *Don't worry. It's not your fault*. The Much Worse was a nice woman with glasses who took notes while Tuesday talked to her, tried to explain that she knew it sounded crazy and maybe it was, maybe IT was crazy, but Tuesday wasn't. Tuesday was fine. Tuesday was sane. Tuesday missed her friend, of course she missed her friend, but regardless of how she was processing her grief (or not), it didn't change the fact that *her best friend was dead and now everyone was more concerned with Tuesday being crazy than with finding out who killed Abigail Hobbes*. The Much Worse was Oh my GOD, why won't anyone believe me, why won't anyone listen, why won't anyone *do* something? *Why won't you help me find out what happened?* The Much Worse was one conversation after another, with her mother and father and her brother and that otherwise nice woman in glasses in her nice office that was so pale and nonthreatening it may as well have been fog. It was always the same conversation, but no one heard it. No one listened. No one believed her, and it made her so sad to be so misunderstood. To be so invisible. Tuesday felt herself floating away. She started to doubt or forget things about herself. It was like she'd woken up in a glass box, and the world was in another glass box, and the person she thought she'd been was in another glass box entirely, so everything was flat and cool and sealed under glass and she could see that other her, sometimes, from the outside. She could watch her own self screaming and pounding inside the littlest glass box, the one at the heart of her, and she would think, *That girl can pound and pound, but I bet that glass will never break.*

The Much Worse was her brother treating her like she would break, or had already broken, like she had to be kept on a high shelf and not be played with, ever, because if she broke any more she'd have to be thrown away. The Much Worse was the ghost of Abby Hobbes never shutting up, talking and talking and talking and not telling her anything she didn't already know.

The Much Worse was that Wednesday in Mr. Mulrooney's homeroom the week before Christmas break. Salem was a small town. It had been two weeks since she'd met with Detective Finch. She'd seen the woman with the glasses who took notes only once, but the rumors were already out. The stories. The information. She'd seen it doodled in Sharpie in the third stall of the second-floor girls' bathroom:

Someone else had decided this was too subtle, and clarified:

She had a test later, sixth period. Physics. She'd barely studied at home, and was trying to catch up before morning announcements when Santa Claus arrived. His pillow-stuffed costume filled Mulrooney's doorway, he ho-ho-hoed, shook his hips more than his belly, and proclaimed he had holiday cheer to deliver. Candygrams. Tuesday had never gotten one before, but then, she'd never sent one either. She turned back to her physics. Santa made his merry way around the room.

Then he placed a candy cane, tied with a red ribbon and a card, on the corner of her desk.

Tuesday's hands tingled as she pried open the card.

Someone had drawn a cartoon ghost, like the ghosts in Pac-Man, surrounded by stars. MERRY CHRISTMAS FROM THE GREAT BEYOND! DON'T GIVE UP.

It was signed *xo, Abby*.

It was cruel. It was bizarre. It was perversely everything she wanted to hear.

In Mr. Mulrooney's homeroom, on a Wednesday morning when she had never felt more alone, or less like herself, Tuesday cried. She covered her face with her hands and her shoulders shook and she cried, sort of but not really quietly, all through the announcements, and at least no one laughed at her. But no one helped her either. Not even Mulrooney.

She had disappeared.

In January, when the skies were gray and Salem was covered with dirty snow, she gave up. She couldn't do it anymore. She couldn't listen to Abby, couldn't pretend she wasn't crazy, because she didn't have the power or the energy to do anything about it even if it was all true. Even if Abby was murdered. Even if Finch had a theory. She could not be this girl anymore, this sad, breakable, hysterical girl, this girl she had never really been inside, but if that's what she looked like, she must be, right?

And Abby would not. Stop. Talking.

At thirteen minutes after midnight on a Friday, she slid the planchette over Abby's Ouija board to spell I'M SORRY. I LOVE YOU. GO AWAY.

Uh, Tues, said Abby. **For real?**

Tuesday spelled PLEASE LEAVE ME ALONE.

Abby took so long to respond that Tuesday wondered if it had really been that easy. Then she said, **You know, it doesn't work that way.**

Tuesday snuffled. Her head felt like it was peeling apart down the middle, halving like an orange.

"How does it work, Abby?" she said.

I'm part of you, said Abby. **Forever. You're like a radio – even if you're not tuned to the right station, I'm, like . . . here. Always.**

Tuesday didn't know what to say to that. It made perfect sense and no sense at all.

"Can I turn myself off?" she mumbled.

Yes, said Abby. **You know you can.**

Tuesday went to sleep. She didn't dream. When she woke up, Abby's voice was still there, fainter, more echo than anything, but when she asked how Tuesday was feeling this morning, Tuesday couldn't answer. She didn't feel good or bad or hungry or hot or cold or hopeful or worried or afraid or happy. She felt – nothing. She felt blank. She felt empty. She didn't want anything; nothing mattered, because there wasn't anywhere to go from here. She knew her name was Tuesday. She knew she had once loved witches and magic with her best friend, her best friend who taught her what it means to disappear, her friend whose body hadn't been buried but was probably dead, who didn't know who had killed her. Nobody understood or recognized who Tuesday was now.

Not even Tuesday.

She had lost herself.

12

CAUGHT UP

Dex didn't check his phone until he left the office at five – early for him on a Tuesday, but he had The Date and he was nervous about it. By the time he saw the text, or rather the *series* of texts, it was too late. The damage was substantial.

According to the time stamp, Tuesday had begun texting at twelve forty-three.

Hey

I have bad news

Dex?

Well I'm just going to tell you

I've been holding it inside for hours and I'm ready now so you're going to hear

What I have to say

The time stamp jumped a half hour, to one-fifteen.

I got fired

They fired me

Nathaniel ducking Arches turned over the binder of research
I did on his family

That I gave to Archie

I think the fucker sold me out

And of course that whole binder was like

A terrible violation of patient privacy

Hospital policy

General decency

Everything

So Mo fired me

Tuesday followed this with several rows of crying-face emojis.

I don't even blame her

My ass deserved it

God why am I so 🔥 FUCKING

🔥 DUMB 🔥

The time stamp then jumped to three-thirty—

I need alcohol meet me at McFly's as soon as you can

—and by four fifty-two had devolved into:

DEX DEX DEX DEX 🐬

WHERE ARE YOUUUUU I'm going to make some 👀 VERY BAD CHOICES tonight

I would hate for you to miss it 😎 💩

Dex didn't know which was more distressing: the fact that this was the single longest series of texts Tuesday had ever sent him, or the content of the texts themselves.

This was how Tuesday Mooney asked for help.

He flew to McFly's.

When he arrived fifteen minutes later, Tuesday was sitting at the bar. More like leaning against the bar on a stool, her body rubbery as a noodle, one foot propped on a red and white Staples copy paper box. A lit cigarette between her first and middle fingers sent a column of lazy smoke to the ceiling.

"You're not supposed to smoke," said Dex, because he was too shocked to say anything else. "I mean, inside. In here. Also, you don't smoke."

"I'm just holding it," she said. She knocked her head back toward the bartender, a tall guy with no hair and a gut that stretched the Sox logo on his T-shirt into a thigh-high. "Nick said it was okay." She waved the cigarette in the air. "It makes me feel so goddamn cool. I get it. I *get* it, Joe Camel. I feel like Bette Davis. *And* Joan Crawford. I feel like Baby Jane and Blanche had a baby, and she is me." She clenched her teeth in a terrible impression of, perhaps, Faye Dunaway *as* Joan Crawford. "I want to eat a man."

"Wow," said Dex. "I'm torn. You're super-fun right now but also clearly in a lot of pain." He looked at Nick. "Nick," he said, "we'll talk about your culpability later, but right now can I get some bourbon? Neat."

"We are not fucking around today," mumbled Tuesday. "No we are not."

Dex took his drink and Tuesday by the elbow and steered both to a high table in a dark corner. *My stuff!* she said, waving the cigarette at the Staples box, and Dex, understanding this, *this*, held all her worldly office possessions, dutifully retrieved it. He had never seen her quite like this. Her head literally lolled. She bobbed and jerked like a bird, weaving the cigarette through the air and exclaiming with glee at the smoke patterns. It had been a minor shock to see her intoxicated two Fridays ago, but this was something else entirely. This was self-medicating drunk, this was *it fucking hurts* drunk, this was *the only way I know how to survive being alive right now is legal poison in my body* drunk. Dex wasn't much of a hugger, or an expresser of earnest personal emotion – he was expressive, sure, his whole life was one extended urge to Madonna-style express himself. But when he really *felt* something, he was much more likely to keep it to himself, to keep it down deep, to turn it over and over in his soul like the Precious. Which, he had always assumed, was probably why he and Tuesday clicked in the first place. They suspected how deeply the other felt things, and it was almost too deep to talk about. So they didn't.

But after he set down her box – it was so light! – he wanted to hug her, hug her hard and not let go, and he thought, for the first time ever, that she might not stiffen into a block of ice if he tried. She might go boneless. She might cry. He almost went for it. He would have, if she hadn't stubbed the cigarette out on the table at that moment and followed it with a wet raspberry.

She turned to him.

"Well fuck," she said. "I'm already drunk and trivia doesn't start for hours."

"Obligatory question," Dex said. "Do you want to talk about it?"

Tuesday wiggled her nose. "Maybe? Ask me."

"I just did."

"Ask me a different, more specific question."

Dex slid a gulp of bourbon down his own throat.

"Okay," he said. "How do you feel?"

"Oh! That's easy!" She finger-flicked the crumpled cigarette off the table with an audible *fap*. "I feel awful. I did something bad. Am I a bad person?" He shook his head. "But I did something really bad. I snooped in Nathaniel Arches's medical records to satisfy my own curiosity, which is one hundred percent illegal, and also just kind of . . . gross. All because I got caught up—" She flapped her hands in the air. "Caught up in this bullshit, in the Archeses – es – Pryce, this *game*. I forgot I'm a real person with a real life who has real bills, and now I'm really mega fucking screwed."

Dex nodded. "That's good," he said. "That's surprising – uh, a surprisingly clear, mostly sane grasp of your situation."

"I need another drink," said Tuesday.

"Maybe later. Next question: what are you going to do now?"

"Obvies," said Tuesday. "Go to Disneyland."

"Seriously," said Dex.

"Seriously. By Disneyland I mean Pryce's funeral." She slammed her fist on the table so hard the bourbon jumped in his glass. "That – that *Archie*." She grabbed his sleeve, twisted her fingers deep in the fabric. "We were supposed to – tonight. But Archie ghosted me, Dex. I left him the binder of research and somehow his brother got it and used it to get me fired and now Archie's not answering my texts. He's—"

Dex had never, ever seen her like this.

"He disappeared," she said in a very small, very un-Tuesday voice. "Will you go with me? To the funeral?" She whispered, as though there was anyone else in the bar who might care they had a secret. "What should we do with our *combined* twenty-six thousand dollars?"

"Tuesday," Dex said, and cleared his throat. "Uh, you should know I—"

He didn't know, exactly, how to tell her.

He'd had a terrible day at work on Friday, and not just bored-to-death terrible, actively soul-blackening terrible. During a monthly meeting with the investment managers, meant to update the staff about trends – what they were buying, what they were selling or excited about – everyone had been jazzed about investing in a new pharmaceutical company with a promising treatment for type 2 diabetes. Because instead of looking at diabetes as something to cure, to manage, or as a symptom of something greater – instead of investigating genetic factors, or the industrial food supply, or, hell, big pharma's vested interest and influence in increasing diagnoses, or at the most basic level remembering that diabetes is a real thing that affects the lives of real individual humans – instead of doing *any* of that, Dex and his colleagues used *the fact of diabetes as a trend* to make money. And the more people who got diabetes, the more people who needed this drug, the more money Dex and his colleagues would make for their already wealthy investors, and they were so fucking pleased with themselves for being clever when what they really were was disgusting.

Dex felt disgusting.

So he took a very, *very* long lunch. He left the financial district, passed through Downtown Crossing to the Common, filling with students and escaping office drones like himself. Enjoying what could be the last warm Friday lunch break of the year, tossing Frisbees to each other on the rolling hills, sitting up on their elbows on blankets, leaning back with crossed legs on benches. The Thought that was always there, waiting in the wings, muscled its way to center stage in his brain: how had he become this person? This person who worked in an office selling promises, abstract ideas about money that he barely cared about – who made a living *exploiting opportunities*, which might as well have been investment code for *screwing people who weren't paying attention*? And he wasn't bad at it. Which wasn't a prerequisite for not doing it, but was its own bleak truth.

He did not want to make a living like this.

But he didn't know how else to live.

The other Dex, the showboater, the singer, the dancer, the idiot dreamer, wouldn't have a nice place in the South End. Wouldn't have this beautiful shirt. Or these shoes. Or his retirement savings, his daily freedom from want. *Ha*, he thought. Free from want. He was entirely *made* of existential want, and guilt, and this horrible flickering feeling of fading out, his self snuffing like a candle. He wanted to be himself again. He wanted all these other parts of him to be seen, to live beyond this narrow life.

He wanted to be of value to someone.

He thought about the game. About Vincent Pryce. A billionaire, self-made. He pulled Pryce's obit up on his phone. *I have arrived at death's doormat with a full heart and full pockets. I regret the latter.*

Dex looked up at the high sun. His heart was full, all right.

He knew how he was going to spend Vincent Pryce's thirteen thousand dollars.

"What," said Tuesday. "Dex. What's going on in your head? There's a lot going on."

"I've already, uh." He swallowed. "Committed the capital."

"What?"

"I spent it."

"You already spent your thirteen thou – you mean the funky irons? That you had in the fire?"

Dex curled away from her, though he wasn't ashamed. He

didn't regret what he'd done, which was refreshing. But Tuesday was so hurt, so tender at the moment, he had the feeling the faintest suggestion that he'd made plans that didn't include her would be an injury. All the years he'd known her, he had never once worried about hurting her. Tuesday was goddamn impervious, assured and contained, too remote to wound. But maybe all that time—

Maybe all that time she'd been pretending.

"Yes," he said.

She bugged her eyes at him.

"Are you – going to tell me?"

"Yes," he said.

"You're killing me, Poin" – she swayed – "dexter. I know ... I know I was a jerk, the way I kept the whole Archie-isn't-Nathaniel thing a secret. At first." She swallowed.

Dex thought, *Not unlike everything else that goes on in that deep dark pit of an inner life you've got there.*

"Sorry about that," she said. "It wasn't that I didn't trust you."

"I know," said Dex, not because it was true, but because that was what she needed to hear. Of course she didn't trust him. Of course Dex was lumped in with all the rest of humanity, in the great pool of Things Tuesday Mooney Doesn't Trust. But maybe, lately – lately it felt like that had been shifting. Just a little. Shockingly. But now, the person she didn't trust, if he was playing armchair psychologist – which, let's be honest, when *wasn't* he playing armchair psychologist? – was herself. What she didn't trust was that she meant something to other people. That she had the right to insist on her own worth.

"I didn't want to be wrong," she said. "And I just – wanted to keep it my own secret for a little while." She looked down at the table. "He brought me pastry."

"That asshole," said Dex. Making jokes was a reflex.

She covered her face with both hands.

"Okay!" He clapped his own hands together and she jumped a little. "I'll tell you! It's a crazy plan! Are you ready?"

She peeked over the tops of her fingers.

"I bought two bespoke suits," said Dex. "Of armor."

Tuesday lowered her hands.

"What?" she said.

"I bought two bespoke suits of armor."

"I guess I heard you the first time."

"Chain mail, breastplate, gauntlets, helmet with a big old plume. The whole ye olde Ren Faire package."

She dipped her head to the side. Opened her mouth and held it open. The edges twitched like she wanted to laugh.

Good.

"Let me explain," said Dex.

She *did* laugh.

"You'll recall I met Bert Hatmaker last week to return Lyle Pryce's beverage tumblers, at the library," he said. "He took me up to see the murals on the second floor. They're all – Holy Graily. Galahaddy. He expressed an interest in knights and quests, and also me."

"Called it." She mimed lifting a glass, an empty toast to her own wisdom.

"Yes, you're a genius. I'm going to ask him to go to Pryce's funeral with me. Tonight. I'm meeting him for drinks in—" He looked at his watch. "Fifteen. What he doesn't know is that drinks will then segue into a fitting for said bespoke suits of armor, from a costume designer I found online – be proud of me, I learned from the master – who lives in Malden, and paid double to work quickly. Because we need costumes for the funeral this Friday. Oh!" He'd almost forgotten. "He knew about the underground theater. He asked me if I'd found it."

Her eyes had been open with interest before, but now they nearly hopped out of her skull.

"Way to bury the lede," she hissed.

"But we knew he knew," said Dex.

"We knew he knew more than he was telling us," she said. "But we didn't know he knew. Now we know he *knows*." She smacked Dex on the forearm. It hurt more than he thought she meant it to. "He's Pryce's helper. Pryce's living agent." She stubbed her finger into the table like she was crushing another cigarette. "We're cracking this thing wide open. We're cracking it *tonight*. You text that man to get his cute butt here for a predrinks drink right now."

"Hold up," he said. "Just, wait a second. It's clear that Rabbit—"

"Rabbit? Did you – did you just call him *Rabbit*?"

Dex continued. "It's clear he knows at least a bit about what's going on. More than we do. More than Lyle, even. But he—"

Tuesday had not stopped muttering to herself. Dex heard "—not a person, he's a precious moment" and felt a strange stirring in his chest that could only be protective instinct. And not for Rabbit, or at least not Rabbit alone.

"Tuesday," he said. He turned her by the shoulders to face him. "You're my friend. For years now. But I've never seen you this – *caught up*." He flapped his hands as she had done. "You seem like you've lost not just your job, but your goddamned mind." Tuesday's face twisted. She cringed like she'd been struck, and Dex felt terrible, because that had been a low blow, even if it were true. He softened his voice. "I like this man. I like him a lot. I'm going to ask him to meet me here because I don't want to up and leave you, and I realize this has been the worst, just the worst day for you, but please." Dex took both her hands and squeezed. "Remember he's a human. Not a database or a file or a whole filing cabinet to dig through."

Tuesday sat very quietly and stared at him.

"All humans are filing cabinets," she said finally. "Some are just better organized than others."

"Tuesday."

"And some have way more files than others. Like, some have big fat files full of amazing shit."

Dex sighed.

As ideas went, this was not a great one.

"Poindexter." She squeezed his hands back. "I'll be gentle."

◆

A job and a mind were two different things. Just because she lost one didn't mean she was going to lose the other.

Bert – Rabbit – Hatmaker sat across from Tuesday Mooney on his own wobbly McFly's stool, drinking his own shitty bourbon. Sweating. His upper lip shone. The high line of his forehead glistened. He was sweating like a bastard in an argyle sweater vest, because it was sweater weather and Bert Hatmaker was the kind of bastard who would wear an argyle sweater vest and smile shyly at her like he didn't know she knew *everything*. Like he had any kind of poker face. Tuesday had a poker face. Right now she had a drunk face, which was close to her poker face but more assertive and – Bert Hatmaker was sweating all over whatever the opposite of a poker face is.

Tuesday hated him a little.

She didn't know why.

"Hey," she said. She interrupted the pie-eyes Bert was making at Dex and Dex was making back. "Hey, aren't you a music teacher?"

"Yes," Bert said, only it sounded like a question: *Yes?*

"How much does *that* suck?" Tuesday asked.

"Tuesday," said Dex.

Tuesday hoisted her arms and her shoulders so high she lost her neck.

"Just a *question*," she said. "Just trying to make *conversation*."

Bert glanced at her (mostly empty) glass, then over at Dex, who sighed.

"Parts of it suck," Bert said, turning back. "A lot. A *lot* of the job is disheartening. I knew that going in, though. No one chooses to be a music educator for fortune and glory. At least, not in the traditional sense."

"The sense of fortune as money," said Tuesday. "And glory as, what, renown? Respect? Fame?"

Bert nodded.

"So you're saying," said Tuesday, "that you feel underpaid? Undervalued? Underappreciated?"

"Well, of *course.*" Bert laughed. "I mean, every administration I've ever taught under considers the arts – all the arts, but music especially – essentially disposable. The first extracurricular subject to get the chop."

He looked, when he said this, genuinely pained, and Tuesday tried very hard not to listen to the sympathy ringing in her ears, which was next to impossible when she was drunk. When she was drunk, she was both her most anesthetized and her most sensitive.

And Rabbit, she could tell – Bert – whatever – she'd noticed it at brunch, but now it was pulsing off his body in waves: *he* was sensitive. Probably, as a kid, too sensitive. But he'd grown up into this man – this Rabbit – who could sit in a bar with a man he liked and that man's drunk and unpleasant friend, and treat both, simultaneously, like they were worth his attention and respect.

He believed other people were valuable, and made them feel it.

She felt the corners of her eyes prick.

Rabbit had the capacity to really love Dex, if Dex didn't fuck it up.

"But the other parts," Rabbit was still saying, "the parts of the job that are actually about the music – watching a kid blow her guts into a trombone and figure out how to move metal, to bend air into sorrow, madness, pain, joy. I love that. I *love* that. That, most of the time, makes up for all the other bullshit."

"Other bullshit," Tuesday murmured. The word got stuck in her brain.

All of this bullshit.

"And what do you do, again?" asked Rabbit.

He couldn't have known. He hadn't meant to bury a letter opener in her heart, a blunt knife designed for opening things, but he had done exactly that.

So she opened.

"I dig. I find. I take what isn't mine," she said. "I share secrets."

Rabbit made a *huh* face. "So you're a spy?"

Tuesday saw her opening. "Takes one to know one," she said.

Rabbit's eyes narrowed.

"We know," she said lightly. "We know you know about Pryce. And now that we know, and we can only assume you don't want anyone else to know, we want to know everything. Else. So we can all know what we all know."

Rabbit looked at Dex, half amused, half confused. Dex looked back.

His face said, *Never mind the crazy girl.*

"Oh my God," she said, pounding her fist on the table so hard the silverware jangled in its plastic Sam Adams bar caddy. She pointed at Rabbit. "We know."

"Tuesday," said Dex.

"Stop playing," Tuesday said, "stupid *games*."

"Tuesday," said Dex, "we talked about thi—"

"What did he give you?" Tuesday asked, burning now, furious. She hurt all over, so she asked Rabbit again, her voice turning into a shout, "Why? Why did you do it?"

"I—" Rabbit began.

"You don't have to tell us," said Dex.

"Yes he does," said Tuesday.

"No, he doesn't," said Dex, "not when you're being such a bitch—"

"No," said Rabbit. Firm, loud enough for Nick at the bar to look up from his copy of the *Herald*. "No, I should tell you. I should – oh my." He covered his mouth with his hand. His eyes leapt from Dex to Tuesday.

Back to Dex.

Back to Tuesday.

"You have to promise," Rabbit said.

"I promise," said Tuesday.

"You have to *promise*," Rabbit repeated, "that I can trust you. Not to *tell* – I mean, *I've* been dying to tell. For weeks." He dropped his voice to a harsh whisper. "Dying, but freaked, because I—"

"Broke the law?" whispered Tuesday.

Rabbit turned a whiter shade of pale, which was goddamn impressive given he already had the pallor of a cocktail napkin. He *was* sensitive, maybe even – still, in adulthood – a goody-goody. "I'm the banker," he said.

"No," said Dex. "*I'm* the banker. Or at least I work with the bankers. You—" He gestured up and down in the space between them, trying to indicate everything – everything – about Rabbit, from his fancy sneakers to his wrinkled trousers, his argyle to his slightly overgrown Caesar. "You are not a banker."

"I'm not *a* banker," said Rabbit. "I'm *the* banker. For Life After Death. I was always the banker, when I'd go over and—" He clasped his hands and drew lower on his stool. He took a deep breath. "Vince and Lyle and I had a standing game night. Just the three of us. Lyle's parents are dead. I'm the closest friend she carried over from her old life to her new one – she wanted Vince and me to know each other. So we played games.

Mostly board games, parlor games. Puzzles. Cards. Parcheesi. Backgammon. Hours and hours of Monopoly. Vince *loved* Monopoly. And I was always the banker. I like being the banker, keeping everything sorted and neat and running smoothly. Vince said I was the straightest arrow he'd ever met."

"Pun intended?" Tuesday muttered, and Dex kicked her under the table.

Rabbit ignored her. "One night, Vince pulled me aside and told me about the aneurysm. That he could drop any day, at any time. What did he say – something like, he was 'going to die, soon, and for the rest of his life.' He needed my help." Rabbit held his hand flat against his chest, like he was pledging allegiance. "God help me, I'm a sucker."

No fucking shit, Tuesday thought.

"So what did he ask you to do?" Dex said, leaning closer, chin on his curled hand.

"Set up that fake brick wall in Park Street, for one." Rabbit ran his hand through his hair. "That was – terrifying. Vince gave me bribe money and a contact, an old lady who'd worked for the T forever but hadn't had a raise in years. Told her I was an artist, like Banksy. She said she loved Banksy, turned the security cameras away long enough for me to slip down the tunnel with a duffel of quick-drying cement, fake bricks, that stuffed mannequin and jester's cap. I've been waiting for the Boston PD to kick down my door for weeks."

"That's – *that's* why you looked so familiar at brunch," said Tuesday. "You were there."

"Where?" said Rabbit.

"There. In the T." She remembered now: a girl playing tenor saxophone for change on the platform, a man dropping a dollar bill in the girl's open case. "On the night the obituary was published, when Archie—" It stung. It stung like a black fly to say his stupid name. "When we found the first clue."

"Well, yeah. Of course I was there." Rabbit kind of smiled.

"I'm the banker. It's my job to make sure the game runs smoothly."

"Was it your job to make the underground decoder room?" Dex asked.

"We did that first. Vince and I, together. He owns the building. Vince sat in the middle of the room and pointed, and I ran around and painted all the symbols." Rabbit's smile went full grin. "That was a *blast*."

"What else?" asked Tuesday.

"What else what," said Rabbit.

"What else did you do?" She lurched toward him across the table and her brain sloshed in her skull. "What else have you done?"

He counted on his fingers. "Chalked the code on the outside of the Steinert building. Printed and left funeral invitations all around town, with a few strategic anonymous comments – on Reddit, Twitter, Facebook – asking the crowd to spread the word. Hired the caterers and the band for his funeral. Booked the permits, so we can have a big party on Boston Common." He rubbed his hands together. "A few other things that I swore to a dead man I would never tell, until the time was right."

"A few other things that you didn't even tell Lyle?" said Tuesday.

Rabbit sat up straight. He shook his head. "She knows I'm the banker. I couldn't not tell her that."

"You didn't answer my question. You didn't say *why*," said Tuesday, as Dex was shushing her.

"I've had some odd things happen to me," Rabbit said, "over the course of my life. I've learned to embrace the mysterious. Because the strange, the extraordinary – those experiences that make you look at the world like you've never seen it before, really pay attention to it – the strange changes you. Shows you new things about yourself. About life. Other people."

Tuesday huffed. "Get to the point."

"The point," Rabbit said, "is that Vince was strange. And Vince made Lyle, one of my favorite people, happy. The happiest I ever saw her. I did it because he was dying and needed my help. Strange called, and I answered."

"You did it," said Tuesday, cold, "because he asked."

"Correct," said Rabbit.

"He didn't – he didn't pay you any money."

Rabbit shook his head.

"At all."

"Nope," said Rabbit.

"A dying bajillionaire asked you to commit assorted acts of light criminal mischief," Tuesday said, "and you did it." She crossed her arms. "For free."

It didn't make any sense.

Or did it?

She didn't know.

She did not know.

She felt sick and sad. There sat Rabbit, an adorable fuzzy bunny of a person, and Tuesday still couldn't say why, but she could barely stand the sight of him. The fact of him. And Dex was twittering at him, glowing, reflecting the rays of Rabbit's sainted selflessness.

"You are too good to be true," Dex said.

Tuesday watched them smile at each other, and if she hadn't been drunk, if she hadn't been soul sick, if she hadn't been predisposed that day to find everything good and sweet and objectively optimistic a terrible crock, and if she hadn't felt so keenly, at that otherwise cozy table, that she was the odd one, the invisible one, alone on the outside always always always, Tuesday might have been able to control herself.

But she was drunk and soul sick and predisposed to find everything good and sweet and objectively optimistic a terrible crock.

"Rabbit," she said, "you are full of shit."

"Tuesday!" said Dex.

"But it's been nice meeting you. Knowing you" – she looked down at her watch – "for the twenty-five minutes left before Dex self-destructs this relationship. I hope you like paying attention to him, because he needs *someone* paying attention to him more desperately than he needs any other thing in the universe." She smacked Dex's arm. "I'll be waiting over here, like always, your relationship methadone, for when the high wears off."

She lifted her glass. "Cheers," she said.

◆

Dex and Rabbit, outside in full dark, McFly's behind them, walked down the uneven bricks of Charles Street toward the Common, looking for a cab. Dex was fuming. Normally, he didn't fume so much as seethe, quietly, privately, until the trigger for his rage dissipated: slow walkers, distracted tourists, people who clogged up the left side of escalators by standing when they ought to have been climbing – so, really, anyone who impeded the speed of his movement through the world.

But this was a good, legitimate fume. And *Tuesday* had brought it on. Tuesday, his oldest adult friend. Who had been acting lately like she wanted to be closer – who had, just today! At a moment of personal crisis! *Reached out to him!* It was almost possible to imagine they were, at last, going to be – well, let's not get carried away – *better* friends. These facts made his fume much more intense. His *better friend* had not only acted like an asshole to the man he was (casually, why even label it) dating, she had acted like a complete asshole to *him*. Dex usually loved parading his paramours around Tuesday. Not only did he value her critical opinion, but she made him look phenomenal by association, that he should count this brilliantly weird woman as one of his intimates. And, sure, maybe it was easier to be mad at her for being cruel than it was to feel guilty about making funeral-going plans that did not explicitly include her (though of course, of course, they would go together) ... on the day when she lost her job because of this insane game. This game that Dex brought to her attention, not that she wouldn't have found out about it herself, but *he* had wanted to play. He had egged her on. He had handed her the rope to hang herself.

And she had turned around and shot him in the face.

He didn't know what he did or did not owe her, but he was fairly certain he hadn't deserved *that*.

"Hey," said Rabbit, nudging him. "Are you okay? That was – rough. Back there."

Hell.

"I'm not an attention whore," Dex said. "I mean, I like attention. Who doesn't."

Rabbit said, "Okay."

"I'm just – what Tuesday said. That's not why I – that's not." Only it was.

Of course it was.

"Dex," said Rabbit, "I know. I grew up with theater kids. Who became theater adults."

"And I'm not, like, self-destructive."

Only . . . he was.

She knew exactly who he was.

"She's not normally like that. That's not her." (Only: he knew her too; and while that wasn't all of her, it *was* her. She was never not herself.) "I knew it was a bad idea to invite you to the bar. She got fired today," Dex said. "Because of this goddamn game."

"What?" Rabbit's feet stopped.

"She fucked up, but she fucked up because she got caught up. In Pryce and the Archeses and all this – *this*." Dex kept walking. He heard Rabbit's feet start up behind him. "And now *she's* self-destructing."

"We don't have to go out tonight, we can—" Rabbit touched his elbow. "You could go back to her."

Dex shook his head. He didn't want to. And Tuesday was already gone. "She's going home," he said. "She *should* go home. She's been different lately. Like . . . off-her-meds different." He sighed.

"What's her story?" Rabbit asked softly, and Dex had to shrug his shoulders.

"She's from Salem," he said.

"What does that have to do with anything?" Rabbit asked. "Unless she's a witch."

"She's pathologically independent. She knows *everything*. Other than that, she's a mystery," Dex said. "I honestly – I wish I did. Know her story. I wish she'd tell me."

"When was the last time you asked?"

Dex stared straight ahead and blinked. "I'm sorry," he muttered. "This night hasn't gone exactly as planned."

Rabbit perked. "There was a plan?" he said. "Beyond drinks?"

"There still is," Dex said. The thought of salvaging the night, of the surprise still to come, lifted something in his chest. "We're a little late, though."

"For what?"

"First, I have something to ask you."

They didn't stop walking. Rabbit moved closer, brushing his arm against Dex's.

"Fire away," said Rabbit.

Dex had asked men to parties before: holiday gatherings for work, weddings – once, he'd even bought two tickets to one of Tuesday's benefit galas for the hospital. But this felt different. This all felt different, and he couldn't say why, other than – all of this was different. All of this, with Rabbit, in his life at this precise moment, was familiar but unlike anything that had come before.

"Will you be my date to the funeral?" he asked. It came out all in a rush. "If the banker can have a date, that is."

Rabbit slid his arm through Dex's.

"If you're okay with meeting the banker at the funeral, then yes, the banker can."

"I've never dated a banker before," said Dex. "I've generally made a point not to."

"Is that the plan? The whole plan?"

"No, there's more." He reached into his coat pocket for his phone. "I got us costumes," he said.

He felt Rabbit's arm tense.

"What?" said Dex.

"I already have a costume," Rabbit said. "Vince – had something in mind."

Dex sunk a little. But only a little. "You don't even know what it is yet." He turned the image on his phone up toward Rabbit's face. "Ever had a bespoke suit before?"

Rabbit gasped, then laughed, then let it die. He clutched Dex's arm.

"Hey," he said. "Hey, stop for a second."

They were at the corner of Charles and Mount Vernon, in sight of the 7-Eleven, with its fancy wood-and-gold-leaf sign, because the tony denizens of Beacon Hill had decreed that even the 7-Eleven in their midst mustn't look cheap.

"Look at me," said Rabbit, and Dex did, and saw that Rabbit looked absolutely awful.

Guilty.

"Stop," said Dex. "It's fine that you already have a costume for Friday. We'll wear these – Saturday. Or next Halloween. Or around town, for, like, kicks."

Rabbit snorted. He still looked distraught.

Dex continued. "And I didn't tell you about Tuesday getting

fired to make you feel bad. It's incredible what you did for Vince. Scurrying around in the T. Setting up that theater underground." Rabbit blushed. "*You* didn't get her fired. Sure—" Dex turned his palms up. "Did you create the basic circumstances that eventually led Tuesday to become the architect of her own downfall?"

Rabbit winced.

"You're just one person. You don't have the power to get her fired, but you're acting like a Swiffer for guilt. Does the guilt naturally cling to you? Are you Catholic?"

"No," said Rabbit, "but I get that a lot."

Dex beheld him and thought, *It's a good thing you never worked in finance, because that hyperdeveloped conscience of yours would have been the death of you.*

"You'd make a terrible real banker," is what he said.

◆

Tuesday sat on the cold wooden bench at the Charles/MGH station and waited for the train.

The station was elevated, outside and open to the air; the tracks followed the Longfellow Bridge across the Charles, carrying passengers between Boston and Cambridge. If the sky hadn't been so overcast, and the city lights so ambient, she might have been able to see stars. She was still drunk – she'd consumed enough booze tonight to remain drunk for the next two days – but what she felt more than anything was—

She didn't know.

She felt slack. Tired and grumpy. She should have been satisfied, full up with the scoop that Rabbit was the banker, and yet she didn't; she felt bad. Dex was pissed at her. He was right to be pissed at her. But she was pissed at him too, and hurt, because he was going to fall in love. Dex was going to fall in love with Rabbit. Move in with him. Maybe even get married;

so long as he didn't move out of Massachusetts, Dex was the marrying kind. She could see it clearly, and she was thrilled for him. She was happy he had found what he'd been looking for, but she was worried too – selfishly worried – that Dex would go away. That she'd just picked her head up and realized what knowing Dex, having Dex as a friend, meant to her, and now – *poof!* Gone.

She was a monster. She was a cruel monster to be mad at him for being happy, for being worried that things would change. And – think clearly, Tuesday, think: Dex wouldn't *abandon* her. And hadn't she herself been anxious, two weeks ago, that Dex was getting clingy? Jesus, what was her problem? She was a mess. Life was change, constant change and uncertainty, and she couldn't help it, despite knowing this was just the way things were – she didn't know how to understand this irrational—

Fear.

She sniffed. She was cold. Her coat was too light for mid-October, but she hadn't anticipated being out this late, because she hadn't anticipated being fired this morning, because she hadn't anticipated being caught, and she hadn't anticipated Nathaniel Arches or Archie – she hadn't anticipated Archie, period. She hated him. A lot. She wanted him, or she had, a lot, when she left Pryce's apartment on Friday, and left them both hanging, wanting more than either of them had already given. She wondered again, for half a second, if something awful had happened. If he hadn't ghosted her on purpose. If Nathaniel – had done something.

She was too exhausted to go back up the Hill to Vincent Pryce's apartment, to see for herself. But she should try texting Archie again.

She sat up, reached for her phone, then got dizzy and super-extra-tired and decided to snuggle her Staples box instead. She laid her head in the crook of her arm.

The outbound platform was empty. A train had pulled away as she was stepping on the escalator, and even if she'd cared enough to run, she would have missed it. Now she had to wait. Though not for long – the announcement had just told her that the NEXT TRAIN TO ALEWIFE was NOW APPROACHING, which was nice but unusual. It was past rush hour. The trains weren't supposed to come this frequently.

"Your lucky day," she told herself.

She felt a rumble and closed her eyes until the final brake screamed. Then she stood. She had positioned herself perfectly to walk straight into one of the opening doorways.

The Red Line's cars were huge, each one a long metal breadbox. She was the only passenger on board. She decided to sit in the middle seat with her back to the platform, so she could look at the city skyline as the train crossed the bridge.

It wasn't until the doors thumped closed that she realized she'd left her Staples box on the bench.

"No," she murmured, standing, staggering as the car jumped, jerked, and caught. She hooked her arm on the pole closest to the entrance and accidentally swung around it so fast that she smacked hard into the door. "No," she said again, but yes: there, visible through the scratched window, was her stuff, abandoned on the bench. There were her slippers and her Spam and her pictures and that brand-new box of Rollerball pens that she'd chucked in at the last minute, because she freaking loved those pens and it wasn't like they could fire her a second time, and the car was moving faster, faster, the train left the station, the train was over the bridge and her box was gone and for one second she thought about pushing the emergency call button or yanking that silver lever that was supposed to do something but she suspected did nothing – but it was just stuff. Things. Objects. They weren't important. And yet, in their abandonment they suddenly felt like the most important, most symbolic artifacts of her life, as if that box held everything she was or had been or even liked about herself, and she had been careless enough to lose it.

She had been careless.

She wobbled back to her seat. The car braked and she lurched hard to the right, an object in motion trying to obey Newton.

The intercom fuzzed.

"Traffic ahead," said the conductor. "We'll be moving shortly."

"Oh fuck you," she told the empty car.

The intercom clunked off.

Tuesday folded herself in half, knees up to chest, arms tight around her shins, heels balanced on the edge of her seat. All around her, the car was breathing. Humming, huffing, electric, pneumatic.

She rubbed her eyes. Peeked over the top of her knees out the window opposite, across the other track and the Charles River beyond. There, visible through the low glare, was the Boston skyline, all six inches of it, from the Pru to the Hancock and back again. It was little but she loved it. She did. Oh, she did she did.

With a sudden sigh, the electricity, the fans, the wan fluorescent lights in the car, all died and Tuesday was alone in the dark on the train on the bridge.

The buildings in the city beyond got brighter.

Who needed real stars? Those lights would be her constellations.

She crossed and knelt on the opposite seats, propped her head in her hands, and looked out the window. Tuesday loved being alone. She always had. As a kid, it had never scared her, even after Ollie accidentally locked himself in the closet in the spare bedroom and was crying so hard when they found him that her dad had to help him breathe into a paper bag. In fact, because that incident guaranteed her brother would never come looking for her there, Tuesday started hiding in the closet on purpose. Snug in the back, between a box of Christmas decorations and a shoe rack that had been repurposed for keeping winter gloves accounted for and matched, she read books and drew cartoons and wrote poems that she didn't care if anyone else ever read. That time alone in the dark, time alone with her self, traveling near and far through books, living in her mind, was what gave her the strength to go out and live in the real world.

And there was no place on earth like a city for being alone. That was why she moved to Boston in the first place: no one there knew, when she first arrived, that she was Tuesday Mooney and that for a while she had talked to ghosts. The city had remade her into a glorious unknown, and she had enjoyed, for years, the perfect company of strangers.

She pressed her hand flat against the window and felt cool, solid glass.

She loved, and felt loved by, this city.

The train popped, flickered – once, twice – then burst back to life beneath her. In the sudden fluorescent glare the skyline disappeared and all she saw was a face reflected in the window.

A pale face with deep-set eyes that she didn't recognize.

It was the first time since Mo fired her that she'd had to look at herself.

"Kendall MIT," said the intercom. "Next stop, Kendall MIT."

The car began to move, but Tuesday stared, hard, at the face.

It was the face of someone who had broken the rules and been fired. It was the face of someone who had no job, no income, no way to continue to pay to be a part of this city she loved. It was the face of someone who didn't know what she'd do or who she'd be tomorrow if she wasn't a researcher or a commuter or a nine-to-fiver. And now, looking at this other woman, she realized she'd *liked* being those things. Had loved them maybe. Her boredom, her curiosity, and her restlessness, her desire to play that stupid game wasn't worth *this* – this feeling of being so completely outside, unwanted, unknown – this wasn't what she'd wanted. What had seemed boring once had become infinitely interesting, essential even, now that it was gone.

It was the face of someone who had been cruel to her friend.

It was the face of a woman alone.

It looked haunted.

It looked dead.

The train followed the tracks as they dove back underground, and took Tuesday down with it.

13

DEATH AND THE NEIGHBOR

Dorry pulled her cheek flat. Her hand, the hand holding the eye pencil, was shaking. She had never purposely put anything this sharp near her eye before, and she had three days to get this right. Three days until the funeral, to practice her makeup. Three days to make her costume perfect. Ned had a theory that the costumes were part of the game, that what they wore to their audience with the widow was important. "We gotta dress the part," Ned said. "The part of what?" Dorry asked, and Ned said, "The part we want." Then he wiggled his fingers in the air like a magician.

"Okay," she told her reflection. "You can do this."

She pulled down the right side of her face. Pressed the sticky tip of the eye pencil against her lower lid, starting at her tear duct, and pushed, gently. The point was surprisingly soft. She traced the bottom of her eye and stopped, blinked, and then drew a small spiral on the flat of her face above her cheek, curling off the outside corner of her eye.

It looked kind of . . . amazing.

Bolder now, she closed her eye and traced the edge of her top lid – it was a lot harder, because she didn't want to press down into her eyeball, and her lid kept twitching – and then did the same to her left eye, without the spiral off the bottom. She stood back. She couldn't believe how grown-up a dark smudge around her eyes made her feel. Looking into the mirror was like looking into the future, her own future, and it was exciting and terrifying and she wished her mom could see it. She wished her mom could see a lot of things, but this especially.

She was wearing black tights, her black Docs, a black skirt, miniish – it was higher than her knees, but her butt was covered. She didn't know how much bending or squatting or climbing she would have to do in it, and she wanted to be prepared – a black tank top, and a too-big black denim jacket she and Ned had found yesterday at the Garment District for fifteen bucks. The final touch, other than the makeup, was the necklace: a heavy silver ankh on a piece of black leather. It had been her mom's. She'd found it a long time ago, stashed in the same box as her mom's *Sandman* comics.

Her hair wasn't quite right. It was still *her* hair, dark brown and straight and flat unless it was humid. She spread her fingers, rooted them close to her scalp, and pushed up on both sides of her head.

"Death's got way bigger hair," she told her mirror-self.

She was going to need hairspray. Or some kind of gunk. Her mother had used makeup, but not much for her hair. Her father's idea of personal care products started and ended with toothpaste and soap. Mish, back at her old school, had been getting into complicated hair junk when Dorry left, but it had been a long time since Dorry had talked to her, and it would be way awkward to text her about this.

Ned? Ned knew all sorts of things. Because he was a year older, and because he was the kind of person who collected information, and knew stuff that didn't apply to him, like – he probably did know about junk for long hair even though he didn't use it himself. They'd taken the 85 after school yesterday, on Monday, to go shopping for costumes for the funeral. Ned spent the whole bus ride talking about all the ideas he had. He needed help choosing. He couldn't decide how literal to be. "Like," he said, "do I dress up as Poe, you know, with a white cravat, suit, like a stuffed bird on my shoulder – but I bet a lot of people will go as Poe, it's obvious, it's, like, *pedestrian*. So do I go literal as a black cat? Or do I go comic nerd as, like, the Black Panther, with the – Wakanda!" He made two fists and crossed his arms at the wrists. They were sitting in the first row of seats at the rear of the bus, where the floor was higher, raised over the back wheels, so it felt like they were sitting in a balcony. It was easier, side by side. Dorry couldn't look at his face, which was good, because whenever she looked at him, she felt painfully shy and goofy. Whenever she looked at him, she remembered everything they'd done together, the very day they met. Riding the T downtown. Slipping quietly into the chalk-marked building, and down the stairs, and into that room, that beautiful disintegrating room Dorry had seen on Ned's phone. They were alone, but they could tell other people had been there. The bottom drawer of a big green filing cabinet was half open, half full of envelopes.

And money.

They were going to take it and go when Dorry noticed the ankh painted on the cabinet, and the word painted below it: LIFE. Ned got it before she did. Ned's brain jumped: the chalk on the outside of the building was a code, and all around them, on the walls – like the giant crumbling mural beneath the stairs – were the solutions. Ned's face, when he figured it out, was almost too much; he shone like a lightbulb. They found a generator and some lights, but even if they hadn't, Dorry suspected they could have found every last symbol in that room from the glow emanating from Ned alone.

He was still shining, on the way to costume shopping. Wound up and electric, splashing, spilling over, and Dorry was shrieking laughter on the inside, caught in the spray. "I don't remember the last time I really dressed up for Halloween, put some thought and effort into it," Ned said. "So it feels big. I don't want to blow it. You know?"

"I think you want to keep in mind," said Dorry, "that the costume should be comfortable. Because who knows what we'll have to do." She caught her breath. "To play our hand, I mean." Then she risked looking at him. He was watching her, nodding his head now, eyes half-masted; he was calling her smart. Way smart, girl, he said, and she had to face forward again because she was going to snort-laugh and that would be the end of *that*. She looked down. Peeking out of the bottom of his jeans were yellow-and-orange-plaid socks.

She couldn't believe that this guy thought *she* was cool. That *this* guy was the guy she'd had a secret adventure with. It was beyond. *Beyond*. She threw herself into it, because sooner or later Ned was going to figure out Dorry was just Dorry, that she was, at best, medium cool, and she wanted to enjoy this wicked-cool boy wanting her attention as long as it lasted.

And it would last at least as long as it took Dorry to introduce him to Tuesday.

Dorry fluffed her hair again. It fell, resolute, straight down. Tuesday probably had some kind of hair gunk.

She was embarrassed to go over there. She was scared to talk to Tuesday. Things were still strained, and Dorry knew she'd made them worse by skipping Tuesday Thursday. Not feeling good, cancel? she'd texted, which was a total lie, but there was no way she was going to text the truth: *squashed in rush hour on the T, $13,000 in my bag, Ned's arm against my arm is super-warm.* She was vaguely grossed out by what she'd done, name-dropping Tuesday to get in with Ned, and also by the fact that she had no intention of introducing them, or telling Tuesday that Ned even existed, or that Dorry was his partner and would be attending Pryce's funeral as his date (!), until – she didn't exactly know. Until it was too late. Until they were all at the funeral, and there was nothing to do but see it through to the end.

Dorry had information. The information gave her power. The power to move people around on the board, move them to the spaces that allowed her path – her path to the Earhart goggles, to the dream, the chance of seeing her mother again – to be clear. It would be dangerous to go next door and ask Tuesday for big-hair styling tips. It would be the first maneuver that might require a direct lie.

It would be the first test.

◆

Tuesday woke up the Wednesday morning after she was fired, and for the space of a breath, for as long as it took to open her sticky eyes – which took a long time; she had the category of headache that makes you wish, with the very first flush of consciousness, that you weren't – for one final moment, she did not remember.

Then she did.

The memory walked up her body and settled heavy on her chest and got heavier and heavier until her lungs were crushed flat and she couldn't breathe.

Then her headache reasserted itself, and she closed her eyes and pressed her palms hard against her temples, which usually did something, but today did nothing other than shoot orange stars across the black backs of her eyelids.

The mattress jiggled as Gunnar hopped up by her feet. He walked up her body and settled heavy, but not as heavy as the memory, on her chest, then tucked his front and back paws under and began to purr. She got up and fed him. She scooped his litter. She sat down on her red love seat and said, "Well that's enough for one day." Her voice felt like an echo in her mouth.

She had been so mean to Dex.

Why had she – who had she been yesterday?

Who had she been these past few weeks?

She wasn't wearing any pants, but she still had on the shirt she'd worn to work. Button-down and basic black.

Her last work shirt.

Stop being so melodramatic, said Abby.

Tuesday pulsed numb.

She hadn't—

No. No no no no no no no no—

Yes, said Abby. **Yes yes yes yes yes yes yes.**

Tuesday sat up straight. "It's just my head. It's just my stupid head," she said. "It's not real. It's stress, it's a stress, uh, manifestation." Gunnar gazed up at her. "Of course I'm stressed. Of *course* I'm stressed, this is – this is – I need some coffee. And a plan."

You do that, Tues, said Abby. **Drink all the coffee. Make all the plans. I'll still be heeeeeeeeeere.**

It was *uncanny*. How well Tuesday's deepest brain could reproduce that voice. That voice she hadn't heard in half a lifetime. That voice she'd recognize until the day she died. And the voice itself didn't frighten her. The voice itself—

On that morning, that awful morning after, hearing Abby's voice softened the raw edge of her heart.

Maybe it wouldn't hurt to listen for a while.

I'm sorry about your job. I mean that. I really do. For an auditory hallucination of terminally undigested grief, Abby did sound legitimately sorry. **You gonna tell your parents and Ollie?**

Tuesday fell sideways on the love seat, covered her head with a pillow, and screamed into the seat cushion.

She certainly *could* tell her parents. She could call and talk to them both right now, at home, before they went to the store in the afternoon. She could tell them that she'd been reckless, that she'd fucked up. She had lost her job, and she could tell them why and how. She could listen to the monologue that followed, that did, to its credit, begin with concern (*Oh Moonie, we're so sorry, are you okay?*) before it segued into implicit blame and disbelief (*How could you, you know better—we know you know better—!*) and dipped into their anxious code that was, for once, completely correct (. . . *have you been . . . hearing . . . anyone?*) before it rounded the corner to the finish line: You can always come home. If you refuse to settle down into a recognizable adult life (which, obviously, was best defined as a spouse, a house, two cars, two and a half kids), you may as well settle down with the store.

She could email Ollie, but her brother was terrible at keeping secrets, especially from their parents. Which she had always thought was kind of funny, but that was Oliver Mooney: you squinted at him, and he confessed to crimes you didn't know he'd committed; often that you didn't even know were crimes.

So, yes: she *could* tell her family. But today of all days she couldn't bear to give them the satisfaction of knowing that she had entertained the idea of returning to Salem. Working at the store. It was entirely possible she had burned all her professional nonprofit bridges forever, and unless she wanted to lose whatever soul she had left to finance – the only other experience on her résumé – she had no direction. No path. No purpose. No prospects.

Other than Vincent Pryce.

His game.

His money.

Atta girl, said Abby.

She took a shower.

It woke her up. And now that she was awake, she was halfway between terrified and galvanized. Maybe getting fired was what she needed. Maybe it was *good*. She could wear comfy jeans and a T-shirt. She could put on a fresh pot of coffee, good coffee; she wasn't beholden to those crappy off-brand coffee pods they had in the office. She could do the work she *wanted*.

All she had to do was shove a certain voice to the background.

Dude. Rude, said Abby. **I'm not a certain voice. I'm your best friend.**

Tuesday looked at her phone, silent and dark. She wanted to apologize to Dex, and while she knew texting was his preferred medium, it felt wrong. Inappropriate, given the gravity of the situation. She wanted to take back everything. She wanted to tell him, and Rabbit, that they deserved each other, and the tonelessness of texting would only reinforce the sarcastic, nasty way that sounded in her head—

It does sound pretty sarcastic, said Abby.

She thought about Rabbit the Banker. She thought about the underground decoder room. She thought about thirteen thousand dollars. She thought about the queen of diamonds and fifty-one envelopes.

It was Wednesday. Vincent Pryce's funeral was two days away.

On her desk, under an electric bill she hadn't paid yet – not because she'd been worried about having the funds, but because, before yesterday, she'd had the luxury of laziness – was Pryce's wax-sealed manila envelope. She turned it upside down. The stack of bills and the playing card flopped out.

Tuesday, said Abby. **You're rich.**

"I'm not rich," said Tuesday.

No, said Abby. **You are.**

"Thirteen thousand dollars will last exactly six minutes," said Tuesday, "in this town."

I bet you can do a lot, said Abby, **in six minutes.**

"And it's not the point of the game for me to keep it. I don't – at least I don't think that's the point." Tuesday inhaled. "It feels . . . not right." She examined the queen's face on the playing card. "What the hell am I supposed to do with you?" she asked the queen. She flipped it over. The back wasn't a recognizable brand; no cupids on bicycles for Vincent Pryce. It was a custom design in red: a border of large rectangles, and in the center a circle with many spokes. A pie cut into twelve pieces. She focused on the circle and let the rest of her vision go a little lazy. She stared at it so long and so hard, the pattern began to wiggle.

She had seen this somewhere before.

Where had she seen it?

(Had she seen it?)

She put the card down.

"Abby," she said, "what would you do?"

The math, said Abby.

"What math."

***All* the math.**

Tuesday got out a pencil and paper.

Hours later, she didn't know how long – research, or more specifically, the internet, had a habit of swallowing great swaths of her life; she could only mark the time by pots of coffee (three), thoughts about ingesting *more* than coffee (four), sandwiches made and consumed (one), texts from Dex or Archie (zero), and albums played on Repeat (only one, because the CD happened to be in her stereo and *OK Computer* fit the mood) – someone knocked on her door.

Tuesday didn't hear it. When the knocking started, she'd moved on from the math – 51 envelopes times $13,000 equaled $663,000, over half a mil free-floating around the city – to more general research, into Edgar Allan Poe, the other Vincent Price, and for a while she'd gotten sucked into the long and storied history of playing cards—

Knock.

Someone was knocking on her door.

She shook her head. Who the hell would be knocking? It

was barely five. She stood up, stretched, rolled her neck on her shoulders. Had someone buzzed a FedEx guy in? But she hadn't – she didn't *think* she'd ordered anything online. If she had, and had forgotten, she was going to have to send it back. This was not the time for impulse internet spending.

She opened her door and Death was on the other side.

"*Ohmygod*," she said, and ducked, coffee-juiced, back behind the door.

"You like?"

Death was Dorry. Just her tweenage neighbor home from school, dressed up like Dream's perky goth sister Death from *Sandman*, because it was almost Halloween and also the universe was a bastard. Tuesday stepped out from behind the door. Her heart was a hammer, but she smiled.

"I like," she croaked. "I like a lot."

"I like your glasses," said Dorry. "I've never seen you wear them before." She paused. "I heard the music. Home sick?"

"Yes," Tuesday said, without even deciding to lie. "Been napping, so I never put in my contacts." Truthfully, she didn't remember what had happened to yesterday's contacts – if she ever found them again, they would be someplace bizarre, like in the toe of her slipper or under the dome of the butter dish. She hoped Gunnar hadn't eaten them.

"I'm sorry," Dorry said. "You're not contagious?" She covered her face. "I hope?"

Ha! said Abby. **Don't sneeze your crazy all over her.**

Tuesday shook her head. "Not the way you mean," she said. "Come on in."

◆

Tuesday was lying to her. Dorry felt it, really *felt* it – Tuesday was home in the afternoon and she wasn't sick, at least not the kind of sick that you could see. Dorry made a list in her head of everything that was off, so she could think about it later: Glasses. Lying. Not sick. And now, by inviting Dorry in, forgetting what she'd promised Dorry's dad. Or maybe deliberately disregarding. She was stunned. It made her bolder. Dorry, since her dad had freaked about Tuesday's picture in the *Metro*, had been toeing the line (literally): she hadn't so much as put a toe inside her neighbor's apartment for any reason other than tutoring. Now she stepped in for hair goop.

"Do you have any, like – my hair." Dorry held her hands out on either side of her head, miming the bigness that was missing. "Should be a lot bigger."

"I've got some paste, I think." Tuesday disappeared into the bathroom and returned with a flat, round jar. "Maybe try drying your hair upside down? I'm sure there are videos online that tell you how to make your hair big." She handed the container to Dorry. "I'm lousy when it comes to this stuff. If you can't figure it out online, I'll ask—"

She froze.

"Dex," she said, and sniffed a little. "He's the guy for proper product deployment."

Now that Dorry had, in her hands, what she'd come for, and it had involved so little subterfuge, she went from bold to worried. The music didn't help. It was odd, something Tuesday hadn't taught her about yet. It sounded hurt and nervous. The guy's voice was high, barely a whisper.

Her Tuesday would have already asked eight million questions about her costume and where she was planning to wear it. This Tuesday was – not defeated, maybe, but definitely distracted. Dorry had been braced for a duel of wits with a tiger and she'd gotten a drowsy housecat.

Tuesday's forehead wrinkled. "Hey," she said, "I have a question for you."

Dorry smiled, so happy to see a recognizable Tuesday peek out, she didn't care if it gave her away.

"Yeah?" she said.

"What would you—"

Tuesday stopped. Looked not at Dorry but toward the corner of the room, and her eyes were far away, and her face was still. Like she was listening to something.

Something that wasn't the music.

Dorry had seen a lot of things in Tuesday since the day they met, and before that, when she was the anonymous woman in black haunting her apartment building. She'd seen a friend, a teacher, someone cool who knew all kinds of cool things. She'd seen a kind of future that looked great.

But today Dorry looked at Tuesday and saw someone who wasn't quite herself. Who had lost control and focus. Today Dorry saw someone she could fool. And move around the board. To get what she wanted.

Tuesday Mooney, Dorry saw today, was her competition.

Dorry went very still. As a realization, it shouldn't have been shocking; it made sense – this was a game they were all playing, wasn't it? Hadn't it been a game from the beginning? The point of games, and of teams, was that you were playing against each other. To win. And since her dad had decided she couldn't play with Tuesday anymore, and Tuesday had agreed (silent partner, her butt), and Dorry went out and found another partner for herself – that meant Tuesday was her rival.

"What would you do with thirteen thousand dollars?" Tuesday asked.

Dorry blinked at her.

Was Tuesday honestly going to pretend Dorry didn't know why she was asking that question?

Dorry's brain thumped, pounding like it had traded places with her heart.

"Just, like, off the top of your head." Tuesday shrugged lightly. "Today. What would you do?"

"About what?" Dorry said – too fast, she couldn't control her voice.

Be cool, she thought. *Be ice.*

Tuesday said, "Not about, with. With thirteen thousand dollars. Cash."

"Vincent Pryce's cash, you mean," said Dorry.

Tuesday froze again. Like an animal, cornered. "Yes," she said. "Of course. Didn't I – didn't I tell you? What the – rules. The game?"

"I read about it online," said Dorry, which was, technically, not a lie. "The *Globe* has been posting little bios. Of anyone who comes forward as a – player." The *Globe* had been covering the treasure hunt with something like glee. Short profiles of treasure hunters, those who chose to self-identify, had been appearing all week: Two brothers from Southie, both carpenters. A sound engineer and her boyfriend, a boot camp trainer. A redheaded writer from Somerville. An ancient woman, kinky silver hair yanked back from her high forehead, wearing a high-necked blue sweater and an antique silver necklace of linked stone scarabs; she owned an antiques shop in the Back Bay. Her name was Verena Parkman, and Dorry immediately liked her best. She looked like a witch. And like she was playing to win.

Dorry and Ned didn't identify. Instead, the two of them gathered as much information on the other players as they could find. They collected the data in a glorious poster-sized chart Ned drew in purple ink and taped to the back of his bedroom door. Dorry had seen the chart because she had been in Ned's room. After they came back from the Garment District, pink plastic bags full of costume loot.

Ned's bedroom was a museum. It was hard to look at any one thing. There were shelves and shelves of books; of stacked white cardboard boxes he'd labeled, in as many colored markers and fancy letters as there were boxes, COMIX; posters for things Dorry had never heard of, and didn't know if they were comics or movies or what, but one – her head went light – she did: *Sandman;* and one wall, the entire wall, floor to ceiling around two windows, was a painting of the tops of the houses across the street, the edge of a tree in full summer leaf, birds, a cat watching from a high balcony, as though the wall itself were one huge window. "I do a new one every year," Ned said. "This was my first tramp loyal," and Dorry spent a good hour that night online, figuring out that he was saying *trompe l'oeil.*

Dorry was still processing that afternoon's information. The notes about the other treasure hunters were just part of the overload. Ned's chart had columns for name, age, residence, job (if known), alone or team, and size of team (if known), intensity (casual or dedicated), possible Pryce connections, game strategy, and, last but not least, card suit and number, drawn in corresponding red and black. The chart was beautiful. What it contained was a mess.

Game players, card players, whatever you wanted to call them, were people of all ages, with a slightly higher tendency to be students, undergrad and graduate, but also a dental assistant, a teacher, a mail carrier. There were people from all over the city (Dorchester) and the state (Peabody) and the country (Flagstaff, Arizona) and the world (exchange students from Belfast). Some of them had clear strategies – to spend the money on another item for Pryce's collection, or on fancy costumes for the funeral; to save the money for college or a house; to donate the money to a charity. Some of them had no idea whatsoever – *I'm still working that out* – and some of them were keeping their plans to themselves (from a crew of Harvard students: *We could tell you, but then we'd have to kill you*).

The chart revealed no obvious answer. There was no clear path. No one, as far as Dorry and Ned could tell, had figured it

out yet. Not even them. They'd decided to split the thirteen
thousand between them and save most of it for college. Neither
Dorry nor Ned felt right doing anything else, though it seemed
like too boring a solution to be what Pryce was looking for. But
Dorry had a hunch that what they did with the money was only
part of the solution; Vincent Pryce valued stuff – things, but
also ideas and actions – other than money. They still had to play
their hand with the widow, which meant collecting all the cards.
"The pattern is going to be in the data," Ned said. Between the
Globe and the Black Cats and their own private knowledge,
they'd only tracked down twenty-six teams; a lot of the chart
was empty, and they didn't know for sure how much they were
missing. "What we need," Ned said, "is more data."

Tuesday had more data.

Tuesday *was* more data.

"What's your card?" Dorry asked her.

Tuesday tilted her head again, like she was listening, and
swiveled back to Dorry.

"Don't tell your dad," she said.

She handed Dorry a queen of diamonds.

The music was fading out at the end of a song, the singer
was howling that *he lost himself, he lost himseeeeelf,* and Dorry
wanted to smack Tuesday's giant old stereo, rip the plug out
of the wall, make it fade faster. She looked at the card, at the
front and the back. It was the same deck, same design, as hers
and Ned's. She didn't understand it any more than she understood their own.

"Diamonds," Dorry said, handing it back. "I'd buy thirteen
thousand dollars in diamonds."

Tuesday wrinkled her nose. "Really?" she said.

Dorry didn't do anything but return her gaze.

"I guess." Tuesday joggled her head from side to side. "I
guess 'seeking well' could mean – seek the good life. Live high.
Drape yourself in diamonds."

Vincent Pryce would not have thought that. Dorry knew this because she'd done the research – she saw her report's shiny plastic cover peeking out from a pile of paper on Tuesday's desk – and she couldn't believe Tuesday didn't know it too.

It was almost like Tuesday hadn't read her report.

Tuesday sighed. "Well," she said, "I guess it's a better idea than mine. Which was keeping it for myself."

Wrong. Dorry almost laughed. That was the *wrong* solution. Vincent Pryce thought living well was *using* what you had, your money, your life, instead of stashing it away. Being curious and adventurous and hunting for weird things. Looking for them, trying to find what was impossible. Like Dorry searching for her mother's ghost.

Which, she realized like a slap in the face, had to be a *correct* solution.

Dorry almost felt sick, she was so excited, so abruptly. She'd been right all along. *All along.* She had figured it out herself, without any help. And Tuesday had tried to—

Tuesday slumped down on her desk chair. Her shoulders caved forward. Her legs were wide, her feet turned in. She looked like a puddle of unspooled thread.

The next song wasn't really a song but a list of things recited by a robot, and it was horrible, there were horrible, sad, skittering sounds underneath and on top, it chilled Dorry, and Tuesday acted like she didn't hear it at all. Or like she'd heard it so many times before, she could no longer hear how horrible it was.

Dorry squeezed the flat jar of hair paste in her hand. She'd gotten what she came for.

"I should go," she said.

"Wait," said Tuesday. "You read – you read the profiles? Of the other players?"

Dorry nodded. "It's been all over Facebook," she said. It was the most casually calculated half-truth she'd told yet. Sure, it was probably on Facebook; but Dorry wasn't, and hadn't read about it there. And Tuesday knew it.

But she didn't notice.

"What did you think?" Tuesday asked. "Gut reaction."

Dorry looked at Tuesday and Tuesday looked back. The full truth seemed like it couldn't possibly change anything, so Dorry told it.

"It's like they're all playing a different game," she said.

14

GAMES PEOPLE PLAY

Go for a walk, said Abby.

Tuesday didn't want to. Once Dorry left – spacey and vague, whatever she'd been hiding all week, she was still hiding – all Tuesday wanted to do was dig up those profiles in the *Globe*, see for herself what Dorry's excellently sensitive gut had intuited. And speaking of her excellent gut . . . where was that report she'd written about Pryce?

Tuesday, said Abby, **leave your apartment.**

"*You* leave my apartment," muttered Tuesday.

Great idea! Whither thou goest, I ghost. Abby paused. Then cackled maniacally.

Tuesday pulled her eyes away from her computer. This was going to go on for some time if she didn't do what Abby said. And Abby had a point. The farthest she'd walked today was the thirty-five feet from her bed to her kitchen and back again, and she was jittery, over-caffeinated, anxious. Walking would burn that off. It wasn't too cold out; it was a perfect late-October early evening. She would go for a walk to Porter Square. She would walk and she would think.

And try not to think about the fact that neither Dex nor Archie had texted her.

Still.

It was scarf weather. She bundled herself up, and it was–

comforting. The sun was low and bright, and Abby had been right; a walk was what she needed. **Told ya,** said Abby, and Tuesday slipped her earbuds into her ears. If anyone passed her on the sidewalk, she wouldn't look like the insane woman talking to no one that she was.

"Don't get cocky," she said.

I'm never cocky, said Abby. **You must be thinking of someone else.** She paused, like she had after her stupid ghost pun, then said, sotto voce, ***Cocky,*** and burst out laughing again.

"It's good to know my mental illness has managed to retain her adolescent sense of humor."

Cocky, said Abby again, still laughing.

Tuesday walked down Summer Street, past the community hospital, past Somerville's ribbons of triple-deckers and tiny front lawns, scattered with dead leaves and lawn statues, benches, birdbaths, the Virgin Mary half-shelled in bright blue plaster alcoves. She thought about how everyone playing Pryce's game could be playing a different game, all at the same time. The game was open-ended. Pryce *wanted* there to be variety. He had funded fifty-one potential start-ups, to see what they would do.

He'd built an experiment with fifty-one variables.

Who *could* all be playing a different game, legitimately. There was, in this one game, the possibility of many. She paused at the corner of Summer and Linden – at a house with not only a polished metal gazing ball and a small windmill but a very large lawn shrine to the Virgin Mary, snug in her surrounding plaster shell – and thought, *Nested.* In one game were many, nested. That's why the instructions were so vague. Pryce wanted every player to do what *they* wanted to do. And depending on what they wanted to do – she supposed, the wording of the funeral invitation was as vague as the game instructions – was there to be another round? Was "the audience" the card players could have with the widow an interview, a test before moving on to the next level? And between the card player(s) who'd spent their thirteen K on, say, a Swarovski-encrusted Green Bay Packers cheesehead and the card players(s) who'd transformed their assets into socks and long underwear for a homeless shelter, whom would the widow choose?

Blinged-out cheesehead, said Abby. **Definitely.**

Was the widow enacting her own or the dead man's wishes? Which could be, based on past evidence – built a castle on Nantucket, collected several million dollars' worth of occult doodads – a little more flamboyant?

That was the key, then, and all she had to do was figure out which game she, Tuesday, was playing.

Depends on who you're playing it with, said Abby.

"Archie. Or Dex." Tuesday had reached the parking lot of the Star Market. She crossed the plaza. "Or myself.

"Archie's game," she said, and dropped her voice; there were more people here, milling around the grocery store, the dry cleaner, the bookstore, after work. "Is tied to Pryce, at a deep family level that I still don't understand, because Archie is keeping his cards ridiculously close." She turned right at the Dunkin' Donuts onto Mass. Ave. "Dex's game is – well, he's already playing it with Rabbit, and it's a fantastic kind of . . . romance. It's a romantic game."

That leaves you, said Abby. **And your game.**

"I know," said Tuesday. She sounded terse, even to herself.

You forgot someone, said Abby, and Tuesday was about to ask her who when she saw the banker.

Through the window of the Newtowne Grille.

Rabbit Hatmaker was sitting in the first booth visible from the sidewalk, next to the door to the takeout lobby, and Tuesday's first instinct upon recognizing his face – haloed in yellow and red from the neon hamburger buzzing in the window – was to drop to the pavement like a stone made of shame.

She pressed her back against the exterior of the restaurant and crouched on the sidewalk. Someone had graffitied a small red heart on the concrete a few feet away from her sneaker. Her own heart was pressed up against her larynx.

Super smooth, said Abby.

Tuesday didn't think Rabbit had seen her. Rabbit was, after all, the sort of person – kind, caring, entirely adult – who would come outside to make sure she was okay, if he *had* witnessed her diving to the sidewalk outside Porter Square's oldest established watering hole.

She'd been inside the Newtowne once or twice. It was your standard townie bar: shouting TVs, glowing blue Keno screens, a dining room on one side and a dark, cozy bar on the other. On a Wednesday night, without any big sporting events, it would be slow and empty, the handful of requisite townies bellied up but none of the students and hipster yuppies who would clog it on trivia nights, the sports fans who preferred the atmosphere – low stakes, low expectations, a relic of another time, like someone's uncle's basement – to other Celtics and Sox and Bruins viewing venues.

So why was Rabbit Hatmaker here?

And did that mean – did that mean Dex was here too?

She wanted to melt into the concrete.

Still crouched, doing her best to ignore the stares of those commuters hustling home along the street who *did* notice her, Tuesday slid beneath the window and peered in at the other side of the booth.

It wasn't Dex.

It was the widow.

Lyle Korrapati Pryce looked much as she had the last time Tuesday saw her, at her townhouse in Louisburg Square, swaddled in sweats at brunch. She was wearing a light gray hooded sweatshirt, well worn, frayed with love. The bare minimum of makeup, her hair held back in a bird's nest of a bun, skin glowing, eyes shining in her bright face. She was listening to Rabbit with some intensity. On the table beside them was a large cheese pizza, floating on a pizza stand, and a pitcher of beer from which only Rabbit had poured himself a glass.

Pregnant, said Abby.

"I know," said Tuesday.

The sunset was deepening. Tuesday hoped it was bright enough to effectively blind both Lyle and Rabbit. She inched up a little higher, high enough to see what else was on the table.

It looked like a house of cards.

What the – said Abby.

Tuesday inched higher. Yes, it was a house of cards. Built precariously on the table between them, between their individual plates of pizza, three stories tall and growing. Rabbit sipped his beer. Lyle lifted a card from a neat pile by her silverware, looked at it, then turned it for Rabbit to see. She laughed. Tuesday couldn't hear her, but her lips were easy to read.

Found it!

It was the ace of diamonds. When she flipped the card back over, Tuesday recognized the pattern on the back. It was the same pattern, borders nested around a twelve-spoked circle, as on Pryce's bespoke playing cards.

What game are *they* playing? asked Abby.

Tuesday didn't know what it meant, only that it had to mean something. It had to mean Dex's boyfriend knew even more than they thought he knew. She had to talk to Dex. Or maybe Dex – already knew? Tuesday's lower back kinked. She straightened without meaning to.

Lyle saw her. She made direct eye contact over the house of cards.

After a beat of confused surprise, Lyle smiled.

And Tuesday bolted.

She flew down Mass. Ave., dodging commuters and cars

through the shopping plaza parking lot. She ran up Elm Street across the city line between Cambridge and Somerville. She ran, her chest burning, past the school. The pet store. She turned left at Linden and slowed to a brisk walk up the hill, then right on Summer, and again she was running, heaving for breath, up the street. Up the front steps of her building. Keys jangling, lobby door open – up the three winding flights to her floor, steps creaking, Tuesday sweating, her lungs tight, her heart fit to explode—

And Archie was waiting for her.

He was sitting on the carpet, his back against her door, wearing his ripped motorcycle jacket. His legs stretched the width of the hallway.

His face was ruined. Swollen and purple, nose crusted with blackened blood.

Tuesday stopped.

Breathing.

"Lost my phone," he said.

◆

Archie coughed. It hurt.

Tuesday stood completely still at the end of the hall. She didn't come closer. Her face was bright red, shiny, like she'd been running. Away from someone, maybe.

And here he was, waiting for her in her dim, dark hall. The wood trim was coal brown. The walls were close, the blue paint dingy. There was an ambient stuffiness, old smells of food. The carpet was muddled blue, blackened from decades of dirt, probably, and he was rubbing his ass on it.

In all that gloom, backlit by weak fluorescent light, Tuesday burned.

"Feels pretty good," he said. "To not have a phone. But without it, I didn't know – how else to."

She wasn't moving.

He pressed his tongue against the tooth Nat had loosened, and tasted warm salt.

"I didn't know how else to warn you," he said.

Tuesday wobbled. As Archie watched, her face drained from red to white.

And she fell to the floor like a pile of loose bones.

Archie had seen people faint before. One Christmas, when he was eight and Emerson twelve, and furious she hadn't gotten the compound bow and arrows she'd been asking for – but Nat had – she'd tried to pierce her own ears. At the time, Archie thought putting two tiny holes in her body was a strange way to show their parents how angry she was. But in hindsight maybe it was Emerson's way of channeling a furious desire to hurt someone by turning it inward, into something fashionable, even. He watched, worried, as she numbed herself with an ice cube. She wedged a cork from one of her mother's bottles of Merlot behind her earlobe, and she didn't flinch when she stabbed her own ear with the sewing needle. But when she saw the smears of blood on her fingertips, her eyes and her head tipped back and she rolled gently off the couch. Later she would tell him, with some pride, that she'd managed to train herself never to faint at the sight of blood again, her own or anyone else's; Archie did not ask how. In the moment, though, her faint was quiet and quick.

So he had never seen a body faint like Tuesday's. She went down, *bam*, like she'd been shot. It stunned him for a second. And then he pulled himself up – he was one bone-deep ache all over, but he could walk – and staggered to her.

"Tuesday." He patted her cheeks, which were dead white. Two days ago, when he'd been bloodier and arguably less conscious, his sister had slapped him with much less tenderness. But then, he was her brother. "Tuesday, wake up." He knelt beside her body, straightened her tumbled legs flat down the hallway. "Tuesday," he said louder. Was she even breathing?

Was he going to have to call an ambulance? His phone was long gone. Crushed. Probably still under a sofa at the Mandarin. *"Tuesday."* He was shouting now.

Where did Tuesday's neighbor girl live?

How many doors would he have to knock on before he found someone who would help? *Would* anyone help?

Tuesday made a sound that wasn't quite a word.

"Hey!" Archie, for the first time, understood he was sweating. He was shaking. Every cell in his stupid body was screaming and he was only now bothering to listen. "What are you – saying?"

"Arn," said Tuesday. Her eyelids twitched. "Hee?"

"Okay," said Archie. "Okay, let's – can you stand?"

"No." Emphatic. "I. Here." Her chest rose. "Usta. Min."

Archie sat back on his heels. Leaned against the wall. The edge of his vision flickered. He—

"Move over," he said, and lay down flat on his stomach beside her in the hall. He listened to her breathe and tried to match her breath for breath. In and out. In and out.

His sister was going to be furious.

His sister probably *was* furious, at this precise moment. Archie had no idea what time it was, but it was late, the sun had set, Emerson would be home at the Mandarin by now, wondering where the hell he'd gone. Why he'd vanished as violently as he'd appeared. Back in her life after six years gone, for two nights only, leaving behind nothing but a bloodied pillowcase. He couldn't remember the end of the beating (Nat never let a loss of consciousness stop him), but he remembered his sister slapping him, trying to wake him, dragging him from the living room to the condo's bathroom, half conscious, spit-spraying the blood still pouring out of his nose, Pollocking the pure white porcelain tile. Nat, blessedly, was gone by then. Emerson cleaned and drugged him up – he had no idea what she gave him, but it wasn't OTC – poured a glug of bourbon down his throat, reset his broken nose. He remembered her reciting a litany of things she was going to do to their brother: slow-poison his whiskey, razorblades in his Italian leather shoes.

"I'm going to stab him in the eye with a seafood fork," Emerson said. Archie didn't say anything, because he couldn't tell if his sister was kidding. She had a dry sense of humor. Perfect for hiding the sharp blade inside her.

He didn't know how much she knew.

Which was why he had gone to his family's condo at the Mandarin Hotel in the first place. He'd read Tuesday's binder of research, about his mother, about what she had done at Arches Consolidated (in a word: manage, and make decisions as though its employees were actual humans). He read about his sister, his mysterious sister, who Tuesday had only been able to sketch in outline: fragments of a public personality, vain and spoiled, that didn't amount to a full person. Tuesday suspected it was a carefully controlled performance. It was enough for Archie to remember all that he'd forgotten in his fear and his haste: that his sister was the most coolly competent person he had ever met, and it was vain and self-defeating and just plain *dumb* to take on his brother without her help.

"Look at you," Emerson had said. She turned him toward her, her finger on his chin. They were back in the living room by then, which showed, in the parlance of every procedural cop show ever, Signs of a Struggle. End tables were tipped. A green glass lamp lay in shards, smashed. Archie's phone was – somewhere, also smashed. Moments before Nat threw the first punch, Archie had been fiddling with it, panicking that he ought to text Tuesday an SOS.

That punch had come as a crushing relief. They'd only been playing brothers for about ten minutes, but every second of it had been an excruciating eternity.

He'd gone to the Mandarin on Monday evening, after five.

Archie figured his mother would still be at the office, but Tuesday's research said that Emerson's role at Arches Consolidated was looser, advisory, which meant she could be anywhere. Like home, at the condo. By herself. Archie wanted his mother and his sister back in his life, desperately, but he was also desperately ashamed – of running, of being such a goddamn coward – and he didn't think he could handle seeing both of them, for the first time, together.

He never thought his brother would be the only person at home.

Nathaniel opened the door and every nerve in Archie's body went dead, but he was so good at pretending, they were both so, so good at this game – they had been before their father disappeared, and they were even better at it now – that Archie actually felt his face smile. He smiled at his brother, and his brother smiled at him. *Eddie—! How the – how the hell are you, man!* is what Nathaniel's mouth said and his arms opened and he pulled Archie across the threshold into the condo and cracked his open palm hard against Archie's back.

Nat wasn't supposed to be at home. Nat stopped there on his way to a dinner to pick up something he'd forgotten – a file, a folder, hell, he could've come home to do a line of cocaine – but now that his little brother was back, back home, well, he'd – he'd cancel! *Sit down, man. I'll get us some beers.*

Archie sat on an unfamiliar couch in the living room, great glass windows overlooking Boston in the gloaming. So many windows. Who knew who might be watching. *Please*, he thought, *please let someone be watching.* He took out his phone. Thought about calling 911. Thought about texting Tuesday. But what would he say? What would he—

Help I'm trapped in my family's luxury condo with my brother who murdered our father and he knows I know and he's going to kill me too was not the stuff of a text.

Especially not on a flip phone.

Then Nat, walking back in with two sweaty bottles of beer, saw the binder. Archie had forgotten he'd brought it, had set it down on the glass coffee table. He thought his sister would think it was funny. That he'd needed a dossier to be reminded whom he was related to.

Nat, not so much.

"Nice binder, bro," said Nat, handing him a bottle. Cold and slippery. Good for shattering. "Gonna ace the exam?" Nat sat and pulled the binder into his lap. Opened it. Flipped through it. "Well, this is revolting." He straightened his tie. "That girl dug all this up?"

Archie didn't respond.

Nat set his beer down on the table. Archie closed his fist around his own bottle.

"Eddie," said Nat, and shook his head. He leaned forward and flexed his fingers into fists. He looked at Archie. "I thought we agreed you weren't going to come back."

"We did," said Archie. He sat up straight.

"That's funny," said Nat. "You're funny." He slapped his palms down on both knees, gathered himself, and stood. "Stand up."

Archie stood and thought that this, at least, was a new game.

"I didn't come back for y—" was all he got out before Nat socked him across the jaw.

Later, with Emerson, half drunk and drugged but still feeling more pain than seemed biochemically possible, Archie looked at his big sister, really looked at her, for the first time since he ran away. She looked older. Sharper. But so familiar it hurt.

He'd forgotten there were other people in the world who looked like him.

"Nat did it," said Archie.

"I know," said Emerson.

That first night, Monday, they didn't say any more than that.

For most of Tuesday, Archie was asleep in his sister's room. He woke a few times, though afterward he couldn't parse his waking memories from dreams. Once, he swore he heard his father's voice vibrating through the wall behind his head: *Get over here, Junior.* Another time – and this had felt alarmingly real – he'd gotten up to use the bathroom and, on his way back to bed, bumped into the bottom drawer, half open, of a small dresser. He opened it wider and looked inside. It was full of blue and white postcards, stiff and shiny. On the postcards were photos of yachts. Yachts moored majestically. Yachts plowing the ocean, the sky perfectly puffy-clouded behind them. He crouched on the carpet. The drawer was full of post-cards, stacked neatly and waiting to be sent. He reached for one and flipped it over.

Scrawled on the reverse in red ink: *I WILL RUIN YOU.*

He woke up later, without remembering how he got back in bed, thinking of yachts. Sweating.

Their mother was in North Carolina on a business trip; Archie would have missed her no matter what. At least Nat didn't come back. "You're safe," Emerson told Archie that night. "He has a model in town. That's where he's sleeping." Emerson made dinner and he tried to bring it up, to make *Nat did it* more specific – he tried to say, *I watched Nat kill our father, and yes, our father was a monster, but I think our brother's worse* – but Emerson shushed him. "Later," she said. "When your head is clearer." This was a game the Archeses played too: the game of not saying everything. The game of assuming what the other person knows is what you know too.

Wednesday, after noon, his head was clear, all right. Clear enough to realize he had no idea what had happened to Tuesday's binder of research. Clear enough to grasp that it was possible his brother had taken it. And was armed now with a specific reason to hate and hurt Tuesday.

Not that Nathaniel Arches ever needed a reason to hurt anyone.

He couldn't call her. He didn't have a phone anymore. Even if it hadn't been pulverized, he didn't know her number. The only thing he knew was where she lived.

So there he went.

And here Tuesday was, exhaling on the hall carpet beside him. He felt her body move and heard her lick her lips.

"Warn me?" she said.

He lay with his head turned, ear pressed to the carpet, protecting his tender nose, and opened his eyes. He saw her cheek, her hair. She had two little commas etched into her earlobe, empty piercings. He was as close as he'd ever been.

If only it were possible, ever, to get closer.

"About my brother," he said.

Tuesday turned her head so they were nose to nose. She wasn't as pale as before, but there was a strange flicker in her eyes, a startled kind of sadness.

He was too late.

◆

Go through his pants, said Abby.

Not that you haven't already.

"Har har," Tuesday muttered.

She heard the shower turn on. She pulled her duvet up around her cold shoulders.

Archie's pants were on the floor. And his shirt and socks. And his boxer briefs, because of course he wore boxer briefs.

Go. Through. His. Pants, said Abby again.

Tuesday rolled on her side, facing the pile of Archie's discarded clothing. If she thought sex – and it hadn't been great sex, but good enough sex, sex with potential (she had to imagine it would be much better when Archie's body hadn't been so recently pulped) – would take her mind off anything, she was wrong. It had sharpened something. Made her hungrier. Desire, in Tuesday's experience, was a feedback loop.

She reached across the floor and snagged his shirt with a finger.

I said pants, said Abby, and Tuesday said, "Would you relax."

Tuesday slid her legs out from under the duvet. She pressed her toes into the rug and pulled Archie's T-shirt over her head. He'd explained it was one of his sister's nightshirts, an over-sized concert T from a Mighty Mighty Bosstones tour in the late nineties that Tuesday couldn't imagine Emerson Arches ever wearing un-ironically. When she asked why he was wearing his sister's shirt, Archie's eyes darted back and forth. "Because," he finally said, "my other shirt got blood on it."

"Blood from where?" Tuesday asked.

"My face," Archie said.

He is infuriating, said Abby.

Tuesday picked up his pants. Felt the pockets. No phone, but he did have a wallet. Credit cards. Insurance. License. A few bedraggled bills. Tucked deep into a fold, a small brass key. **PO box,** said Abby. "Interesting," said Tuesday. She folded his pants neatly on her dresser.

With the shower still running, Tuesday lifted his ripped jacket off her living room floor. Inside the lining there was a deep, zippered pocket.

She pulled out a spiral-bound reporter's notebook and a small silver envelope. Addressed to Archie, no surname, at a post office box in downtown Boston. Stamped and canceled, also from Boston. The date of the postmark was one day after the Auction to Abandon All Hope. One day after Vincent Pryce died.

The return address wasn't an address but a symbol:

Tuesday considered for a moment what she was doing. Standing in the middle of her living room wearing only a prodigal billionaire son's sister's Bosstones concert T, with said prodigal billionaire in her shower, having just had decent-sex-with-potential with said prodigal billionaire – about to violate said prodigal billionaire's privacy.

Hadn't she just gotten fired for this?

The silver envelope had been slit clean across the top. She slid her finger inside and pulled out a single sheet of creamy correspondence paper, letterpressed at the top with the same symbol as the return address, in bright, bloody red ink.

The dead man's typewriter had misfired here and there.

```
Dear Archie,
   If you are reading this, two things mus
be true: one, you still hold the post office
box k y I gave you, long ago. And two, I
am dead.
   So I am dead! Gracious, what a thought.
It is not a surprise — can death be a
surprise, rea y, to anyone? — but still it
is strange to imagine these words being read
after m death. It is wonderful to imagine
them being read by y u. You are one of my
heirs. I send this letter in hopes that
both the news of my demise and this letter
may reach yo .
   In the afte math of y death, you, and
every ne you know, will be invited to play
a game. It is imperative tha you do so, and
t at you not do so alone. Why? Because I
am a horribly old man and must hav a dying
wish. Humor me. In playing my game, know
that you honor my last equests: that you
```

make your way through this world with curios
ty and courage, that you follow strange
clues, make detours, and that you do not p
ay it alone. Find a partner or two or three
or f ur. Cross and crisscross your paths
with the paths of others.

I only had the pleasure of being your
friend for a short time, but you and your
family mean a great deal to me. I have
thought of you often, and always hoped,
someday, you would find your way home. Despite
everything — in spite of certain circumstances — you were dealt an extraordinary
hand. Let this be the beginning of everything
you ha e yet to becom .

I ave enclosed a key to my home on Pinckney
Stre t. No one will find you there.

Your f iend always,
Vince

Tuesday looked up.

At some point, the shower had stopped. At some point,
Archie had walked out of her bathroom. He stood in front of
her now, hair dripping. He didn't look mad. Or surprised,
even. If anything, his battered face was a mixture of fatigue
and relief. His bruises had gone livid in the hot shower, red
and purple nebulas swirling up and down his sides and his
lower back. Nat, he'd told her when they were lying in bed
and he was trying not to let on how much it hurt to be touched
– Nat knew where and how hard to hit him, to make him hate
every cell, every muscle and bone in his body, for not being
stronger, harder. For not being impervious to pain, for never
being able to give as good as he got. That was Nat's perverse
superpower and always had been: whenever his brother beat

the living shit out of him, Archie always ended up hating himself.

Well, not just himself, he said. He hated Nat too.

Now he was standing in front of her, holding a towel up around his waist, as close to naked as Tuesday thought he was capable of being.

"This is why," she said.

"Why what?"

"You're playing. Because Vince" – she smiled a little – "was your friend. Playing was your friend's last request, and you hired me because he told you not to play alone. What else did Vincent Pryce ask you to do?"

"Nothing," said Archie.

"Who was this man," she asked him, "who could get people to do so much for him, for so little?" She paused. "What game are *we* playing?"

"I don't know."

"You do," she said. "You don't want to tell me."

Archie took the notebook and the letter out of her hand, stuffed them both into his jacket, and tossed everything on her love seat. He stepped closer. Slid his palm, still damp, to cup her face.

"If I ask you to trust me," he said, "will you lie and say yes?"

Tuesday was tired of lying. Kissing him, while still a game, at least felt like a form of truth.

15

DEAD MAN'S PARTY

Dorry had been to exactly one funeral before the funeral of Vincent Pryce. Two, if you counted the funeral of the goldfish she won at the Topsfield Fair when she was eight.

The other funeral had been her mother's. She didn't cry at her mother's funeral at all. At least, she didn't think she did. Large sections of that day, those days, she did not remember. The things she *should* have remembered, she didn't. She didn't remember what her mother's face looked like in the casket. She didn't remember what her mother had been wearing. She remembered *she* wore a white shirt, because she read online that it was traditional at Buddhist funerals to wear white instead of black, and though her mom was only sort of Buddhist, she liked the idea. She remembered eating a Lorna Doone. She had never heard of, never even *seen*, a Lorna Doone before. There was a small basket of cookies and crackers beside the tissues in the family parlor, off the main room with all the chairs and the big line of people who showed up to shake her hand and tell her How Sorry They Were. She knew there were plenty of things in the world that she didn't know, but those alien Lorna Doones, cheerful yellow wrappers shining side by side with the Oreos, made her feel like she'd slipped into another dimension. Lorna Doones didn't exist in her world. This had to be another world entirely.

Vincent Pryce's funeral was another world beyond that.

The lawn of Boston Common, the low sloping part from the merry-go-round and the frog pond to the road that cut between the Common and the Public Garden, was a crowd. Of all sorts of people, old and young, black and Asian and white and brown, skinny and fat and short and tall, and they were all in costume, and because they were all in costume, it was like looking straight into their hearts at what they loved or who they wanted to be. There were Poes and ghosts and cats and ravens and Spider-Men and mermaids and fairies and grim reapers and Leatherfaces and a freaky good Jason Voorhees – he was huge, scary huge; when he passed Dorry, she was eye to belly button – a bat, an Uno card, Dracula vampires, *Twilight* vampires, their faces brushed with glitter, some Red Sox, some Bruins, a Celtic who could have been Kevin Garnett, but she couldn't get close enough to tell for sure. Someone was dressed as Mayor Menino. Someone was dressed as Kermit the Frog. Someone, a guy, Dorry thought – he had big shoulders and an Adam's apple – was dressed as Cher, which Dorry got only after Cher came up to Ned and said, "Prince!" and Ned said, "Cher!" and they hugged, because even though they were strangers, they knew each other.

She hadn't known what Ned's costume was until then. He was wearing a purple jacket with big shoulders and skinny black pants and a curly wig, and he'd grown a scrubby little mustache that shouldn't have been cute but was stupid adorable. Maybe because he was still wearing his glasses. He had blobs of red makeup smeared all over his face, which she still didn't get (was he zombie Prince?). But he'd known right away who she was – "Hey, Death!" he said as she walked up to the bus stop by the Dunkin' Donuts on Highland – so she was too embarrassed to ask who he was trying to be.

Ned's big sister, Cass, was dressed as Nefertiti. Dorry recognized her right away; she'd been obsessed with ancient Egypt in the fourth grade. Cass was a junior at MIT and had the best posture of anyone Dorry had ever met. Her eye makeup was like Dorry's, only much better. She wore a white toga with shiny gold belts wrapped around her waist and under her arms, and sandals, and a short denim jacket, because, despite the pretty warm weather, it was still October. When they got off the T at Park Street and stepped into the cooling night, Cass bobby-pinned a large, blue and gold paper headpiece over her hair. She kept reaching up to make sure it was secure.

Cass and her friend Lisa Pinto were the two other members of their team. Ned had asked Dorry, shyly, if they could come – he and Dorry had cracked the code and found the money, but Cass and Lisa Pinto had organized the Black Cats; it didn't feel right to leave them out. Plus, Cass was his sister. And a better chaperone option than his parents. What could Dorry say but yes? Nothing else about this date was normal, so why not bring along two other people? Lisa Pinto introduced herself to Dorry using both names, and when Ned talked about her (and he did, a lot; he'd for *sure* had a huge crush on her once), he used both names too. Lisa Pinto was dressed as the back half of a two-person horse costume. "It's sort of abstract," she'd told Dorry, snapping the suspenders on her shoulders as she leaned back against a pole on the Green Line. "But surprisingly comfortable, warm—" She raised her eyebrow at Cass. "And practical. It's basically a kangaroo pouch. I'm holding a great deal of useful stuff."

"That's Lisa Pinto," said Cass. "Always thinking with her ass."

Cass and Lisa Pinto had been showing off from the second they boarded the 88 bus. Like Dorry was someone special, someone they needed to impress, or at least make laugh. It took half the ride to Lechmere for her to catch on. At first she was just amused, because they were obviously good friends, the kind of friends who were fun to watch, they were so easy with each other, quippy and quick. But then Tuesday's name came up, and came up again, and something inside Dorry snapped into place, like when the eye doctor was showing you different lenses: a window, clear, that showed her what she was really looking at. She was looking at two game players. Two players who looked at her, Dorry, with hunger. She wondered what they thought she knew that they didn't. She wondered if the only thing they saw when they looked at her was a clue, and what they might do to get it out of her.

It was an echo of that awful feeling she'd had at Tuesday's. That urge to compete, to protect what she had – to keep what she knew secret, to be a spy, to lie, even to a person she . . . but *could* she say she loved Tuesday if she felt like this? Tuesday had scared her. She had been – strange. Tuesday had reminded her of that horrible sinking, that woozy dark place, that, once upon a time, Tuesday herself had seemed capable of vanquishing.

Dorry hadn't seen her since that day. She told Ned what she'd found out – Tuesday's queen of diamonds – and though Ned was full of other questions (What's her costume? What does she think is going to happen at the funeral?), Dorry deflected. And she sure as heck didn't mention Tuesday or the funeral to her father. She built the details of a lie around the truth. She planned to tell him she'd been invited to a slumber party at her new friend Nadine's, and Nadine was really into Halloween, so it was sort of a costume slumber party. Fifteen minutes before she had to leave to meet Ned at the bus stop, she'd dressed and gunked up her hair; she'd gotten the lie all ready in her mouth, had rehearsed it – not too much, she didn't want it to *sound* rehearsed – but when she'd walked into the living room her dad was flopped on the couch, watching a scary movie on TV; there was screaming, someone was being chased, and Dorry was pretty sure he was drinking. The last time she'd seen him drinking was after her mother's funeral, and he got so drunk he couldn't stop crying. He rolled into a ball and made a terrible sound like he was dying, and Dorry hid in her room and called Gram, and Gram came over and took care of him. Now, on the floor, within reach of his curled hand, was a bottle with a red screw-top cap. His other hand was balancing a glass of clear liquid on his stomach.

"Hey," she said, and he pressed his head against the couch's arm to look back at her. He didn't say anything about her outfit.

"I was invited over to someone's house," she said. "They're having a party."

He turned back to the TV. "Curfew's at ten," he said.

"It's a sleepover," she said. "I'll be back tomorrow."

"Okay," he said.

She left.

She walked down the hall, past Tuesday's silent door, down the curling stairs to the lobby, feeling relieved and guilty, guilty and relieved. She should probably tell someone, call Gram – but then again, Dad was a grown-up, he could do what he wanted, and the fact that he wanted to drink tonight was none of Dorry's business. The more important fact was this: Dorry had done it. Dorry had *made* it. She was closer to winning than she'd ever been, and even if her father were sober, and could drive, and cared enough to come get her – *she would get to the funeral first.*

Dorry felt – it was crazy, right? She knew it was crazy. She couldn't explain it, but she felt close. Close to her mother. Close to seeing her again. The closest she had felt since her mother died.

And now she was standing with Ned and his sister and his sister's friend, watching Vincent Pryce's funeral come to life all around her. There was a big, black-and-white-striped tent where people could get drinks and snacks, a stage with a band playing a song that sounded familiar but twisted up, remade. The field was lit with bonfires in tall metal stands with colored glass panels that threw red and blue and purple and orange and green firelight across faces, feathers, wings. There were – Dorry counted – twelve stands, all in a circle.

She nudged her elbow against Ned and he nudged back. Twelve, she wanted to say. Twelve like a clock.

But she didn't. It was a dream, and in a dream you don't have to speak to be understood. Everyone seemed happy. Buzzing and laughing, talking too loud, louder than they would have if they were wearing their nondream skins. It didn't feel like a funeral, or at least not like either of the funerals Dorry had been to before. It wasn't lonely. It wasn't a blurry, surreal blank. It was a party with food and dancing and strangers hugging each other.

A wish flickered across her mind: that her mother's funeral had been like this. A party. A concert. A place she could imagine her mother grabbing her hands and asking her to dance, and even though her mom could be sad, and angry, and sometimes she had been so painfully uncool it made Dorry's teeth hurt, her mother had known how to be happy. And when she was happy, it sort of radiated out, like a campfire, and could make you happy too. Yes: if her mother's funeral had felt like remembering it was possible to be really happy – that, Dorry knew, she never would have forgotten.

The blue bonfire burning above them snapped and threw down sparks. Dorry ducked and then laughed, embarrassed. Ned put his arm around her shoulders and asked if she was okay.

She leaned against him and felt new and brave.

"Where are we—" he started.

The fire snapped again.

"What?" said Dorry, leaning closer.

"Where are we meeting up with Tuesday?" Ned said.

"She said she'd find us," Dorry said, automatically, because the more lies you told, the more secrets you kept, the easier the lies and secrets became.

◆

Dex squinted at the crowd through the scrim of his false lashes.

He knew – he knew that girl. The little girl dressed all in black, with the Horus eye painted on her face. Well, she wasn't a little girl, she was smack in the middle of the Britney Spears Venn diagram (not a girl, not yet a woman), but he knew her, and he couldn't figure out how. Maybe it was costume distortion. And his false lashes and the jangle of the band against his nerves. The singer was a skinny white kid with perfect skin and raccoon-blacked eyes and legs like swizzle sticks, and he was merely a shade above decent, by Dex's admittedly exacting standards. The crowd jostled him from all sides. He wasn't far from the park bench where he once drank coffee from a borrowed tumbler and contemplated the high of having only just met one Rabbit Hatmaker, but he might as well have been on another planet. Boston Common was teeming. Overrun.

And he was all by himself, alone in a crowded funeral.

He shivered.

He was supposed to meet Rabbit by the food tent in fifteen minutes. No – he checked his watch. Thirteen minutes. He took a step toward the tent and lost sight of the Horus girl he thought he knew, and as soon as she was gone, swallowed by the throng, he forgot he'd even seen her. His mind was having trouble holding on to things. There was so much to see. To hear. The air was dense with distraction.

"Girl," said a deep voice to his left, and Dex twitched and spun toward it. "That mug is beat."

The voice belonged to a stunning six-foot-something drag Cher. Dex took it as the extreme compliment it was, and drew his fingers back on either side of his cheeks, contoured and blended. He batted his eyes, dark and false-lashed, traced his filled brows, pursed his red lips. He was painted for the very back of the house, and it felt good, better than good, to be noticed by a professional.

Dex had discovered, when he was a freshman in high school,

after someone's well-meaning but tragically Revloned mom botched his makeup for his first featured role in a drama production (Bottom), that he loved the way a little colored paste and powder, skillfully applied, gave him an entirely different face, and that he was naturally skilled at applying it. Because it was the early nineties, deep in western Mass., he knew to hide that talent; he carefully fixed his makeup in a bathroom on the other side of the school, far from the bustling preshow auditorium – reddening his lips, blending his foundation so it didn't trace his jaw blunt as a coastline. He lined his eyes. Tamed his brows. When he was in full costume later, that same well-meaning mom told him gosh, she'd done a great job! He was beautiful! Dex gave her the butchest thumbs-up he knew how to give.

He was a headliner (Rolf the Nazi, Nathan Detroit, and Henry Higgins, for the record) who did his own eyeliner for the rest of high school. He refined it in college, on the stage, at parties. But adult life had less space for this face; he painted it only a few times a year. It made him a little sad, now, to see this other face he had, that he showed to no one but his mirror and the infrequent dark club. This face that he had never shown to Patrick, or to any of his exes, unless they happened to be dating on Halloween. It was a face for occasions – it was too much work, to put on and take off, to wear every day. But that was part of why he loved it. It was dramatic and haunted, his own face but better, the face he wore when he wanted to feel more alive.

Or feel like Madonna, an urge that overtook him like gay clockwork every Halloween. Over the years he had been club-kid Madonna, *Evita* Madonna, Marilyn Madonna, and once, memorably, pleather bondage Madonna. This year he was wearing a short blond wig with finger waves, a wireless over-ear mic, a blue pinstriped pantsuit with enormous shoulder pads – the top of his body was an inverted triangle

– and a pale pink bustier. And a monocle, of course, dangling between the fabric cones of his faux breasts. The irony was consciously unintentional, but Dex's subconscious was a dire conflagration these days: in his business suits, he couldn't express himself.

"Put your love to the test," sang Cher, disappearing back into the crowd. Dex's gut trembled.

A gust of cold wind whooshed. Cloaks and wings fluttered. People shrieked, chilled but happy. Dex shivered again and decided to just go to the food tent and wait. Milling made his anxiety worse. He needed somewhere to perch and something to drink. He needed—

Tuesday.

Tuesday was standing about twenty feet away. Not looking in his direction, but it was unmistakably her – her dark head and her pale cheek and her tall body, all dressed in black. Her hair looked beyond fantastic, shining over her shoulders. So that was her costume: woman in black. Dex snorted. Typical, typical Tuesday. The last thing she'd want to do after getting fired was spend money on some dopey dress-up clothes. Even though he was still pissed at her, and sore, and awash in anxiety about Rabbit seeing him in drag for the first time, he knew it wasn't her fault. But she certainly hadn't helped. Tuesday had shone a klieg light on his naked need for attention, and what was drag – what *wasn't* drag, really? Drag was punk, drag was protest, drag was performance and art and fantasy, drag was as many things as there were people who practiced it – though for him, what was drag but a sequined scream? *Look at me. Really look at me, please. I dare you to look at me and know me and love me.*

Despite all that, seeing Tuesday in her un-costume gave him a small bump of amusement.

Nice effort, babe.

A tall drink of dark and damaged was standing next to her.

Archie. What Dex could see of his face was a ruin. Bruises, yellow and purple, going sour along his jaw. A fat lip, split. If it was makeup, it was fantastic. If it wasn't, something had happened that Dex half wanted to know, half wanted to stay comfortably ignorant of. Maybe he was dressed as – Dex didn't know, a fight club playboy or something, in a ratty red smoking jacket. Archie leaned down to whisper in Tuesday's ear. Something about the way he touched her shoulder and she curled toward him made Dex inhale.

No wonder her hair looked fantastic.

It was sex hair.

Dex was a mess and he didn't know how to sort himself. The fact that they were obviously sleeping together, and Dex could read it from across the crowded Common, rose as a gleeful silent cackle in the back of his head. The fact that Dex hadn't even tried to contact his supposed friend since she'd been an asshole – when she was blind drunk after one of the worst days of her adult life – drained some of that glee. But whose job was it to be the better friend right now? Who was responsible for making the first move?

Dex looked at his watch. It was time.

He addressed the first bartender under the *Beetlejuice*-striped tent and ordered a gin and tonic, hold the tonic, and stood, sipping quietly, waiting for Rabbit to appear. Dex hadn't told Rabbit what his costume would be. Since it wasn't going to be the bespoke suit of armor – well, Dex sniffed, it was still *a* suit of armor, in a manner of speaking – he told Rabbit he'd have to wait and see. Which had the potential to be a little brutal, perhaps.

To both of them.

Dex saw Rabbit before Rabbit saw him. He came around the corner from behind the tent, eyes searching. He was dressed in a swallowtail coat, top hat, white spats, and red bow tie, with his pockets turned inside out. A luxuriously fake white mustache crouched on his upper lip. So Vincent Pryce's plan was for the banker to dress as the Monopoly man. Because, clearly, Vincent Pryce had known how dashing Rabbit would look in a tuxedo.

Dex sipped and watched Rabbit search.

It didn't take long.

Rabbit covered his mouth with his hand and walked over. Dex didn't know how to read that. Rabbit's eyes looked like they wanted to laugh.

Maybe?

"What do you think?" said Dex, and realized he was going to just do it, say it. Force the issue. "Too much?" He gestured to his wig, his face, his entirely other body.

Rabbit lowered his hand. He was blushing furiously above his mustache.

They beheld each other, a fake old man and a fake young Madonna, until Dex couldn't take it any longer.

"Does it freak you out?" he asked.

Rabbit's mouth went up, down, worky without actually working.

"It has, in the past, and I won't name names. Let's say Drag Dex has been received with varying levels of enthusiasm." He felt his throat close a little.

Rabbit smiled at him. It didn't feel like enough. But then, that was one of Dex's problems, wasn't it, that for whatever reason, logical or il-, the world, in one way or another, never felt like enough. This Dex was his favorite. This Dex, painted for the gods (or at least the Madonnas), was a dead-serious joke, the ghost of who he thought, once upon a time, he was supposed to be. A singer. An actor. A light on a stage who could share infinite other lives for a moment with strangers, easing the sting of being so very finite indeed. This Dex was a reminder that he had lived long enough to have known other versions of himself, that the self he was now wasn't permanent, or didn't have to be; this Dex was many, and could become someone else still. The gulf between this Dex and the other Dex Howard, the Dex who shaved his face in the morning and knotted his Armani tie and slid feet into his Gucci loafers (every bit an act of drag as what he was currently wearing) – that gulf was deep and wide and dark. Every time he passed through it, every time he remembered the cost of all those hours spent being that Dex, Office Drag Dex, Part of the Problem Dex, Cynical Dex, it was that much harder to go back. But to stay, to be, to remain *this* Dex – too open, too loud, too femme – was terrifying too. He was never in more danger than when he allowed himself to be *most* himself. When he was most himself, he ran the constant risk of being entirely Too Much.

The kind of Too Much that could get the literal shit kicked out of you.

"I know, I know," Dex said. *Pop the moment*, he thought. *Pop it like a balloon.* "Just another needy queen, begging for attention."

Rabbit's white-gloved hand slipped into his own and squeezed. "You're astonishing," he said.

Dex wanted desperately to believe him. But that would have required believing it himself first.

◆

"Madonna at twelve o'clock," said Archie.

Tuesday turned to look.

"That's him," she said. Her voice was small. She didn't move. Dex looked at his watch, closed his eyes as if bracing himself for a blow, and about-faced to the food tent.

Tuesday's face was very flat. Then she twitched, and tilted her ear forward like she was trying to catch a voice in the crowd. She'd been doing that, tilting and listening, for the past two days – in her apartment, when there were no voices other than their own. When Archie asked her about it, she said she was thinking, not listening. Archie decided if she could agree to (mostly) stop badgering him about his family and Vincent Pryce, then he could stop badgering her about this tic.

So he did. But he didn't stop wondering. Or worrying.

Or aching. His body was wrecked. He touched his lip, amazed that it was still so swollen (making out like insane teenagers probably hadn't helped). And something was wrong with his neck now; he couldn't turn all the way to his right without feeling a sharp pinch. But his bruises were fading. And he wasn't dead, which meant he probably hadn't been bleeding internally this whole time.

Though maybe he *was* dead. That would explain the way his brain was floating, how when he looked around him – at this crowd, this party, this funeral – he had to remind himself it was real and that he was real too, that he was in his body and he was standing here. Archie had the sensation of being outside time. Able to observe the yawning pit of his life from a distance, without judgment but also without the deep burn of shame and fear that a reckoning typically triggered. He'd followed Vincent Pryce's direction to play his game, and not play it alone, and now his life had loosened. Shifted. Tomorrow he could be anyone.

But today he was still himself. He'd ghosted his sister – hadn't so much as emailed her, even after Tuesday correctly pointed out it was childish to vanish. "You don't do that if you have any choice in the matter," she said. "You *do not do that* to people you care about." He tried to explain it was because he cared about Emerson that he'd disappeared. He didn't want her to know where he was or whom he was with, because the less information she had that his brother could get, even tangentially, about his whereabouts or his intentions, the safer everyone was. Tuesday told him that was a steaming pile of self-deluding horseshit, and he knew it.

"You of all people," she said – they were sitting on her tiny red sofa watching the other Vincent Price's *House of Usher* (well, he was watching; Tuesday's fingertips were flicking furiously across her laptop, like she was casting a spell) – and shoved him, hard enough to hurt. "You of all people should know how it feels for someone to vanish without a trace. Your father was a complete bastard, but don't you want to know what happened? For sure?"

Archie held his tongue.

Tuesday had been online for hours. They'd hatched a general plan for what to do with the money, after which Tuesday said, curtly, she would take it from there. She'd taken it, all right. The rapid patter of her fingertips was both soothing and hilarious; Archie, who had never officially learned how to type, thought it sounded more like she was pretending to type than actually typing. Every once in a while he asked what she'd found, and she'd say, Not yet. I haven't found it yet. Until she said, There, I found them. And he had to agree that she'd found something perfect.

"There are ways to let people know that you haven't vanished off the face of the earth," Tuesday continued. "And the whole 'the more people I let in, the more people I put in danger' thing is superhero vigilante crap. I'm already in danger. Your not telling me everything actually puts me in more danger, because I don't know what we're up against."

Archie smiled at her.

"You said 'we,'" he said.

"Also," she said, "it's patriarchal bullshit. If I were a man, would you feel as compelled to protect me?"

"You're not a man? This whole time, when we met—" Archie shook his head. "I just assumed."

"Don't get cute. When we met, do you know what I recognized in you? What I saw?"

"My cuteness?" He shrugged. "It's hard to miss."

"You live every day with an unsolved mystery," she said.

Archie held his tongue again, and though it seemed that she was about to say more, so did she. Until:

"Roderick Usher Real Estate owns a Gilded Age mansion in Brookline." She turned her laptop to face him. "Roderick Usher owns a *lot* of property in and around Boston, not just the condo in Beacon Hill. But this one is . . ."

"What?" The Google satellite image looked like any other giant old house on the edge of Brookline adjacent to the Emerald Necklace, the string of parkland southwest of the city.

"Special." Tuesday clicked over to a browser tab with the property record. "Look at the sales history. Roderick Usher bought it six years ago from NA LLC."

"Not applicable," Archie joked.

"NA LLC bought it a few years before that from ACE Real Estate Investments. ACE REI has the same corporate address as Arches Consolidated. It's a subsidiary." Tuesday's voice was speeding up. "And ACE sold it to NA for exactly one dollar."

"Is that like *The Price is Right*?" said Archie. "One dollar!"

"Real estate that passes from buyer to seller for one dollar typically means it's an interfamily transfer. Your family company sold this old house to a private corporation with a family or personal connection. And NA sold it to Roderick Usher, for a lot more than a dollar, and a lot more than the surrounding properties are worth – possibly – or possibly not – knowing that Roderick Usher Real Estate traces back to Vincent Pryce."

"NA." Archie didn't want to even say his name. "Is my brother."

Tuesday inhaled. "That's my guess," she said. She was already typing furiously again. "But why this house? What *is* this house? Did your family ever live in Brookline? Do you recognize the neighborhood, or the property?" She paused.

"It's almost like there's an – undergame. Like the surface of Vincent Pryce's adventure is a dash around the city, all codes and playing cards. But there's another game underneath it, festering. And it's all about" – she jabbed a finger at him – "your family. And I can't figure it out."

Archie didn't say anything.

"Yet," she said.

Archie didn't have to ask, once they were standing in the humming crowd at Vince's funeral, whether Tuesday had figured it out yet. It was clear that she hadn't. She was too distracted still, too uneasy. Too raw.

"Aren't you going to talk to him?" Archie asked, nodding toward Dex and the food tent. Tuesday was acting funny about Dex too, preoccupied and hesitant. When he'd asked if Dex was meeting them at the funeral, all she'd said was *We need to look for a Madonna*. Then she'd cocked her ear again, and listened, and muttered something that sounded like *nested*. Tuesday was a still point in the center of the Common, thoroughly distracted, but not, he suspected, by the tumult around her. Her brain was looking inward, turning over details and trying to make them fit. Trying to reach, through the thicket of Vince's game, a satisfying conclusion. But Archie knew Vince. And by now he knew Tuesday well enough to think that they might have competing definitions of what made a conclusion satisfying.

Vince was everywhere at his own funeral. In the hundreds of revelers strewn across the grass, in the circle of colored bonfires, in the woodsmoke and music on the breeze. In the very air, crackling with weird potential. It made Archie feel sick. Because Vince was in a movie at the back of Archie's brain too. And in that movie, Vince was looking at him across the crowded ballroom of the Four Seasons Hotel. Exactly as he had looked at him, as they had looked at each other, in the moment before Vincent Pryce died. It was the first time they'd seen each other in six years, since the summer Edgar Arches Senior disappeared.

It was also the summer Edgar Arches Junior had been disappearing by degrees. Had been becoming, thanks to Vincent Pryce, a man named Archie. Who believed he could live a different life than the one he'd been born to.

And it was the summer his brother changed his life forever, but not in the way Archie thought Vince meant.

In the movie in Archie's head, Vince stood up and screamed. Then he opened his eyes in shock, in horror, at Archie standing in the back of the ballroom.

You and your brother, screamed Vince, *have one thing in common.*

The funeral music stopped abruptly, midsong, like someone had yanked out a cord.

A squeal of feedback shot through the dark.

"Friends, freaks, all and others, I welcome you. To my funeral."

The crowd broke into applause and whistles. Archie, hearing Vince's voice – everywhere – all around – his knees softened. *I killed you,* he thought. *I didn't mean to. I'm so sorry. But it's what an Arches does.*

An Arches kills.

He bumped into Tuesday and held on to her.

"Usually at a funeral – well, usually, at a funeral, the deceased does not speak." Vince's voice came from the sky and the ground. Vince's voice was in Archie's bones. "But this is my funeral, and I can say whatever I please. I'll start with thank you. Thank you for coming. I hope the food and the music are excellent. I hope tonight you drink and dance and laugh and hold one another close and in the midst of my death feel very much alive."

Archie breathed.

"And some of you, tonight – I hope some of you cross over."

The crowd cheered, and the sound was very far away, like it was coming from the other side of the world.

"You began playing this game when you didn't know for certain what you might win," Vince said. "You played for the sake of playing. You played for the hope of a great fortune shared. Now you are one step closer: for, should you be one of the thirteen chosen, you shall be driven from this place in a horse-drawn hearse to one of my most prized possessions. Not all of the objects in my vast collection of the fantastic and phantasmagoric fit inside my house on the island. Some of those haunted objects are themselves—"

"Houses," hissed Tuesday, and squeezed Archie's arm.

"Houses," said Vince, as though he'd been listening. "Should you pass the widow's interview, tonight you will sleep in a haunted house, not far from here, with a view of Olmstead's emeralds. And tomorrow, should you listen to the spirits, let them rattle and lift you, you may awaken anew. You may rise the recipient of wonders beyond what this world knows."

Vince cleared his throat. The crowd whistled.

"I make a point," he said, "of putting a serious question to a person whenever I meet them. The hour is late and the time for words without meaning is past. I am deeply sorry I am not here tonight, in a form more corporeal, to hear your responses. But still I wish to ask of you all:

"What are you looking for?"

Tuesday's grip on Archie's arm tightened.

"Well." Vince laughed a little. "That's all. Have fun. Take care of one another. This is my party; like my life and yours, it too will end. Not very long ago, I found myself wondering whether it was time to seal myself into my own tomb. I had lost a dear friend, and I had, in my grief, retreated from the world, with nothing left but to set my affairs in order. But then one mystery led to another, and led me back to myself, and I found I had yet more life, and more people, to love. Do not stop. For you, there is still time. To do the work. To reckon with the past. To shed light, and to become it; to make and remake this world and to imagine and build others. Yes, for you there is time, because you, unlike me, are not dead. Please, if not for my sake then for your own—"

Archie was shuddering. He saw Vince across the ballroom. He saw Vince's eyes widen. He saw Vince see him, in his last seconds. Know him, in his last thought.

Blame him, with the last beat of his heart.

"Act accordingly," purred the dead man.

16

INTERVIEW WITH THE WIDOW

"You're not going to run away this time, are you?"

Lyle was sitting in a deep-red velvet wingback chair, purpled by shadows, her body buoyed by yards and yards of rustling black fabric. She was a widow in black lace. The dress was true black, rich black, the kind of black that ate light, with a high neck, puffed sleeves, and shiny black buttons to the elbows. A veil floated around her face. A layer of black fringe hung heavy along the hem. A black parasol, collapsed, leaned against her chair.

It couldn't be the most comfortable thing to wear, especially when you were pregnant. But it was boss as hell.

"No," said Tuesday. "I—"

Don't even bother, said Abby, and Tuesday snapped her teeth together.

"Have a seat," Lyle said. Tuesday sat in a matching red velvet wingback across from the widow. Behind Lyle, not so close to the tent wall to be a fire hazard, was a fireplace. On a faux mantel above sat a white marble bust of, presumably, Pallas. Lyle passed Tuesday a plate heaped with chocolate chip cookies.

"Cookie?" she asked.

Tuesday took one.

Archie sat in another wingback, tipped slightly askew over the uneven grass.

Lyle blanched.

"That's Vince's," she said. "That's Vince's robe. How did you get Vince's robe?"

Ooh, delicious, said Abby.

"This isn't funny." Lyle moved to the edge of her seat. "Whoever you are – how did you get my husband's robe?"

"I knew him," said Archie. Painfully, like the words were a dry cracker stabbing his throat. He pulled the lapels of the smoking jacket tighter. They'd stopped at the condo on their way to the funeral. Archie didn't have a costume, and Vince's robe was the only thing he said he could imagine wearing.

"That's nice. I knew him too." Lyle lifted her chin at one of the security guys posted at the entrance of the tent, and he channeled his attention on the small circle of chairs. "You need to do better than that. This is the part where I get to decide whether you keep going."

"How do you decide?" asked Tuesday.

"Your costumes are part of it. And you're already tanking hard in that respect." She stared at Archie. "Tell me now how you got Vince's robe or you're both out." She looked at Tuesday. "Sorry, Tuesday. Your boyfriend better not screw it up."

"He's not my boyfriend," Tuesday said.

"I knew him." Archie blinked. Swallowed. He'd been distracted for most of the day, but since they'd gotten to the funeral, he had become a human balloon. Without Tuesday to tether him, he would've drifted away.

Let him go, said Abby, and Tuesday shook her head.

"I knew him when I was younger," Archie finally got out. "He was my friend. He – uh." He closed his eyes. "When I got back to town, I – I have a PO box here, just – in case. He sent me a key. To his place in Beacon Hill, and I – got used to wearing this. It's drafty." He tugged on the smoking jacket. "And this is . . . cozy."

Lyle's eyes slid into slits.

"He knew me before – the last time I saw him was six years ago. No – the last time I saw him." Archie wrapped his hands around his kneecaps. "The last time I saw him was the night he died. I was there, at the hotel, in the ballroom. And I—"

"It's true," Tuesday told Lyle. "He was at the Four Seasons. That's where we first met."

Archie made a noise like a wounded bird.

"I killed him," he said.

"What?" said Lyle.

What? said Abby.

Tuesday didn't say anything.

That's impossible, Abby continued.

"I – I know it was an aneurysm, but. The shock of seeing me. After—" Archie dragged both his hands down his face. "He looked at me and knew me and he – I could feel how much I had hurt him. How disappointed he was in what I had done, or not done, really. I—"

What's impossible? Tuesday thought at Abby.

Lyle leaned forward, mouth slightly open, face rapt and still.

Look at her, said Abby. **A man just confessed to stressing her husband to death.**

"So you're Archie," Lyle said.

"Yes," said Archie.

And she's taking it in stride.

"You're Vince's lost Arches. You got the letter I sent to the PO box. Vince kept that box for you all this time," said Lyle. She sat back, voluminous skirts rustling, and stared hard at Archie's face. "I see it now – the resemblance. That shiner threw me off." Then she handed him the plate. "Cookie?"

"What?" Archie said.

Because she knows, said Abby. **She knows better.**

"Cookie." Lyle waggled the plate at him.

"But—" said Archie.

"You didn't." Tuesday's head felt hot. "You didn't kill him."

"No," said Lyle, looking sideways at Tuesday but addressing Archie with her body. "You didn't."

"You can't know that," said Archie. "The shock – you can't know. You can't know, not for sure."

"Believe it or not," said Lyle, "not everything in this world happens because of you."

She knows, said Abby, **that Vincent Pryce didn't die at the fundraiser.**

The hair on the back of Tuesday's neck sprang. How—

Yes.

Of course Vincent Pryce hadn't died at the fundraiser.

The show couldn't begin until the actors were on the stage.

"You didn't kill Vincent Pryce at the fundraiser," said Tuesday to Archie, casually, though the back of her brain was fizzing like a sparkler. "You couldn't have, because Vincent Pryce didn't die at the fundraiser."

Lyle's mouth dropped open. "Well," she said, bright, "I wasn't sure anyone would figure that out."

"Figure – what?" asked Archie. "What do you mean? You mean – Vince isn't dead?"

"No," said Tuesday. "He's dead."

"He is," said Lyle. "Dead."

"Sometime in the last—" said Tuesday. She hovered her hand over her own belly and raised an eyebrow at Lyle. "Eight weeks?"

Lyle's lips pressed together in a flat line that wasn't a smile.

Cool it, said Abby. **Figuring out all the secrets at once won't get you another cookie.**

"Please," said Archie. "Would someone please explain what's happening?"

Lyle turned up her palm and gestured to Tuesday. "The floor is yours."

Tuesday clasped her hands. **You got this,** said Abby.

"An aneurysm is a bomb without a countdown clock," she

said. "It goes off when it wants to. You can't know. You can't plan. Vincent Pryce, faced with that certain uncertainty, decided to plan everything else. Prepaying, preprogramming his funeral service. Elaborately. He set up all the dominoes while he was still alive and trusted his surviving loved ones to set them off.

"The man who died at the fundraiser didn't die," said Tuesday. "I don't quite – know – he must have been an actor. Wearing a Vincent Pryce costume, hired to play his dramatic death scene. We thought we saw him die, but all we actually saw him do was collapse. The doctors who came forward, they were trying to save him still. And the paramedics got there so quickly, I bet they were actors too. You, Lyle – you were an actor. That night."

"Get me in a room full of corporate wankers and I'm already acting anyway," Lyle said. "But you're correct that I had a script that night."

"That's how Vincent Pryce managed to die on cue, when all the dominoes were lined up – guaranteeing maximum publicity, maximum press, and public interest in his death." Tuesday sat back in her seat. "He wanted as many people to know about his game and to play it as possible. I don't know why, exactly. Other than the simplest explanation."

Archie snorted. "Oh great. The simplest explanation." He turned to Tuesday. "Which is?"

"He liked games." Tuesday shrugged at Lyle.

"Vince loved games," Lyle said. "And he thought too many people had forgotten how to play. They'd been brainwashed into thinking the entire point of playing a game – or working or living or doing anything – is to win."

"Isn't it?" Archie asked.

"Not the *entire* point," said Lyle. "Otherwise, the only game humans would ever have invented would be the coin toss. Heads or tails. Win or lose. But instead we have chess and checkers. We have backgammon and craps and poker. We have Clue and Monopoly. We have Risk – we have Settlers of Catan, for Christ's sake. We have Frogger. Myst. Halo. We have *Jeopardy!* and the freaking *Match Game*. You cannot convince me the point of *Match Game* is to win." Lyle raised a beautiful dark eyebrow. "The point of a game is the experience of *playing*. The obstacles and the choices you make to get to the objective. The possibility of winning, the danger of loss, shapes the game. Risk and reward give the game suspense, a plot. But winning or losing is not the whole point." She took another cookie from the plate and bent it into two pieces. "So yes, Vince loved games, and he wanted to make people play. What I wanted was the distraction. I'm a director. That's how I first got to be friends with Rabbit – I directed the high school musical, he conducted the pit orchestra. Vince found out about the aneurysm last March. We both knew it was coming but we didn't know when, and I knew I needed a project to get me through this year, this time after – this time without Vince." She bit into one of the cookie halves and chewed. "Vince died five days before the fundraiser, at home in bed. With Roddy curled up over his feet, and me sleeping" – she closed her eyes – "beside him. Roddy and I woke up, but Vince kept dreaming." She looked up at Archie. "The game is for his heirs; his heirs are anyone who wants to play. But it's also for me. And you, Archie. A lot of it is for you. I mailed that letter the day after the auction. You're the only one who got a personal invitation to play."

Archie, shocked pale, grumbled, "I thought you said not everything in the world happens because of me." He shook his head. "I saw," he said. "I saw him *look* at me—"

"You saw an actor look at you," said Tuesday, chewing thoughtfully, "from across a ballroom, wearing a costume that you recognized. Whatever you saw in his face was your projection."

"How can you be so cool about all of this?" he snapped. And he was suddenly so present, jerked angrily out of his dreaminess, that Tuesday almost told him the truth. That she wasn't cool at all. She was a walking exposed nerve. If she looked cool, it was because cool was the only costume she had in her closet.

Archie still hadn't learned how to see through the way things appear to the way they might actually be.

Lyle coughed delicately into her fist. "I have a few questions," she said.

"Being one of Vince's chosen heirs isn't enough to get us through?" Archie said. There was a bratty sourness in his voice that made Tuesday hate him a little. She didn't regret their partnership, however fuzzily defined that partnership may be. But Archie was more like his brother than Tuesday suspected he'd care to admit; they both had a problem, sometimes, remembering how rich they were.

"It's enough to get *you* through," Lyle told him. "You're guaranteed entrance. The only one."

Tuesday's pulse quickened, but she didn't let her face so much as twitch. "So I brought an ace?" she said.

Lyle paused. She locked eyes with Tuesday as though Tuesday had said something cunning. And intentional.

Think about it, said Abby.

"Can I see your card?" asked Lyle. "Your playing card."

Tuesday handed her the queen of diamonds from the pocket of her dress. Lyle pinched it between her first finger and thumb.

Then she flicked it into the fire behind her.

"Um," said Archie, his voice rising, like this small act of violence was a warning of greater lunacy to come. "Okay."

You brought an ace, said Abby.

"What did you do with the thirteen thousand dollars?" Lyle asked Tuesday.

Fifty-one, said Abby.

Tuesday watched the red pattern on the back of the card blacken. Rectangular border in red, a nested circle. A game, and a game inside a game.

Fifty-one, said Abby, **is one card less than a full deck.**

"And it's not the fifty-one," murmured Tuesday to herself. It was the *one*. The missing one. But which card was it – an ace, and was the ace Archie? Had she already found him?

"Tuesday?" said Lyle.

"I—" Tuesday stared at Lyle. She felt the cushion of the chair beneath her. The slight warmth of the fire.

"At first I thought I would keep it," she said. "For myself. I was fired from my job this week—" Lyle softened but Tuesday held up a hand. "It's okay," Tuesday said. "I mean, it's not okay. But it wasn't unjustified. Anyway, I lost my job, so I thought, what a perfect time for a windfall, while I figure out what the hell else to do. Banked. Done. But."

"But," said Lyle.

"That wasn't the game. That wasn't Pryce's design. To keep the money for myself felt like stealing. I'm not rich, relatively speaking." She turned her head from Archie to Lyle and back again. "But I have savings, I have options. I have time. A strange stranger gave me – gave us – thirteen thousand dollars and told us to use our imaginations. To seek well: to be curious, to find what we can in the world, to *be* alive while we're alive. I thought of that line in his obituary—"

Lyle's eyes glittered.

"—about regretting arriving at death's doormat with full pockets. I felt he was saying – don't hoard what you've been given, because you think it's all you're going to get. Be generous. And be generous *now*, because the future isn't a destination. It's an extension of how we choose to live today. Archie offered to match the thirteen thousand, so we had twenty-six thousand to work with. And I found someone to give it to."

"You found – someone?" Lyle asked. "Who? Where? How?"

"In an obituary." Tuesday grinned. "Her name is Ruby Octavian. She's forty-seven, widowed – it was her wife Lou's obituary. Ruby and Lou Octavian owned a refurbished movie house in a town about this big" – she held her fingertips a hairbreadth apart – "in upstate New York. Lou had a heart attack one night closing the place up. Ruby works in the town's public library. They cohosted movie marathons and classic film screenings and booked bands and dances, and they got married there, under the screen. I don't know what's going to happen to the theater. I know Lou and Ruby both loved it. I know I would've really liked Lou. But Ruby's still here. And so is the library and so is the theater and so are the people in the town who come to both."

"But how did you – did you know them?" Lyle said.

"No, not personally," said Tuesday. "I read a bunch of online obituaries until I found someone I missed without ever having met them. The rest is easily discoverable. Articles, wedding announcements in the local paper, real estate records, Facebook, Twitter. The movie theater has its own website. Ruby's setting up a memorial prize in Lou's name, small grants for kids who want to make their own movies." Tuesday crossed her arms over her stomach. "I thought Vince would've appreciated that, too. Plus, the name of the theater itself – the Castle – felt like a sign. I gave Arch the cash, he drew up a check made out to Ruby, and FedEx will drop it on her doorstep Monday. Inside there's a note saying it's a no-strings-attached gift from a friend on the other side. Signed with a little black raven." She paused.

Lyle was smiling at her.

"What?" Tuesday said.

"Vince would have loved that," Lyle said. "He would have just." She sighed. "Loved that." She clapped her hands together. "You're through. You made it. Your costumes are simply atrocious – like, what even are you, Tuesday? Other than yourself."

She's on to you, said Abby, and Tuesday laughed, and Archie laughed like he could hear the voice inside her head too.

Lyle continued. "But you used your imagination. You used all the money." Lyle sliced her hand through the air. "You would not believe the number of bozos who came here tonight and tried to pay me thirteen thousand dollars to keep going. To buy their way forward. Like, no. Just – no. That might happen in the real world, but this is not the real world. This world is Vince's design, but I'm casting and directing it."

Tuesday raised both brows. "Did you take the money back?"

"Hell yes, I took the money. I'll *use* it." She settled back into her folds of luxurious black. "But the most important box you checked on the checklist—"

"I *knew* there was a checklist," said Tuesday.

"You thought about someone or something outside of yourself."

Lyle looked at Tuesday, and Tuesday looked back. She didn't know Lyle, not really. Not from the details she'd found in her research, not from the brunch they'd shared, and not from this fifteen-minute interview. Lyle didn't know her either. They were their own selves, separate humans living separate lives. But they were aligned nonetheless, linked inextricably, and not just by the death of Vincent Pryce but because all lives are linked, all the world is one tremendous story. And Tuesday felt, for the first time since she'd been fired – for the first time, probably, since – since she didn't remember when—

Tuesday had the distinct sensation of knowing where she was going.

"Crucial point," Lyle said to Archie. "The same isn't true of you. You made it through not because you used your imagination – though you did use all the money Vince gave you plus additional money of your own, noted – but because of your name. You're moving on because you're Edgar Arches Junior."

Tuesday felt Archie's mood darken beside her, a cloud skimming over the sun. "I don't know everything," said Lyle, "but I know enough. Remember who you are when you're in that house. Remember who you are is *why* you're in that house."

Archie inhaled. Tuesday exhaled.

Let's do this fucken thing, shouted Abby.

"Congratulations," said the widow. "You're dead."

17

THIS HOUSE IS FALLING APART

Dorry pressed both hands flat to the rough pine underside of the coffin lid and pushed.

It didn't budge.

"That's okay," she murmured to herself. "That's fine. I can wait. She said it would open when it was time."

"She" was Mrs. Pryce. Vincent Pryce's widow, wearing a huge dress that rustled when she knelt next to Dorry, folds of fabric crowding around her so she looked like she was sitting on a little black cloud. After Dorry settled herself snugly into the coffin – really, it was a wooden box with a pillow for her head; it wasn't even coffin-shaped – Mrs. Pryce asked if she was comfortable. And if she was sure she wanted to do this.

Dorry nodded. She wasn't turning back, not *now*. Cass and Lisa Pinto passed the widow's interview, based on all the questions Mrs. Pryce asked, because they started the Black Cats group on Facebook. Ned made it because Mrs. Pryce took a long look at his costume, then smiled broadly and said, *Bravo. It took me a minute.* Dorry honestly wasn't sure why Mrs. Pryce let her through, partially because she hadn't told the whole truth, and she was pretty sure Mrs. Pryce could tell. When she asked Dorry what she was looking for, Dorry thought, *Mom.* Always. All this time, she'd been looking for her mother. And though, back in Tuesday's apartment, it had seemed so clear that looking for her mom was the right answer, the kind of answer Vincent Pryce would want to hear, she couldn't—

She didn't want to say it. Out loud. She didn't want to admit she'd played this game, in front of Ned and Cass and Lisa Pinto, who were the coolest people she'd met (since Tuesday), all because she wanted some special goggles that would let her see the ghost of her mother. It would sound too silly. Too babyish. And it was just too true.

So instead she told Mrs. Pryce that she'd researched her husband's stuff and thought it was amazing. A second after she said it, Dorry realized it might sound rude, like she didn't care about the dead man as much as all his stuff, which wasn't true at *all*. The widow squinted at her, and Dorry rambled for a bit about how she didn't mean to sound greedy, she just – like, for example, the Earhart goggles, they were amazing. Ned jumped to her rescue and said, "So you're looking to be amazed," and Dorry was so grateful for the save that she almost cried. Real tears that she had to blink back. Which Mrs. Pryce *definitely* noticed.

At that point it would've been mean to hold Dorry back. To not let her go on with the rest of her friends into the next tent, all stacked with pine boxes.

Not that they were her *friend* friends, really. She'd only known Ned for, like, a week, and Cass and Lisa Pinto for . . . hours.

Mrs. Pryce, kneeling next to her coffin, looked worried. Like maybe she didn't believe that Dorry was eighteen, or a freshman at MIT, or named Juliet Mai Huang, which was the name on the student ID Dorry showed when she signed the papers. (Lisa Pinto's horse costume *was* a kangaroo pouch full of very useful things.) Dorry made up everything on the papers except for her address, because she'd heard somewhere that the best lies have a significant percentage of truth.

She pushed the lid again, and still it didn't budge.

At least she wasn't moving anymore. Or rather, being moved. Once the lid had been shut, and she'd heard the bolt on the side of the box sliding home, Dorry rose in a swoop. Then she floated horizontally, her head tipped lower than her feet, like she was being carried by two different people, one tall and one short. She felt the box thump against something solid and slide forward. She heard Ned. Ned was in the coffin next to hers. The boxes weren't very sturdy. She could see light through the edges and feel cool air creeping in. Ned's dampened voice wavered in and out, funny and high-pitched. *Don't have to be rich! – don't have to be cool* – then something that sounded like *I yi yi yi yi yi yiiii—*

"Ned!" she said. She knocked her knuckles against the side. "Ned, it's Dorry. Next to you!"

The yelping stopped.

"Can't get next to you, girl," he sang again. "Can't get next to you."

The singing was because he was scared. The only thing he was afraid of, he'd whispered on their way to the funeral, was that they'd have to crawl through a tight little space; he hated little spaces, hated hated *hated* them. Dorry guessed the coffin counted as a tight little space. At least he didn't have to crawl through it. He sang the whole time they waited in the coffins, which was, according to her phone, about half an hour, and then suddenly she felt a forward jerk, and motion again. She thought she heard the clop of a horse's hooves. Cheering. The happy noise of a crowd, whistling and – honking? Ned stopped singing, or Dorry stopped being able to hear him over the sounds of the world outside her coffin. She curled on her side and double-folded the pillow under her head and let herself be ferried.

She lost track of time. The ride wasn't gentle, but it had a kind of rhythm, and she didn't realize it was over until she felt herself being pulled back and hoisted again. Carried – up some stairs. The sounds of the night muffled. She was indoors. And she was set down again, she knew not where.

That felt like a long time ago now.

She sort of had to pee.

She had heard scraping, the thunk of coffins being set down, doors opening and closing, but not in a while. She couldn't hear Ned singing anymore. Maybe he had fallen asleep. It defied logic that Dorry could be feeling sleepy – locked in a coffin in a haunted house – but she was. It was past her bedtime. By a lot. She felt cozy and warm and dreamy, and she didn't know what was about to happen, but she wasn't afraid. Maybe she should have been. She wrapped her hand around her mother's silver ankh necklace and thought, *No*. How could she be afraid? How could she be anything but excited? She closed her eyes and pictured her mom's face, and it was like a face from a photograph. It didn't move. It was flat, pinned in time like a postcard tacked to a corkboard. The ankh had been cool when she first touched it, but now it was warming up in her hands.

She heard a soft click. It reminded her of the sound the door at her dad's lab made when he swiped his badge.

She pushed the lid and it opened.

Dorry sat up.

She didn't know where to look first. She was in an enormous room, bigger than the basement of the Steinert building but just as old, dusty, and crumbling, a great hall that reached up two stories to a ceiling covered with strange whorls and bumps of plaster. The hall was surrounded on the second floor by a balcony ringed with stately dark columns. An enormous stone staircase poured from the balcony to the floor of the hall, where Dorry's coffin lay in a jumble with several others. She was the only one sitting up. Everything was gloomy. Light came from one side of the hall, from high arched windows on both the first and second floors. The world was blue light and shadow and—

Dorry kicked her stiff legs out of the coffin and scrambled to her feet.

Scattered throughout the hall were squat square pedestals. On each pedestal was an object. She saw a wooden baseball bat propped in a metal stand. A yellowed globe. An old-fashioned microphone, silver and striped, the kind you imagined Elvis singing into.

Strapped to a cloth mannequin head, faceless and soft: silver-framed goggles with big, bug-green lenses.

Dorry took the goggles off the dummy without thinking. The goggles were here. They were right here, not at the end of the game. Or was this the end? Had she won already? Her hands shook. She slipped the goggles over her head and pushed them back up into her hair like a headband without looking through them. It was silly, maybe, but she—

For weeks she'd been thinking of everything she might see through them, but now that her real life had caught up to her dreams, she was painfully awake. Her heart hurt. It was almost too much to be awake inside her own dream. What if it turned into a nightmare?

She reached up and wrapped her hands around the silver of the eyepieces. She held them.

Then she pulled the goggles over her face and opened her eyes.

◆

"Do you hear that?" said Tuesday. "Listen—"

She tipped her ear to the side. She'd been tilting her head like a dog reacting to a whistle for days, only this time Archie heard it too. It echoed through the basement, this dank, fusty basement where their pine boxes had been dumped on the uneven dirt and slate.

"Sounds like." He swallowed.

Tick *tick* tick *tick* tick *tick*.

"A bomb?" he said.

"It's not a bomb," Tuesday muttered. "Vince doesn't want us dead." And then, off Archie's face: "Not literally."

Tuesday pushed herself up and out of her pine box, then turned back to lend Archie a hand. His calves cramped for a second when he stood on them. The basement was a warren of cardboard boxes and old furniture, dust transforming, by volume, into dirt, and curtains of cobwebs. The only light came from a single weak bulb somewhere to their left. It smelled like wet wood and paper, mold and earth.

"I can see why your brother would sell this off," Tuesday said. "If the upstairs is anything like this, it's not an easy flip." Her voice echoed around a corner. "Oh Arch," she said quietly. "Look at her."

Archie came around a tower of boxes and saw an eye: a black eye, deep as a well. Surrounding the eye was a face. It was a portrait, head, neck, and shoulders, of a young woman, sketched in black charcoal. She had dark hair swept off her forehead with a perfectly round pin like a little moon; those deep, heavy-lidded eyes; and a long, boxy nose that made Archie think of bloodhounds. Her mouth was slightly open, as if she were about to speak. Archie couldn't tell how old the drawing was – there was no date, no signature – or why the woman felt so familiar.

Only—

"This is Vince's," he said. "I remember her. I don't remember who she is, but I know her face. It's part of his collection."

Tuesday picked up the frame and held it at arm's length. "If it's part of the collection, and it's here, then that means it's part of the end game." She audibly *hmmed*. "Let's take it," she said, tucking it under her arm. "And let's find your bomb."

Archie's arms and hands were twitching, like his nerves were shorting out. The long ride in the pine box had calmed him after the interview with Lyle Pryce, though he was still raw. Had Vince been toying with him, *using* him, this entire time? Vince had given him the PO box key that summer. *You never know*, he'd said, pressing the key into Archie's palm, *when you might need to get in touch with a friend*, which had struck Archie as odd but, for Vince, typical. Now, it struck Archie as though Vince had placed him like a piece on a board, long before Archie had any idea he was playing a game. What a dupe he was. What a stupid pawn. Archie had actually thought his decision to play Vince's game had been a choice, *his* choice, a tribute to an old friend. Fate, that he should come home just in time to play it – or tragic destiny, that his return should bring about Vince's death, and create the occasion for it. Either way, it had given him, in his first terrifying days home, a direction. Vince's game had seemed so much easier to focus on, in his guilt and shock, than the cosmically, hilariously insurmountable task of confronting Nat.

Nat, who hadn't needed any plan whatsoever to confront Archie senseless.

And the auction, falling for a fake Vince – Archie had let the guilt of shocking Vince to death pickle him for weeks. What else had he seen and believed? What else was a lie? He burned. And Tuesday had been so obnoxiously composed about it all. Her coolness made him feel even more moronic. He was a complete idiot for not seeing it before she did. He'd actually *known* the dead man, after all. Didn't that mean—

"Ah!" she said. "There. There it is."

Tuesday pointed toward the far corner of the basement's ragged brick wall. Dangling from a nail on a long gold chain was an open pocket watch.

"Is that part of Vince's collection too?" she asked.

It wasn't.

Archie's mouth filled with something hot and sour, and he realized, a second later, that he was about to throw up.

He swallowed.

Yes, he'd known the dead man.

He had known both dead men.

The last time he saw that watch – gaudy as hell, too big to be practical – it was on the floor of his father's yacht. It was ticking away face-up on the carpet of the *Constancy*'s main cabin. His father's flailing hand had torn it out of his suit jacket.

"Kind of impractical for a pocket watch," said Tuesday. She propped the drawing of the young girl against a post and drew closer to look at the watch from the right side, the left, above, and below. "It's a showpiece. Lots of gold. Diamond chips? Style is old but it feels new. Reproduction, maybe. It has an inscription on the inside cover – *Tardius lex*."

Tick *tick* tick *tick* tick *tick*.

"'Slow law'?" she said softly.

Archie couldn't move.

Something was odd about the brick wall behind the watch. The bricks, floor to ceiling, were lighter than the age-blackened bricks on either side. And the wall itself was a diagonal, as if it were covering up a corner of the basement.

"This wall is false," said Tuesday, louder now. She rubbed at a line of mortar and it turned to dust at her touch. She looked back at him.

"You want to—" His throat yanked the words back from his mouth, down into his gut. "Knock it down?"

She lifted the watch off the nailhead.

"Have a better plan?" she said.

Archie's plan, six years ago, had been to run away. That was it: his entire plan. It was the plan of a spoiled twenty-six-year-old brat. On the day that his father shoved his mother into the bar cart, and Archie sliced open his finger and his sister stitched it up, and then his brother and his father, the latter already drunk, went to that wine tasting at the Blue Whale in Nantucket Harbor – as soon as Nat and his father were gone that day, Archie had packed a bag. He threw in socks and underwear. A toothbrush. His electric razor. A ruffled paperback of *All Around the Town*. He hadn't read it yet, and he assumed he was going to have a lot of free time in the near future. All his assumptions about running away were improbable and romantic, as if there might be boxcars on Nantucket he could hop to points west. The only facts that seemed germane were these: He hated his family. He hated his life. Escape was change. This was going to be his adventure.

He didn't say goodbye. He didn't think of his mother or his sister. He thought, for a second, of Vincent Pryce, and congratulated himself for a plan he thought Vince would heartily approve of. He grabbed a bag of potato chips out of the pantry and one of his father's best unopened bottles of scotch, and he took his sister's Vespa. He didn't think to leave a note about that either. The theft spoke for itself.

Archie loved the sea. Whenever they went out on the *Constancy*, even when he was a little kid, he spent more time with their various hired skippers than with his family, who preferred not to interact with their staff when there were so many other things – drinks, resentments – to nurse. He knew enough to be able to get the boat out into open water and back to the mainland, where he would ditch it, or sink it, maybe, as a final fuck you, and vanish into the wider world. Which had to be better than the one into which he'd been born.

He quietly boarded his family's yacht and proceeded to get very drunk on his father's scotch. That hadn't been part of the plan, but it hadn't *not* been part of the plan either. The next thing Archie remembered about that day – drunk, he'd rolled himself up into a cocoon of blankets on the floor in the master bedroom and fallen asleep – was the sound of his father's pocket watch hitting the floor. He didn't know it was the watch until later; all he heard was a heavy *thunk*. All he knew, when he jerked awake, was that he was not alone on the boat. And from the gentle bob of the floor beneath him, he could tell he was out to sea. He pulled deeper into the blankets and listened. He couldn't comprehend what he was hearing. A frenzied whistling of fabric against fabric. Low grunts, muffled like a muzzled animal. It was quiet, achingly quiet, or maybe Archie was so drunk he was delusional, but it was so still he thought he could hear ticking: tick *tick* tick *tick* tick *tick*. That was when he thought of the pocket watch. His mother had given it to his father for his most recent birthday, only a few weeks ago in July. It was a reproduction pocket watch of Commodore Cornelius Vanderbilt's, inscribed with his father's credo, *Tardius lex*. The full quote, attributed to Vanderbilt – *You have undertaken to cheat me. I won't sue you, for the law is too slow. I will ruin you* – was his father's favorite. It was etched into a brass plaque on his desk, and now he could carry it with him always. "What are you trying to say?" his father asked, holding the watch high. "Time's up?" He wasn't joking, but Archie remembered his mother laughing anyway.

He hadn't noticed, then, how loud the ticking was. But that night, huddled in the stateroom, it was the loudest watch Archie had ever heard.

The air on the boat altered.

That was how it felt: the air, the very air itself, changed. He felt too sober and slightly sick. He didn't want to breathe.

"You can come out now," said his brother from the other room.

And Archie, shocked biddable, came out. Nathaniel was pinning a body down on the left-hand banquette in the main cabin, knee to chest. He held a large white pillow with a blue anchor, printed off-center, tight over the body's face, even though the body was limp. The body's hand, fingers curled, brushed the floor a foot or so away from the pocket watch, which might have stunned Nathaniel if the hand had been able to swing it with enough force. Nathaniel's own hands were spread, his fingers rigid. They were the only part of his body that didn't look at ease. His face was open and refreshed, his shoulders and legs and arms loose and confident, having performed the work for which he was born and bred, and having performed it well.

"Don't act so surprised," said Nat. "The old man would have done it to me first if I'd given him the chance."

They hid the body in a place Archie had never seen before but Nathaniel, apparently, used often: a smuggler's hole in a false floor beneath the opposite banquette. Their father's body fit the space as neatly as a foot in a shoe. Archie both did and did not remember the hours that followed. Some details were sharp: the white pillow with the jaunty blue anchor that Nat tossed back on the banquette and karate-chop fluffed. The furious redness of his father's face, full of as much wrath in death as in life. "That'll do for the time being," said his brother. Then he remembered Nat telling him, *Couldn't have done it without you.* And Archie remembered thinking, *Did I do something?*

What did I do?

In time, he remembered exactly what he'd done: nothing. He hadn't stopped his brother. Not that night, when he might have investigated what was happening instead of eavesdropping from the bedroom. Or any of the days and nights thereafter, when he could have reported his brother to the police. Whenever he listened to that terrified cry in his brain that said *You have to tell, you can't not tell, the weight of never telling the truth will poison you*, another voice would say: You are a fucking idiot. Do you have any hard evidence, other than what you saw? Why wouldn't Nat produce a credible story of his own to cast doubt on you, his vagrant fuckup of a little brother? Who disappeared the very night Edgar Arches (Senior) went missing, and only *now* starts making wild claims about successful, famous, incredibly powerful Nathaniel Arches? I mean, how did *that* look?

The voice's tone would change when it came in for the kill: And wasn't the old man a monster anyway? Didn't he deserve to die?

Aren't you glad he's dead?

(Yes.)

Nat brought the *Constancy* within rowing distance of Cape Cod. Topside, the wind tearing the words out of his mouth, he told Archie to take the dinghy and never come back. "If you come back," said Nat, "if you show your face to me again, ever, I will kill you."

Archie believed his brother. He never stopped believing his brother. But he came back anyway, because the life he was living, a life without consequence or connections, wasn't worth protecting anymore. And if he was going to do something, now was the time.

Lyle Pryce told him to remember who he was. That who he was, was the reason *why* he was in this house, by Vince's design. Archie'd always thought Vince believed he was capable of a bigger, braver, altogether different life than the one he'd been born to. But maybe the only life Vince ever wanted for Edgar Allan Arches Junior was his own.

So Vince invited him to play a game. A game that led to this house. This house that Vince bought from Nathaniel.

Nathaniel, who hid their father's dead body in a hole.

"Come on," said Tuesday, smiling at him. "This is kind of our thing. Knocking down walls to find the dead bodies of drunk . . . clowns—" She tilted her head, listening. Listening. To someone only she could hear.

She whipped her head back at Archie.

"The missing," she said, "ace." Her eyes glistened, enormous. She put her hand over her mouth.

Archie almost loved her then. He didn't know it was possible to feel understood so easily, the darkest parts of his darkest heart known without having to say a word. Though that was still the coward's way out. If he really wanted to be known, he was going to have to tell something like the truth.

"That watch," he said, "belonged to—"

He was interrupted by a tremendous bang. The entire house shuddered, like a bomb had detonated upstairs. Dust rained from the ceiling in grainy streams. The bricks in the false wall shifted like a pile of teetering blocks, and Tuesday thrust her hands forward, shoving the bricks back into the darkness beyond, into the space behind the false wall. Archie tried to walk to the wall to tear it down with her, but his legs were a thousand pounds apiece. He lifted one. He lifted the other. He turned and the drawing of the young girl with the deep eyes watched him, and with a cold jolt he remembered where he'd seen her. Not in Vince's collection. He had seen her in his own face. In his sister's, and his brother's.

In his mother's.

She was the ghost of the girl his mother had been before she became an Arches. Which was just the sort of sentimental thing Vincent Pryce would do: leave his mother as a sentinel and a witness, even if she was only made of paper.

The bricks fell. The dust rose.

Tuesday started laughing.

She had pushed the top half of the wall down, enough so that she could lean in and look into the hidden corner of the basement. She gestured to him, her body jerking with laughter that was almost lunatic, and Archie went to the broken wall and looked over and down into a round, deep hole in the floor.

Tuesday wrapped her arm around his side and pulled their bodies together.

"Seek," she hissed. She was shaking. Her whole self was chattering. "Seek *well*."

◆

Dex woke up alone.

"Nice, Pryce," he told the empty music room. "I'm aware that I'm sans partner. That I'm playing your little game solo. Didn't have to rub my face in it." He pushed himself up and out of his coffin and straightened his cone breasts and his microphone. Dusted pine shavings out of his wig and off his shoulders. He flipped the lid of his coffin shut with the tip of his shoe.

He was running low on hope. He didn't know why he was here, even, other than by the grace and pity of Lyle Pryce, who, when he admitted what he'd done with the money – what had he said, exactly? Yes, relieve the specific horror of your vanity, Poindexter Howard: *pitching extravagant woo*. He told Lyle he had pitched extravagant woo to a party known to both of them – Lyle nodded – and while his woo was, if not rebuffed, put on hold, he couldn't be mad at Rabbit. Just as he couldn't be mad at Rabbit for not sufficiently convincing Dex that he was cool with Dex's emotional extravagance. It wasn't Rabbit's fault that Dex needed more than anyone could give him.

"Vince would have loved a bespoke suit. Of armor," Lyle told him, and it didn't sound like a conciliatory compliment. Dex could see that it was true; he'd known the dead man for all of an hour, but he'd spent the better part of the past few weeks playing his game. The dead man was nothing if not extravagant himself.

Maybe he belonged here after all. Maybe he was far, far too hard on himself. He looked around. The music room was dark and still, the ceiling high and windows heavily curtained. It smelled like old furniture, dust, and mothballs. He assumed it was the music room because there was a piano, a poor neglected thing, and because the wallpaper was patterned with lutes. Or lyres. Some kind of stringed instrument left over from an ancient civilization.

Beside the closed door, there was an umbrella stand.

Dex crossed to it. It held a single black umbrella, furled tight. The handle was solid wood, curved, worn smooth by decades of hands. The tip was silver and sharp. He hesitated for a moment, but only a moment, because the only bad-luck omens he believed in had to do with the theater, and he only believed in those because they were part of the script. He unclasped the umbrella's tie.

It opened with a sturdy, satisfying *fwoomp*.

"Are you special?" he asked the umbrella. "Haunted by the spirit of Gene Kel—"

He wasn't alone.

Dex's lips clamped shut, and he pressed his ear hard against the darkness. A sliver of moonlight sliced the curtains. His eyes had adjusted well enough to the gloom by then that he could see – what the ever-loving—

The wall opposite, the uninterrupted wall, flat and flush between the lutes, cracked open.

Dex dropped to a quiet crouch and sheltered behind the open blackness of the umbrella. A secret door. *A secret fucking door*. He pressed his fist over his mouth to stopper a hoot. Who was this surprise guest? What did they want? Were they supposed to team up – was Dex not, after all, all alone?

There was a light in the passage behind the secret door. Dex risked a glimpse around the umbrella's edge, quick enough to see that the profile looked masculine. Tall and broad. High forehead, a long, wolfhound nose—

Archie. Tuesday's Archie.

But it couldn't be Archie, because he wasn't wearing that ratty smoking jacket. He was wearing a crisp white shirt, sleeves rolled up to his elbows, glowing gray in the darkness, and he wasn't – Dex blinked; the light was better, and the man turned – his face was perfect. Not a bruise. Not a scrape.

Dex's hand, wrapped tight around the umbrella's handle, began to sweat. He was fairly certain Lyle Pryce would not have cast Nathaniel Arches for a role in her husband's final act. He was fairly certain Nathaniel Arches was here for his own reasons, and he was fairly certain none of those reasons were altruistic.

He was fairly certain he, Dex Howard, in the music room with the umbrella, was the only person in the house who knew it held more than ghosts.

Nathaniel Arches slid the secret door shut behind him with a gentle click.

At that moment something exploded.

◆

"What did you just *do*?" Verena Parkman – the old woman whose picture Dorry had noticed in the *Globe*, who looked even more like a witch in person – pressed a gnarled and spotted hand to the cameo at her throat. "Cassandra. Retrace your steps."

Cass was stunned, which was the only reason, Dorry thought, that she didn't remind Verena, respectfully but firmly, that her name was Cass. Verena called them all by their full names. Dorothea. Cassandra. Edmund. (Dorry hadn't known that was Ned's first name.) Lisa got off easy. So did Marcus and Colin Shaughnessy, the final two in the great hall, brothers with thick Boston accents and huge, stubby-fingered red hands, who restored old houses for a living. Marcus, short, was dressed in red overalls. Colin, tall, wore green. They both had thick black mustaches glued on their faces.

But this – whatever Cass had done, whatever had just happened – stilled the room. Dorry was maybe slightly less bewildered, but only because she was still wearing the goggles. She'd avoided most of the dust and debris that flew out of the wall when it shook and cracked, but it was all over her hair and her costume. She could taste it in her mouth.

"I don't – know," said Cass. She rubbed plaster dust off her nose with the back of her hand. "I was standing here." She stood with her back to the center of the room. "Looking up at the balcony. I stepped. Here." The cluster of people in the great hall gathered around Cass's foot. It was resting innocently on one of the mangy old carpets blanketing the floor.

Cass rubbed the floor again with her toe.

"Perhaps some kind of lever or trigger," said Verena, "beneath the carpet."

Cass nodded. "I think," she said, "we need to see what's underneath."

Verena and Cass had taken charge. As soon as everyone was up and out of their coffins, they led the introductions. Verena had a sharp way of speaking but Dorry liked it; she knew what she wanted to say, and she didn't want to waste time talking around it. Marcus and Colin seemed nice too, though only Marcus spoke. Lisa Pinto asked if they were twins, and they replied *the Irish kind*, which Dorry didn't entirely understand. But they were all adults who took Ned and Cass and Lisa Pinto seriously. They wanted to work together, to do – whatever it was they were supposed to do. Cass said she doubted that they were supposed to just sleep the night away in uncomfortable coffins on the floor of a haunted house. And we discover our purpose here, said Verena Parkman, by determining *who* haunts this house.

Or something like that. Dorry hadn't really been paying attention. She was too lost in what she could see, now that she was looking through the goggles.

Which was nothing.

The lenses were a little cloudy, but with age, not spectral evidence. Everything and everyone was greenish but hardly ghostly. Because this was real life, and ghosts weren't real. The whole thing was *so* stupid, and so was she – to have imagined, even for a second, that she might see a ghost because she had special glasses. Like ghosts were an observable phenomenon if only you had the right tools. How stupid was she to hope she would ever be able to see her mother again. She wouldn't. It was scientifically impossible. She would never, ever see or hear or smell or talk to – her mother was gone from the world, and she had left Dorry behind, and Dorry had known this, she had always *known* this, and that she'd ever, for a second, been able to pretend otherwise – she was such an idiot. She wanted to rip the goggles off and throw them away, because they made her feel like the giant baby that she was. But she couldn't take them off her face. She didn't want anyone, least of all Ned, to see how red her eyes were. To see how hard she was trying not to cry, and how miserably she was failing.

She knew she was being a child. A silly, childish little girl. She knew she should have been listening to what Verena Parkman was saying. It was about the house, and it seemed interesting and important, but a very big part of Dorry couldn't bring herself to care. The game, for her, had been about those stupid goggles. And she'd gotten them. She had held them in her hands. She had *won*. But what she had won, after all of that, was absolutely nothing. No ghosts. No mysteries. No – Mom. The disappointment was so heavy she was breathless.

Verena was standing in front of a big painting on the wall to the left of the grand staircase, beneath the balcony but lit from the open windows opposite. It was a portrait of a woman with silver hair brushed up and away from her face, pale skin, and a black dress whose neckline went up her throat and sort of faded into the background, so she looked like a floating head. With two floating hands. Matilda Something-or-other, Verena was calling her. Only daughter of one of the wealthiest Brahmin families, died mad and alone, died without heirs. Gilded Age fortune never found.

"This was her house?" Ned's voice cut through the humming in Dorry's brain. She blinked and felt a tear pool against the bottom of the right goggle lens.

"I'm saying it certainly appears to be." Verena shrugged. "She lived in Brookline. Adjacent to the Emerald Necklace – that's what Mr. Pryce meant by Olmstead's emeralds. The parks designed by Frederick Law Olmstead are called the Emerald Necklace." She sniffed. "Mr. Pryce was a well-known collector, especially to all of us who deal in antiques locally. I heard through my contacts that several years ago he'd purchased the Tillerman family home, falling apart though it was. Because he believed it was haunted. A genuine haunted house." She looked at Dorry, straight through the green glass of the goggles, and Dorry shrunk a little. "She died here. In her bed. Mad, they said, in her final years. A total recluse at the end, possessed by strange humors, taken up by passions. She was the only human, the only body, discovered in the entire house – a bit decayed, as you might imagine, by the time she was found. She once held tremendous salons right here in this hall, full of the high and the low, artists and men of business, scientists and mesmerists, poor and rich. Until she cast everyone out, shut the doors forever, and retreated from the society of the world." Verena Parkman smoothed the wool of her skirt with both hands. "They said that she didn't trust the banks, that she converted the family wealth from stocks and bonds into gold and silver, and that it was absconded with entirely. *She* said—" She cleared her throat. "In a diary – a colleague claims it is legitimate, but who knows its provenance, truly – but *she* said she would 'take her fortune with her up to the ceiling of heaven.'"

Vincent Pryce would have thought that was a terrible waste.

Dorry twinged. Vincent Pryce. Matilda Tillerman. She knew that name. She knew those names together.

Because she'd done the research.

"I have a theory," Cass said.

"Do tell, Cassandra," said Verena.

"It's Cass," she said gently. "The fact that you know all that, about the house and Matilda Tillerman? That's why you're here. We were chosen to be here for a specific reason, like – Ms. Parkman, you're here because you know the house's history. I'm here because I'm good at organizing people, getting them to work toward a goal. Lisa's here because she's a horse's ass."

"You know it," said Lisa Pinto.

"You two, Marcus and Colin." Cass furrowed her brow. "You know how old houses work. You take them apart and put them back together. That has to be why you're here, and that has to mean – we have to." She looked around at the vast open hall. "Find something. Or do something. To the house itself."

Dorry, still only half listening, walked over to the painting. It was huge. Taller than Dorry. Life-size. It looked like Matilda Tillerman could walk right out of it.

"Why'm I here?" asked Ned. "Feeling a little left out, is all."

"I don't know," said Cass. She wrinkled her nose at him. "Yet."

There were two letters, neatly painted, in the lower right corner of the portrait: MT.

"The artist Matilda Tillerman," Dorry whispered to herself.

"We are missing people too," said Verena. "There are only seven of us, and thirteen chosen. That means there are six more persons somewhere in this house."

"Then let's find them," said Cass. "Ned, Dorry, check upstairs. Ms. Parkman, stay here in case anyone shows up. Colin and Marcus, why don't you see if there's a basement. Lisa, let's start down here."

Cass did nothing after that but cross the floor of the great hall. Away from the portrait of Matilda Tillerman, through the jumble of empty coffins and artifacts on pedestals, toward the wall opposite the grand staircase.

And the wall before her, between two closed doors, boomed and shuddered and spat out dust and plaster and sent a crack spiraling to the ceiling like an upside-down bolt of lightning.

Cass sneezed from the dust. "Gesundheit," said Verena Parkman. The brothers Shaughnessy inspected the cracked wall. The air smelled electric, hot, like a firework. "You think the house is set with charges?" Marcus asked his brother, and Colin shrugged. Marcus continued, "What's the point of blowing up a house when it has people in it?"

"Murder," Lisa Pinto said drily.

"Could have been on a timer, like the locks on the coffin lids. Someone could be watching us. Or. Could've set something off," Marcus said to Cass.

"We must pull up the carpet," said Verena. "To see what is beneath."

Dorry hovered on the edge of the group. They didn't need her help. They didn't need *her*. She was an extra, and despite the fact that she'd won, she'd lost. She felt the painting of Matilda Tillerman watching her from across the room. She could understand why someone would close up their house and push the whole world away. Sometimes the whole world hurt.

Colin and Marcus and Lisa Pinto and Ned knelt along the long edge of the giant carpet and began to roll it up.

And Dorry saw it.

Cass paced back and forth, inspecting the old wooden floor.

"Nothing," Cass said. "Maybe I didn't trigger anything. Which makes me think it was on a timer. Or it was just a coincidence."

Dorry said, "You mean you don't see it?"

Cass looked up at her. "See what?"

"See the—" Dorry went very still. She closed her eyes. And when she opened them, it was still there.

An ankh.

On the floor – large, two feet long, placed so it shot a straight line from the grand staircase to the opposite wall, the wall with the lightning-bolt crack.

She wrapped her hand around her mother's ankh and thought, *Maybe*. Maybe this was how the goggles worked. What if her mother was silver, heavy and cool on a cord against her chest – and a part of the floor, and part of the air, in the world, always, in the details, in everything Dorry was and saw and did? And what if she'd been here all along, all this time, waiting for Dorry to learn how to see her with something other than her eyes?

"There's an ankh on the floor." Dorry pointed, then walked over, knelt, and pressed her hand against it.

"How do you—" Verena peered at her. "Those glasses. It must be those marvelous glasses that you're looking through."

Dorry pulled them off. Her hands were shaking. Though the ankh disappeared once she was looking through her own eyes, she didn't need the goggles. She didn't need them to see or to feel her mother anymore, and she didn't need them to cover her face. She had nothing of herself to hide. Verena looked through the goggles and gave a cry. "So there is!" she said. "Right there! An optical effect, a symbol painted with a special stain." She handed the goggles to Cass, who yelped.

"That's your job, then, Dorothea," Verena said. "You must go and look for what is invisible."

Ned took the goggles from his sister and whistled. He lowered them. "That's amazing and all, but what is it? Like, X marks the spot? Are we supposed to dig here?"

"What if." Dorry's brain was ricocheting around the room. "What if stepping on the ankh didn't crack the wall," she said. "What if it's the other way around." She licked her lips. "What if the wall cracked – on a timer – so we'd look for and find the ankh. And now we have to look for more—"

The closed door to the left of the crack in the wall creaked open. A man stuck his head out. A tall white man with dark hair and a high forehead and a long nose. After a flash of recognition (Archie!), Dorry's gut pinged.

It was Archie, but it wasn't.

"Is it safe to come out?" he asked.

◆

What Tuesday saw, around the edge of the kitchen door, looked like a party. A Halloween party, or the streets of Salem on October weekends, everyone in costume, everyone a little strange to each other but friendly and warm. Recognized. Thrown together by chance and all playing the same game. Mario and Luigi were moving from pillar to pillar in the great hall, inspecting them (for what?). She saw a college-age girl, missing the front half of her horse costume, prowling the perimeter, examining the walls. She saw a short young woman in a banana-yellow tracksuit splattered with red, talking with a man who was even shorter than her, wearing a bright green Hulk costume and purple pants. Actually – no. He wasn't wearing a costume; he was wearing green body paint all over a very muscular torso. Another college girl, with a handmade Nefertiti headdress held up around her afro, stood in the middle of the hall, keeping watch. Sitting beside her on two stacked pine boxes was an old woman who wasn't, as far as Tuesday could tell, wearing a costume at all.

I bet Lyle gave her grief about it too, said Abby.

"I bet she gave Lyle grief right back," said Tuesday.

"What?" said Archie.

Tuesday didn't respond.

They'd come up from the basement to call the police. To call the police and tell them that, based on a series of facts and strange coincidences, and the nudging of a dead man, Tuesday Mooney had a hunch that the body of missing billionaire Edgar Arches (Senior) was buried in a well in the basement. The final resting place of the dead-drunk clown. The missing ace, found. It was the biggest intuitive leap of her life. She did not know how he died. She didn't know how he got there, though she suspected Nathaniel Arches, owner of the property at the time of Ed Senior's disappearance, did. The facts swirled. Nathaniel Arches had sold the property to Vincent Pryce – after all, who better to unload his father's secret tomb to than the crackpot chump with whom he was publicly feuding? It made a kind of sick sense.

It fit.

She didn't know how she felt. About any of it. After the initial wave of triumphant euphoria came a cool, queasy dread, to be standing so close to death. Murder, most likely. The odds of a natural death leading to interment in a secret well seemed low. Besides, murder was easy. It was human. It was entirely ordinary. She had always suspected as much. When she stopped shaking, when her teeth had stopped clacking together so she could speak, she told Archie what they had to do. "We have to call the police," she said. "I think this is a crime scene."

"I know," said Archie.

"I know you know," said Tuesday. "A lot more than that."

Her phone didn't have service in the basement. They climbed the basement stairs, came out through a servant's hallway into the kitchen, and now they were spying on the rest of the players of Pryce's game – Pryce's other game, the one played in the light of day, the game that got bigger and more generous as you played it. Tuesday, for a beat, resented that she'd gotten stuck playing the nasty game within the game, collecting the sick cereal-box prize in its belly. True, she could bring closure, a solution to a mystery. She knew that wasn't without value. But upstairs, in the dusk of the kitchen, watching those other people search and call and laugh with each other, Tuesday found she didn't want to call the police. Not yet.

She wanted the other players to have a chance to finish their game. Maybe there was still another prize to be found. Death was real, but so was life.

Don't get greedy, said Abby.

"What are they doing?" whispered Archie.

"Looking for something," she said. "Maybe more symbols. Like in the underground theater. Like the ones that—"

Dex found.

Thinking of the theater made her think of Dex. And miss him, and wish he were there, with a fierceness that would have surprised her a month ago. But not now. Not after everything that had happened, everything they had done. All the words she had said, and couldn't take back.

Of course Dex, never one to miss an entrance, chose exactly that moment to slide into her line of sight.

He must have been standing on the staircase that loomed to the left, or behind one of the pillars. He wasn't there, and suddenly he was: Madonna – pinstriped, finger-waved, "Express Yourself," David Fincher Madonna – was standing in the middle of the great hall talking to Nefertiti. It felt like watching the moon rise; she was so glad, so very, very glad, that Dex was here. That Dex was playing. He deserved to be. Tuesday didn't make a conscious decision. She grabbed Archie's hand and pushed the kitchen door open.

The girl in the half-horse costume saw them first. She shrieked. Nefertiti had a much cooler head, and only jumped a little to see two new strangers approaching from the darkness beneath the stairs. It quickly became clear that the shriek wasn't out of fear, but recognition. Tuesday wasn't a stranger. She was known to these people. "I thought it was funny that you weren't here," said Nefertiti, after introducing herself as Cass. "Where were you hiding?"

"Basement," said Archie. He shook his head. Tuesday hoped that would be enough to convince them not to investigate.

She looked at Dex. Dex looked back. A long black umbrella was hooked over the crook of his arm. In his hand he held a vintage silver microphone. There wasn't coolness between them, but there was a field. It was electric. Tuesday felt it lifting the hairs on her arm.

"You look wonderful," she said. "This might be your best" – she cleared her throat – "Madonna to date."

The thing between them changed a little. It softened. Dex nodded. "Thank you," he said, and fingered the chain of the monocle looped around his neck.

Archie went rigid beside her. She was still holding his hand, and he squeezed so hard she felt her bones shift.

His brother was walking toward them.

"This is Trudy," said Cass, introducing the short woman in the yellow tracksuit. "She's a sound engineer, works over at MIT. Marcus and Colin, home renovators. Lisa, best friend. Verena, queen of all she surveys." She turned to wave to the beefy, purple-panted Incredible Hulk, who was now on the opposite side of the hall – "Alex, bodybuilder slash Hulk" – who waved back. Archie continued to squeeze Tuesday's hand. "And this," she said, turning back to introduce Nathaniel, "is Archie."

Archie let go of Tuesday's hand. "I know," he said, reaching out to shake his brother's. "He's my little brother."

Nathaniel took Archie's hand in his own. "Nat," he said. "Imagine seeing you here."

Cass moved her head to the side. Tuesday's heart was beating painfully, but still, she smiled. Cass was no fool.

"What are you looking for?" Tuesday asked her. The only thing to do, it seemed, was move things along, hurry them to their conclusions as quickly as possible. "Do you have a sense what the final game is?"

"Invisible things," said the old woman, Verena. She sat up on her stacked coffins, very tall and very straight. "With the assistance of young Dorothea."

"Young Dor—" Tuesday only got half the name out before she looked up. And saw her next-door neighbor.

Dorry was standing at the top of the stairs. Beside her was a nerd version of Prince: a skinny kid, maybe a year older than her, wearing a purple jacket, black pants and boots, with a high wig and black-framed glasses. Dorry was wearing the costume she'd had on when she came over to borrow hair gunk, because of course this was the party she was going to. She'd found a way to get here on her own, without Tuesday's help. She was Death, and she was inevitable.

She had a pair of aviator goggles with green lenses down over her eyes.

The great hall held a small crowd of excited, talking humans, but Tuesday felt the world narrow to a single person, a single girl. A girl who wanted to talk to ghosts. Who had fought her way to a treasure that could only let her down. Who wanted, who needed, to believe an impossible thing.

"Dorry," said Tuesday, stepping forward. She raised her voice. "Dorry, how are—"

Dorry lifted the goggles.

Her face was full of light.

Dorry was a burning warmth Tuesday could feel on her own face. Tuesday walked toward the foot of the stairs, looking up, and thought of the first time they met: how sad Dorry had looked then, how translucent. How she had hugged Tuesday so hard it felt like she was trying to squeeze the life out of her. Now Dorry was the sun. And Tuesday was shocked and grateful for everything Dorry Bones still believed was possible.

Tuesday felt she shouldn't raise her voice above a whisper. "Do the goggles—" she said. "Do they work?"

Dorry fluttered excitedly. "Come on. Up the stairs," she said. "You can see it best from up here." So Tuesday climbed. She was starting to feel woozy. When she got to the landing, the balcony stretching to her right and her left, Dorry said, "First, I need to – uh. Ned," she said, looking at Prince, smiling like she had a secret. "Meet Tuesday Mooney."

Ned smiled at her. His face was smeared with red makeup, his ears stuck out, and he had a little kink to his smile. He was radiating the same light as Dorry. The light was bouncing between them, reflecting.

"It is a pleasure to meet you, Ms. Mooney," he said, shaking her hand.

"It's a pleasure to meet you too," Tuesday said. She appraised his costume. "Prince," she said. Then, after a beat, "Prospero." She smiled. "You've got some red death on your face."

Ned cackled. "I knew you'd get it," he said. "I'm Ned. Ned Kennedy."

"Ned," Tuesday said. Then her breath caught, because she got it again. "Ned Kennedy. You found the clue in the alley. You posted it to Facebook. To that group—"

Ned's mouth dropped open. "No way," he said. "You know me from the internet?" He shouted down to the group on the floor of the hall. "You hear that, Cass? I'm internet famous." He turned back to Tuesday. "She's my sister. She thinks I'm—" Ned laughed. "I don't know what she thinks," he said. "But it doesn't matter, 'cause I'm internet famous."

"You're about to get more internet famous," said Tuesday. "We all are."

Dorry pulled the goggles off her head. "Put these on," she said, "and tell me what you see."

Tuesday slid the straps over her ears. Adjusted the lenses over her eyes. The world was green. She blinked. Her contacts shifted. She saw, in the center of the great hall, a jumble of pine boxes. Pedestals displaying artifacts from Pryce's collection. She saw, directly across from her, a tremendous crack in the plaster of the wall, shooting up to the ceiling, which she saw was old and feathered, cracking. Falling down in places. She saw Dex, fitting the vintage microphone into a stand on its pedestal. She saw Archie – the real Archie – inspecting the other pedestals, and she saw

Nathaniel circling him, stalking him, never taking his eyes off him. Circling—

Circle.

She saw, on the floor, where tattered rugs had been rolled or pushed back, darker than the wood or the tile, a circle of symbols around the great hall. Roman numerals. I. II. III – all the way around, and instead of the numeral for twelve, there was an ankh.

Tuesday shoved the goggles up into her hair.

"You saw them, right?" said Dorry. She practically squeaked. "And the numbers – there's numbers on the pedestals too. They match. We think we have to move them, like, into place. Pedestal to number. Now that you're here, I can guide everyone. There are supposed to be thirteen players. That's twelve pedestals, twelve players, and one to guide them. That has to be it, right? That's the solution to the riddle. *This* is the clock, and with all of us here now, it—" Dorry's eyes were bright. "It equals twelve. Right?"

Tuesday swallowed.

Guess not every clock is a metaphor, said Abby.

◆

"Places, everyone," Dex called. "Places."

It felt very right, directing. Though perhaps what felt right wasn't the directing but being at the center. He had taken charge of the pedestal with the vintage microphone stand mounted on top – the second he saw that microphone, all gleaming striated silver, he needed to hold it – and that particular pedestal was marked VI. The VI on the floor, then, was positioned several feet in front of the foot of the grand staircase, six on the clock face. He formed a perfect line with Dorry's goggles at the top of the stairs, the ankh on the floor, and the crack in the opposite wall. Dex was the beam. In a room of chaos and boxes, costumes and dust, he was part of the spine.

Tuesday was next to him, situated at pedestal V. Under a small glass dome on top was a taxidermied tarantula. The remaining ten pedestals and players stood in a ring around the hall. Ned the Prince was at VII. Cass the Queen had taken VIII. Even Verena, that delightful crone, had taken charge of the ankh-marked pedestal at what should have been XII. Archie was next to Tuesday at IV, and his brother was at III. The pedestals were large – four-foot-tall rectangular columns – and heavy, as though they contained something more than the wood used to construct them. But the only pedestal that didn't seem to be impenetrable was Dex's. A glass knob near the top slid out to reveal a slim drawer. Inside the drawer was a black cord with a headphone jack on one end.

"Before we do this," said Lisa the half-Pinto, over at IX. "Seriously. What are the chances that all of these pedestals are, like" – her voice was flat – "bombs."

"This would be an extremely complicated way to kill people," said Cass.

"I think we can agree that the dead guy was nuts," said Lisa Pinto. "And maybe he *liked* devising extremely complicated – I mean, isn't that the whole plot of *Saw*?"

Dex cleared his throat. He felt the room turn to him.

"Pinto raises a fair point," he said. "If anyone would like to step back or leave, do it now."

Nobody moved, of course.

He opened the drawer. Reached into the inside pocket of his suit for his phone. Snapped the silver headphone jack into place. Opened his music app.

"Everyone ready?" he said. He looked back up at Dorry. She had her arms wrapped around a column, hugging it with glee. He made deliberate eye contact with every soul in the room. Then he set his music to Shuffle.

Gentle flutes, far away, floated to his ears. He heard Tuesday snort.

"Where is that coming from?" Cass asked.

The flutes rose together over a military snare, and Dex's heart followed.

"Dex's pedestal," Tuesday answered. "There must be a speaker inside."

"That would explain why it sounds muffled," said Cass. "Anyone else's pedestal doing something?"

Dex hummed. He mutter-sang to himself. Ahh, Fernando. We *were* young. We *were* full of life. *And none of us prepared to diiie.*

"Prepared to die?" said Lisa. "What the hell song is this?"

The chorus hit, louder and faster. When it did, Dex's pedestal vibrated. And he noticed something interesting: the slightest whine. Feedback.

His microphone was live.

"Hello," he said into the mic.

Ten people twitched and jumped as their pedestals quivered with Dex's voice.

"Whoa," said Trudy, the sound engineer in the yellow tracksuit. "Guys." She squared her hands around her pedestal. "These are speakers. With *very* serious subwoofers, I bet. Wireless." She lifted her chin to Dex. "Can you talk again? High, and low?"

"Sure," said Dex in a helium voice. "What should I say?"

"Something lower," said Trudy. "And louder."

Dex tucked his chin into his neck and summoned a deep bass. "Like this?"

He felt it in the floor. It rubbed the soles of his feet. Another chorus was coming around, and Dex, in heaven, opened his throat and sang. His pedestal trembled. The players shook. On every sustained note, every taffy-stretched *Fernandoooooo*, the thrumming in the floor got stronger. The volume was rising of its own accord, and Dex didn't think it was his imagination.

The silence after the fade-out was whole and still.

Until a giant hunk of plaster peeled away from the crack in the opposite wall. It slid down and shattered into pieces on the floor.

The next thing Dex heard, over the knocking of his heart, was Tuesday. Laughing. Into her hands, covering her mouth.

And then Ned, shouting.

"It's a face!"

General confusion followed. Ned pointed at the wall, at the small section now denuded of plaster. It did – Dex squinted down the length of the hall – it did look like there was a face underneath. Half a face; a face with a beard hooked over its ear. *"That's* why I'm here," Ned was saying. "It's a mural. It's a painting. *There's art on the walls. All around us!"*

All around us.

"Dex." Tuesday was leaning in. "Dex," she said, almost whispering. "Sing the house down."

"Preferably songs with many long, sustained notes," Trudy said, laughing. Everyone seemed to be laughing at once. Like they were all drunk. But they weren't. Dex was sober as a stone. "And bass. Lots of bass."

Dex wrapped both his hands around the mic stand. He closed his eyes. The hairs on his arm rose. His heart filled his throat, so tight he was afraid he was going to choke, because this wasn't karaoke roulette, this wasn't drunk and fucking around. This was something else.

But then:

Look at that little faggot, said a voice, deep, his father's voice, from the general vicinity of the back of his head, a sore spot behind his right ear. Doing a perfect imitation of a Dire Straits song. Like his father even knew Dire Straits existed. *Singing some stupid song. You call that working?*

That's no way to make a living.

Dex's eyes flicked back open. He saw the great hall. He saw the crack, and more plaster dangling, eager to break free. He took a deep breath. Then he pulled his phone out of the drawer and chose a song. The only song he wanted to sing.

When he said "God?" into the microphone his voice was louder than he had ever imagined it might be.

Dex did not, strictly speaking, believe in God. He didn't strictly *not* believe in God either, and when he was feeling particularly self-castigating he told himself his agnosticism was another manifestation of his general cowardice, his disinclination to pick a side, to make up his mind; the proverbial hottest places in hell were reserved for persons such as himself. But then he'd remember what he learned, long ago, at the altar of Our Lady Madonna Louise of Ciccone: the power, the necessity, the elemental beauty of refusing to stop becoming.

This particular song, this song that was her bedrock, that transcended, for Dex, all the other Madonnas – he had lived with this song in his soul for decades, and still, every time he heard it, it was new. As a kid he played it ad nauseam on a cassingle he'd stolen from the Rite Aid. He'd had to steal because he'd borrowed against his allowance and was still in debt, but he couldn't depend on the radio; he needed access to this song whenever he wanted. This song that people talked about on TV as though it were important, it was a song that was *news*, and the news was about Pepsi and black Jesus and Madonna "acting like a fucken whore," his father said, so Dex hid the stolen tape at the back of his desk drawer, where he hid the picture of Michael J. Fox that he sometimes slipped under his pillow.

This song had been haunting his entire life. What had given it that kind of power? First, surely, the music itself: it was many-headed, a pop song and a spiritual. It built and pleaded, downshifting into the minor and then bursting, triumphantly, major. Its power was ecstatic, a direct product of the tension of being one complicated whole, and a release – *the* release, of refusing to be contained and simple and static.

"Like a Prayer" had been trying to tell Dex for years, if only he'd listened, that he didn't have to solidify. All he had to do was recognize and celebrate the pain and the mystery of life, the mystery of being not what one seemed, and not one thing only, but being, *being* nonetheless. And what he was meant to be was an artist, and what he was meant to do was to sing, and to move in the spaces surrounding the definite, between the sacred and the profane, the body and the spirit, the silent and the spoken, the living and the dead. That was his gift. That was what he could give to others.

The practice of this art was the transmutation of love.

Dex thought, like an arrow to his heart: *Yes*. That was how it worked. Love lasted by becoming art. The art made yesterday haunted him today. The art he could make today would haunt the future. There was still time to be who he'd always been, again. As a kid, dreaming, it had seemed impossible to be satisfied with only one life. As an adult, indebted, afraid that what he loved and whom he loved would one day cost him more than he could afford, it had seemed impossible not to protect himself with money.

But he didn't have to be all one thing or all another. He didn't have to live only one life at a time. And a living wasn't something you made but something you did. Again and again, over and over, always, always becoming.

Dex belonged here after all. He was far, far too hard on himself. And even though life was a mystery, and everyone must stand alone – he was everything. He was everything he needed already, in himself.

His voice filled the great hall. His heart caught fire. He came home, at last, to himself.

◆

When the ceiling fell, Archie was looking up. It had been shivering for a while, shedding dust and plaster like snow. Verena

Parkman, wisely, had already removed herself to a position of safety beneath the balcony, which didn't appear to be in danger of collapsing. Mario and Luigi, the contractor brothers, seemed certain of that.

Archie had been trying not to stare at the brothers. He couldn't help it. They were obviously brothers; they looked as alike as he and Nat, but they just as obviously liked one another. As if it were an easy thing for one brother to like the other. He understood it was possible not to live in mortal dread of your sibling; he knew his life wasn't, for a host of reasons, remotely normal. But still, it hurt to see evidence of what might have been simple.

He should have been staring at his own brother. He might have noticed how angry Nat was growing.

By the time the ceiling fell, it was too late.

Dex was back at the helm of Vince's infernal karaoke machine. He'd passed the mic around, but it always seemed to land in his hands. The room had been thrumming for nearly an hour, which had to be part of Vince's plan, royally pissing off the neighbors in the dead of night. The crack in the wall had spread up to the ceiling, shedding giant hunks of plaster like broken ice floes, with assistance from some of the objects on the pedestals – a slingshot, a thrown bowling pin, a Frisbee. Alex, the bulked-up trainer dressed as the Hulk, had slammed his fist into the wall and sent a new crack spiraling up. The more plaster fell, the more they could see the hidden mural beneath. It was a painting of people in fancy dress, overlapping and gesturing and milling about as if they were at a party. "It's Brookline's answer to the Sistine Chapel," Tuesday said. She was pacing, making a tight circle between her podium and his, hugging her arms to her stomach. Alive with discovery, her eyes bright and beautiful. "How much do you want to bet those are portraits of actual historical Bostonians? Circa whenever this Matilda Tillerman died? What if – does it look like Sargent to you? Is it a lost Sargent?" She seemed to have forgotten about the well in the basement. Archie knew her enough to know it was only for the moment.

Dex was now dueting with an enthusiastic girl dressed as the rear half of a horse, on a pop song with a dramatic, drawn-out chorus, something about falling from cloud nine. They were making the speakers, and Archie's sternum, vibrate. And the ceiling – by the time they reached the second chorus, the ceiling had had it.

Whatever sound it may have made at first was swallowed by the sustained vowels of Dex and the half-horse *leeeeetting goooooo toniiiiight*. The split in the plaster shot up the middle like an unzipping zipper and the edges peeled back and rained down, another world entering this one from above. Dex stopped singing. People shouted and ran for cover beneath the balcony. Archie jumped back, but shielded his eyes and stared up.

What lay beneath the plaster was a mural, but it didn't look painted.

Tuesday was beside him now.

"Holy," she said. "Shit."

The ceiling of the great hall was covered with silver clouds and golden sky.

The clouds and the sky shone like metal in the gloom.

"Is that—" Dex coughed. He was crouching on the staircase, hiding under the black umbrella covered with white dust. The air was thick with it. Dex scrambled to his feet and cut the music off mid-verse.

Verena Parkman stood and walked carefully to the center of the room, neck craned. Then she let out a small joyful bark of a laugh.

"So. She did take her fortune," she said. "Her gold and her silver, up to the ceiling of heaven."

And that – *that* was the moment Nat had had it too.

The other players, the kids, the contractors, Trudy, and the

Hulk, stepped back into the center of the hall and looked up. Some of them cheered. Some gasped. Some clapped. Archie only heard them. Because he had turned to look at Nat.

And Nathaniel Arches was livid.

His chin was low, forehead jutting, like a bull preparing to gore someone. His lips were tight. He was breathing hard enough for Archie to notice six feet away.

He looked like their father, right before the first blow.

This was what Archie had come back for. To stop this man.

"Hey, Arch – I mean. Are we really pretending you're your brother?" Tuesday asked, hanging back from the gathering crowd. Tuesday was waiting for him to join the others. Him. Not Nathaniel. He couldn't pretend to be anyone anymore; he had to be himself.

"Nat," Archie said to his brother, "get out of this house."

"It was mine, you know," Nat spat. "I owned it."

Tuesday stilled. Archie felt her attention shimmer, assess, and refocus on what was happening between him and Nat.

"We know," she told him.

"And I sold it," Nat said. "I sold a house *covered* in fucking—"

"We know," Tuesday repeated.

"That—" Nat wiped his mouth with the back of his hand. "That shit Vincent Pryce. If he weren't dead, I would kill him. Right now."

"He didn't know," said Archie. "How could he have known about a hidden—" He gestured at the painted wall, the gold ceiling, and felt like an idiot for trying to defend Vince. Trying to reason with his brother. Trying to talk to his brother like his brother was someone you could talk to.

"Vince didn't know about the mural," said Tuesday. "It's not why he bought the house."

"I would still kill him," said Nat.

"I don't know how, exactly," said Tuesday, "but he knew about the well."

Archie didn't understand, at first, what she had said.

It was impossible to imagine she would have said it.

"What?" said Nat.

"Pryce knew about the well," said Tuesday.

"What?" said Nat again.

"He knew about the well." Tuesday reached into her pocket. "What I want to know," she told Nat, and Archie – this was happening, this was happening, this was what he came back to stop and it was still happening, he was such an idiot for ever thinking he could stop *any* of this—

"Is what *you* know," said Tuesday. "About the well."

She held up their father's pocket watch.

◆

Tuesday, said Abby.

Nathaniel wasn't answering. She hadn't expected him to. He stared at her with eyes that looked dead.

Tuesday, said Abby. **Run.**

No, thought Tuesday.

What are you doing? said Abby. **Seriously. Why did you – what are you hoping to—**

"That's my watch," said Nathaniel.

"It's not your watch," said Tuesday.

"Yes," said Nathaniel. "I am my father's eldest son. My father is dead. It's my watch."

"I thought your father was missing," said Tuesday.

"No," said Nathaniel. He took a step closer. "He's not."

Tuesday inhaled slowly through her nose. She felt her chest fill with air and her head tighten.

Tuesday, said Abby. **Do not go up against this animal alone.**

I'm not alone, she thought back. *I have you*.

I don't count, said Abby.

Nat moved. He collapsed the six feet between them in one long stride and snatched at the watch.

Tuesday was faster. She yanked the watch away and stepped back.

She felt her heart in her chest, squeezing.

Nat raised his hand.

There's a whole room, Tuesday thought at Abby. *A room full of witnesses.* She looked over at the crowd in the center. They weren't paying attention to anyone or anything but the ceiling.

He can't do anything.

Yes, said Abby, **he can.**

Tuesday swallowed.

Nat snatched at the watch and Tuesday yanked it away again, and when she stepped back, she bumped into Archie. Who was just standing there, pale as cheese, stiff with fear.

He's terrified, said Abby.

But Tuesday – wasn't.

She felt for her heart again, felt for it with her mind. It was beating hard, but it wasn't mindless, wasn't trying to fly out of her chest. It was working. Priming itself. Getting ready to—

"Give me back my watch." Nat's voice was low and cold.

"Tell me what happened," said Tuesday.

Nat's face splintered. On another mouth, it might have been a smile.

"You want to play?" he said. "Really?"

Tuesday chose not to respond. She straightened her back.

Nat spun away from her, walking to a pedestal with a tall display mounted on top.

He took the baseball bat out of its stand.

Run, said Abby again.

Nat tossed the bat lightly from hand to hand. It was wood. It made a vicious *whoosh* when he sliced it through the air.

Why are you not running? said Abby.

Nat whipped the bat through the display on top of what had been Tuesday's podium. The bell jar holding a taxidermied tarantula shattered, and everyone in the room, at last, was paying attention. For a heartbeat, the world was silence.

In the silence Nat advanced.

Tuesday stepped to her left. She didn't look away from Nat's face. She felt the floor change from wood to carpet under her feet, and sensed something rising behind her. He was corralling her, forcing her back up against the stairs. She still wasn't afraid. She felt a massive wave building behind her breastbone, a wave of energy. Nathaniel Arches was a bully and an asshole, probably a psychopath, more than likely a murderer, and some of that he couldn't help. He couldn't help that he'd been born to outrageous privilege and never wanted for anything material; he couldn't help the chemistry of his brain, or that his father had been a violent bully. He couldn't help the fact that the world didn't exist solely for his pleasure, that there were other people in it; and he couldn't help that no one had ever tried to teach him to be better. Or stood up to him. Her mental files ruffled, and her brain leaped: *no one other than Vincent Pryce*. When Nat kidnapped her to lunch, he told her his brother had been harassing him, threatening him through the years – with postcards. But it couldn't have been. Archie was a mess around Nat. It must have been Pryce, all that time.

And now Vincent Pryce was dead. He'd left a trap for Nathaniel Arches, and Tuesday was dying to spring it. Because how dare he intimidate her. Threaten her. Make her feel she was anything less than she was.

Fuck. This. Guy.

Tuesday, said Abby.

No – it wasn't Abby. It wasn't Abby's voice.

It was Dex.

"Tuesday," he said again, and she turned from Nat long enough to see Dex standing by her side. He looked shocked. He'd been watching, then. He hadn't been distracted by the ceiling.

He was holding out a long black umbrella.

Collapsed, still dusty. She saw the sharp silver point at the end.

She wrapped her fingers around the handle and turned back and Nat was raising the bat like a cudgel and Tuesday slid the silky umbrella long between her hands, horizontal like a staff, and straightened both arms and blocked the hit.

Her arms shook. Nat was not playing with her.

But she knew that. She'd always known that. None of this had ever been a game.

And now she knew what she was fighting for.

"Get out of my life," she hissed, and shoved Nat and the bat away.

She slid her foot back until it reached the stairs and stepped up. And up. And up again. She moved the umbrella to one hand and held it at her side like a sword.

Like you know how to hold a sword, said Abby.

Nat lowered the bat. He put his foot on the bottom step.

She was focused hard on Nat, but she could hear the other players in the background. Murmurs of disbelief and confusion. *What is he doing? Is this part of the game?* And one voice, a voice she knew, a voice that was – her heart, for the first time, quailed a little – Dorry's. *This is real. Someone call—*

Tuesday took a risk. She turned and ran up the stairs.

Nat's feet thundered behind her and she spun as soon as she reached the landing, umbrella out. Nat was there a second later, bat out, fingers squeezing the wood, squeezing hard.

They faced each other at the top of the stairs. Tuesday's back was to the left wing. Nat's was to the right.

"This is the part where we taunt each other," she said.

Nat swung. She blocked. He swung again and she blocked again, stepping back, stepping back, praying there was no debris, no lump in the carpet to trip over, thanking all that was good and kind in the universe that she wasn't wearing heels. **Like you would ever be wearing heels,** said Abby, and Tuesday thought, *Sometimes* I conform to gender norms, and Abby said, **STOP DEFENDING YOURSELF. HIT HIM.**

Tuesday thrust low and stabbed Nat square in the toe with the pointed tip of the umbrella.

It went straight into his shoe.

He screamed.

Tuesday had never physically hurt anyone before. She might have slapped her brother once or twice when they were kids, but she'd learned very early that physical violence was not her weapon of choice. If Tuesday meant to wound, or even if she didn't, she used words.

She had to yank hard to free the umbrella from where it was lodged. In Nat. The tip came back red.

"Oh my God, I'm so sorry," she said, before she could help herself.

But are you really? said Abby.

She was horrified, slightly nauseated, with her own ability to cause pain. It wasn't a good feeling.

But she wasn't sorry at all.

Nat was doubled over. One palm rested on the end of the bat. The other was pressed against his thigh. He was breathing strangely.

Tuesday raised her umbrella. They had moved about twenty feet around the balcony.

She could see through a doorway and into one of the rooms lining the hall.

There was a long lump on the floor. A bright grass-green lump, splattered with red.

It was a body.

Lifeless and bloody.

Her brain leapt again.

Of course.

Of course Lyle hadn't let Nat in. He hadn't arrived in a coffin like the others; he'd let himself in. He suspected his brother would be here, and he knew what secrets this house contained, knew what needed to be kept hidden. The only problem: the final game involved a set number of players. Nat's solution was to remove one of those players so he could take their place.

She looked away from the bloody body and back to Nat.

He had straightened to his full height. He stared at her.

And smiled.

He was rabid now. He swung and she blocked, again and again. She thought about ducking into one of the rooms, but that seemed like a trap. She didn't want to disappear from sight. The other players were yelling below, cheering when she swung her umbrella around and clocked Nat on the jaw with the handle. Someone shouted that they'd called 911. Tuesday didn't know what good that would do. By the time the police got there, whatever was happening between her and Nat would be over.

Her body was wearing out. Her will was still a shrieking Valkyrie, but she was getting clumsy. Slower. Her throat burned from breathing. Her heart was starting to ache. She needed to end this.

"Nat," she said, holding up her hand. "Stop."

"No," he said.

"Why not?" she asked.

His answer was to haul the bat back with both arms.

Tuesday rushed him. Not with the umbrella, but with her head aimed squarely at his stomach. It worked. Not the rush, but the surprise. He dropped the bat and was knocked just enough off balance that Tuesday pushed him down. She bolted past, back around the balcony toward the stairs.

She felt the toe of her sneaker—

She never knew what her sneaker caught on. It could have been an uneven board. It could have been a twist of ancient carpet fringe. It could have been air, nothing, her great body, exhausted, losing its own balance and pitching forward into space.

She slammed against the ground.

The umbrella flew out of her hands and skidded down the hall.

Tuesday, said Abby.

Her lungs were squashed.

Tuesday, said Abby. Her voice was different. It wasn't alarmed, though it should have been. Nat was still back there. He would get up and come after her. In seconds.

But Abby wasn't scared. She sounded – almost happy. And almost sad.

I'm going to miss you, Abby said. **So much.**

What are you talking—

Tuesday lifted her head. At the top of the stairs, not twenty feet away, her face red from running up the steps, those goggles – those silly green goggles shoved into her hair like sunglasses—

Dorry.

That was the first time Tuesday Mooney was afraid. Because Nat was back there. Nat would always be there, he was coming, and when he was done with Tuesday, Dorry would be right—

◆

It lasted five seconds.

Maybe less.

To Dorry it felt like forever.

She got to the top of the stairs. She put her hand on the column to steady herself, and there was Tuesday flat on her stomach. She'd tripped. All Dorry had seen from below was Tuesday standing and suddenly not, she was gone, down like a pratfall.

Now she was lifting her head. She was looking at Dorry.

And the man who looked like Archie was walking toward her.

And the man who looked like Archie swung high and brought the baseball bat in his hands down fast on one of Tuesday's legs.

Like he was chopping a piece of wood.

Dorry heard Tuesday's leg break.

Her own legs dropped her. Hard. She collapsed on the floor with a jolt. Her goggles slid down from her forehead and she thought: *Thank God. Thank God. I don't want to see. I don't want to see this.* But she couldn't not look. She'd come up here to save – to help—

She had to get up.

She opened her eyes.

She saw the girl.

The girl must have been hiding in one of these rooms, hiding all this time. Dorry didn't know how she and Ned had missed her. But here she was. Walking around the balcony. Quickly. Getting closer. A teenager, a few years older than Dorry. Her face was pale green through the goggles. Her mounds of curly hair bounced with each step. She was dressed in shiny black, with long black gloves and a giant cape high around her neck and shoulders.

The man who wasn't Archie didn't notice her. He was too busy raising the bat to hit Tuesday again.

But he never got the chance.

The girl in black walked straight up to him and pushed him over the balcony.

18

MORE THAN A FEELING

Tuesday opened her eyes.

She was still here.

Here at the hospital. Her hospital – well, it had been her hospital until it fired her five days ago. Or more. They told her she'd been a patient since early Saturday morning. She wasn't sure how many days ago that was, because of all the sleeping and the drugs and the surgeries and the visits. Her parents came. Her brother and sister-in-law came. They brought Olive. It was her niece's first time in a hospital to visit someone she knew, and her eyes went very large when she saw Tuesday in that bed. "I'm not using you as a teachable moment," said Ollie, and Tuesday said, with a snort, "Like hell you aren't." But it felt good to be useful. It was important to see what could happen to people, to see that people could be put back together. And part of putting people back together was reminding them that they weren't alone.

No matter how much they thought they wanted to be.

Her right femur was shattered. She'd had at least two surgeries – she did not remember them – and would need more. For now her leg was stuck full of pins, immobilized in a cast, and locked into a device that made her feel half automaton. Olive's eyes went even wider when she saw it, but not in fear. She looked at Tuesday, at her leg, and Tuesday said, "I know. I'm bionic."

She didn't remember Nat hitting her with the baseball bat. She remembered looking up and seeing Dorry, and wanting Dorry to *get away* and then—

This hospital room.

Which barely qualified as a hospital room. The bed was the same as on every other floor in the main tower, but the room itself was lined with dark wood trim. The door was heavy, and let in no sound, no chatter from nurses or visitors. There were two comfortable, well-upholstered chairs, a pull-out sofa, a small desk, and the curtain covering the window was almost velvet. It was, of course, a single. She was in Webster House, the floor reserved for Certain Patients who required Certain Privacies (from other patients, from the press) and Amenities. International self-payers. Scions of the city and other millionaires. Celebrities. Patriots and Sox. And apparently Tuesday Mooney. What she lacked in health insurance, she made up for in notoriety.

The first time she regained consciousness, her father was asleep on the pull-out. Her mother, she found out later, was at the cafeteria. Tuesday came to slowly, like she was rising from the bottom of a lake. She knew who she was. She knew where she'd been. Her right leg – was wrong. On a wheeled table to her left was a covered tray. Hospital breakfast. And beneath it, a newspaper. Her mental files began to flutter. She reached for it.

TREASURE HUNT ENDS IN DISCOVERY OF LOST ART, FORTUNE was the headline. PLAYERS OF PRYCE GAME UNCOVER SOLID-GOLD CEILING. There was a group photo taken beneath the full fresco on the back wall. She didn't see Nat. She was missing too, but they'd reprinted that fantastic picture of her coming out of the Park Street T, cropping out the cops. Archie's broken face was identified, mysteriously, as William Wilson. There were quotes, from Ned Kennedy: "We don't even know how much art is hidden all around us." Verena

Parkman: "Thus Mr. Pryce's legacy, his true gift to the city, is revealed." And Lyle: "The Tillerman mansion will be fully restored and open to the public, and will serve as the head-quarters of the Raven Foundation."

Tuesday didn't get to find out what the Raven Foundation was, or count all the gaps in the story, looking for everything that had been left out, because Ted Mooney's gentle snoring had stopped. He was awake. His glasses winked at her from across the dim room. When he said her name, she slammed her mental files shut. The only thing she wanted to know was that her dad was okay, and her mom was okay, and she was okay. Despite all contradictory evidence.

And she was; she was fine. She was alive and safe and being repaired by some of the best doctors in the world. She was lucky.

So today, when she opened her eyes, it wasn't the first time she'd woken up in her room in Webster House.

But it was the first time she'd done so to find Emerson Arches sitting beside her bed.

"Hello," said Emerson.

Tuesday stared at her. Her dark brows and pale skin, her white-blonde hair, yanked back tight in a ponytail, were all as uncanny as ever. She smiled. Her small pointed teeth caught on her lips. She was dressed entirely in black, black cigarette pants and black flats and a mod black turtleneck, which Tuesday appreciated, though she was certain Emerson wasn't doing it in tribute.

There were many things Tuesday wanted to ask. And say. But what came out first was "Where's your brother?"

"Feeding your cat," said Emerson. "He wanted to help."

"That's not the brother I care about."

Emerson paused. "Really?" she said.

"I didn't mean—" Tuesday inhaled. Matching wits with Emerson required a clearer head than was chemically possible at the moment. "This isn't fair," she said. "I'm on a lot of drugs."

"What makes you think I'm not," said Emerson.

Tuesday felt her face contort into a grin. She coughed.

"That is, actually," Tuesday said, "very helpful of Archie. I appreciate it. Though I wonder if the primary attraction for him wasn't being helpful but my empty apartment. To squat in."

Emerson's eyes gleamed. "You've got his number," she said. And then: "My other brother won't bother you."

Tuesday watched her eyes. The gleam was gone.

Something had replaced it.

Relief.

"He won't be bothering anyone," Emerson said. "Not anymore."

Or was it triumph?

"What happened to him?" Tuesday asked. "After he hit me."

Emerson's gaze was flat and steady.

"He tripped," she said. "Fell over the balcony railing."

Tuesday jerked. "He what?"

Emerson lifted and lowered her shoulders. "I wasn't there for that part."

"Did he – when he fell, did he—"

"He lived," said Emerson. She examined her manicure. "My other brother, Eddie, Archie, whatever you want to call him, said Nathaniel fell over the edge of the balcony. Landed in the great hall and didn't move. In the confusion of calling the police, the ambulance, attending to *you*, apparently – at some point our brother's body disappeared. Nathaniel must have gotten up. And run away."

"Or he could have been dragged," said Tuesday. "Away."

She looked hard at Emerson.

"Were you there for that part?" Tuesday asked.

Emerson didn't respond at first.

"It's a poetic disappearance," Emerson said at last, lightly. "Like father, like son. Wherever they've gone, I like to imagine they're together."

The skin on Tuesday's arms tingled, cold.

Maybe there were some things she didn't have to know absolutely everything about.

"What did you know—" Tuesday was fuzzy. But not afraid; Emerson was not her enemy. If she had been, Tuesday would already have been vanished herself. "Pryce's design was two games in one. Rabbit was the banker for one. And the other game, the undergame—"

"I'm not a banker," said Emerson.

"The undergame didn't have a banker." Tuesday swallowed. Her mouth was hospital-dry. "It had a blackmailer."

Emerson didn't move.

"Nathaniel said – he said that someone had been harassing him for years," Tuesday said. "He thought it was Archie. And it got worse suddenly, which he thought meant his brother was in town. Archie *was* in town, but I think that was a coincidence. I think the harassment got worse because Vincent Pryce died. He was the blackmailer – the first blackmailer – but then he died and passed—"

Emerson smiled at Tuesday with her teeth. "You have an exceptional imagination," she said. "Pryce passed the torch?"

"Not the torch," Tuesday said. "The postcards."

Emerson flared slightly.

They stared at each other.

"I'm here today" – Emerson slid forward to the edge of her chair – "because my brother told me you had something that belonged to us."

"Which brother," said Tuesday, "told you?"

"Does it matter?" Emerson blinked. "A pocket watch," she said. "I assume it's in your effects. The things you had with you when you were admitted."

"That's evidence," said Tuesday.

Emerson said, "Of what?"

"I'm not . . . sure," said Tuesday.

Emerson opened the drawer by Tuesday's bedside, and Tuesday didn't stop her. She took out the gaudy reproduction watch. Held it tight in her palm.

She looked at Tuesday.

"Imagine, with that exceptional mind of yours," Emerson said, "a woman. Her husband is a brute. She's borne it as best she can for many years, protected her children as best she can, in a life that feels, husband aside, like the best she can expect. Then she meets someone. She makes a new friend. Who reminds her that much of what she accepts in her life is *un*acceptable, and that she has a choice. So she chooses to imagine another life for herself. For her children.

"Now imagine her husband, as he gets older, is getting worse. He's always been a brute but he's beginning to pose a mortal threat not only to her – that, she can handle – but to her grown children. Imagine this woman's new friend owns a company that makes custom reproductions, gadgets, gizmos, and imagine this woman owns – and knows intimately – a powerful conglomerate that acquires hot digital tech. This woman, by the way, is a fucking genius. Imagine that. On the record.

"Now imagine this woman asks her friend for help."

Tuesday had to remind herself to breathe.

"The friend makes a watch. The woman gives him a miniature transmitter to hide inside. A recorder, tiny, like a nanny cam. The woman gives the watch to her husband for his birthday. The woman and her friend sit back and wait to record something irrefutable, something prosecutable. Which is exactly what they record, far better – or worse – than they ever hoped. One night, at sea, they record a crime. A crime that one of her sons commits, and the other son appears to help cover up." Emerson paused. "Suddenly they are caught in a very, very bad bind: the one son is cruel and violent, dangerous, and now there is proof, something prosecutable, to put him away. But it looks just as bad for the other son, who isn't entirely innocent but is far from being his father's child. To hand the recording over to the police, as the friend insists, would implicate them both. The woman cannot bear this. She and her friend fight. Their friendship does not ever recover."

Tuesday said, "Imagine," and Emerson's eyes flashed at the interruption. But she waited. To see what Tuesday would say.

"Imagine," Tuesday said, "the friend, in an attempt to settle his affairs before his impending death, approaches the woman's daughter. He's created an elaborate blind, a game, an adventure, in part to torture the father's son. And he can't do it alone; he needs help. But he won't cause his friend, the woman, more pain. Because he loves her. He never stopped. She didn't either."

Emerson did not react. Tuesday took a breath.

"So he will ask the woman's daughter," she continued, "who is very able and very willing to play. Willing to needle her brother, rile him, maybe lure him directly to the final stage. Dangle – something. The watch itself, maybe. The threat of evidence against him. The best friend needed a blackmailer he could trust to make sure the game-within-the-game's objective was carried out after his death. To reveal the father's son as the criminal he is."

Emerson shook her head. "That may have been the friend's objective, but it was never the woman's. The woman means" – she palmed the watch – "to bury the past."

"What does the daughter mean?" said Tuesday.

Emerson grew still.

"The daughter," she said, and stared at the floor. When she finally looked up again, her eyes were neither smiling nor triumphant. They were tired. They didn't know what they were looking for, but they were eyes that hoped they had earned the right to see for themselves.

"The daughter means to live her own life now," Emerson said.

"Imagine that," said Tuesday.

Emerson almost laughed. Her lips twitched, then flattened. She stood, tucking a blood-red Birkin bag into the crook of her arm. She slipped the watch inside and turned toward the door.

"Imagine that," she repeated, quietly, to herself. Then she turned back. "Tuesday Mooney," she said. "Take care of yourself. Once you're back on your feet, I'll make sure my brother invites you over for cocktails."

Tuesday didn't respond.

"Mother," said Emerson, "makes a mean Corpse Reviver."

◆

Dorry came to the hospital after school on Thursday. She brought her homework with her.

"We don't have to talk about bio," Dorry said. "I feel pretty good for my test tomorrow."

"I can still quiz you," said Tuesday. She raised her eyebrows. "I love the parts of a cell."

They looked at each other. Dorry was smiling, but too hard. Her hands fidgeted with her biology text. Tuesday wouldn't have called the air tense, but it was full of words waiting to be spoken.

"We can talk about what happened too," said Tuesday.

Dorry raised the book to her face and let out a whoosh of breath behind it.

"Thank God," she said, lowering the book. "I'm *dying* to talk about it, but I didn't want to stress you out. Or, like, make you feel worse, or remind you of what that – guy – *did*—"

Tuesday pointed at her immobilized leg. "Believe me," she said, "I remember what that guy did."

"Archie just said, that, uh – to go easy on you." Dorry

blushed a little. "He's staying in your apartment." She bugged her eyes. "He's, like, my new neighbor."

"Don't get used to it," said Tuesday.

"Is he your boyfriend now?" Dorry asked, leaning closer.

"He's my cat sitter," said Tuesday.

Dorry took that in. She sat back in her seat for a second and then hunched forward again.

"So," she said, "I think I have a cat sitter too?"

"It wasn't a euphemism," said Tuesday. "But anyway. You mean Ned?"

Dorry nodded. "He's so cool," she said. "I like him. *So* much. I'm just – like, glad that I know him. He's the first boy" – she paused dramatically – "friend I've had in as long as I can remember, and I'm pretty sure he wants to be my boyfriend and I want to be his girlfriend . . . but maybe not? I don't know. For now, we're just – friends."

"I hate that," said Tuesday. Dorry looked stung, and Tuesday put a hand on her arm. "I hate that phrase. I know you don't think of being friends with Ned as being *just* anything." Her voice felt thick and she coughed it loose. "Don't cheat your friendships. Don't ask them to mean less to you than they do, or think they only have value if they're a stop on the way to a *real* relationship." Dorry rolled her eyes. "All relationships are real," said Tuesday. "Friendship can be as deep as the ocean. It's all a kind of love, and love isn't any one kind of thing."

They smiled at each other.

"These drugs are making me deep," Tuesday said, nodding toward the heavy IV bag.

"Deep as the ocean," said Dorry.

Tuesday felt her eyes fill. She blinked and moisture pooled at the corners.

"Oh, don't cry!" said Dorry. "I can't believe I said that. I didn't mean to make you cry. Archie *told* me—"

Tuesday laughed and sat up as straight as she could and

opened her arms and Dorry leaned in. And they were both here, alive, together for the moment in the in-between.

When Dorry sat back she was rubbing at the corners of her own eyes with her thumbs. She sniffed and asked if Tuesday would quiz her for a little bit. There's no cure for feelings, said Tuesday, like separating the endoplasmic reticulum from the mitochondria. They studied. Dorry was, as she said, perfectly prepared for her test the next day. They talked about the Earhart goggles, and everything Dorry had and hadn't seen through them. For the first time since she'd known her, Tuesday heard a degree of calm in Dorry's voice when she talked about her mother. The shock seemed less severe, the pain less acute. They talked about Dorry's dad, and how he was more relieved that she was safe than pissed that she'd snuck out to Vincent Pryce's funeral without his permission. And impressed, even, by what the game had revealed.

"I had to tell him about what happened to you, though," said Dorry. "He got a little *I told you so, I knew it was dangerous* then. But he says hi. And he hopes you get better soon."

"He knows where you are right now," said Tuesday. "Right?"

Dorry nodded. "And – like, all the stuff about – that guy hitting you." Dorry's brow darkened. "We agreed, all of us, not to – it would have been one thing if he died. Then we would have had to report it and everything. But he didn't. He got up and ran away. We didn't want that jerk to be the story, you know?" Dorry looked pained. "But now he's, like, out there. And he got away with this. I guess we should have asked you what you wanted."

"I don't think he got away with anything," said Tuesday. "And I would have wanted that." Regarding Tuesday Mooney, and why she was absent from the group photo, all the papers said was that she'd suffered an accidental, nonfatal injury. Which of course made the press rabid for more, and which was why she'd been put up in the hospital equivalent of a four-star Hilton – on Lyle Korrapati Pryce's dime, which seemed vaguely like a hush payment. Tuesday had decided she didn't care. Her leg was getting fixed and she didn't have a whiff of insurance. It was the least Lyle could do.

Not that it was Lyle's fault Nathaniel had wormed his way into the final thirteen.

Tuesday's mental files fluttered.

"Dor," she said, "hand me that paper."

Dorry passed her the *Globe* with the front-page story about the mural's discovery. She wanted to see the group photo.

Tuesday remembered what she'd forgotten.

"There she is," she said. "Number thirteen. I forgot – I forgot I saw her. For a split second, in one of the rooms upstairs, when Nat and I were fighting, I saw what looked like a dead body." She sighed. "My first thought was that he'd killed her so he could take her place as one of the thirteen. She was wearing a green dress and it was bloody. But that must have been her costume." She turned the paper around to Dorry, with her finger at the girl's face. She was tall, standing on the end of the back row. Her reddish hair was pulled back, and she was wearing a sixties-style grass-green dress, high-necked and curvy and splattered with red.

Dorry peered at the photo. "That's not her," she said.

"What do you mean?"

"I—" Dorry blinked at her.

Tuesday turned the paper around to look at the photo. She counted thirteen heads. She matched the names in the caption with the faces. Dex. Ned and Dorry. Cass and Lisa Pinto. Warren Wilson, née Archie. The old woman, Verena. Colin and Marcus, the Mario-Shaughnessy Brothers. Trudy in the yellow tracksuit. Alex, the ripped Hulk. And Kat, the girl in the bloody green dress, missing number thirteen. Not pictured: Tuesday Mooney.

"These are the thirteen players Lyle cast in the final act," said Tuesday. "Nat hit Kat over the head so he could take her place."

"That's not." Dorry was shaking her head now. "Then who did I see?"

"Who did—" Tuesday set the paper down on her lap. "Who *did* you see? Where?"

"She had." Dorry licked her lips. "She had curly hair. Lots of it. I couldn't really tell what color it was because—"

"Because why?"

"Everything was green," Dorry said. "I was looking through the goggles."

A moment hung silent between them.

Dorry stuttered. "I – it was – at the top. Of the stairs. I ran up, after you fell down. I ran up to help you. That's when I saw her. She was wearing—"

Dorry closed her eyes.

"She was wearing a dark satiny dress with a big cape and long satin gloves. She walked right up to that guy. And."

"And what?" Tuesday asked.

It was impossible.

"She pushed him," said Dorry.

It couldn't have happened.

"I think he would have hit you again. And again," Dorry said. "I think she saved your life."

Dorry could not have seen her.

"I didn't tell anyone what I saw." Dorry's lower lip trembled. "I couldn't. At first I thought I – I had to protect her. Because she protected you. And later, when all the craziness was over, I started to wonder if I saw her at all. If she was in my imagination."

"But . . ." prompted Tuesday.

Dorry sat up straight.

"I know what I saw," she said. "I can't explain it. But I know I saw a curly-haired girl in black satin save your life."

"I believe you," said Tuesday.

"Should we tell someone?" said Dorry.

"Who would we tell?" asked Tuesday. "What would we tell them?"

Dorry sat with that.

"If she wasn't this Kat person" – Dorry's voice rose – "who was she?"

I'm going to miss you. So much.

It was impossible. It couldn't have happened. Dorry could not have seen her. And yet.

"A friend," Tuesday said.

◆

Abby was gone.

Again.

It took Tuesday a few days to notice. At first she blamed it on the drugs and her lack of consciousness. But when her head finally cleared, it was – clear. Empty as the open blue sky. *Abby*, she thought. *Abby, where are you?* But no response came. Tuesday's head had reset, purged itself of its delusions. She was cured.

She felt strangely hollow. Her skull echoed, too spacious, like a longtime tenant had pulled up stakes and left behind no forwarding address. When Dorry told her about the curly-haired girl in black satin, for one moment Tuesday almost believed that's exactly what had happened: that the ghost who'd been haunting her for sixteen years had made herself corporeal to save Tuesday's life. It was the kind of thing, living or dead, that Abigail Hobbes would have done. Strange and unprecedented. Wildly improbable. A noble act at the climax of the film.

A dead girl saving her best friend's life.

It was a great story, and though she couldn't quite believe it, Tuesday liked telling it to herself. It had dramatic heft and resolution, more satisfaction than the logical, loose-ended alternative, for, if Dorry saw what she saw – and Tuesday believed that she had – there was simply a fourteenth player. A girl who snuck into the house just as Nathaniel had, who took action when she saw Nathaniel attacking Tuesday. It could have been Emerson in a costume and curly wig. But for all practical purposes, it had been a stranger: a stranger saved her from anything worse than a pulverized leg, and Tuesday would never get a chance to thank her.

That's not why she did it, Dex texted. For the kudos

Though if I ever push an asshole over a balcony to save your other leg

You better BELIEVE I want credit

Abby might have been gone, but Dex was there. Every day.

The doc says my legs are going to be two different heights, Tuesday texted.

I'll never walk in heels again

You're going to be the leaning tower of Tuesday, replied Dex. C'MON EILEEN

He came to her room after work on Friday.

"Hospital happy hour!" he said, and handed her his flask. He didn't sit. He was too busy examining the furniture, rubbing his thumb over the velvet nap of the curtains, opening and closing the drawers of the desk. "Though on this fancy floor," he said, "wouldn't be surprised if there's an actual wet bar around the corner."

He'd visited before, when Tuesday was still foggy and her parents had been around. It was the first time her parents had met Dex, and Dex had met her parents. Later, after Dex left, her mother leaned close to Tuesday and said, with the straightest of faces, "He has a very old, powerful spirit. I think he might be a witch, only he doesn't know it yet."

Today Tuesday and Dex were alone.

"Dex," Tuesday said. "Dex, stop fluttering."

"Tuesday," said Dex. "I can't help it. Hospitals make me flutter."

"My mom thinks you're a witch," she said.

That had the desired effect. Dex froze, flattered.

"A what? A witch? Your mother?" He smiled. "Well, she would know."

"She said you have a very old and powerful spirit." Tuesday moved to one side of the bed as best she could, given her leg, and patted the empty space. "But you don't realize it."

Dex sat. She slipped her hand into his. She hadn't known she was going to do it until she did. At first he pulled away – out of surprise, Tuesday thought, not discomfort. He relaxed.

"Are we going to talk about feelings now?" he said, low.

"I'm sorry," she said, "I was so nasty. To you and to Rabbit. I felt like shit that day, but that didn't give me the right to take it out on you."

"It wasn't *un*true," said Dex. "What you said."

"It doesn't matter," said Tuesday, "if it was true or not. I was a dick."

Dex laughed then. "You sure were," he said.

"I am truly sorry," Tuesday repeated.

"I forgive you," said Dex, and Tuesday's throat caught.

"Wow," she said, a little choked. "That's a powerful feeling."

"I'm not – I'm not exactly going to thank you, for being a dick." Dex drew his shoulders back. "I don't want to reward objectively bad behavior. But I thought a lot about what you said. That I need attention, that I need the world to love me. You're right."

"We all need to be seen."

"Some," he said, "more than others. Anyway, I thought about it and I realized, as I was belting away in Vincent Pryce's karaoke demolition machine" – Tuesday snickered – "who I was searching for, dating all those creative boys, those ballerinas and singers, even Rabbit's a musician. It was me. I was looking for who I used to be. For the ghost of myself. What I used to love, what I spent my life doing. So." He squeezed her hand. "Why don't I become the person I'm looking for?"

Tuesday passed her free hand in an arc, a shooting star swiping through the air.

"The more you knooow," she sang.

"You're hysterical," said Dex. He dragged his own free hand across the outside of his wet eyes.

"Does this mean you're going to quit your job?" she asked.

"Not today," he said. "Not tomorrow. But maybe soon." He tipped his head back, like he could see the blue-black autumn sky through the ceiling panels. "And for the rest of my life."

They sort of glowed, quietly, at each other.

"Dex," said Tuesday.

"Yes?"

"I—"

She thought of Abby. She thought about what Abby would do. It wasn't the same as having Abby's voice in her head, but it would suffice.

"The last time I had a friend like you," she said. She looked down at their hands and then up, up at his face. "A best friend."

Dex's lips sprang back in a grin.

"I lost her," said Tuesday. "And then I lost my mind."

"That sounds serious," said Dex.

"I'm a serious person," said Tuesday, deadpan.

Then she cackled. Because she was with Dex, and Dex was

with her, and because she remembered – after all these years, she remembered – this was how it felt to be safe with another person. A person who laughed with you, and sang with you, and held your hand, and handed you an umbrella when you needed to defend yourself. A person who deserved to know you, all of you, as you knew them. She wanted to tell him everything. Everything about Abby Hobbes, about how Abby vanished and about what happened after. But also everything that had happened before. How it felt to be a girl growing up in Salem, a strange girl on the outside, who didn't know it was possible to find other people in the world to love, and to trust, until she did. She wanted Dex to know who she'd been, where she'd come from. She wanted Dex to meet her first best friend.

"Her name was Abby Hobbes," said Tuesday. "She was a witch too."

19

HEART ON A STRING

Tuesday stood outside the Tillerman house, juggling her crutches under her arms. Behind her, she heard the Green Cab she'd taken from Somerville splatter away through the river of slush on the road.

It looked smaller in the daytime. The house had metastasized in her mind these past three months – or – had she even seen the outside of it, the night of the funeral? She hadn't. Tuesday shook her head. *Hello, Tillerman house*, she thought. *Nice to see you for the first time.* It was an imposing box of warm sandy stone, brownish in places with dead moss and creeping vines, surrounded by naked winter shrubs and trees that had been cut back from the circular drive. And while it may have looked smaller than expected, it was still an enormous house, built to grand proportions, built to last lifetimes, wearing its wealth in its bones, in the gleam of its windows, in the marble of its portico.

The high whine of a power saw, muffled, sliced the air.

Tuesday sniffed. She pulled her phone out of her coat pocket. She was fifteen minutes early. She knew Lyle would appreciate promptness, but there was such a thing as being too prompt. Too eager. Though that's what she was – eager. Desperately curious. Lyle had invited her to the house for lunch, to discuss "some things," whenever Tuesday felt ready.

She was more than ready. This was, officially, the farthest Tuesday had ventured on her own since being discharged from the hospital two and a half months ago. She'd had regular appointments at physical therapy, dinner with her parents and her brother on Sundays, plus get-out-of-your-apartment trivia and karaoke nights with Dex twice a week. Recently, she and Dorry, when it wasn't too snowy or icy, had been walking around the block on Thursdays instead of eating takeout in her apartment. But this, today – answering Lyle's cryptic invitation – was Tuesday's first step back into the real world on her newly uneven legs.

She was having trouble. Not with walking, necessarily – at least, nothing worse than the kind of trouble you'd expect when you have to relearn how to walk on a shattered leg – but with accepting. Accepting that her right leg, the only one she was ever going to get, had changed. It had been altered forever by a careless, violent man, who, not coincidentally, looked a lot like the man who'd been squatting in her apartment when she'd first returned to it. Archie, to his credit, had done an excellent job taking care of Gunnar in her absence; her cat even seemed to like him. The first afternoon she was home, Gunnar sat on the back of the love seat behind Archie's head, chewing on his hair. And it wasn't just Gunnar Archie had cared for. He'd filled her freezer with individual servings of homemade soup and vacuumed and kept everything tidier than Tuesday likely would have kept it herself.

He felt terrible. He was trying. She wanted to give him credit for that too. She didn't want to wake up at two in the morning from nightmares she couldn't remember, feeling very fragile and very mortal, but she did, and if she texted Archie, he came over. He came over and wrapped himself around her and it helped. It also helped that he'd gotten his own place. "You're rich as hell," Tuesday told him. "And you're no longer a lost son. Stop stealing and sign a lease."

So he signed a lease on a loft in Cambridge. He had nothing to furnish it with. They went to the antiques shops along Charles Street and bought a bed and a table and chairs and a couch. They went to Target to buy essentials, shower curtains, a bathmat. Archie embraced cleaning supplies with such unbridled joy – she had never seen a human being so thrilled about a self-wringing mop – that Tuesday could almost pretend they'd met like ordinary people, and that whatever they were to each other, now or in the future, could be easy. Then another part of her said, *You never wanted ordinary or easy, and you know it.*

Nathaniel did not reappear. There was an article in the *Globe* about his absence, but the story, probably through Constance and Emerson's influence, was buried near the obituaries. His second-in-command at N. A. Arches was promoted. The world continued to spin. And Archie was officially reinstated as an Arches, at least privately; he was seeing Emerson fairly frequently, and his mother every week for Sunday dinner. When Tuesday asked how those dinners went, Archie went flat. That was when she knew, for sure, that he knew. Everything. He'd known the whole time what had happened to his father, and now he knew what had happened to his brother, and he knew what his sister and his mother and Vincent Pryce had done. He wore it like a brick tied around his neck. She could imagine one day being strong enough to share the fullness of that weight—

But that day was not today.

She looked at her phone again. Now she was twelve minutes early. The power saw paused and started up again.

She swung forward on her crutches. She could finally walk around her apartment without them, but they helped when she was unsure of the terrain or how far she would have to walk. She wasn't very good on them. They didn't feel natural, and not just because they were a constant reminder that her body was different now.

She maneuvered up the short steps of the portico. There was a giant door knocker: a brass lion's head, mane luxurious, with a metal ring clenched in his teeth. She clanged it against the door.

Lyle opened it almost immediately.

"Tuesday," she said. "You finally decided to come in?"

"Were you watching me?" Tuesday said.

Lyle nodded.

"I was – I was processing."

"There's a lot to process," said Lyle. "Come on in." She pulled the door back and stepped aside. She was wearing jeans and yellow work boots, dusted with plaster, and her ever-present hooded sweatshirt. Clear plastic safety goggles were pushed up into her hair. They were in a small, dark vestibule, with a short flight of stairs leading to a room that Tuesday recognized from the wedge visible through the doorway: the great hall. The power saw was much louder in here, and she heard voices, rustling, activity. "You okay with the stairs?" Lyle asked, extending her arm. Tuesday hesitated.

"I'm not great on these," she said. "Not sure I ever will be, honestly. I can't seem to adjust to them. My arms are too long, or my legs are too – something."

Lyle tapped the side of her chin. "Wait here," she said. She scurried up the stairs and disappeared into the hall. Tuesday rested on her crutches. A man passed by the doorway, hefting a two-by-four over his shoulder.

She squinted.

It was Marcus Shaughnessy.

Even without the Mario costume, she knew him.

"How about this?" said Lyle.

She was holding the black umbrella. Someone had cleaned Nathaniel Arches's blood off the sharp silver tip.

Lyle descended the steps and held the umbrella out to Tuesday. "It's sturdy," she said. "And tall. Try it."

Tuesday remembered how good it had felt in her hands. How solid and true. She handed Lyle her crutches and wrapped her right hand slowly around the black fabric. She squeezed her palm around the wooden handle. She pressed the tip firmly against the floor.

She took a step.

"Perfect," said Lyle.

It was.

She followed Lyle carefully up the steps. The great hall was even more of a mess than the last time she'd seen it. There were drop-cloths everywhere. Some of the columns were braced, being replaced with new wood or stone. The fresco on the wall opposite the grand staircase was almost entirely revealed, but protected by a giant plastic sheet. She couldn't see the details clearly, but even so: it was a monumental work, a mural of life-size figures spanning two, three stories. Tuesday pressed her hand to her chest. It was a party, or some kind of gathering. The figures were dressed formally, holding drinks or platters, in old clothing, full skirts and high collars, laughing and talking. Some were dancing. Some were fighting. Kissing. The wall writhed. It washed over her like a tide; everywhere she looked, she saw something new, something alive.

Lyle waved to Marcus, and Tuesday saw it wasn't Marcus, but Colin. He waved back. Both brothers were here, along with a whole crew – Tuesday saw everyone now, a fleet of workers in steel-toed boots and hard hats and goggles, digging into the house. "The Shaughnessys were a find," said Lyle. She continued walking along the wall, beneath the balcony, toward the left side of the grand staircase and the kitchen beneath.

"It'll be quieter in here," said Lyle, pushing the door open. "Kind of using this space as headquarters for now. Ah!"

Verena Parkman was sitting at the oversized kitchen table, surrounded by papers and ancient ledgers. She looked up when Lyle and Tuesday entered.

"Well." Verena's face crinkled happily. "Look who's up and about." She nodded at Tuesday's umbrella. "I see you've got your trusty bumbershoot."

Tuesday wasn't sure how to react.

"Give us a minute?" asked Lyle. Verena rubbed her hands together happily and rose. "Almost time for elevenses anyway," she said, and left through another door, disappearing into one of the house's many chambers.

"What's going on?" Tuesday asked.

Lyle gestured toward the stools at the table. Tuesday sat. Lyle sat beside her.

"I'm putting together a team," Lyle said.

Tuesday tilted a little.

"What?" Lyle deadpanned. "Regular people can't put together teams?"

"Are you regular people?" asked Tuesday.

"Girl," said Lyle. "Please. You know regular is relative."

"A team to do what?" Tuesday asked.

"Lots of things," said Lyle. "Bring the house back to life. Figure out who Matilda Tillerman was, and how and why she painted all of that, and share it with the world. Preserve the fresco and the gold and silver ceiling, open it up to the public, make it a space that brings people together. Vince didn't have the time, but he had the money. I have the money now. I have the time. To use this money to do something to help, put something good into the world. Because the world, my goodness." She rested her hand on her belly, which was very full and very obviously pregnant. Tuesday wondered if Lyle even knew she was doing it. "Has problems. Of some magnitude." Her chest rose as she inhaled. "But!" She brightened, and it wasn't false cheer. It was an act of hope. "If there's one thing I've learned in my forty years on the planet." She fixed her eyes on Tuesday. "No one can change it alone."

It was a good speech. Tuesday said quietly, "What can I do?"

"Find stuff," said Lyle. "Information. The way you found that movie theater. I need someone who can find people and places all over the world."

"To anonymously donate money. Like" – Tuesday felt herself starting to glow – "angel investing. Crossed with micro-financing. Crossed with . . . MacArthur fellowships?"

"I was also maybe thinking of turning the castle on Nantucket into a national lottery-based performing arts and humanities boarding school. Sort of a real Hogwarts, but completely free," said Lyle. "Did you ever think about that, like, does Hogwarts offer need-based tuition assistance?"

"What?"

"I have a lot of ideas," said Lyle. "I need someone to bounce them off. Anyway." She coughed into her clenched fist. Then she brought both hands together, fingertip to fingertip. "I would like to formally offer you a job," she said. "Finding people. Organizations. Places, institutions, and situations where we, the outrageously fortunate, might be of assistance, either monetarily or – I don't know, some other way we haven't imagined yet. I need a friend with a moral compass and a sharp head who can help me find—" Lyle's impassioned roll skidded to a stop. "Look," she said, "I'm not so naive as to say we're going to find the answers. But you know how to look. Maybe you can find some clues. And maybe you can help me figure out how to strategically and responsibly die, God willing many years from now, totally broke."

Tuesday pointed at Lyle's belly.

"What about the baby?"

Lyle didn't even blink. "The bab*ies*," she said, "already have a trust fund. They're fine. And they're going to grow up learning how to share." She paused. "Do you babysit?"

"I know a dependable fourteen-year-old who might be interested," Tuesday said. "And also a dramatic thirty-four-year-old who loves a captive audience." This was all – this was so much. It was – taking it in was making Tuesday lightheaded. "Was this whole – was the whole point—"

"Was what," Lyle said, "the whole point?"

"You hired the Shaughnessy brothers to renovate the house, Verena's" – she gestured to the old books on the other side of the table – "doing something archival, from the looks of it. Who else is stashed away in this—"

She almost swallowed her tongue. It was too pertinent a question to ask aloud, too much to know and not tell. She would have to, at some point. But not right now. She tried again.

"Who else is on this team you're putting together?"

"I gave each of the thirteen a choice," Lyle said. "A half-million-dollar cash prize up front, hooray, you won the game, no strings attached. Or." She grinned. "A job. With salary, consulting fees, benefits, whatever you need. Future fortunes yet to be discovered. You're the last of the thirteen I'm asking."

"The *last*?"

"Ned Kennedy and Dorry Bones and Ned's sister and her friend are going to work here once the house is fully restored – after-school job, community outreach organizers – but they also took the payout, all four of them. To split with the Black Cats, that whole Facebook group. I know, I made an exception. They were a special case." She counted on her fingers. "Archie took the payout. Which I gave to him on the condition that he drop it into a trust for Dorry, though I'm not sure Dorry knows that yet." She cocked her head, appraising Tuesday's open-mouthed shock. "Frankly, I'm *astonished* Dex didn't spill the beans. He took the payout a month ago. Rabbit made him promise to keep it secret, but." She made a face that Tuesday interpreted as *You know Dex*. Which she did, and so did Lyle now, too. "I'll let him fill you in on his grand plans. Of course you're free to take the money too, but I'm giving you the hard sell. I want you with us."

"Was this all—" Tuesday didn't know how to wrap her tongue or her mind around what she had done, what game she had played, what she had won and lost since that October day when she watched an old man pretend to die in the ballroom of the Four Seasons. She landed on the matter at hand.

"Was all of this a job interview?" she asked.

"Is anything," asked Lyle, rocking back on her stool, "ever only one thing?"

It was a good answer.

"Come on," said Lyle, shouldering a quatrefoil-splattered Louis Vuitton bag the size of a pumpkin, "we're picking up lunch for everyone. We can talk more about the job on the way." They returned to the great hall. It rang with banging and sawing, destruction and creation. Tuesday's head was full of clear light. She was going to take the job. It was a decision she wasn't even conscious of making. Of course she would take this job, but not only because she needed one. She would take it because it was a mystery. Because it was with Lyle, and the other people who had answered Vincent Pryce's call. Because it was in this house, at the end of this game, and everything that had already happened was always, still, the beginning of what came next. The air smelled electrical, and of freshly cut wood. Lyle pulled off her plastic goggles and they tangled briefly with her ponytail.

The silver tip of the umbrella made a wonderful click when Tuesday pressed it to the floor with each step.

Lyle dug into the giant bag. Her brow creased.

"Must've left my keys in the kitchen," she said. "I'll be right back. Hang here. With Matilda."

She left Tuesday in front of the painting of Matilda Tillerman – the self-portrait still hanging on the wall beneath the balcony. A protective sheet of plastic had been stapled over it, pulled tight and shining. Tuesday regarded Matilda, and Matilda regarded her right back. How on earth had she managed to paint a towering fresco without anyone discovering it for over a hundred years? Had she done the ceiling too? The painting's eyes were very dark and very alive. Her lips were parted slightly, as though she were about to speak. Tuesday's eyes moved down to her shoulders, to the details of the black dress she'd painted—

And she saw Abby.

Abby Hobbes, reflected in the taut plastic sheet, was staring back at her.

Her hair was red, massive with curls. Her eyes were gleaming, as surprised to be seen as Tuesday was to see her. It was Abby. To see her, to see Abby's face, with her own eyes and not the eye in her mind – to see her instead of just hearing the echo she'd left in Tuesday's memory – Tuesday could not explain it. Tuesday could not doubt it. Abby hadn't aged. Abby was sixteen. Abby would be sixteen forever. She'd forgotten how much child was still in Abby's face, how full her cheeks were, how her freckles cascaded down either side of her nose. There was a wayward curl floating off the top of her head, crooked at an angle. The corner of her mouth twitched, like she wanted to react – to smile, to laugh, to say something – but was too stunned to do anything but look back at Tuesday. At the human she used to haunt. The friend she'd had to abandon to save.

But here they both were, still.

Tuesday turned around.

No one was there.

Abby wasn't there, because of course she couldn't be. Wouldn't be. But neither was there a member of the Shaughnessys' crew, who happened, when you caught her curly-headed reflection in a sheet of plastic, to bear a passing resemblance to the first love Tuesday ever lost.

The string that her heart had always been following.

Tuesday turned back to the painting. Abby was gone. She

saw her own face reflected. She saw workers in the background, moving with tools, standing with their hands on their hips, talking with each other. She saw Matilda Tillerman's face, painted, silent, beneath the plastic. She heard nothing but saws and hammers. The thud of a heavy object falling. Footsteps approaching. Lyle's keys jangling.

"Whoa. You okay?" Lyle said, stopping short. "Look like you've seen a—" She laughed. "In this place, who hasn't?"

Tuesday had been holding her breath.

"I'm good," she said, and let it go.

ACKNOWLEDGMENTS

You hold this book in your hands

◆

because Bonnie Nadell and Austen Rachlis, no matter how many bananas drafts they read (and boy were they bananas), saw what this book could be, and helped me to see it too. Because Naomi Gibbs saw it and brought it fully into itself, and was a joy to work with, like everyone at Houghton Mifflin Harcourt: Larry Cooper, Chrissy Kurpeski, Liz Anderson, Michelle Triant, among others, who took my weird visions and made them manifest, and beautiful. And because Andrea Schulz, years ago, when she first heard about my day job, said, Oh, you should definitely write about that. Thank you, Kayla Rae Whitaker and Amber Sparks, for your words and your kindness.

You hold this book because I lived in Boston for eleven years and worked in both fundraising and finance, and had a LOT to process. Thank you, MGH and the Prospect Research Team (2010–2014), especially Angie Morey. I loved the work, but I loved working with you all even more. You are an astounding group of human beings. Thank you, Michael and Deanna Sheridan, Wendy Price, Barry Abrams, Heather Heald, and Eddie Miller, for the years before MGH, the days of RFPs and

BlackBerrys (those who know, know). I didn't always love the work itself, but working with you was a gift, and it changed my life. Thank you, Grub Street, which I am thrilled to work for still; thank you to Michelle Hoover, Alison Murphy, and Chris Castellani, and to all the thoughtful, visionary, funny, and immensely talented writers and people in the Grub universe.

You hold this book because of my friends, who are my family; and my family, who are my friends. It exists because I didn't stop, and I didn't stop because of the people I'm lucky to know and to love. You keep me safe and sane; you make my life rich. My beloved Bostonians: Laura Q. (my common-law Boston marriage) and Mike Messersmith, Jason and Karen Clarke, Jenn and Dave Wolff, Nam Nguyen, Alyssa Osiecki, Kristin Osiecki. Lit Team Boston Forever: Rob and Karissa Kloss, Steve Himmer, Sage Brousseau, Kevin Fanning. The cheering section: Bob Erlenback, Eric Rezsnyak, Louise Miller (I am so happy to be your friend), Gina Damico (WHY DIDN'T WE HANG ALL THE TIME WHEN WE LIVED IN BOSTON), Rachel Fershleiser and Liberty Hardy (you are both champions for books and it is a glorious thing), Margaret Willison (your enthusiasm, your sheer light, is a force of nature, and I am beyond grateful to know you), Kathryn VanArendonk (dolphin gif goes here), Joyce Hinnefeld, Josh Berk, Domenic Breininger, Kiera Wilhelm, Shannon Aloise, Mary Jo Lodge, Kirsten Hess and Christa Neu. My Bethlehem-by-way-of-Buffalo family: Jenna Lay (with whom I've shared so many, many adventures; none of this without you, always); Sandra, Garret, Elena, Zoey, and Oliver Lau (Elena, someday you'll get to read these, and I promise you'll be glad you waited); Manda Betts (by way of Rochester). You hold this book because my mother and my father never said, Writing is not a job. Because the Racculias and the VanSkivers taught me the tremendous value of words and stories and art and music. Because the

Bach Choir of Bethlehem helped me put down roots in my new home, and the Bethlehem Area Public Library made those roots deeper. And because Bruce Coville wrote back to the fan mail I sent him when I was eight, and showed me that ghosts were people and so were writers.

Thank you for reading; thank you, thank you, all.